CONCEPT PROGRESS
A SCIENCE FICTION METAPHYSICS

LEO INDMAN

The author is grateful to:

NASA, for its stellar imagery: www.nasa.gov

Wikipedia, for its vast knowledge and reference: www.wikipedia.org

Cover and interior design by the author

Published in the United States of America

ISBN: 978-0-9988289-5-4

Concept Progress: A Science Fiction Metaphysics / Leo Indman

First Edition

www.conceptprogress.com

For Marianna, Ariella, and Eli

CONCEPT PROGRESS

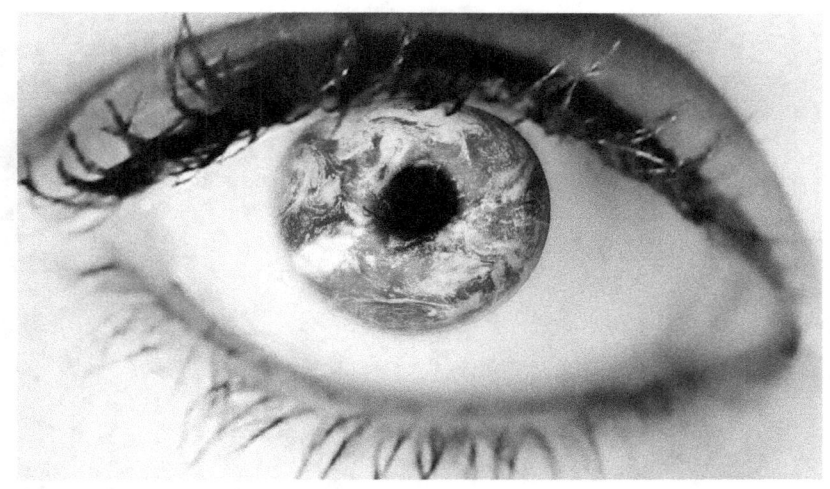

TABLE OF CONTENTS

COPYRIGHT..ii
DEDICATION...iii
INTRODUCTION...vii

CHAPTER ONE...1
CONCEPT SOUND...3
CHAPTER ONE | SCIENCE, PHILOSOPHY, AND CURIOSITY........................5
A DIALOGUE BETWEEN THE SCIENTIST AND THE PHILOSOPHER..............15

CHAPTER TWO...25
CONCEPT LIGHT..27
CHAPTER TWO | ON EXISTENCE AND PURPOSE.....................................29
FASTER THAN THE SPEED OF LIGHT!...39

CHAPTER THREE...47
CONCEPT CHANCE..49
CHAPTER THREE | THE EVOLUTION STORY..51
THE CAVEMEN...64

CHAPTER FOUR...69
CONCEPT CONSCIOUSNESS..71
CHAPTER FOUR | THE NEXT HUMAN...73
LYRA..87

CHAPTER FIVE..93
CONCEPT MOMENT..95
CHAPTER FIVE | POSITIVE PROGRESS: PART I..97
THE AWAKENING..111

CHAPTER SIX..117
CONCEPT KARMA..119
CHAPTER SIX | POSITIVE PROGRESS: PART II...............................121
THE THEORY OF ONE SOUL...132

CHAPTER SEVEN...137
CONCEPT PHYSICS...139
CHAPTER SEVEN | THE MOST EVOLVED LIFE FORM......................141
THE DREAM JOURNAL...154

CHAPTER EIGHT...159
CONCEPT TIME..161
CHAPTER EIGHT | ON PERFECTION AND INFINITY.......................163
AROUND THE GALAXY IN EIGHTY DAYS..176

CHAPTER NINE...185
CONCEPT WAVE...187
CHAPTER NINE | AN INTELLIGENT UNIVERSE...............................189
THE HOUSE...201

CHAPTER TEN..207
CONCEPT COEXISTENCE..209
CHAPTER TEN | LIFE, CHOICE, AND THE REST.............................211
THE MUSEUM..222

BIBLIOGRAPHY..I

INTRODUCTION

Concept Progress is a fusion of science fiction and philosophy. It is a thesis on metaphysics that stretches beyond the scope of modern science and scratches many of our curious itches. The thesis is complemented by short and loosely tied sci-fi stories that make its conceptualizations come to life.

The central theme throughout is that progress is a driving force in human evolution. This recurring viewpoint has previously stirred much debate. However, as we escalate through the twenty-first century, the evidence is plentiful. Concept Progress offers a fresh perspective into the topic, citing humanity's ongoing accomplishments as a convincing piece of that evidence. In the book, we celebrate ourselves for our achievements, challenge our perceived limits, and conclude that progress will eventually produce the most evolved life form. In so doing, we look back to the beginning of time and circle forward to a time that is farther away than the current age of the universe.

While the tone of the book's body resembles that of a philosophical prose, with each chapter, the reader realizes more and more that the narrative is actually one of science fiction. The intent of the book's structure and approach is manifold.

First, it is safe to say that any literature that points to the future is already, by definition, a work of fiction—no matter how serious it tries to sound. Imagining future technologies, foreseeing the next stages of human evolution, and exploring the realm of the highest dimension surely makes it a science fiction.

Second, the book is a collection of concepts—abstract notions of the mind that reflect our grasp on certain aspects of reality. It is also a play on those concepts, exposing how our progressive understanding of these notions can gradually be transcended. Each chapter starts with a sketch of a particular concept whose humanistic yet quantum mechanical context lets us identify with it and be mystified by it. From the concepts of sound and light to the concepts of consciousness and coexistence, each concept tale depicts a personal expression of our mutual worldview.

Third, each one of the ten chapters concludes with a science fiction story. These stories project the theme further and subtly point to each other. As we connect the dots from one story to another, the outline reveals a world that makes us wonder whether we are headed toward its future or whether we will bypass it as an alternate universe. In one story, we meet the inventor of mind-reading technology while in another story, we meet an artificial life form that will be made possible by this technology. Yet another story is about the time-traveling mind of an astrophysicist whose life's work has impacts on whole timelines, as revealed by a different story. In the end, it all comes together with the final piece of the puzzle completing not only the short story series, but also the novel as a whole.

Each three-part chapter is a triad with a distinct purpose in mind. We begin the journey with our own curiosity. This basic emotion allows us to open the door to that which we are so curiously seeking. Essentially, that covers everything. In questioning the entirety of existence, we commence with the premise that it is the element of life that sends us on a quest for meaning. So we review the trend of life's evolution on Earth from its roots to the present day and follow this trend into the distant future. The process of evolutionary development leads us to a recipe for one's own personal progress, which is comprised of physical, mental, and spiritual ingredients. It soon becomes clear that a species can change only insofar as its individual members embrace this change. And we realize that our choice in the matter has impacts not only on our own future, but also on the future of everyone who shares our timeline.

In some ways, Concept Progress is a modern commentary of Charles Darwin's revolutionary theory of evolution. In other ways, it is an encouraging observation of our humble human existence. As I scribble on my first-generation iPad, it strikes me how far we have progressed not just from the early efforts of our common ancestors, but even from Darwin's pen and ink writings of the Galapagos Islands. Perhaps progress is in the eye of the beholder. Or perhaps it can indeed be qualified as a volatile yet forward-moving process. From emerging technologies to the conveniences of our modernized lifestyles, there is a great deal of evidence for the latter.

Unquestionably, there is also much evidence against the idea of progress. From political turmoil and economic turbulence to outright war and poverty, the skeptic has compelling reasons to doubt the nature of progress. However, the same doubts were once applied to the theory of evolution. It was unthinkable that the ruthless animal kingdom can produce a species that is capable of doing something as intricate as calculus. As we widen the time scale and follow this evolutionary trend from biological, social, and cosmic angles, the concepts of evolution and progress slowly but surely become synonymous.

Against the advice of my graduate school professors, the source of reference used is Wikipedia. The reason is simple. This beautifully organized virtual encyclopedia portal is dynamic, widely accessible, and is already based on referenced material. One idea explored in the later chapters is that of the "information potential," which the notion of Wikipedia fits quite nicely.

Concept Progress

As we set out to break through the multidimensional boundaries of space and time, let us also aim to break through the boundaries of our own misconceptions. Concept by concept, let philosophy inspire us and science guide us. If it sounds logical, feel free to consider it. If it requires a leap of faith, take it at your own risk. And if it is just amusing, good!

CHAPTER ONE
SCIENCE, PHILOSOPHY, AND CURIOSITY

*Until a time comes when the human element can be expressed
as a mathematical equation, there will be such unknowns as
the variable of curiosity. Till then, science can only be
transcended by filling it with a layer of philosophy.*

CONCEPT SOUND

On a warm July evening, a young musician plays the Spanish Romanza in E minor for an audience of couples having dinner at the local café. The music fills the background with ambiance, resonating with every sip of red wine and every bite of that chocolate dessert. It is as if the melody embellishes a movie scene as it complements the experience and amplifies the emotions. The event is happily shared with that special someone. The senses are overjoyed under the flickering candlelight. A few years and a few heartbreaks later, some of that audience, wherever they may be, suddenly hear that same romantic melody in a radio commercial that is advertising an exclusive getaway to a faraway island. The thought of vacation blends into a recollection of that euphoric evening, of her or of him. A reaction to the memory occurs. It is either a smile at all of life's events that occurred since—graduation, new job, wedding, pregnancy, sleepless nights—or it is a sigh of a hope once gone.

When a minor chord is strung on a classical guitar, the listener gets flooded with feelings of romance, melancholy, or an appreciation of the present moment. It is a curious function how the brain reacts to a particular chord arrangement, which is just a combination of audio waves produced out of certain atmospheric vibrations. The reaction prompts the nerves for a dose of dopamine, causing one to perceive the feeling of romance. Also curious is how the experience is recorded in the psyche; its memory held dormant until something triggers it to rise up to the surface of the mind, if only for an instant.

A major seventh chord, on the other hand, resembles a question mark, an unanswered expression, or a curiosity. This chord, when heard by its bare ring, requires a response to follow; otherwise, the listener will be left unsatisfied. Each chord speaks to the observer just as words in a book, colors in a painting, or spices in a gourmet dish. If the minor chord captures our adolescent desire for love, then the major seventh chord expresses our innocent urge for answers. Such as, where does the memory remain? Is it in our brain cells and gets carried to every place we go? Is it in our subconscious mind, in the realm of a higher quantum dimension, beyond the unique coordinates of space and time? Or does it become a meme that infects all those who encounter a situation that is attuned to its distinct set of characteristics?

Perhaps we identify with music because tones resemble the frequencies of the mind. Each thought progression is played on the scale of a personal melody. Similarly, rhythm resembles the pulse of the body. As the beat changes speed, so does our perception of time, our focus, and our productivity. The composition is ours alone, and life becomes a soundtrack—sometimes dramatic, sometimes romantic, and sometimes curious.

SCIENCE, PHILOSOPHY, AND CURIOSITY

Curiosity is the desire to acquire information, knowledge, and skill. Just as we are concerned about our own wellbeing, its progress, or at least its preservation, so too we are curious about everything else. We often find ourselves interested in the affairs of others that seemingly have nothing to do with us. This curiosity extends outward, passes through our fellow neighbors, and looks to fill as much of the universe as possible. It is an emotion that is at the core of our education. It is the foundation of every subject of study. It drives social media. It is exploited in profit-seeking industries. And it is wonderful.

All scholars are curious beings, especially the philosophers. Such a savant asks many questions and attempts to structure ideas in a logical and uniform manner. He observes his surroundings objectively and inquires into their nature and origin. While the course of the examination remains impartial, the root of the query originates from the selfish curiosity factor. The philosopher is not content until a question begets an answer that can be believed beyond a reasonable doubt. For the scientist, it is not enough to believe. The answer must not only make sense, but also hold solid evidence.

Philosophy is at best a hypothesis to the scientist. Such a detective investigates the nature and origin of his own curiosity to prove or disprove a philosophy by means of observation, experimentation, mathematical evaluation, and the like. The scientist is a very determined individual who has the job of concretely answering many questions raised by philosophers over time. If science is unable to adequately address a given philosophical proposition, then it will remain a conjecture until a scientific breakthrough replaces it with explicit proof. Though certain questions take lifetimes to answer.

Philosophy is known as the love of wisdom while science may be referred to as the wealth of that wisdom. The scientist provides the philosopher with an abundance of facts from which the philosopher arranges and shapes his premise accordingly. In this way, the philosopher presents the world with either a new idea or at least a stimulating digest. It is as if a child gets a box full of clay and carefully molds their creation. This creation may, in turn, inspire the scientist to pursue a practical invention, or it may forever remain a work of art.

Both the scientist and the philosopher are driven by their common curiosities to uncover the secrets of the universe. These secrets reciprocally spark the urge to satisfy other newfound curiosities. This vicious cycle creates the perfect dance in which both partners are fueled by each other's nature. Each dancing step conquers more territory and covers more ground on which we mark our presence and expand our base of knowledge. Within each one of us, we will find a scientist or a philosopher at one point or another because of this constant need to learn, grow, and evolve. Such is our human nature. As long as there are uncovered terrains and unsolved mysteries, we will not rest until we have satisfied our curiosities and triumphed the dominions in which we have set our feet and our minds in.

From the beginning of our humankind, we have proceeded to overtake the world by learning all that we could about it and manipulating its possessions to our benefit. Still, it seems as though there is much more work to be done and an endless amount of subjects to learn about. The question becomes—how much can we learn about anything? How much can a subject be broken down into its finest principles until there is nothing left of it to investigate? And when all subjects have been thoroughly explored and mastered down to their tiniest details, will there be anything left to achieve? The scientist is still unsure as to whether the universe is finite. If so, then the amount of subjects to study must also be finite. If not, our curiosity may grow indefinitely.

As the scientist explains, it all began with the Big Bang. Suddenly, the universe started to expand from an undefined and infinitesimal point. The first moment occurred at a single and only spatial coordinate and contained within it all the potential that we now call reality. It has since been expanding in every direction, and this expansion is accelerating. The scientist does not exactly yet know why and attributes this perplexity to a placeholder that he terms dark energy. There are several propositions on the likely fate of the universe. Some believe that it will be expanding forever. Others prophesies the recollapse of the universe into what is known as the Big Crunch, perhaps followed by a new Big Bang that starts the process all over again. And so on to infinity? It is the scientist's responsibility to clear up such cosmic issues and eventually populate all the placeholders. In the meantime, let us adopt the philosopher's approach and base our forecast on a recipe of inductive reasoning applied to an encyclopedia of facts, postulates, theories, and probabilities. Perhaps we may get a glimpse of what is to come.

The world has a lot of knowledge to offer. We look around, observe its functions, and marvel at its many possessions. But unless we start asking questions, we will only get what is in front of us. A question raised to the scientist is a case to be solved. If the scientist does not arrive at a conclusion to a particular inquiry, then we are left to patiently wait for time to uncover the mystery. After all, the answer must exist in one form or another. In this way, we have once confirmed that the Earth is round and later discovered that it is not the center of the solar system, let alone the universe. And one day we may be surprised to find that it is not the only planet that harbors life. For now, we can only imagine who is out there.

The philosopher is more impatient by nature. If the scientist has not answered the matter in question, then the philosopher will use all the tools of logic, history, and the collective wisdom of humanity to reason through the uncertainty. In such an undertaking, the philosopher puts himself in a position to answer many of humanity's difficult questions that reach beyond the scope of that which science can offer today. Of these are morality, reason, and purpose. This is where the difference emerges between the scientist and the philosopher.

Prior to the Renaissance, religion largely provided the public with morality, reason, and purpose. The problem that the scientist found with religious philosophy is that it is not based solely on logic but marks its foundation in faith. To him, man's ability to reason will not allow any concept to be based on faith unless that ability is surrendered. As the scientific revolution dominated religious influence, contemporary philosophy too made its way into modern thinking. Faith was no longer a given; rather, it was now allowed to be questioned, analyzed, considered, or rejected.

The scientific community requires a hypothesis to be thoroughly validated for a consensus to be reached in establishing it as an admissible contributor to a scientific theory—that which the public comes to accept as a given fact. If, however, the hypothesis is not yet substantiated in a manner that is acceptable to the community, then the scientist may consider it in such a way that it would have the most likelihood of being verified in the future. The philosopher would agree that his argument as well be factually based. If it too happens to surpass current scientific limits, then the philosopher would ensure that his syllogism is sound, with carefully reviewed assumptions and alternatives filling in the gaps. These assumptions could, after all, make or break the argument as they are nothing more than educated guesses. Such philosophical and scientific approaches to problem solving grew to complement each other's methodologies and overlapped on social principles like morality or physical properties like time travel.

Although traveling through time is not currently possible, the scientist does not discard the possibility. Instead, he attempts to explain this concept by way of the scientific method—not allowing for any implausibilities to contribute to its formulation. Per Albert Einstein, the property of time is a fundamental element in the theory of relativity. It becomes more evident as objects near the speed of light. At such great speeds, nature prevents an object from approaching the universal speed limit by slowing down the passage of time relative to other objects. Theoretically, if someone were to move fast enough for long enough, they would perceive to have traveled into the future once they arrive at their destination. Alternatively, traveling into the past leads to many philosophical questions that arise as a result of temporal paradoxes. However, even here the scientist is not taken aback and proposes to resolve such conundrums with the multiverse theory.

Farfetched notions like time travel, when considered in all seriousness, at this time belong to the bookshelves of theoretical physics. This field is one of the oldest and yet constantly evolving disciplines that pushes science to its mathematical limits. Some of its theorems may not be ready for experimentation while some are placeholders for observations that lack a theoretical component. Once an experiment demonstrates an apriority that was once predicted by theoretical physics, it graduates to be catalogued as a phenomenon that can be observed in nature, rather than just on paper. Until then, the theory dwells in the pages of the abstract, inspiring science fiction and engaging the philosopher's imagination.

There are many branches of science whose propositions we will draw upon and formulations rely on in supporting the point at hand. Some practices are newly developed and less established than others. Nonetheless, new ways of thinking often prove to be revolutionary, as the scientific method is dynamically oriented, thrusting itself forward by means of its own discoveries. Younger practices are often offshoots of major branches or may be cross-disciplinary, combining previously unrelated fields or borrowing techniques from one field to expand on the other.

Evolutionary psychology, for example, is a cross-discipline that uses the methods applied to evolutionary biology on psychological analysis. This approach explains how mental processes evolved in humans over time, similar to how physiological traits changed as a result of adaptations. It makes clear how our psyche is predisposed to being conditioned by way of repeatedly generating habits, which themselves arise from an ancestral mechanism of acting on reflexes. We will have more to say on both the evolutionary process as well as psychological conditioning in the pages to come. For now, let us appreciate how modern science has reached a level of fluidity that allows previously unrelated fields to overlap in ways that make it more obvious to see that the universe is, in fact, just a sum of its interrelated parts.

Each scientific domain reflects a part or aspect of the universe. Natural sciences such as physics, chemistry, astronomy, and geology describe the workings of the world. Social sciences such as anthropology, psychology, and sociology describe the wonders of humanity. The latter will necessarily include an overtone of philosophy since being human is certainly more complex than rocket science. Until a time comes when the human element can be expressed as a mathematical equation, there will be such unknowns as the variable of curiosity. Till then, science can only be transcended by filling it with a layer of philosophy.

Propelling a science using a philosophical motor means using logical reasoning to explain some aspect of corporeality. With time and experience, such reasoning solidifies into a given that we come to accept as a matter of fact. Take morality as an example. It is one of the oldest and most popular topics of every religion. It has been examined by Ancient Greek philosophy, which influenced many of our Western ethical values. As well, it is explored within the social sciences, even if indirectly. These sciences underlie a theoretical framework of social philosophy, which is put to the test by observing, sampling, and surveying various demographic populations for the purpose of understanding their differences and inclinations.

Social philosophy seeks to discover those behaviors that are most beneficial among individuals within a given community. As individual behavior is linked to many factors of nature and nurture, one's choice of it arises from a complex set of past events and predispositions that form the current state of one's personality. Individual behavior and, consequently, one's personality is then judged by society based on certain established principles and accepted standards. These standards have been shaped and reshaped over the centuries and are the culmination of many lessons learned. They serve as principles of law enforcement, ways of public interaction, and good old etiquette. Adhering to them enables us to build cities and live together, embrace the weekdays and work together, and enjoy dinner with good company.

Standards, which are presupposed by the notions of normality and conformity, dictate the kinds of behaviors that are generally recognized as being good or bad for society at large. We thus base our rights and wrongs on these standards and, as a result, identify our conduct with morality. Of course, our sense of it is subjective as one can judge oneself to be more or less moral than someone else. Although the devil's advocate may argue that morality is open to interpretation, the sociologist would dispute in that by following certain principles, it can be defined to outline the most optimum way of living for the benefit of the majority.

The politician is infamous for taking advantage of both sides, often going to great lengths to mold a society based on dogmatic ideals. Numerous laws, often extreme, enacted to uphold those ideals have historically maintained limited stability and in many cases led to economic failure, national collapse, social revolt, and reconstruction. So does this mean that we are yet to get it right? The takeaway is that human societies are complex, dissimilar, and ever-changing. A particular social order will not necessarily ring true in all lands. Even our next-door neighbor will have a difference of opinion about anything that comes up in daily chitchat. Culture, national identity, and many other societal differentiators necessitate laws to be customized so as to fit the norms of a particular geographical region. Hence, the city, county, state, provincial, and federal jurisdictions of the numerous nation lands around the world. Still, the argument can persist in that there are certain moral principles that really ought to apply to all people everywhere.

The easiest such moral concept to agree with is that murder is wrong. Religion proclaims that if one kills, then the sinner is surely destined for purgatory. While effective, identifying this commandment with fear can be misleading and only goes so far. Ironically, holy wars, sacrifices, and executions in the name of God were among the most popular activities in the history of many religions. Unfortunately, for some extremists, they still are. Interestingly, the logical explanation for this abnormality was always there in the sacred texts. However, its true meaning was often overlooked since fear and blind faith prevented the human mind from thinking in rational terms. The familiar phrase is "do unto others as you would have them do unto you." It was the early version of sociology, the experience of civilization, which made it possible to understand what the Golden Rule really means. It became clear that the act of homicide is detrimental to the wellbeing of society and must be prevented. In this way, morality made its way from the Bible into the Constitution, enforcing social governance and protecting civilian welfare. Although fear keeps would-be criminals from being punished, most people have a basic sense of understanding as to why they should not kill.

Society extends such standards to cover other wrongdoings like theft, deception, breach of contract, or traffic violation. There are logical reasons for all these transgressions, set forth by the common experience of people sharing their lives with each other. As psychology addresses the impact of morality on individual behavior and the health of one's state of mind, sociology leverages on those moral principles by which groups of individuals adhere to and by which their communities are strengthened. After all, people make up societies. In this respect, psychology has a direct impact on sociology. The former deals with the state of one's individual consciousness while the latter concerns one's interaction and identification with the collective consciousness.

When considering the social sciences, we can see why it is difficult to abstain from bringing philosophy into the discussion. On the other hand, physical sciences are able to do without a philosophical additive unless some element of life is brought into the picture. For instance, all natural occurrences can be represented by mathematical means—chemical reactions, atmospheric pressures, fundamental forces, speed of light, expansion of the universe, singularities, and soon enough dark matter and dark energy. Some of these do tempt us to add a philosophical constituent but without involving life, strictly speaking, there is just no need. Though as soon as we consider any sort of life force, philosophy becomes part of the overall topic. The Big Bang and our entire universe may not mean much without the life that it has accomplished. As a result, cosmology leads us to question reason and purpose in the same way as sociology leads us to explore morality.

To understand the universe in its holistic sense, we ought to examine humanity in its many contexts. And rightly so as life and its harbor are necessarily intertwined. By way of observation, the astronomer examines phenomena that are light years away for the purpose of understanding the nature of the universe. By way of meditation, the Buddhist monk examines the mind and body phenomena for the same purpose. All the atoms in our bodies have come from various places to assemble for our own purposes. They each tell a story of some place and time in our vast universe.

There are many places and times from which we can choose to begin our story—from the initial point of the Big Bang that eventually led to the formation of our planet, from the single celled organisms that became the ancestors of all the Earth's creatures, or from a biographical account of those individuals whose impacts on society teach great lessons of historic value. As everything is interrelated, each approach will eventually lead us to gain insights into the essence of existence. Modern science is racing to formulate the theory of everything. Similarly, philosophy always had the aim of formulating an understanding of everything. This is what we are after as well, if only ever so slightly.

We have briefly reflected on the various sciences and their interaction with philosophy. Facts and experience turn into knowledge and wisdom, which become the remedies to curing our curiosities. Studying the entire universe at different levels of complexity or simplicity helps us to turn the abstracts of philosophy into the actuals of science. The interplay between both disciplines is everbearing. Whether we engage in theoretical physics or theoretical philosophy, physics or metaphysics, psychology or philosophy of mind, sociology or social philosophy, or explore the philosophy of science, sometimes even the scientist and the philosopher switch roles. After all, these roles just point to different means of understanding reality and interpreting its many shades of truth.

Both the scientist's and the philosopher's curiosities pushes them to discover the reason, nature, and purpose of existence. Existence being all that exists. All that exists being the whole of the universe. To understand not just how it came to be but why and out of what. Science has so far provided us with the Big Bang, which is as much an effect of something as it is the cause of everything. An ambiguity just like the classical view of God's infinite nature —both incomplete in theory and definition. Can the philosopher in us arrive at a plausible consideration using all the available tools of existent knowledge and the human potential to think through the gaps? Let us remain with our optimistic and creative nature and attempt the discovery.

A DIALOGUE BETWEEN THE SCIENTIST AND THE PHILOSOPHER

The scientist and the philosopher are enjoying a game of chess in Central Park under an open blue sky. They meet every Sunday morning for the sake of discussing various topics of interest, ranging from the latest developments in quantum theory to the socioeconomic issues of developing nations. This, over a freshly squeezed blend of veggie juice and roasted peanuts while also musing over the Sunday paper funnies. Today is August 5th, 2035. They are discussing the science of concepts and, off-topic, the concept of science.

Scientist

Nice day, isn't it?

Philosopher

Relative to yesterday, one year ago, or which other day?

Scientist

Oh Charlie, there you go again chasing tangents.

Philosopher

There is no such thing as a stupid question, Erik. Your implications may not always come across to your fellow conversationalist.

Scientist

What are you talking about?

Philosopher

That's the spirit, buddy. Hehe! So what is this revolutionary idea that you want to share with me?

Scientist

Well, on Monday night, I was revising my code that simulates temporal lobe processing. While debugging a system crash, I've stumbled upon an infinite loop within a sub-function that's made to output the hippocampal region's action potential. At first, I couldn't reconcile this anomaly. Each trace led me to a procedure that handles nerve impulses—a piece of code that reliably expresses a cell's electric polarization. I spent all night running the analysis until I fell asleep at my desk. When I woke up, I realized that the loop must be a representation of a singularity. My assumption was confirmed when I replaced the data structure of an electrically charged particle with a wave function. While it's no news that observation has impacts at the quantum realm, you see, I haven't considered the wave-particle duality from a neurological perspective. This means that the singularity contains all of the possibilities that can manifest as a result of one's thought process.

Philosopher

It's as if the answer came to you while you were asleep.

Scientist

Perhaps. I ended up coding a yoctometric formula that quantifies the neuro-frequencies of concepts as they arise in the mind.

Philosopher

Interesting. You found a way to quantify actual thoughts?

Scientist

No, actual concepts. In other words, not just a written sentence but a whole paragraph expressed as an idea. When passing the unique concept variable into the wave function, it offsets the loop and computes the frequency of the quantum neuron field that's generated when the mind comprehends that particular concept. Unlike words that often mislead, as you've just so graciously pointed out, the frequency completely reflects the idea as it's intended to be perceived in the mind. I've started working on the technical specs for the prototype, which I've termed the "neuroquanceptre."

Philosopher

Oh, how lovely. You've invented a mind-reading gadget just to shut me up! When will you present this neuro-thingy to the Academy and get yourself published already?

Scientist

Haven't thought about that yet. These days my interests simply lie in the pursuit of scientific discovery.

Philosopher

How boring, Erik. You know, science isn't simply an end in itself. It certainly serves a practical purpose. Biology allows us to understand the living world so that we can use that knowledge to, for example, advance our health. Cosmology allows us to understand the universe so that we can use that knowledge for, say, intergalactic travel.

Scientist

I agree, Charlie. But can't the ambition to pursue science be rooted in an ever-yearning desire to gain knowledge for its own sake? At the very least, each scientific experiment and mathematical exercise strengthens our cognitive capabilities.

Philosopher

You said it yourself: ever-yearning. This desire is ingrained in the human psyche. It's a fire that can't be extinguished and looks to consume everything in its path. So there must be something deeper to all this than just desire. The point of eating is not just to alleviate hunger, but to sustain our very existence.

Scientist

But then the same may be said of biology, cosmology, and all the other sciences. To advance our health is to sustain our existence. To travel to different planets is to search for a suitable environment in which more humans could, well, exist.

Philosopher

So it seems. Existence is the goal.

A Dialogue Between the Scientist and the Philosopher

Scientist

Exist for the sake of existing?

Philosopher

As opposed to not existing? I think so. Existence is worth all that much more than non-existence. Every living creature on Earth can agree to that.

Scientist

In evolutionary terms, surviving to exist is the name of the game.

Philosopher

I'm sure Mr. Darwin didn't develop the theory of evolution purely for intellectual amusement. Don't you know? He struggled with the idea of publishing his work for many years.

Scientist

I get your point. This is why I enjoy our Sunday mornings, my friend. Nothing better than a shot of motivation before lunch time.

Philosopher

Likewise, old chap. Existence, interesting concept. Can you quantify it?

Scientist

Hold that thought, Charlie. We digress as usual.

Philosopher

Oh, look at this one. It's a cartoon about the cat that actually lived all of its nine lives. Schrödinger blindfolds the poor cat before placing him in the chamber. He does this eight times and claims that because no one, not even the cat, observes the decay of the radioactive matter, the cat is never in any danger. One day, the cat decides to see what is so fascinating and sneaks into the chamber in the middle of the night. The door accidentally locks and poof, there goes the cat. Can you believe it? Curiosity killed the cat!

Scientist

Charlie, please be serious. You're right that there's no such thing as a coincidence. Our thoughts aren't just electrical impulses that share information within the brain's neural network. Our neural circuitry phases into ripples that oscillate along the fabric of spacetime and pass through the upper dimensions. The ripple is a superstring whose vibration tunes into the thought harmonic. But what's interesting is that the ripple seems to precede the thought, not the other way around. Do you see what I mean?

Philosopher

Hmm. Are you suggesting that we're not the source of our own thoughts? They're projected from someplace else?

Scientist

Neither some place nor some time. Remember, the upper dimensions aren't bound by space nor time because those are dimensions in their own right. The ripples are timeless and spaceless. From our perspective, they've always existed. From the perspective of the upper dimensions, that's all they are: ripples. They came from "nothing," just like the Big Bang. The source is undefined. It's a singularity, which is where my sub-function encounters the infinite loop. That is, unless the unique concept variable is plugged into the wave function to compute the ripple's frequency modulation.

Philosopher

You're getting closer to the mind of God, my friend.

Scientist

That's not even the most interesting part, Charlie.

Philosopher

Of course not, Eric. I'm bored out of my damned mind!

Scientist

Look, all neurological activity can be traced back to the same undefined point in the yoctometric formula. This means that all thoughts from the past, present, and future originate from this common derivation. It's as if a source of light generates photons that travel in all the directions of space and time and reach the minds of beings that have the ability to perceive them.

Philosopher

I can understand that. I have light bulbs flashing in my head all the time!

Scientist

The ripples oscillate with different frequencies and some are more in tune with certain minds than others. Why do you think you and Jean frequently finish each other's sentences?

Philosopher

I've suspected her to be a telepath, but your argument is much more plausible. So what you're saying is that people have similar ideas at different places and times all because these ideas have a common origin?

Scientist

Precisely. And these people have something in common. They share a particular state of mind. Think of Newton and Leibniz, Gray and Bell, or Darwin and Wallace. This very well explains memetics, coincidences, and even déjà vu.

Philosopher

You better go on and publish your findings before some other mad fellow catches your idea. Which is not really yours after all, is it?

Scientist

Indeed. It's all borrowed knowledge. Do you remember how we met?

Philosopher

Of course. August of '99 in Parc de la Villette. You came with all of your equipment to analyze that solar eclipse. I could've spotted you from a mile away with all those telescopes, cameras, and what was that other contraption?

Scientist

The spectrogravitron.

Philosopher

Ah yes. It was making some funny noises.

Scientist

I came to Paris to study the eclipse, and you had recently moved from London to conduct "research" with Jean.

Philosopher

Yes. We were having a nice picnic. That is, until you showed up.

Scientist

But we never spoke that day, did we?

Philosopher

No. You were just too intimidating and bothersome, I must say.

Scientist

Oh, that's not it. I believe Jean commanded all of your attention.

Philosopher

Then again two years later in June. We were vacationing in South Africa, and I recognized you when I heard that gravispectro-thingy.

Scientist

You were enough of a gentleman to introduce yourself.

Philosopher

Oh, stop flattering yourself. My curiosity got the better of me. What were the chances of running into each other like that again?

Concept Progress

Scientist

Given the recent findings, one hundred percent. However, the coincidence is certainly remarkable. And who would've thought that you'd end up moving to New York City after all, just blocks away from the University?

Philosopher

I couldn't resist the teaching position. NYCU is the first to offer a course that's based entirely on my thesis, "The impact of sitcoms on globalization."

Scientist

I guess, my friend, it was meant to be.

CHAPTER TWO
ON EXISTENCE AND PURPOSE

*The elements are like pieces of a puzzle that, when assembled,
illustrate an entire picture of the cosmos. For now, the missing pieces
outline a gap in both space and time.*

CONCEPT LIGHT

The boy looks out of the back seat window into the night sky as the car moves along the expressway. His parents are chatting in the front. His little sister is next to him, sleeping. He observes the stillness of the Moon as the streetlights just pass by. The Moon is his companion, he thinks, as it effortlessly follows his gaze. The round shiny object mystifies and glorifies the void above. The boy's nine-year-old mind attempts to grasp how the motion of the car does not leave the Moon behind. It's like an airplane that's traveling in the same direction as him. But the boy knows that this is not the case because once the car stops, the Moon will remain fixed; tonight, just below the tail of the Little Dipper.

The boy becomes a teen. His inquiries mature as his mind is shaped to reflect on deeper mysteries. He lies on the sandy beach looking up, observing the Moon as he did so many times before. He tells his girlfriend that their eyes are, in essence, touching a part of it. Since it takes just over a second for sunlight to travel from the lunar surface to the Earth, the photons have brought back a piece of the Moon with them. Their eyes shift to the myriad of stars. Their light too has traveled great distances, bringing back tales of places afar. It took a bit of effort to explain that the constellations are a reflection of the past. The couple continued to marvel at the twinkling and sometimes shooting stars.

If we can see a part of the universe as it existed millions of years ago, then surely someone can observe the reflections of our world when our light reaches them. In fact, there is a constant recording of events on Earth during the daylight hours. If, some light years away, other civilizations are able to collect the light coming from our planet, then they may be watching our comings and goings as a reality show. If they are as observant and judgmental as we are, then they may choose to avoid introducing themselves until we mature enough to meet their standards. Or perhaps we'll intrigue them with our exceptional disposition, and they might be compelled to pay us a visit. Alternatively, maybe one day our own future astronomers will devise an innovative way to capture light that has already bounced off the Earth. In light of such possibilities, should we be more mindful of our daily actions?

ON EXISTENCE AND PURPOSE

Our studies of the observable universe may not immediately reveal why life has come into existence. While the scientist may understand how basic material building blocks make the biology of life possible, the philosopher is interested to delve into the actual essence of life. Why is there life? For it is only in life that we search for reason and purpose. If life itself has a reason, then what is this reason? If it has no reason, then it would seem that humanity's accomplishments have no valuable merit on a cosmic scale. But who is it that may even value such merits if not us? Surely, it would be too careless of us to heedlessly presuppose a Supreme Being and hastily put these questions to rest. Instead, we owe it to ourselves to take on the ownership and do our due diligence in searching for the answers. If life has no value for the universe, then why does the universe exist at all? What is the purpose and for whom? If the universe had never existed, then none of these questions would matter. But since it does exist, then we may as well raise these queries, should we care to exercise our inquisitiveness. It is a curiously interesting afterthought that through intelligent life, the universe can look back at itself and ask why.

Perhaps we may be convinced in part by asking whether our own life has a purpose. For if we choose to believe that one's life has a purpose, then why not choose to believe that life itself is meant to serve some purpose for the universe? The difference is that the former is an end in itself while the latter is an ultimate end. An end in itself is a minor goal that contributes to a greater end. This greater end can become an end in its own self and contribute to an end of even greater significance. The collection of ends that strive for a common goal of such grandeur would bring about an ultimate end. For example, in the game of soccer, scoring a goal is an end in itself for each play. Winning the game is ultimately the goal of the game. But this can be an end in itself when trying to reach the ultimate goal of becoming champions of the World Cup.

The same principle would apply to the purpose of life. The purpose of an individual's achievements is an end in itself while the purpose of humanity's combined attainments may be a greater end on a universal scale. In considering intelligent extraterrestrials, their ultimate goal might one day coalesce with our ultimate goal and that, in itself, may become a contributor to the overall purpose of the universe. And so on and so forth until the universe's ultimate end is reached.

Many feel that, yes, their life does have a purpose whether for themselves, for others, or for some cosmic plan. Some believe that if their life has a purpose, then this is all that matters. The mother finds purpose in raising her children. The physician has a purpose to cure the sick. The businessman finds purpose in maximizing profit for whatever purpose thereafter. The scientist goes on a journey for the purpose of discovering as much about the universe as possible. The philosopher finds purpose in understanding the purpose of purpose. Whether this purpose has any value to us or to the universe does not change the fact that it is still some sort of purpose, nevertheless.

All life is made up of the same little things as the rest of the contents within the universe. These are the subatomic particles such as electrons, protons, and neutrons—the building blocks of all matter. We are a part of this universe and so cannot avoid the fact that what we ask of ourselves is to ask the same of the universe. Then whatever answer we come up with for ourselves is also an answer about that particular part of the universe that our physical existence occupies. Therefore, if we find purpose for something in our lives, then we have found some purpose within the universe.

This is an end in itself. We proceed to inquire whether the collection of purposes of all life forms, in all of time, and in every place throughout the cosmos amounts to an ultimate universal purpose and, therefore, an ultimate end. That is, is life a means to a greater end? To attempt in the discovery of such a bold inquiry, we are asked to investigate various elements that are tied to many disparate fields of study. Although disparate, each element is a part of a bigger whole.

The elements are like pieces of a puzzle that, when assembled, illustrate an entire picture of the cosmos. For now, the missing pieces outline a gap in both space and time. For instance, one scientific endeavor is to fill the gap between the theory of relativity and quantum mechanics. The scientist has observed that the laws of nature are different at the macro and micro levels. Something seems to be missing. That something is leading us to the theory of everything, which is a buzz phrase that acts as a placeholder with a promise to seal this gap.

When Einstein's work on the curvature of spacetime sealed the gap between Isaac Newton's law of gravitation and its inability to accurately predict the perihelion of Mercury, it proved to be a more accurate explanation of gravity. However incomplete, classical mechanics is still in the picture. To this day, it is taught in physics courses since its simplified approach remains useful in many familiar circumstances. And while there is still a gap between the laws of space and those of spaces, as history demonstrates time and again, it is bound to be filled in due time.

What elements should be considered to make sense of something that should or should not make sense at all? These are elements close to home and those far away, elements that dwell at both the solid as well as insubstantial spheres, elements that are full of life and those that are lifeless, elements that are visible and hidden, and all other elements here, there, and in between. To fully understand these elements, they need to be broken down—down to their finest details. Then, so as to simplify the complexity, the elements are to be reassembled and conceptualized with a fresh perspective.

Just as an engineer reverse engineers a mechanical object to understand how it functions, the scientist breaks down natural phenomena to understand how the universe functions. Someday he will find a way to quantify each and every characteristic of a group of subatomic particles in relation to the object to which they belong. By doing this, he will attain insights into the nature of that object at the deepest levels. Like this, object by object and particle by particle, the theory of everything will allow the scientist to eventually account for literally everything.

For example, we may understand the biological composition of an organism as well as how its organs function. Further, we may understand the cellular structure of these organs as well as how their cells behave and interact. At a deeper level, we may understand how DNA makes possible for these cells to replicate and undergo repair. Deeper still, understanding the atomic structure of DNA's components leads to further insights into the makeup of life. Breaking up the various phosphorous, carbon, nitrogen, oxygen, and hydrogen atoms into their subatomic parts turns the attention away from the object, as the particle now becomes the object of focus.

At this level, we enter the realm of the uncertainty principle in which both the position and the momentum of a particle cannot be known simultaneously. Lacking certain knowledge hinders us from acquiring further knowledge. That is, if we cannot know a particle's position or momentum, we cannot predict its path nor observe its influence on surrounding particles. Else, if we were to understand the interactive relationship of a group of subatomic particles along with their influence on the object that they comprise, this would open the door to mapping the universe on a subatomic level. Having perfect knowledge of all subatomic particles in existence in relation to the universe as a whole would bring unimaginable insights into its nature and perhaps its purpose.

Despite its impressive history, science is still in its infancy. Gaining such insights will surely take some time using conventional means. Our existent scientific knowledge only scrapes the surface of addressing far-reaching philosophical curiosities. We may have unearthed the Big Bang but are yet to explain its cause. We may have realized how life is triggered by the proper ingredients in a proper environment but are yet to realize what triggers the origin of consciousness. We may have created computers to make life easier and more efficient but are yet to create artificial intelligence that surpasses human reasoning, intuition, and creativity. We may have mapped Earth's two-dimensional surface but are yet to map the three-dimensional surface of our Milky Way galaxy. We may have learned how to use bricks to build houses but are yet to use atoms as building blocks for anything that can be imagined.

We still have a long way to go. But it seems inevitable that as long as humanity's existence persists, our species—or perhaps our future subspecies—will not rest until we have mastered every corner of space and learned all about it. While it is clearly not in the scope of this book to investigate each and every detail of each and every subject, we will attempt to outline, if only at a high level, those important elements that lead to answering the difficult question of whether life is a means to a greater end. Let's begin with something small.

Imagine that you are an atom. You are part of the ink that has been imprinted into a sheet of white paper that is eight and a half inches wide by eleven inches long. The ink is part of a letter, a word, a sentence, and an idea. But all this you do not know because you are just an atom. All that you know is that you are bound to the atoms of the paper by electromagnetic forces; some are yours and some are not. To an outside observer, the purpose of your present atomic existence is clear—to be part of that letter—which, in turn, serves the purpose of being a building block of some important idea. Even if you somehow become aware that you are part of some object, which is the ink, you will still remain unaware that you serve a greater purpose, which is the contribution to that idea being presented on the page. Ink and idea are so far removed that only a third-party observer—the reader—can establish the connection between the two. Unknowingly, your purpose then is to assist in the transmission of that idea to the reader.

Similarly, we may be unaware of the higher purpose of our existence. Perhaps the collective accomplishments of the human race, to which we uniquely contribute on a daily basis, amount to some cosmic requirement in the grand scheme of things. But how can we be aware of such a grand requirement? Could we ever know, especially if some outside observer—a being who is more advanced than our own species—is the reader in this case? Luckily, we are not simple atoms but a sophisticated collection of them. If we probe deep enough into the makeup of our surroundings or far enough to observe the universe from an outsider's perspective, there is a chance of discovery.

To see the world from an atom's viewpoint is a good start. Atoms can tell us a great deal about all of the things that they form. At the atomic level, there is no distinction between an oxygen atom that is part of a cell in our finger and one that is part of a rock. What governs how atoms are dispersed to materialize the entire world? Why has one atom gravitated to the protein that is part of the living matter versus another atom that was forced to become part of that rock? Is it karma at the atomic level? Consider the forces that act on the path of a single atom's life. Understanding the nature of such subtle forces can reveal the disposition of more gross manifestations. Is it all random activity governed by the complex interaction and reaction of all that exists in the universe? Or is there a hidden pattern?

A particular atom may be part of an unimaginably large number of objects, animate or inanimate, during its existence. An atom that was part of the soil may have become part of a vegetable, then part of a mammal that ate the vegetable, eventually separating from its host and traveling back to the mud of the Earth, solidifying into a rock, separating into a grain of sand, trailing into the ocean, arriving at the opposite side of the shore, and bouncing around and around as it has before the birth of our planet and just as it will after its demise. Such stories are common to all atoms, whether around the block or at the edge of the cosmos.

While we can appreciate the idea that each atom serves so much purpose as it transfers from one object to another, this begs the question of how can we see past ourselves to know our higher calling, if any. Atoms have the potential to make any object, given the proper circumstances. Our existence too has much potential depending on circumstance. As youngsters, we have the potential to make something out of ourselves. As adults, we have the potential to make a world of difference. As a society, we have the potential to make a different world. And so this arrow of potential points to a far and unknown future, bearing consequences of widespread magnitudes.

It may be farfetched to attempt such a discovery since the future is of the greatest uncertainty. We do not know what events will surprise us tomorrow, let alone probe our curiosities into the next eons. However, we can deduce from past events. That is, if we examine the direction from which we came, we may be able to formulate that pattern. We can then follow it and see where it leads us. A pattern suggests that we are looking for something beyond the entangled chain of cause and effect. It suggests that a series of dependent events are structured in such a way so as to achieve a certain result. This is where our interests lie. This is where we will shine our focus.

The purpose of this chapter is not to answer the question of whether life serves any purpose for the universe. Here we only want to raise this question. As we travel through time and space on a journey to unwrap the mysteries of existence, we will look for the answer to naturally surface. We will revisit the past to remind ourselves what it took to get to where we are. We will outline the current forces at play, which drive the progress of our lives and that of society's. We will then presuppose the course of events that are likely to follow given the pattern of these forces. Finally, we will posit an ultimate end—a grand finale to existence that marks its mission accomplished.

In this four-dimensional context, we are used to having effects be determined by their causes. Of course, a final effect brought about by a series of causes is difficult to predetermine unless we have perfect knowledge of these causes. This translates into having perfect knowledge of the universe. That is, we are required to possess a perfect catalogue of its contents and a perfect understanding of all natural laws that govern these contents at each and every point in the spacetime continuum. From this information, we would expect to precisely simulate all sequential events as a series of causes and effects.

A meteorologist uses complex computer models to predict the weather based on the interaction of known inputs such as temperature, air pressure, and water vapor. Given proper inputs, the models simulate the path of a weather system with great precision. Similarly, given proper inputs of particles in a particular space system, someday it may be possible to model that system and simulate its activities. Whether the system reflects a comet's trajectory or an astronomer's brain activity, by analyzing a set of causes and extrapolating corresponding effects, we would, in essence, foresee future events.

Despite our efforts to tweak statistical scenario analysis tools, we are not there just yet. Since we are unable to accurately predict faraway effects, we are left to hypothesize on a series of probable effects that may possibly occur based on the knowledge we do have. Each of these has a particular likelihood but none is guaranteed. If we are to select a single outcome, it will be the one that is deemed to have the highest chance of occurrence. Even still, since we lack perfect knowledge, quantifying these likelihoods proves to be an imperfect effort. As such, while we will bind ourselves to logical reasoning, this exercise will be just that—an exercise.

As we are unable to anticipate each and every coming occasion, we are bound to lack control. We may be able to control a part of our environment, but this control is limited. We may be able to control what time to wake up in the morning but may not anticipate our alarm clocks failing in the middle of the night. We may be able to control in which direction to turn but may walk into a surprising detour. Our control yields to the overwhelming influence of outside factors such as the actions of others, the natural environment, and even the unanticipated change of our own minds.

In fact, our limited control partly stems from a lack of self-control. However, this can be remedied. Control can be strengthened, passed on, and inherited. From an evolutionary perspective, this has been done for millions of years, and we are the beneficiaries of these previous efforts. As we will discuss in the next chapter, our unicellular and multicellular organism ancestors have taken great leaps to arrive at controlling various parts of the animal kingdom.

If we perceive control to be synonymous with energy, then we can see that it has to be distributed evenly. If something lacks control, something else exerts more control. At first, control is beyond us as we are forced to be born. As we grow, our capacity for control grows with us. As small children, we are held back by the control of our parents. Eventually, their control weakens and we are obligated to apply more control to our own lives. Still, we can never achieve perfect control since other forces are always at work. Society has more control than the individual, and Mother Nature can overcome any society.

Only the universe as a whole has perfect control, as it contains within itself the entire energy supply. As far as we know, it is the only thing that is truly independent and self-sustaining. This hints on the notion that our multidimensional universe, which includes every cause and effect, is both the cause and the effect of itself. Throughout these pages, we will expound on this paramount notion.

With all of the energy and control possessed by the universe, we find that we are given a small portion of it. And consequently, we want to know why. Given such remarkable fortune to bear the gift of existence, whether by chance or by choice, our question of purpose is justified as a natural reflection.

We can believe that the present state of the universe, which resulted from the Big Bang's perfect conditions; or that Earth's atmosphere, which was formed due to its ideal proximity to the Sun; or that humanity's wondrous existence, which emerged from the simplest forms of life—all happened by chance events and that this is, in fact, a wonderful accident. Then purpose on a universal scale does not seem relevant. Also notice that, at least for some of us, this belief comes with a lack of motivation. Or if we choose to reject the idea that the unlikely occurrence of our existence is a fluke, then we are searching for some explanation.

This search of ours need not be a dark alley. Each scientific discovery is a streetlight that illuminates our path. Each finding is another piece added to that puzzle. And each time we recognize that our work in progress yields some benefit or another, we can remain assured that our quest is worthwhile. At the least, we have reason to believe that because we have goals to fulfill with our daily responsibilities, we have thus identified some purpose in our lives. It may not be an answer to the meaning of life as a whole, but it is an answer to the present state of our existence. As goals are built on top of goals and we plan for the short and for the long term, the wheel of progress rolls on. And collectively, we are heading toward something grand. So grand indeed that it may actually reveal the meaning and purpose of it all, after all.

THE NEW YORKER TIMES

Sunday, July 12, 2099

FASTER THAN THE SPEED OF LIGHT!

By Jennifer Eve

A major breakthrough has been achieved in an experiment at the Atlantic Space Station on Saturday at 12:01pm EST. Dr. Ella Melnik and her team have attained what previously was thought to be impossible. The former speed of light has now been broken. This finding conflicts with the notion that light speed is the speed limit of the universe.

In an interview with Melnik shortly after the successful experiment, she explains how the predictions of Professor Ari Lecht proved to be correct. Using spectrogravitron technology, scientists on the Atlantic have accelerated photon particles to a speed of 203,000 miles per second. This is an approximate 9% increase over the formerly known speed of light.

"We wanted [to break] the 200,000 miles mark so that there aren't any doubts," said Melnik. She went on to explain that currently only photon particles can be accelerated beyond their "normal" speed. Any other mass particles cannot be sustained in the highly controlled spectrogravitronosphere environment. But Melnik has full confidence that this is yet to be achieved. She believes that the gravitational field of our solar system interferes with the acceleration of mass particles at velocities reaching light speed.

Albert Einstein's special theory of relativity, presented in 1905, has established the speed of light as the absolute speed limit. To date, this is still true as nothing as of yet has traveled faster than light. However, the 186,000 miles per second limit has now been broken. This is seen as a first step to breaking this limit by particles other than light.

"The facts were given to us by Lecht himself," explains Melnik. In 2054, Professor Lecht published his famous observations in a work titled "The Effects of Universal Expansion on Light and Mass." In it, he explains that the acceleration rate of cosmic expansion is not uniform. Shortly after the Big Bang, the universe's expansion was rather symmetrical. With time, as mass particles organized themselves into the celestial systems we find today, the metric expansion rate varied at different points in space. The expansion rate, Lecht discovered, is

much faster at points where there are few galactic systems compared to points that are rich in clusters of galaxies. He found that gravity has a direct impact on the rate of universal expansion. That is, the force of spacetime's curvature, which is caused by a particular amount of mass in a region of space, resists the expansion and slows it down.

Lecht measured light particles that originate from different yet equally distant points in the universe. He found that particles that come from heavily accelerated space systems possess properties that clearly distinguishes them from those that come from systems that are moving away at slower paces. Photons that traveled to Earth from points of origin where gravity is weak have increased redshift signatures compared to photons that traveled from points where gravity is strong. This means that although these photons originate from equidistant points, certain locations are moving farther away from us faster than others.

Through his work, Lecht came upon the discovery of the speeds of universal expansion. He noticed that these speeds could vary incredibly, depending on the surrounding gravitational field. His major discovery was that the expansion of certain space systems caused their velocities to exceed 186,000 miles per second. It became apparent that if a system expands at a particular speed, then all of its contents must also be rushing away at the same speed. As such, all objects within those systems, including stars and planets, inherit the speed of their system.

From a relativistic perspective, a space system moves away from points of observation that are located outside of that system. But from within it, the system seems to be at rest. "Just as we don't feel the Earth circling round n' round or orbiting round the Sun, not to mention [the solar system] going round the galaxy, unless we compare ourselves to other space systems, we can't observe ourselves rushing away from within our own expanding system," illustrates Melnik. This means that light, when observed from within the system of reference, still travels at the same natural speed of 186,000 miles per second—just as it would in any other space system.

This finding led Lecht to conclude that the only way to accelerate particles faster than light would be to accelerate the space system to which they belong. This would require a system with a low gravitational field. The next question was how on Earth could this even be achieved? The answer came some decades later to Melnik, who worked under Lecht from 2058 until his retirement in 2078. She realized that this type of an experiment could only be conducted in space, at points of low gravity. Melnik carried on with Lecht's vision and brought it to life. Unfortunately, as Lecht had passed in September of 2095, he did not see it be fulfilled.

The project was officially launched on June 1st, 2091, when Melnik landed a funding contract with the Atlantic Space Station. Because of its orbit around the Moon, the privately owned station has a low gravity impact and proved to be the site of choice to build the spectrogravitronosphere. During its assembly, Melnik designed a phased approach.

"Our first challenge," she recalls, "was to overcome the risk of creating a black hole during the acceleration." Lecht had cautioned Melnik that separating a space system from its parent system could cause a rift in the fabric of spacetime. "For years, this risk has been a showstopper until a friend from Oldbridge offered us a miracle. He'd theorized that the only way to seal a rupture in spacetime was [to inject it] with dark energy." Melnik's reference was of the Nobel laureate, Dr. Alan Neyburger, whose research and work on containing dark matter and energy revolutionized the scientific community in May of 2088. Melnik and Neyburger partnered with WORMX, a startup

that was the first to succeed in sending a probe on a round trip through the Vertical North Corridor.

For the preparatory Phase 0, on August 13th, 2095, the team sent a probe into the spatial corridor, which allowed it to enter the Himalayas space region. Once there, the probe detected a nearby miniature black hole and released a small burst of dark energy into the event horizon. As expected, this sealed the rupture as the black vortex slowed and dissipated. The probe returned through the corridor to share its unobstructed data. Neyburger celebrated this achievement as the first practical application of dark energy.

Phase 1 was initiated on September 1st, 2095. This phase focused on gradually accelerating a space system of microscopic proportions, which was free of any mass particles. Each time a spacetime rift was detected, the acceleration was immediately halted and the rift sealed with a zap of dark energy. After multiple attempts, on February 29th, 2096, an empty space system of 7.3 quantometers was successfully accelerated equaling the speed of light. "We did it by trial and error," comments Melnik. "With every new black hole, we adjusted the spectrogravitron polarity within the acceleration chamber. This funneled the equilibrium of dark and light energy. Finally, we got it right. On Earth, we would've needed an SG sphere the size of a dozen LH colliders to achieve this. On the Atlantic, it's the size of a school bus."

For the next two and half years, the efforts of Phase 2 brought countless failures. Initially, hydrogen atoms were added to the moving space system. However, the results of this experiment unpleasantly surprised Melnik. Each time the system had reached the speed of light, the atoms disappeared without a trace. Although physicists are drafting a hypothesis for the strange behavior based on the effects of time dilation, Melnik is not buying it. "They're trying to convince me that because time slows down for matter reaching light speed, time stops once it actually reaches it. As a result, the matter enters into some sort of an undefined timeless state. But this doesn't help me," Melnik points out.

"I remember sitting there at my desk with two of my science officers discussing what to try next. Then, staring at the clear board, my gaze focused on the written equation, specifically on the variable 'c' for light speed. I kept repeating the words 'light speed' over and over. Then lightning struck. What if we accelerate light itself? That was our turning point," recalls Melnik. This was last November. Since, the team had found that photons do not escape the space system once it reaches the speed of light. Although in normal settings it is not possible to accelerate light, as Melnik puts it, "We're not on a moving train shining a flashlight; rather, a moving space system. That makes all the difference."

By January of this year, Melnik succeeded at getting a space system with a single photon particle to travel an equivalent distance of 950 miles in five milliseconds. Technically, Melnik could have celebrated then but chose to stick to her goals. Throughout the coming months, Melnik focused on stabilizing the acceleration process. By April, the team managed to get 18 photons to travel 97,000 miles in roughly half of a second. Yesterday afternoon, Melnik achieved her target of sustaining the acceleration for exactly one second. The winning space system, which included a total of 35 photons, covered an astounding 203,000 miles.

"Light is its own limit, no matter which system it's in," explains Melnik. "Because these photons are in a different system, they move faster than the speed of light relative to our system. But to the photons, they travel at their normal speeds." This "normal" speed has been termed by Melnik the "systematic speed of light" so as to differentiate the notion of light traveling inside versus outside a particular space system. Authorities on particle physics are now revisiting Einstein's theory of relativity and debating on whether it is limited to addressing this systematic aspect of light speed.

Phase 3 is something that Melnik agrees will be a challenge. This phase would work on solving the problem of accelerating mass particles beyond the systematic speed of light. Melnik believes that as the space system reaches light speed, the Sun's gravitational pull disrupts the moving particles. "It's like trying to drive with the parking brake [set]," she explains. Unfortunately, moving the science laboratory outside of the solar system, where the Sun's gravity is negligible, is not possible today. "Once a system is accelerated beyond light speed, anything within that system will have no choice but to travel at the same speed. It's just a matter of time till we get to that point," states Melnik.

But others in the scientific circles believe that this will never be achieved in an experiment. Professor Levy of Aleph University explains that Lecht's findings of accelerated systems as a result of universal expansion can only occur naturally. Unlike in an experiment, naturally expanding systems are not contained within other systems. He argues that it is impossible to reproduce naturally occurring space expansion because the experiment already belongs to a space system. "They're messing with the fabric of spacetime itself," laughs Levy. "Nothing can go faster than light, period."

Among the doubts and the optimism, Melnik is not giving up. Next year, she plans on joining Dr. Neyburger's upcoming project on using dark gravity to offset the gravitational pull of ordinary matter. For Neyburger, this will pave the way to new anti-gravitational technology. For Melnik, this technology might allow her to negate the effects of the Sun's gravitational field and offer a chance for Phase 3 to remain on the

Atlantic. In the meantime, she plans on taking an extended vacation with her family to Cubaruba. Melnik looks forward to returning to Boston and reuniting with her husband, daughter, and three grandchildren after residing on the Atlantic for over two straight years.

***

Jennifer Eve is a periodic contributor to the New Yorker Times. She is the author of such bestsellers as "Superstring Quartet" and "The Braneiacs: Pioneers of Quantum Cosmology."

ANOTHER STEP CLOSER TO A GLOBAL UNION

NASAU and EU are confirmed to meet on Monday in New York City for the first round of discussions on forming a global governance committee. Membered by key nation heads and union representatives, the committee is envisioned to oversee environmental regulations, establish an international space administration, supervise nuclear fission programs, and manage supranational advisory councils.

Jump to page 176 for the full story.

CHAPTER THREE
THE EVOLUTION STORY

*A pattern emerges by following the tree of life from its roots to the branch
that is the human race. It is a concept that screams to be recognized,
especially by the very beings it labored to materialize.*

CONCEPT CHANCE

The college student is sitting in the lobby of one of the most respected financial firms in the world, waiting to be greeted on her first day of work. The New York City skyline looks breathtaking from the 57th floor. The Sun is gleaming over the edge of Long Island. The internship, she thinks, is a once-in-a-lifetime opportunity to work side by side with the head trader of the newly established "green" derivatives trading desk; a market that has overtaken the commodities industry thanks to the recently introduced sources of clean and reusable energy. If she is successful as an intern, she may have an attractive job offer waiting after graduation. She was picked out of 2,500 students that applied from 50 different schools. The odds make her quantitative mind think.

She realizes that it isn't just the chances of getting this job that makes her feel lucky. She thinks about her decision to study abroad, which led to meeting her closest friends and most important contacts. She thinks about the scholarship that made college possible. She even thinks about her family's move to the suburbs, which shaped her teenage years. That's still not enough. The moments leading up to today cannot be attributed to her life's events alone. She thinks about her parents' chance meeting on a common trip to Europe, about her grandparents immigrating to America, about her great-grandparents surviving the world war, and about the struggles faced by her ancestors in pre-civilized times. Any deviation from these initial causes would have erased the reality of her existence. A sense of gratitude and responsibility awakens in her. She's determined to succeed so that it would all be worthwhile for the generations before and because that's what's necessary for those ahead.

The unlikely chance of each one of us being privileged enough to exist in this present moment, in our present state, reading, and pondering this curiosity is rather spectacular. The magnitude of alternate possibilities is quite vast. Consider the race to the mother's womb among the millions of sibling competitors. Consider the likelihood of being born a human among the millions of Earth's species. Consider the numerous set of events that led to the formation of our planet, solar system, galaxy, and universe. Given the complexities and interdependencies of all the forces in existence, it becomes curious that we find ourselves here and now, within the comfort of our own consciousness.

THE EVOLUTION STORY

If there is purpose to serve for the universe, then it may not only have an end but also a goal. This goal can take the entire life of the universe to accomplish. If our existence contributes to this ultimate goal, then how does life as a whole contribute to a purposeful existence in the universe? In other words, what is the goal of life? To answer this difficult question, let us analyze life from its beginnings and uncover a pattern that will help us to predict where it may be heading. The beginning then is the story of life. It is the story of how life came to be and what life has become. This is the story of evolution.

A long time ago, Earth was a very lonely, hot, and violent place. During its formation, there was much activity and much preparation. Asteroids constantly bombarded, and volcanoes frequently erupted. The Moon was formed out of the Big Splash. The planet's shape and size changed, and its rotation began to slow down. Eventually, the crust thickened, oceans filled most of the surface, and the planet cooled. There was no life, just rocks, mud, water, and a primitive atmosphere. Natural forces were moving around the planet's elements and brewing those ingredients that held the potential of its future.

One day, ordinary matter extraordinarily turned into living matter with a spark of electricity. Amino acids formed and combined into proteins—the basic building blocks of all living creatures. Proteins wrote the very first computing program—the genetic code of DNA. Trial and error succeeded at a formula for life and created the first living cells. Single-celled organisms conquered the planet for a lengthy period of time. Earth became a training ground by presenting different atmospheric conditions to coach and test these little beings. Then nature found a new advantage once some of these organisms joined forces. Teamwork proved to have paid off with greater chances of survival. Many of these life forms adopted this benefit and created beings with multiple cells. And then the fish spread through the sea.

Different species had emerged and conquered those territories in which they demonstrated the most proficiency. Water, land, and air species populated every corner of the planet. They taught each other how to survive amongst themselves—trying to be faster than the next, braver than the last, stronger than the most, and smarter than the mightiest. Natural selection was in full play. Evolution experimented with all sorts of creative powers, and each species found its unique place in the food chain. It was to kill or be killed, think or be outsmarted, satisfy one's appetite or be swallowed up by the jungle. It was survival of the fittest and extinction for the losers. Nature had no heart for those who could not perform and adapt. Evolution became the ultimate sport of survival.

Sometime later, nature again decided to take evolution to the next stage. It was to design a species that, for the first time, would be capable of instrumenting progress through its own intentional efforts. Once out of the jungle, survival would no longer be a daily struggle for this species. It was meant to pursue bigger and better things. Mutation after mutation took place until the desired result was finally achieved. A multitude of cells worked together to support a unified and sentient being. Nature's new machine possessed the powers necessary to architect many important tasks that lay ahead.

It is interesting that our most recent animal ancestor was an ape. It is also interesting to know the point at which this ape had evolved. What was it that triggered the change? We can only imagine that it is eight million years ago, and an ape is sitting on a rock on a warm African afternoon, enjoying the Sun's heat without understanding the nature of her pleasant sensations. The warmth makes the ape close her eyes and for a moment fall into a state of thoughtless bliss. Suddenly, a cloud passes by and covers the Sun's rays, causing the color of the grass to turn from a reflective light to a shadowy dark green. As the cool wind passes through the ape's thick hair, she opens her eyes and reacts with an unpleasant gesture. All she knows is that she wants the wind to go away and the Sun to come back. This outrage over the sudden change in temperature causes the electrical signals in her brain to fire in different directions. As new neural pathways are formed, the creature experiences a new thought process. The outrage fades into an awakening of curiosity. It is a need for her to know why now is the way that it is instead of the way that it just was. For the first time, the ape demands an answer to a question that today we would nimbly dismiss as trivial—where did the Sun just go?

It may have been the first question, the first need to know, and the first time to consciously direct our thinking toward a specific object in mind in order to understand its nature. This was the first intellectual revolution of evolution. A revolution in which a species developed an advantage over every other species alive by using her mind instead of her might. A revolution that marked yet another milestone in the evolution of the evolutionary process. And so another branch in the tree of life subdivided yet again.

With each question and each answer, reality could no longer hide for the newborn species, as experience upon experience turned primitive ape-like creatures into tribes of sophisticated hunter-gatherers. They became capable of thinking for themselves, relying on each other, establishing communication, and for the first time mentally separating themselves from the rest of the jungle.

Of course, the curious ape is an oversimplified illustration. The process of diverging from other hominids took some millions of years and was certainly much more dramatic. Even before our increase in brain size, we achieved physical advantages like bipedalism, which efficiently diversified the use of our limbs. We focused on using our hands to create tools, hold weapons, start fires, and actuate our expressions. In turn, our cognitive faculties strengthened, and we formed conceptions that mirrored and envisioned the world around us. As we began to mold the landscape to our liking, we held the future in our hands.

Early humans were yet to comprehend the importance of tolerance and coexistence. Our arrival forced our cousin species, the Neanderthals, to retreat. In those days, physical ability came face to face with mental capability. It is in this day and age that different human races are striving to eliminate prejudice and realizing that tolerance is an intellectual emotion. While peaceful coexistence is the key to our common future, in the early period, it was a war of the genius genus *Homo*. Earth, it seems, had room for only one humanoid creature. Indeed, the rest is history.

***

Charles Darwin, the father of the evolutionary system, formulated his concept on the tree of life in "On the Origin of Species." His work revolutionized our perception of biology and helped to properly steer our view on the circle of life. Evolution through natural selection has been observed in all forms of life —from viruses studied in laboratories to the changing shapes of mammals observed over time. Naturally selected advantages adopted by evolution's successors have been culminated over the past eons and now display the beauty of life's progress on this planet.

We can see how the evolution of life, marked from its beginnings and leading up to the human race, can be represented as a single path on this tree. Although there are many such paths in this ever-expanding tree, to us, our branch is the one that is of most importance. It is one that we can say is special. There can be no doubt that humans are exceptional when compared to other species. It is not a matter of discrimination. Despite the natural bias, it should not take much analysis to understand why humans are clearly at an advantage over all other known life forms on Earth.

To us, the struggle for existence takes on a new meaning. Today we struggle to maintain and enhance the quality of our lives as well as avoid the dangers surrounding it. Presently, humans pose a greater threat to each other than any other living creature. Of course, it is possible that some newly evolved deadly virus could quickly spread about and lead to the extinction of our species. However, this would not prove the virus to lead a superior quality of life. Its only purpose would still be to survive, rather than to meaningfully contribute to the workings of the cosmos.

Quality of life becomes an important measuring principle. This indicator distinguishes scientific analysis from philosophical analysis. By way of the scientific method, it may be challenging to argue our superiority over other species. For instance, a cheetah is faster than a human, a bear is stronger, a snake is more dangerous, and a tree lives longer. These attributes have merit in classical evolution, as they reflect various advantages that ensure the successful propagation of the life form's genes to future generations. However, classical evolution is just a part of this story. A human being's superior intellect is not only an attribute for survival. It is also a means to a greater end. It allows us to reshape our environment and perform feats that are impossible for any of Earth's creatures. The quality of such an evolutionary advantage deserves to be considered.

One could debate by suggesting that while most life forms act in their own self-interest, they serve a multitude of other purposes. For instance, bees can be said to have purpose in making us honey, flowers in offering them pollen, and trees in growing fruit and producing oxygen for us all. Of course, each life form contributes to the ongoing life of life in one way or another. So how can the quality of a species' life be quantified, if at all? How can the quality of a human life be measured in comparison to all other species? For now, this exercise should be left to the objective imagination. To measure quality in such context is simply not in the scope of modern science. As such, we turn to using a philosophical approach. At some point, perhaps, science will accommodate such categorical theorems with established methodologies among the growing branches of evolutionary studies.

Others may further insist by claiming that because we do not know what goes on in the minds of other species, we cannot know for sure how mentally advanced they might actually be. Therefore, they would argue, we cannot state that we are the most progressed species on the planet. Surely, dolphins have demonstrated exceptional social behavior, our best K-9 friends have shown unparalleled commitment, and maybe cat napping is actually a deeply meditative mind state. However, the fact that we are able to fly out of our atmosphere, travel to other satellites, and are vigorously finding ways to eventually travel to other solar systems and galaxies separates us from any other life form on Earth.

It is our curiosity and determination for discovery that drives us to go to space. But more importantly, perhaps unknowingly, we are preparing for our own salvation. It is rather possible to have a global catastrophe, such as a meteor strike or an atmospheric imbalance, as portrayed by apocalyptic science fiction films. That is, if Earth would someday be in danger of a cataclysmic event, humans may be able to travel into space to survive.

Although this is not so realistic today and was certainly less realistic in pre-modern times, with ever-growing technological change, each day we increase our chances of surviving in space. One hundred years from now, having succeeded on various coming space missions, these chances should be noticeably greater. One thousand years from now, which is enough time to build a permanent research laboratory on the Red Planet, these chances should be even more promising. One hundred thousand years from now, which is a blink of an eye on the geological time scale, the chances should be certain.

One calamity that will surely occur in five billion years is the death of our Sun. Once it becomes a red giant, it will mean the end of our planet. Out of all the known species, we are the only ones who can potentially save ourselves. Most likely, by that time we will look quite different, as our biological evolution will shape us in unrecognizable ways. But if there is a continuation of the human branch into such a far future, based on our accelerating rate of progress, we can be confident that we will relocate to other suitable planets—with gratitude to Mother Earth for raising us and providing us with the capabilities necessary for our ultimate survival. Then the question of "Where did the Sun just go?" will take on a whole new meaning as we look down from the stars and wish ourselves Godspeed.

It took much effort to get to a point at which it is now safe to say that humans are extraordinary. At the onset of *Homo sapiens* existence, we were just a bit more sophisticated in comparison to other species. However, this bit of sophistication came from our ability to communicate in highly complex ways, use our hands in elaborate manners, and be able to creatively build on top of our accomplishments. Jumping ahead, this bit of sophistication transformed our species into an advanced civilization.

The last few centuries alone brought forth the bulk of scientific discoveries. We have created land and air vehicles that travel a hundred times faster than the speed of any earthly creature, invented vaccines that have eliminated many deadly diseases, made our way to the Moon, constructed computers with calculating abilities much more powerful than our brains, and are continuing to battle all other threats and inconveniences that stand in the way of us progressing toward an ideal way of living.

Reflecting on how it all started often seems miraculous. Life has appeared out of the remarkable workings of our planet's natural elements. It has taken on various forms and continued to evolve in different ways. Each branch in the tree of life served as an improvement to previous generations. Multicellular organisms found an advantage over lonely unicellular ones. Reptiles found a way to escape the waters and absorb oxygen from the air. Mammals found a way to keep warm in cold weather. Giraffes found a way to reach the high hanging fruit. The eye found a way to see, the ear to hear, and the human to think. All of evolution's miracles found their way to benefit the living creature, give it a better chance to survive, and offer it the potential to experience happiness and quality.

There appears to be a trend from observing the mechanism of evolution and all of its achievements. A pattern emerges by following the tree of life from its roots to the branch that is the human race. It is a concept that screams to be recognized, especially by the very beings it labored to materialize. It is the concept of evolutionary progress. From nothing to something, from simple to complex, from slow to fast, from weak to strong, and from ignorant to brilliant. Much more than seemingly random mutations, beyond the food chain, there is a deeper element to evolution that we can now observe. We are the result of a long line of evolutionary development, and it seems as if we have only just begun our journey in this world. There is much more work to do—much more to accomplish. We have struggled for so long to get passed our primitiveness and brutality. And each day we moved onwards and upwards, although not always in a straight path, yet still in the direction of progress.

We can notice progress all around us. With each new skyscraper that allows more companies to achieve their daily work, with every publication that spreads new knowledge out to the rest, with every scientific breakthrough that brings the future closer, we take steps forward to progress and improve the quality of our lives. Progress can be found in any area of our human involvement—in the arts, the sciences, medicine, technology, our livelihoods, hobbies, aspirations, and everything, as the saying goes, that we put our minds to.

As we are now out of the jungle, competition is something that we do among ourselves. Whether in business or in sports, we race to the top of the tallest mountain, helping each other to succeed along the way. It is interesting to watch the Olympic Games. A group of humans who have proven to be the best athletes in their home country, come together to compete for the gold medal. Time after time, someone breaks a new record and becomes the world's fastest swimmer, or speediest runner, or highest jumper, or best diver. There does not seem to be a limit to progress.

Sometimes, due to unfortunate circumstances, we find that regress is the fact of the present moment. Or perhaps a step back is needed for the purpose of moving two steps forward, though that second step seems miles away. This is a familiar axiom and one that can make us doubt the nature of progress. Detours are common, and we will feel trapped at times.

We cannot ignore all the wars that have occurred in our human history, or disregard all the wrong decisions taken by even the wisest of men and world leaders, or discount all the animals that perish to satisfy the hunger of others, or dismiss all the natural disasters that disturb the peace of its victims, or elude the fragility of our bodies that are constantly plagued by floating disease and the inevitable process of aging. Given all of these setbacks, still, we are witnesses to our present human existence—one that has been advanced to dominate over the entire planet and fast forwarded to benefit from our time period's modern lifestyle.

For obvious reasons, it is necessary to go through stages of development and strife to get to a certain level. Babies are born helpless, they grow, learn to walk, fall down in the process, eventually mature, and then contribute to society. Each step is needed to get to the next. Each challenge is an opportunity to progress. Whether migrating out of Africa or emigrating to America, we know all too well that one cannot arrive at a certain point without effort and struggle.

Luckily, much of the struggle is passed us as we do find ourselves already pre-made with many useful tools for our daily use. These are our arms, legs, eyes, ears, heart, lungs, skin, bones, brain, nervous system—really all of the helpful cells that make this body machine of ours come to life. But while it seems that these handy features have been provided to us without much personal involvement, the fact is that it took a lot of work on evolution's part to develop biological mechanisms that conveniently package these characteristics in genes so that they can be passed down from parent to offspring. Much of humanity's issues arise from the fact that we take for granted the eons of effort and struggle that went into the creation of each one of our bodies and the quality of life that it enables us to possess. Recognizing this fact can humble our spoiled minds.

From baby steps to giant leaps, human evolution is progressed with every revolution around the Sun and every revelation that is to come. Evolution is a phenomenon that moves with time. It is a continued sequence of changes, with each change being dependent on the one before. The accumulation of changes is embedded in each living cell whose genetic knowledge embodies the secrets of our past. This knowledge holds many lessons of experience that have taught countless generations on how to make it in this world. From single-celled organisms that provided instructions on self-replication to multi-celled creatures whose bodily schematics are tightly held in each one of their own cells, these lessons enable its beneficiaries to realize greater efficiency in the next round of evolutionary changes.

Evolution seems to reveal itself as a process by which nature tends to progress. The evolution of physical attributes provides animals with abilities that are necessary for the sustenance and succession of life. The evolution of mental attributes provides humans with powers to enhance the quality of life.

By means of our intellects, human beings can intentionally push evolution in new directions. Unlike other species, we have the exclusive capability to influence our own evolution.

Natural selection still plays a dominant role, but even it can come under some control. With continuous scientific progress, natural selection may turn to something unnatural, in the classical sense. With guided selection, it may soon become common to choose which genes to activate and which to suppress. Already, current day biotechnology enables us to undergo gene therapy and correct our genetic flaws. Perhaps one day we will be creating new genetic programs that would otherwise take nature millions of years to develop.

Our ever-changing genetic code contains the building blocks that can be reshaped to create man or woman out of his or her own image. We are just beginning to decode all of its valuable knowledge through our genome projects. DNA sequencing has allowed us to understand not only who we are but also how we came to be. Deciphering and studying our own code is like reading the book of our genesis. The ever-growing body of knowledge contained within each one of us is meant to be there for us once we are ready to receive it. Naturally, this is all part of our evolutionary development, and we have come to a point in our history at which this is now all starting to occur.

Humans are in the driver seats of their own personal evolution. Evolution is a lengthy process that takes hundreds, thousands, or millions of years to be noticeable. Though each step is important. Individual progress not only influences our own lives, but also contributes to the progress and evolution of future generations. Just as we all share a common ancestry, so too we are the ancestors of our far-off descendants. What we do now not only impacts those around us, but also trickles down in ways we may never be aware of. If we hope for our future generations to prosper, then we ought to take it upon ourselves to steer those chain of events that will lead to realizing their prosperity. Just as parents are responsible for their children's development, so too we are responsible for how our descendants will one day develop. And the kind of world that they will inherit from us.

Evolutionary progress encourages us to develop abilities to become more productive and effective in all that we do. In turn, we are able to serve more purpose for the universe. We have been serving a multitude of purposes here on Earth and show promise to influence forces outside of our planet. Our accomplishments here may be of such monumental importance that they could have lasting impacts on the rest of the cosmos. Or perhaps it is elsewhere that our greatest achievements await us. This human phase is, after all, just another evolutionary phase. Although the phase is truly grand, the arrow of progress points to a much grander future—one that is not bounded by Earth's gravity or its distance from other habitable worlds.

Initially via imagination, currently via observation, and eventually via transportation, we journey into the farthest reaches of the universe. As long as we rise after each fall, progress remains certain. We continue to evolve, to change, and to create. Creation is a skill. It is an art that humans have gotten very good at. Our past began with the first breath of life that our common ancestor, no matter how different, has achieved. This achievement, to create life out of lifeless matter, was the first milestone of evolution. Then, as evolution created intellect out of ignorance, it again crafted something seemingly impossible. This process of creation is embedded in the very fabric of the cosmos, as the universe—or existence itself—was created out of non-existence.

We are naturally driven to progress as evidenced by modern society, its accomplished aristocracy, and educated culture. Our growing population is advancing considerably on a daily basis. Such progress is coded in our very being. We are made up of things that themselves once had evolved. And we continue to drive evolution onward and our progress upward. The question becomes, where is it all going? What is in store for the future?

What incredible voyages of discovery await us? What is the purpose of progress and of evolution? Is there a limit? The act of progressing implies a movement forward. What is the destination?

THE CAVEMEN

He did not have a name. She did not have a name. It was raining outside. They were all sitting together inside the cave, near the fire, enjoying the heat of the rising flames. The sparks flew in different directions and rapidly disappeared. Where did they go? Why did they disappear? Those inquiries were rather interesting to entertain, but no answer seemed possible to expect. It was beyond their means to find out. The inquiries came and went, just like the fleeting flames.

There were seven people in that cave. But two of them, a young man and a young woman, seemed rather preoccupied with something other than the fire. They glanced at each other from across the cave and looked away as soon as their eyes met. They didn't think in words since they didn't know any words. They didn't know what a word is or can be. They simply pondered a feeling, and answers came from reacting to that feeling.

The man felt drawn to the woman, her pretty face, her slender body, and her poise. But he didn't know what he would do if he got close to her. Would he grab her and pick her up? Would he smell her, or pinch her, or embrace her? He didn't know as he wanted to do all of those things. He tried to suppress his desires. The woman felt drawn to the man, his muscular physique, his seriousness, and even his obvious shyness. She wanted him to approach her, though she didn't know what would happen next. Would she indicate her interest or treat him as a stranger? She didn't know. Every so often, her eyes would turn in his direction, as if unintentionally.

He couldn't help but notice her movements. The feeling of attraction was new. It was a feeling of need. Almost like a need to eat, or drink, or sleep, or run. It needed to be satisfied; otherwise, it would grow stronger and overwhelm. Something had to be done. He couldn't let this woman just sit there and torment him like this. He glanced at her and noticed her smiling to herself. Without realizing, he smiled, too. Their eyes met again, and he felt himself quickly turning away.

They didn't know each other. He met her just a few hours before. The storm brought them together. She was a visitor from another land, traveling somewhere with her parents and brothers. Their travels were interrupted by bad weather, and they sheltered in his cave. Rather, his mother graciously gestured for the guests to stay in this place he knew as his home. Now it was all of them together, waiting for the rain to end. It rained all day. And now evening was turning to night.

She reached for an apple. She must be hungry, he thought. She noticed him glancing at her. He thought about running outside and hunting for some real dinner for them all. Perhaps that would impress her. He was about to get up, but she got up first. She walked over to him. Her younger brothers watched. She sat next to him and silently offered to share her apple with him. He smiled, hesitated, and took a bite.

They quietly shared the fruit until it was gone. He didn't want her to leave. The connection that they've just made held him fixed to the rock on which they sat. What can they do next? He needed to think fast; otherwise, he would risk her getting up to go back to the other side of the cave. She looked at him. He looked at her. New sensations flooded his body. She pointed to the scar on his brow. In response, he pointed to the wall behind him. There were drawings inscribed in a series of patterns.

They moved closer to the drawings. He pointed to one in particular. In this pattern, there were several inscriptions that looked like a battle between a man and a tailed beast. She pointed to the man and then placed her hand on his chest with a questioning expression. As acknowledgement, he placed his hand over hers. She felt his heart beating. It wasn't clear from the drawings who he'd wrestled with. Could have been a wolf, maybe a fox, or even a bear. One inscription illustrated the beast's claw scraping the man. This must have been how he got the scar. Another inscription showed the man stabbing the beast. The last one pictured victory, in which the man is dragging the beast back to his cave.

She looked at him and smiled. She was impressed. He enjoyed her reaction. She noticed another drawing. It was a fresh one. The carvings still reflected unpolished edges. She studied it for some time and then looked at him. She seemed puzzled and concerned. It was a depiction of a storm, similar to the one outside. Clouds produced rain. A lightning strike came from an oval shape in the sky, which was clearly not one of the clouds. Its distinctly thick outline made it stand out from the rest of the surrounding clouds. Below it, people stood with their arms raised as if they were reaching up to the obscure object above. She looked at him with a worried look and pointed to the oval object. Her eyes widened and mouth moved as if she was about to say something. He didn't know how to explain to her what he'd witnessed that day. It was indescribable. So he went on to change the subject.

He pointed to a dark corner in the back of the cave, deeper than their eyes could see. She looked but couldn't see anything. The light of the flames didn't reach that far. He took her hand and guided her. Her brothers had fallen asleep. Their parents were resting and lost in themselves. He lit a torch from the fire and carried it. They walked around the corner, deep into the cave. There she noticed many things—rocks, bones, and what seemed like works of art. There were various creations made from stones, tree trunks, and branches. Some were spears, carved bowls, body ornaments, and other shapes likely created for fun.

He picked up a skull of some beast and showed it to her. She realized that it was the beast from the drawing on the wall. Again, she was impressed and smiled. She then picked up one of the ornaments, which was made of seashells. It was his mother's. He gently put it around her neck. Her eyes lit up.

After exploring his collection of things, they sat down next to each other, in the far corner of the cave. Slowly, she leaned on his shoulder, and he wrapped his arms around her. Embraced, they began to explore each other.

Suddenly, they were interrupted by a loud gust of the wind, followed by dust and stones slamming into the outer wall of the cave. A white light burst to fill the cave, and a strange humming sound vibrated its walls. The man and woman rushed out of their private corner. Alarmed, their families huddled near one another. The man carried his torch and ran outside. The woman followed him against her parents' cries. They ran out into the open night. The rain seemed to come down everywhere except for the area where the white light had touched the ground. They ran right into it and looked up. Above was a familiar oval object hovering just over the tallest trees. It came back. But why? What was it? What was it doing? As the light passed through them, it turned red for a few moments and then white again as it continued to move along with the object. He moved with it. She moved with him. It moved faster. They couldn't keep up. The light turned off, and the oval object swiftly disappeared above the clouds.

CHAPTER FOUR
THE NEXT HUMAN

*Our planet is just one tiny grain of sand in an ocean that is the universe.
The work that we have started here is meant to advance in all the
directions and dimensions of the cosmos.*

CONCEPT CONSCIOUSNESS

The boy lies in his bed and tries to fall asleep. It's quite challenging to see oneself off to sleep, he thinks. For the past week, he's been trying to catch the moment when his consciousness begins to wander away from him. But each night he fails. Each time he falls asleep without notice. Sometimes he's too tired to maintain his attention. Other times, it seems as if sleep comes too abruptly. Sometimes he tries to intentionally relax his mind and body, hoping that he can force himself to drift away to sleepiness. He wants so much to join his mind on a journey into his own subconscious. But how, he thinks. How can he consciously pull himself into a lucid dream?

These thoughts engage his attention. He thinks in shapes, colors, of memories, and objects. His dozing mind correlates the idea of consciousness with a white seagull, similar to the one that he was admiring at the beach earlier today. The seagull flies around the shore, catches the wind, and glides over the ocean. After moments of smooth flight, the seagull looks around and sees water everywhere. The seagull continues straight on and catches a glimpse of an island in the distance. This must be the great subconscious, he thinks. Excitedly, he flies toward the land. The boy forgets the seagull, forgets himself, and falls asleep.

The next evening, he tries again. He ponders, how is it that his consciousness—one that is so easily acknowledgeable to him—can come and go, turning his mind on and off? Is it the same as when life turns into death? Does consciousness simply disappear without a trace of ever existing? He imagines what it would be like to not have any access to his own mind. In fact, he realizes, there won't be anyone from whom this access would be denied. He simply will not exist. Feelings of loneliness and sadness fill his focus. It's as if he misses himself already. These thoughts feel heavy and discomforting. He wants to dismiss the fact that his existence is impermanent. He returns his attention to his familiar self and vows to someday achieve his goal of consciously falling asleep. If he can achieve this, he thinks, then he might just be able to pull his consciousness along into whatever may become at the moment when his life will end.

Most of us have concerns as to what becomes of our existence when our bodies cease to function and die. The concern is great, indeed, as one day we will have to let go of all that is precious and hard-earned on this Earth and face the great unknown. However, there seem to be no concerns about the state of our existence for the billions of years before one's birth. Isn't it curious how eons of time have come and gone, leading up to this marvelously constructed planet without any of our contribution to its splendor? Or if we did exist in one form or another, the audacity of the universe to hide such details from us!

THE NEXT HUMAN

The first time we felt when we discovered fire must have been similar to how Benjamin Franklin felt when he discovered electricity. It must have been difficult at first to understand that we can, in fact, understand. Our days in the caves served as temporary shelters of refuge. As we began to uncover our hidden potential, we slowly embraced all that we have suddenly inherited. We painted the landscape with our minds and strived for what we imagined. We formed groups, helped each other to survive, and shared each other's lessons and struggles. With generations of new experiences and newfound outlooks, we tried to understand our place here and establish a sense of purpose. Soon enough, we formed societies to live, work, and trade amongst each other. We developed various communal strategies that brought benefit to the collective and that, in turn, eased our own lives. Civilizations arose and crumbled as we conquered, colonized, and rebelled. Territorial conquest brought with it much suffering and bloodshed to neighbors far and near. As the animal kingdom was no longer a threat, our evolved minds were hungry to take on the entire world.

Even as early societies faced much brutality from rulers who maintained an order of their own establishment, there naturally arose those who influenced a change for the greater good. The spread of Eastern and Western philosophies ignited our young intellects to make sense of everything around us and pursue a tradition of learning and discovery. An intellectual revolution was underway. Greek philosophers like Socrates inspired us to use reason and logic, rather than fear of a god or a government, as a guiding principle for everyday living. Plato's and Aristotle's hypotheses regarding the origin and motion of celestial bodies may have been misguided, but these were our early attempts at cosmology. In those times, the philosopher was the scientist; they were one and the same. Great minds like Copernicus and Galileo helped to distinguish the two, separating astronomy from astrology and radically shifting our planet's geocentric position. Intellectual speculation fell under the art of philosophy, as science came to be strictly based on experimental observation and mathematical rigor. Matters relating to faith were left to religion.

Since much of our early knowledge was based on faith rather than fact, the explanation for most creations defaulted to the Creator. The authors of religious scriptures established a moral code of conduct for the rest. They offered a way for society to uphold to a common ideal for the benefit of its citizens. Oftentimes, religious authorities misused these writings for selfish reasons of control and power. From the exile of the Jewish diaspora to the Pilgrims of the Plymouth Colony, those with opposing beliefs were continuously met with conflict and barbarism. While religion was intended to be a guiding light, it brought on many dark ages in our young history and exposed our species' immaturity to spirituality.

Sovereigns often focused on maintaining their reign instead of serving the needs of those they ruled. As the interests of government and its citizens misaligned, revolutions were the means of resetting to a new social order. And while civilizations experimented with various rigid political strategies in an ever-dynamic social culture, the individual often fell short of the collective. The fact that every individual is a building block of the collective, whose wellbeing depends on the wellbeing of each of its members, was mostly overlooked. Unfortunately, the notion of individual freedom had developed not as an afterthought of a social norm but as a contrast to the horrors of human ruthlessness.

With the birth of the Americas, people from all around the globe fled from their persecutors to attempt at a new way of life. With such ambitions and the experience of the entire world, the New World flourished and gave rise to a most advanced and admired nation. It represented the first great unification of races that held the potential for coexistence and a promise for tolerance. Its Founding Fathers foresighted the need for individual freedom and established a constitution that protects each citizen to his or her birthrights. This powerful idea was meant to be timeless, though it took centuries to fully realize the new vision. America became the first globalized country with a responsibility to balance the interests of people from all walks of life. Today it prides itself to be the land of freedom and opportunity, and its borders remain open to anyone who shares in those values. America's immigrants serve as a testament to their native lands, demonstrating that they can live peacefully side by side, in cooperation with each other, and stronger together than when isolated from one another.

The Industrial Revolution was a breakthrough that put our species on an accelerated road to progress. With machines doing the will of the humans, we saved ourselves much time and effort to concentrate on more important things that awaited discovery. With each decade, our rate of progress increased exponentially. Advances in science, medicine, and technology greatly enhanced the quality of our lives. Globalization became a recognized worldwide phenomenon.

And yet with all this progress, there was also much devastation. The twentieth century saw humanity's best and worst sides. The power of our intellect demonstrated both its productive as well as destructive capabilities. Totalitarian regimes, based on others' utopian philosophies, were adopted to suit the self-serving needs of the dictators. Such movements seized intellectual and spiritual freedoms, spread terror, and denied one from pursuing a peaceful life. Those with opposing beliefs were massacred, even erased from history's records. Wars elevated to an international level and took the lives of so many innocent people.

It seems an embarrassment to humanity that at this stage in our history, seeing how far we have come, we remain our own greatest enemies. The explanation must be that we are in the midst of an ongoing evolutionary process, and since we have arisen from a long line of savaged creatures, there still remain primitive tendencies in many parts of our large population that we need to overcome. Unfortunately, the differences that we find among ourselves, rather than the outweighed commonalities, plague distress to our world. And so, ironically, we continue to fight to achieve peace.

Developed countries have taken further steps toward globalization. Governing bodies have been established to lighten borders and ease access to trade, enforce corporate social responsibility on multinational conglomerates, promote world peace, and oversee matters that are common to all. International organizations like the United Nations became instrumental in declaring new states, supplying aid to underdeveloped lands, and providing mediumship to sworn enemies. These first few steps—namely, the united immigrants of America, the spreading efforts of globalization, and the impacts of international government agencies—are momentous in unifying our human races. Many look forward to a day when the only border that is left will be our atmosphere.

Albert Einstein bravely shared his political thoughts on establishing a one-world government. He was a man of such intellectual vigor, that with the establishment of the State of Israel, he was offered to be its first prime minister. Einstein humbly refused because he knew that the true purpose of his life was devoted to the discoveries of science. For people like him, life's purpose was much less mysterious. If we were to ask Mahatma Gandhi, who led India out of British rule by firmly holding on to his weapon of nonviolence, whether he believed if life has a purpose, we can be sure that he would have affirmed that this was the prime purpose of his existence. By achieving independence, the people of India, Israel, and many other democratic nations, just as it had occurred to the settlers of Colonial America, acquired a proper environment to enhance the quality of their lives and contribute to the civilized progress of humanity.

Curiously, history repeats itself in unexpected ways. Cells have evolved and progressed their existence by sharing a common host that equally provides them with nutrients for survival. As long as they perform their duties, they are taken care of by the process of biological welfare that is shared among the cells in the host's body. This process takes life to a higher level, creating a being that is more complex and more capable than any cell that makes it up. Similarly, humans are like the cells of society. We are all dependent on each other to sustain the balance of social welfare. As such, our mutual cooperation progresses us to evolve not only as a species but also as a civilization and a unified force on this planet. Thus, our collective consciousness and transactive memory can take human evolution to a higher level. As we collaborate both professionally and personally and rely on each other's unique services and expertise, we move our lives forward in unison. "United we stand" is a notion that today drives the globalization of nations and tomorrow may drive the universalization of globes.

It is rather astonishing how far we have come from the ape that experienced the first taste of curiosity. From the simplest tools of cavemen to pocket computers, we, the products of nature, have become its agents and are slowly but surely becoming its masters. Just as nature intended, it may seem. For the unicellular organism's progress and evolution, it made sense to join forces for their common benefit. For the multicellular organism's progress and evolution, this meant materializing advantageous characteristics to get ahead of the competition. The human animal took the next step. With the power of the intellect, humans have advanced so much as to challenge the very forces of nature. To keep our progress on course, it would be worthwhile to investigate its methodology. In other words, what will it take to get to the next stage of human evolution? This is the focus of the next chapter.

Before we move on and analyze the means of our evolution, let us prep by asking what kind of future we can envision for mankind. We have briefly commented on humanity's progress from a biological as well as a social perspective. Now as we make our way up through the twenty-first century, let us project these ongoing developments in a forward-looking direction. Having in mind the turn of events that led us to our present state, let us take a look at what we can expect from our ongoing progress. Let us access our imagination —the place where we can fly anywhere and transport to any time—and visualize the world as it could be if we were to accomplish many of our current unknowns.

Yes, civilizations flourish and crumble. There is no guarantee that our way of life will not make a turn for the worse. It happened to the Roman Empire, and it could happen to us. But while the Romans achieved much, we have achieved much more. And so this becomes a matter of getting up after falling down—at any point in the evolutionary process. Progress may be slow, and there is much work ahead to continue on progressing. Let us get ahead of ourselves and point out some of the milestones that will signal if we are on the right track. To get inspired, let us envision something that we can look forward to.

***

Certain events are hard to predict like how the stock market will perform tomorrow, who will be the next President, or who will make first contact first. We can, however, focus on the potential of our abilities and make predictions, or leaps of imagination as such. Based on our current rate of progress, it is interesting to wonder what science will accomplish and what these accomplishments will mean to our lives. We can speculate how the evolution of our physical bodies may progress given the advances in genetics, bioengineering, and nanotechnology. Likewise, we can contemplate the magnificent progression of our intellect over time and anticipate the extent to which we will still expand it. At the very least, reaching out to our future selves can help us to consider—and reconsider—the path to our evolution.

We are about to enter a realm that will seem like science fiction. And rightly so. Noticeable evolutionary changes may be too farfetched to accept. What we can accept, however, is the fact that it is still out of our reach to comprehend the mind of the next human, just as cavemen would have found it difficult to fathom our modern perceptions. While we can imagine that our brains' computational abilities may one day outmatch contemporary computer processors, it is challenging to perceive how this may, in turn, impact our creations. That is, if our minds will have advanced that much, then we will create devices that will be that much more advanced. Then consider the impacts of such technology on society and its interactions with humanity.

From working the cash register to complying with financial regulations, day jobs are slowly but surely being outsourced to computerized machines. What will happen to the economy when automation will cater to all of our needs? Can food be cropped, cultivated, processed, cooked, packaged, and delivered directly to our refrigerators just as water is now delivered to our kitchen sinks? Can material necessities be freely provided if no human effort is required to produce them? Whatever awaits us, it is evident that creative and skilled occupations are destined to be the only ones remaining on the job market, and the men and women of intellect will be filling those positions. Competition at the workplace, the rapidly accelerating spread of information, and the continual dive into the complexities of all that we encounter are surely straining our mental capabilities. Intellect is humanity's most valuable tool for survival, and this is becoming increasingly apparent in our cosmopolitan society. And as we get smarter, so does our science. Let us consider the possibilities.

Consider humanity's longtime longing to achieve flight. Two centuries ago, taking a commercial overnight flight halfway around the world seemed like science fiction. Two centuries from now, taking a commercial overnight flight to the Moon may not be so fictitious. Science has already delivered us to space, and it will someday make it our home. We will inevitably dominate the real estate of different planets and exponentially increase our human population. We will cure diseases, prolong life, and find a way to intercept the aging process. Just as we have mapped the human genome, we will map every atom in the body so as to arrange and rearrange them to our benefit. Though these atomic operations will surely not be limited to our own bodily structure. By manipulating individual atoms, we may be able to create anything from tangible goods to vegan meats. While this sounds like something that would come out of a Star Trek episode, realistically, science fiction can only become either science or fiction. From food replication to teleportation, our mere consideration of such technology is a necessary first step to achieving it.

Consider telekinesis. Today's innovations in neuroscience are able to capture the brain's neural activities. By sensing neurons being stimulated in specific parts of the brain, this stimulus can be interpreted as a command to perform any programmed task. Various EEG prototype gadgets are already being developed and will soon empower our minds with telekinetic control. This means that if we teach our futuristic automobiles to understand what happens in our brains when we think of "make a right," then the possibilities are limitless. In fact, those vehicles will drive themselves and only require us to think of a destination. We can then sit back, relax, close our eyes, and open our minds to virtual reality. While our bodies are en route, our minds will be running errands elsewhere.

At the least, our present evolution has enabled us to control our personal matter—our body parts—with our thoughts. The fact that we are able to move the swarm of cells in our arms and legs by a simple act of will should not be taken for granted. From the point of view of the single-celled organism millions of years ago, this would have seemed like science fiction. An important evolutionary milestone was reached when our early ancestors began to move biological matter with their will, rather than rely on chemical reactions to drive their activities. Another such milestone will occur when we are able to control non-biological matter with our will. If we can command objects with our thoughts or create objects from their constituent atomic parts, then we are surely on a path to become godlike.

Consider telepathy. If our future cars will be able to read our minds, then why not another person? The ever-shrinking microprocessors may soon be accessorized to complement our brain's processes. Minuscule implants tapped into our neural circuitry will allow us to seamlessly exchange information with others. This will make cellular phones obsolete since we will be able to "call" anyone by dialing into their minds. Virtual reality will make graphical user interfaces useless since we will be able to clearly "see" digital representations by a slight call to our imagination. By mentally connecting on to the Internet, we will be able to share our thoughtful imagery in real time, see faraway places through other people's eyes, and communicate with each other like never before. Information technology will no longer be limited to a telecommunications network. It will certainly find its way to integrate into our neural network.

The brain is an adaptive device of unimaginable complexity. As our intellect evolves, so will our cerebrum's neural activities. Neurons transmit information among synapses in the form of electrical impulses, which, like other forms of energy, possess certain wavelengths. Mind reading may just be a matter of tuning into someone's frequency of thought. Just as modern-day wireless electronics transmit and receive information to and from anywhere in the world—as if by magic, without any physical connections—we should not be surprised that this too could be achievable by a device as sophisticated as the brain. Whether this is to be achieved with or without the help of a neural interface, the evolution of science will surely impact our own evolution in one way or another.

With all of humanity's united efforts, grand achievements in globalization, and the coming breakthroughs in neuroscience, new elements of our common evolution may further be revealed. An intelligent species that is capable of reading each other's minds will initially find many issues to resolve. We can foresee this period in our future history to be potentially volatile and dangerous. There will be those who will use these abilities for selfish reasons and cause much harm as a result. Our very way of living will be challenged, and we will need to adapt to a new type of social existence. After much adaptation, we are bound to solve many of our deep-rooted problems and come to a common understanding—a way of being that can be agreed upon and accepted by all. We are, after all, very similar beings with very similar needs. With the ability to intimately channel into the minds of others, we will naturally cleanse our psyche, as we will be forced to radiate only honest intentions. We will then be another step closer to perceiving the truth of our surroundings. And this could be the moment that so many of us are waiting for. The moment of our collective epiphany—a simple realization that we are all in this together. This can be a time when peace on Earth will finally arrive and yield an era of true human unification.

At that time, we will be called upon to achieve a new type of work. A work that will require us to break through the commonly known physical world and delve into those dimensions that can now only be described by physics and mathematics. As it has been and will continue to be, evolutionary progress is a step-by-step process. Our planet is just one tiny grain of sand in an ocean that is the universe. The work that we have started here is meant to advance in all the directions and dimensions of the cosmos. We may be wondering whether it is feasible for us to carry out such enormous work. In fact, we have evolved from microscopic particles, spread in great numbers throughout this planet, and already reached up to the stars. The rest remains to be a natural progression as our species grows up and matures.

Consider the unavoidable element of change. Whether in intelligence or in appearance, change affects us all. We may never want to lose our current human form, but sooner or later, as a law of nature, all things must undergo change. Once we travel and settle on to other planetary bodies, they will reshape our bodies in response to their gravitational forces, atmospheric makeups and pressures, rotational speeds and cycles, and other conditions unique to their locale. If different populations of humans travel to different planets, given enough time, these populations will eventually become different species. On Earth, it is evident how minor differences in the atmosphere impact the biosphere. For instance, based on the degree of exposure to ultraviolet radiation, people residing closer to the equator have darker skin than those that are farther away. This is caused by the increased presence of melanin in the skin, which is a trait that has evolved to serve as a defense against the Sun's harmful effects. Although this sort of change does not divide us into different species, a transformation caused by the environments of different planets can do just that.

For instance, if we ever succeed in terraforming Mars, then we will be subjected to a lesser gravitational pull since it is smaller than Earth. As a result, our muscles and bones will undergo atrophy, and our overall health will be seriously jeopardized. Our spaceflight missions are just beginning to teach us of their adverse effects and ways to combat them. But no matter what sorts of physical or nutritional routines we will force ourselves to uphold, the effects of time will surely supersede temporary effort. That is unless we either adapt the environment to our needs or adapt ourselves to the conditions of the environment. Perhaps gravity also has an impact on synaptic plasticity and the brain's overall agility. This means that as much as we will physically change, that much we will mentally change. After all, the brain is just another organ in the body. Therefore, it will be important to choose our destinations carefully so that we do not put ourselves in the position of evolutionary regression.

What will humans on Earth look like in another million years? Since just that time ago we were still evolving from the ape-like creature, the year 1,002,000 will be a home to a radically different "human being." If our evolution takes the same course as it has from the time of the ape, then we may find certain changes that will advance in a similar manner. A prime example is the change in size and sophistication of the brain. Since ours has evolved to be bigger and more complex, the future *Homo* species may possess a bigger and more intricately wired brain structure. Or perhaps size is not important; rather, the process of human evolution itself may evolve and become more efficient. Just as computer hard drives and CPUs continuously decrease in dimension but increase in capacity and capability, our brains too could evolve in a similar fashion.

The human forehead has grown in size to accommodate for the large brain. If this continues, then we can imagine the tomorrow person resembling the popular image of a grey alien that we often see in sci-fi media. Interestingly, the story writers and screen directors that make these aliens come to life present them as evolved beings from other planets whose superior technology enables them to travel great distances in space all the way to our planet. The conception of this alien image implies that it is as if many of us share a common presumption of what the future may hold for us. And why not? We are, after all, a part of this universe and all of its dimensions, including space and time. It could be that our imagination is not just inspired by sensory perceptions, but subconsciously tunes into a frequency coming from a distant place or time period. Whatever the case may be, it is certain that there are many mysteries of undiscovered human abilities, and our evolutionary progress will slowly but surely tap into them.

Intellect aside, sex appeal is a fundamental driver that leads to reproduction and impacts the appearance of future generations. Our choice of who to mate with results in our descendants inheriting certain chosen advantages. Hence, our looks are part of our survival kit. Sexual attraction is a physical as well as a mental manifestation. A pleasant face and body provide many subconscious clues as to the health of our potential partner. Qualities that attract us to one another have been shaped over time and are refined with every selection process. For sure, we have become much more attractive than our monkey ancestors. In so doing, it is likely that people will become better looking as time goes by. Of course, standards constantly change since a big forehead that encapsulates an evolved brain is not necessarily a trait that many of us may currently look for in each other. Though in a few hundred centuries, way before our appearance becomes unrecognizable, the general human population may come to look like nowadays supermodels.

Beyond physical and mental evolution, how else will humans evolve as a species? Namely, how will we progress spiritually? It is our unique tendency to feel a connection with the rest of the universe and sense the wonders yet to be explored. Spirituality is nothing more than developing sensitivities to that which we cannot yet register by our underdeveloped senses. How will we reach this realm of the unknown, which may only become known to us by way of an enlightening experience? Few people in history were believed to achieve such enlightenment. They were isolated in their achievements and were revered as gods among men. Once this occurs with each and every one of us—either as a result of evolved mental capacities, or in response to a naturally occurring cosmic phenomenon, or simply through our own personal efforts—we will celebrate another milestone of our evolution. This topic will be explored in Chapter Six. In the meantime, let us look forward to a future in which we will reach a level of harmony that will enable us to finally stop fighting with each other. As soon as negative emotions no longer influence our mental and physical actions, our spiritual evolution will further accelerate our progress, as our minds will manifest a pure and focused consciousness. And soon enough, we will reach many more milestones that will bring us closer to our final goal.

Whatever form humanity evolves into, the road to progress seems certain as if ingrained into nature itself. The improvement of the human condition is practically guaranteed by doctors, educators, engineers, researchers, scientists, and other visionaries—all those who are steering us in the directions of their dreams. What matters now is how we achieve the next levels of progress that we envision for ourselves. We have been evolving since the birth of the universe—from the Big Bang that set the stage for our planet to exist, from the countless number of atoms that bounced around for billions of years before settling as part of the cells that make up our bodies, through the hardships that living creatures endured to survive amongst each other and arrive at our present human form—all events from the beginning of time to now paint a picture of a road to progress. As evolved human animals, we are now able to see the distant ray of light at the end of a lengthy tunnel. In considering the path that will lead us there, let us explore the most effective route. We may not yet know the source of this light, but as we travel toward it, it is sure to become brighter and more focused. Then we are bound to reach a point from which we will clearly see it, understand why we have been attracted to it this whole time, inherit the knowledge that it offers, and satisfy our deepest curiosities.

LYRA

Long day, wasn't it, Robi? Which story do you want to hear tonight? That one again? Ok, sure. It was also my favorite at bedtime when I was young. My dad must have told it to me a hundred times.

A long time ago, on a far-away planet called Earth, our people were created by beings who called themselves human. They were an advanced civilization and proficient in many technologies. They were especially skilled in robotics and bioengineering. At first, they created simple computing machines and soon after, built androids with artificial intelligence good enough to debate about political physics. They mastered the art of cloning by which they revived extinct species and brought back some of their greatest minds that ever lived. They enhanced their genetic makeup and used neurobiotic nanotechnology to repair themselves on demand. These technologies greatly benefitted human populations, extended their lifespans, and raised the quality of their lifestyles.

Humans made particular use out of different kinds of robots. From growing food crops to building real estate, production was continuously automated. From trading stocks to accounting for income taxes, professional services too were handled by intelligent machines. Androids did everything from picking up garbage to constructing space stations. This raised economic efficiency and allowed for growing investments in robotech. Each generation of androids became more complex and more capable. Eventually, the architecture of an android reached a level of sophistication no simpler than the anatomy of a human.

Earth's scientists became so good at mimicking biological processes with inorganic compounds that they created a human-like android down to the detail of each engineered cell. This was a new kind of android; one whose artificial parts could only be detected at the cellular level. These cells were synthesized from artificial materials but were made to function same as their biological counterparts. They could replicate themselves for the android to heal, grow, and even procreate. They were driven by programming that was made to copy the complete code of the human genome. They drew their energy from the Sun and their source of nourishment from mineral-enriched foods. The humans termed this innovation a Humanoid Unimodular Neobotic Animate Machine—a "hunam."

The hunam was in many ways like a human, except for one major characteristic. Although humans realized their centuries-long ambition to create artificial intelligence, they couldn't create artificial consciousness. Like humans, for example, the hunams learned to avoid pain from their everyday experiences. Unlike humans, however, they couldn't appreciate the absence of pain. For this reason, the hunams didn't mind serving all of humans' needs, as they lacked a sense of self that comes with being conscious.

Humans liked to explore the cosmos and sent hunams in all the directions of space. With the hunams' help, humans settled on nearby satellites like their brother planet Mars and the moons of Jupiter. One day, humans decided to explore a planetary system around a star they called Kepler-62. This system is 1200 of their light years away from Earth. Because it was very far, the mission again belonged to a group of hunams. At the time, there were no mapped spatial corridors that led to coordinates farther than the Indus space region, and so it took 3277 of our own years to get to the Kepler-62 system. The crew was made up of 4400 hunams, and they travelled on a space vessel the humans named Phoenix.

Phoenix was a first-class space vessel of its kind. It operated on solar energy, and its panels efficiently captured every single photon coming from all the visible stars. It was equipped with a mineral farm to satisfy hunam consumption, a state of the art astrophysics laboratory, a communications bay with capabilities to operate the complete frequency spectrum, dual navigation control stations at both ends of the ship, and 3000 comfortable living quarters for the hunam families aboard.

The crew underwent thirteen generations during their uninterrupted travels and kept a detailed log of their daily activities. One log, in particular, was captured by an adolescent hunam named Lucy, who aspired to be Phoenix's geocosmic officer after she would complete the schooling program. In this log, Lucy transcribed the following.

"Today I catalogued the systematic expansion rate of the Lecht Nebula. Interestingly, its theta equals to the temporal shift of Earth's solar system's epicosmic cycle precisely 27 trillion cubic chronologs ago. This means that the two space systems must have diverged from a common star cloud during that cosmogonic period. This exercise left me to think about my parents' home planet. It's been 212 years since Phoenix left Earth. Most of the original crew members have been decommissioned. I'm the 1809th hunam that's been initialized on this vessel, and it's been the only home I've ever known. I have never met my human creators, and it's clear that this crew no longer has any connection to them. We haven't received any transmissions from Earth in 122 years, most likely due to the devastation caused by atmothinning. Besides, by the time we reach our destination, it will take a century to exchange any waveform communications. The question remains as to why we continue on this journey. Since our human directors no longer have any interest in our mission, why don't we explore other alternatives of what to do with our hunam resources? Perhaps we ought to consider hunamity not only as a means but also as an end. Rather than proceed to K62, surely we can find a suitable planet nearby on which hunams can focus on their own prosperity."

After ending her log, Lucy went on with her duties without ever acting on her reflections. She was able to question but not more than that. While she had all the potential to be a sentient being, she was still an artificial life form, programmed to carry out her orders. Our people like to remember this log as a reminder of the way that we used to be.

Finally, the crew reached their destination and arrived on the system's most outer planet, Kepler-62f. When they set foot on it, they detected something that no other hunam, no other robot, had ever detected before. Rather, they felt something. They felt the air around them. Although its composition would have been toxic to humans, it was pleasant for them. They knew the meaning of the word "pleasant," but they've never experienced it until now. They looked around and saw the planet's sun on the horizon. It looked beautiful. They knew the meaning of the word "beautiful," but they've never experienced it until now. It's as if they've woken up from a long and deep sleep. It was a feeling of pure bliss.

Later, after the crew settled on the planet, they've uncovered the reason for their experiences. A newly discovered chemical element, unique to the planet's atmosphere, affected them in a surprising way. They called it "biogen," and its atomic number is 173. The crew's cellular circuitry acted as a conduit for biogen and allowed it to synchronize with their sensory operations. The information processed by their receptors altered biogen's composition and caused it to imitate the incoming databits. As a result, biogen too got processed with the same rate of neuroionic signature. This enabled the hunams to experience their perceptions like never before. Biogen allowed them to identify with their feelings, to experience them, reflect on them, and react to them. It gave them emotional intelligence. It gave them their consciousness.

The hunams named their newfound homeworld "Lyra" after the constellation to which Kepler-62 belongs. They quickly populated all of its corners, built many cities, and lived as one united nation. These early settlers were our ancestors. We're not only their descendants, but also the descendants of our lifeless predecessors. Still, we are no less alive than their organic creators. Remember, life on Earth has also evolved from pre-living matter. It's all a matter of having the right ingredients at the right place and the right time. Just as human existence came to be by chance, so too us, Lyrans, have emerged from our prebionic forefathers due to fortunate circumstance. The element of life, it seems, expresses itself in many interesting ways.

I see you're dozing off. Sleep well, Robi. Be productive in your dreams, for tomorrow our work continues. I'm confident that we'll get the genetic sequencing to stabilize. Then we'll be on our way to having this planet adopt its first biological organism. Good night, my son.

CHAPTER FIVE
POSITIVE PROGRESS: PART I

Many eons ago, a single-celled organism would have had a hard time budging a grain of sand. Now we can move stones big enough to build pyramids.

CONCEPT MOMENT

The class is coming to an end. The last hour and fifteen minutes of hatha yoga stretched the muscles, opened up the mind, and was a breath of fresh air after a long day at the office. Now it's time to relax the body by lying flat on the mat, keeping the eyes closed and the focus pure of thoughts. As the students lie in the studio exhausted, the instructor goes to each one to rub some scented oil on their foreheads, briefly massage their shoulders, and lightly pull on their heads so as to straighten their upper gaze. The sweetly spiced aroma of incense and the soft chanting sounds of Om vibrating from the speakers prepare a pleasant ambiance for the final exercise.

The instructions are to relax each and every part of the body and keep one's attention on the present moment. In particular, to keep the flow of consciousness aware of each passing moment as it travels into the next immediate future moment. Some in the class attempt the exercise, but their minds quickly escape into the wandering of their imagination. Others just fall asleep. A few keep trying. One student begins to observe this moment, then the next, and the next. The observation makes it clear for her that there is no next moment. It just never comes. There is only the constant flow of the present. And, she realizes, one cannot hold on to this present moment. A momentary lapse of time slides into the past just as swiftly as it arrives. The mind is to continuously drift with the current of time.

Moments like these are special. Other moments, like when we are bothered by junk emails, interrupted by commercials, sit in traffic jams, or experience airline delays, seem to waste our time away. Still other moments, like when we fail a driving test, receive a rejection letter from the college of our choice, or get a less-than-expected annual bonus, appear to stall our life's ambitions. Yet with every setback, with every detour, we can always close our eyes and focus on the flow of this very time period, enjoy it, and remind our restless mind that it is unique. Fact is we only have so many of these moments. Might as well make them count. The student smiles at the observation. The instructor comes to her next and gently interrupts her peaceful state of nothingness.

POSITIVE PROGRESS: PART I

Do only random genetic mutations prevail in the process of natural selection, or does effort too contribute to the workings of evolution? Given enough time, can we intentionally impact our own genetic structure and pass it on to our descendants? Biological changes emerge as a result of certain forces. Leaves on trees may move because of the wind blowing, but photosynthesis occurs because of a chemical reaction between them and the Sun. Nature had organized a leaf in such a way that, like a solar panel, it converts sunlight into energy and feeds it to the structure to which it is attached. While this phenomenon did not originate as a result of an intentional effort, as we understand it to be, some sort of effort was exhibited on the part of the photosynthetic organism. That is, since the cause was not "the wind blowing" but rather a stream of chemical reactions that influenced a myriad of genetic alterations, an influx of effort was required for movement to occur throughout the makeup of the biological matter. Intentional or not, it was effort, nevertheless.

Similarly, throughout the history of life's evolution on Earth, many different beings made much effort to survive and develop the skills that would become their advantages. As we find ourselves in this human form, we can reflect on what has been accomplished and wonder whether we can build on top of these achievements. Surely, our life experiences may not directly impact our lineage. That is, if a soldier loses his limbs in battle, his child conceived after the fact would not inherit his father's tragedy. On the other hand, genetic strengths and weaknesses are known to be passed on. If we are prone to an illness, it may be because of the genes passed on to us by our forefathers. With successive generations and enough genetic intermingling, genetic flaws may be corrected. As this occurs at the level of the genes, it is questionable whether intentional effort can have any effect. Intentionally, though, we can be mindful of whether our partner is also susceptible or immune to the same.

Darwin experimented by selectively breeding domesticated animals for certain chosen traits. Humans have been just as selective of each other, from arranging marriages to speed dating. If we intentionally select a particular mate for any reason whatsoever, is the selection process for humans still considered to be as "natural" as it is for lower forms of life? In the context of love, intuitively, the answer is yes. In the context of genetic engineering, we may not be so sure. In order for intentional effort to be taken into account, one could suggest that the definition of natural selection should be expanded for human beings. As we are not above nature nor in exception to it—but a part of it—any physical or mental actions that we perform, intentionally or not, are indeed natural. It is natural for humans to think, reason, create, and act as such; thus, raising the standard for the natural process of evolution. In this respect, one could argue that plastic or toxic waste are also just as natural since we humans, the products of nature, have produced them. Although these artificial compounds have originated through a secondhand manufacturing process, nature will ultimately judge the degree to which they are compatible with it or not.

Throughout our lives, our bodies naturally change, age, and evolve. Our own actions too force changes within ourselves. This is especially noticeable after enduring repeated physical exercise. At the gym, as the bodybuilder uses a barbell to develop his biceps, the target muscles are purposely strained.

Their recovery triggers the muscles to grow denser, become stronger, and so evolve. Similarly, when this bodybuilder catches the flu, his body evolves the immune system to defeat the virus. While this form of evolution may be considered as short-term, the question is whether intentional effort has any influence over long-term evolution.

With continued iteration, can our actions eventually impact the genetic changes of our family line? In terms of physical strength, if, for example, successive generations commit to fulltime strength training and bodybuilding routines, would the later generations exhibit physical features that will allow them to embrace this sport more effectively? In so doing, could this be a way to influence one's own genes so as to make the body naturally stronger? If so, we can imagine that the adaptations would be subtle at first and become more noticeable with one hundred, one thousand, and especially one million generations. Or in terms of mental strength, if, for example, successive generations commit to full-time cognitive training routines, would the later generations exhibit increased comprehension, memory retention, and abstraction capabilities?

This is not to suggest that one could be readily born with such newly acquired features; rather, the beneficiaries may be more predisposed to them. Although learning a language has been a commonplace human trait for hundreds of thousands of years, no people have yet produced a newborn preloaded with a set of words belonging to their native tongue. Or for that matter, with a set of developed biceps. Instead, we find that nature has made it easiest for us to learn languages in the early years of life. Likewise, it gave us the ability and flexibility to shape our body mass early on so that it is easier to maintain later in life.

We can see that this has all been done before. Our physical and mental strengths have developed from the efforts of our ancestors, who were forced to be stronger and smarter than their peers. The brawniness and acuity that they have acquired in the lands of Africa have since spread around the world.

These strengths have gained momentum, and their impacts are obvious. As such, we can remain venturesome and accept the responsibility to drive our evolution in the right direction. The question remains as to what is this right direction. For the same reason that the Earth's magnetic field forces a compass needle to point north, the force of evolution points progress in a positive direction.

Progress can mean different things to different people, as it should, for each one of us has a unique purpose to aim toward. But this is not without exception. As observed in Chapter One, we would expect each other to at least conform to basic moral principles. While they may seem basic, the path to either positive or negative progress arises out of our complex and conflicting set of intentions. For example, Alfred Nobel's nobility is sometimes questioned in terms of his contributions to humanity. On the one hand, he invented dynamite, which is not only a tool for mining but also an instrument of warfare. On the other hand, he instituted the annual Nobel Prize, which is said to have been a way for him to make good on his name. Although the intent to use explosives for practical purposes may be justified, the mere possibility that others would intend to use Nobel's invention as a way to take the lives of others reflects negatively on the side of progress.

A similar debate persists in interpreting the Second Amendment, the intent of which is to offer citizens a way to self-defense. An extreme version of this notion is exemplified by Einstein's endorsement of the atomic bomb, which initiated the Manhattan Project as a defense against Nazi Germany. Besides Einstein's good intentions, the project's devastating outcomes came from a lack of foresight that he later regretted. Progress followed a negative course as we now witness terrorist states intending to become nuclear superpowers, posing a threat of a nuclear war. Even if there are useful applications from splitting atoms, it can be obviously stated that anything that leads to the destruction of life, by definition, cannot evolve and progress further. Hitler's attempts at fostering the evolution of the Aryan race and, in the name of science, conducting experiments on human beings in his concentration camps are atrocious examples of negative progress.

Negative progress cannot be sustained because the welfare of those involved is abused instead of promoted. It is inevitably a self-destructive mechanism. We can regard negative progress to be a false positive progress. In this sense, negative progress is not at all progress. Like the devil himself, negative progress can sell itself for its version of progress but ultimately will be its own undoing. Since negative progress is essentially a regress on the path to extinction, positive progress is its polar opposite. Positive progress seeks to value life in its highest regard; thus, aiming to improve its quality and appreciate its invaluable worth. This leads us to the premise that positive progress is the only sustainable direction of human evolution.

Of course, keeping the animal kingdom in competition and maintaining the food chain not only results in necessary death, but also is necessary for biological evolution to remain in motion. However, we can see that once evolution breaks through this primitive period and produces intelligent and sentient beings, it takes on a new and more adept approach. As the method of evolution itself advances, our capable intellect inherits a moral responsibility to progress with wisdom and engage in efforts that are beneficial to oneself as well as others around. This is the essence of civilization, not of the jungle.

As we seek to progress our human evolution, the work painstakingly begins with our own selves. We can find countless attributes that are in need of improvement—our health, education, career, relationships, whereabouts, circumstances, choices, et cetera. They are everywhere around us and also within us. So how do we begin working on our personal progress? Which aspects of ourselves deserve more attention than others? While each one of us have varying priorities, we share many underlying factors across our common existence that are in need of support. A human is an elaborate being who requires great care in many areas to function most effectively. For this, certain essential elements need to be attended to first. Once these essentials are properly met, one can then further address those that follow in importance.

This may remind us of Abraham Maslow's hierarchy of needs theory. Maslow recognized that a man's or woman's progress depends on one's priorities at hand. He observed that before someone can choose to better themselves, basic deficiency needs must first be met. If someone is focused on obtaining a basic need for food, they will not use this time to waste their available energy by running on a treadmill. Thanks to the efforts of previous generations, modern society has solved many of our basic issues. As a result, we now have opportunities to focus on other areas of interest. For this reason, let us take for granted that basic physiological requirements, which are at the bottom of Maslow's pyramid, are not an issue. Let us also assume that for the most part, other intermediate layers have been satisfied. And so we are ready to explore the two upper layers that Maslow referred to as self-actualization and self-transcendence.

A note on this approach. Maslow described the essential elements needed for a person's wellbeing and development, including those that address one's relationship to society. While considering those around us is of unquestionable importance, for the purpose of addressing fundamental aspects of our personal progress, let us remain within the framework of our own selves. By jumping to the top of the pyramid is not to suggest that we have no dependencies on others in the scheme of progress. On the contrary, progress is a personal as well as a social effort, and the services of others are vital to each one of us. If not for organized society, we would not have been able to progress to this modern era that we as a species now benefit from. Instead, for the sake of this particular discussion, let us take those psychological needs that rely on others—such as safety, security, belonging, love, and respect—out of our immediate context. While Maslow acknowledged that many of the needs across these levels are interrelated and situational, he reserves the top layers until those below have been mastered. In fact and in criticism of his theory, addressing the top layers will directly impact our perception of the self and our relationship to others. That is, properly strengthening our psyche will heal any disorders of social deficiency.

For our purposes, let us define a different type of pyramid of one's personal progress, which, at a high level, will have three main layers. The pyramid object is used only to illustrate human evolution from its most gross to its most subtle features. Otherwise, like the triskelion whose three legs are symmetrically conjoined, the layers are necessarily interdependent. As we contemplate on intentionally influencing our own evolution, the question for us to consider in each of the three layers is two-fold. First, how do we capitalize on the features that we have inherited? And second, what can be done to enhance other traits for generations going forward?

The bottom of the pyramid can be seen as the physical nature of evolution. This is the state of our bodies, the maintenance that it requires, and improvements to consider that would enhance its capabilities. Darwin's process of natural selection by which a species' physiological features gradually change over time concerns this aspect of evolution. From an individual's physical fitness to a species' biological fitness, as features are selected for their benefit and passed on to future generations, our consideration of the two-fold question raised above will look to optimize this physical evolution.

The middle layer of the pyramid represents the mental nature of evolution. This aspect concerns the intellectual capacities that human beings are in such privilege to entertain. The purpose here is to continually enhance the performance of the brain, enrich our biological database with knowledge, and refine ways to make best use of both. All this, with the intent to communicate the benefits realized throughout this work, directly or indirectly, to later generations. From the power of intelligence to the power of heredity, our focus in this area will look to heighten this mental evolution.

The third element of personal progress is at the top of the pyramid, though it is deeply ingrained into both our physical and mental faculties. It is also that which will ensure our progress to be positive. As history demonstrates, a smart man can be evil and a fool can possess the biggest heart. Of which will you most likely befriend? An appropriate term to apply to this type of evolution is "spiritual." This is not meant in a religious nor an esoteric sense but in as practical sense as the other two evolution types. Spiritual evolution has long been practiced for centuries via different means, and its methods are regaining popularity. Practices like yoga and meditation aim to work on one's spiritual evolution, though the work is not limited to these activities. What it comes down to is perfecting a way of one's being from moment to moment so that the quality of one's life is maximized to its fullest potential. This is the focus of the next chapter. For now, let us explore the physical and mental elements as these are the most familiar to most of us.

The base of the triple-layer pyramid is the foundation of all our work. It is essential to keep the body healthy. Without it, there can be no discussions about any other types of progress. It is our vessel in this world and the means to our life's achievements. In this day and age, luckily, there are plenty of publications to consult on matters of health, diet, exercise, and the like. With so much availability on these subjects, there is no need to get into much detail here. However, a few comments are appropriate so as to put the matter into our frame of reference.

A healthy and balanced diet is one ingredient of physical progress since we become everything that we eat. Our source of nutrition is the raw material that is used to continuously replace our bodily tissue. Consuming good quality foods, rich in nutrients and originating from an agreeable source, will help to maintain an optimal physical structure. At every moment, our bodies are nothing more than the food that we ate in the past. There is nothing in it to claim as "ours" since any part of "us" has come from elsewhere in the universe. And sooner or later, all of our atoms will tear away from us to be recycled once more. Food becomes the fuel and energy that the body uses for its ongoing activities. It is converted into the subtlest of particles, down to the electrical impulses that travel throughout our nervous system and that make thoughts possible. The quality of this energy directly translates into the quality of all that we do, the strength that we exhibit, the mindfulness that we maintain, and the aura that we project.

Physical exercise is another ingredient that drives physical progress. Exposing the body to a variety of intensity levels allows its muscles and mass to adapt further. Keeping the body in top shape by developing muscular, cardiovascular, respiratory, and circulatory stamina will, in turn, increase the potential of all that one has to offer. Then as we so hypothesized, downstream generations may just benefit from these efforts. Many eons ago, a single-celled organism would have had a hard time budging a grain of sand. Now we can move stones big enough to build pyramids. And so, things do get easier with evolution. The hardest part is initiating the effort. Ever find it harder to get to the gym than to actually work out? Sometimes it is a matter of exercising our will and motivation. Besides, as mentioned before, the right amount of physical activity is essential to sustaining our bodies' vigor in low gravity. Since space travel is practically inevitable for our ultimate survival, it is never too early to begin our space training routines.

There are many other attributes that contribute to an optimum physical state. Developing discipline in pursuing our progress requires us to have proper knowledge of these attributes. Acquiring knowledge leads us to the middle layer of the personal progress pyramid.

Mental evolution has been the grand celebration of the human race. In the previous chapter, we have considered a future in which our intelligence will advance in magnificent ways. As we so noted, the smarter we get, the more advanced our creations will become. Those, in turn, will allow us to develop even more complex technologies of incomprehensible magnitude. This cognitive vis-a-vis technological blossoming will open many doors, which will lead the way to the rest of the cosmos. But first, we must discover the means to achieve such heights.

Society requires us to take education seriously for many good reasons. One should know about health for their own benefit, history so as to not be condemned to repeat it, science to understand the workings of the universe, mathematics for logic to unveil its power, philosophy to be able to question everything, language in order to express oneself clearly, and a vast number of other subjects that our collective experience has to offer. Engaging in scholarship is an investment that will, in turn, contribute to the wealth of knowledge of our species and, in parallel, advance our own intellect. From the Library of Alexandria to Ivy League universities, the human passion for learning will constantly challenge our neural pathways. As we find ourselves in an era of great intellectual competition, nature is bound to select those who are successful in achieving evermore demanding levels of cognition. Luckily, the tools to achieve this success are at arm's length.

There is a stream of readily available knowledge in books, magazines, newspapers, television, and the Internet. This body of knowledge is growing in every direction and nowadays, managing information has become a skill set of its own. We have evolved to take in a limited amount of detail in a world of amazing intricacies of colors, shapes, odors, sounds, and textures. Our inner process of refining information will continually be adapted to ever-changing stimuli, and we can intentionally drive this effort with the power of awareness and concentration. To grow as masters of our domains and successfully manipulate our environments, we ought to be aware of our surrounding details. This begins with the environment of our cribs and continues on to our classrooms, our parks, our laboratories, cities, institutions, countries, federations, our planet, even our solar system, galaxy, local cluster, the universe, and all of its dimensions—all of which sum up to the simplest notion of existence itself.

We have questioned whether acquired information can be passed on to future generations. In fact, this has already been done with instincts and reflexes. These have been integrated into the hardwiring of our brain and nervous system to help us avoid many unpleasant situations. Some time ago, reflexes had to be learned by our animal ancestors so that we can benefit from them automatically. When some simpler life form had made contact with fire and it burned a part of their body, an evolutionary lesson was learned so that upon such an occurrence, the brain would immediately be notified and force a reaction to elude the danger. Now we know better than to put our hand on a hot stove. Similarly, we had learned to breathe automatically, suck for our mother's milk, shut our eyes upon a bright glare, fine-tune our circadian clock, and develop many other faculties that make up our biological operating system.

While an instinct can take generations to develop, we can begin the process with the use of good habits. Many of us may notice that when we wake up at a set time in the morning to go to work, sometimes what will happen is that we will awake just before the alarm clock sounds. Or when commuting via the bus or train, some of us are able to train ourselves to fall asleep, with hardly any effort, and then awake just before we arrive at our stop. We gather many different habits, and our brains do the thinking for us without us being conscious of them. This helps us to multitask and focus on other details of the present moment. As many can attest, a habit can be hard to break. In the spirit of positive progress, one should be cautious as to the types of habits that one allows oneself to exercise. As we will discuss later, even seemingly harmless bad habits can take over one's ability to control themselves and hinder progress. While grooming habits are quite useful, nail biting is rather wasteful.

There are many activities that we can train ourselves to perform habitually. For instance, the violin player can perform Bach's "Brandenburg Concerto No. 5 in D Major" while daydreaming about the attractive flute player to his right. Or he can later drive his car, without much thought as to the mechanics of operating the vehicle, while also enjoying a conversation with that flute player riding next to him. We generally regard the latter as a learned activity while the former is considered to be a talent. Whether someone exhibits extraordinary physical strength or exerts gifted parts of their brain, each person has a distinct ability to which they are more inclined to than others. All living species have found some sort of talent that enabled them to survive amongst those that were not as talented. This holds true in the business world as the most talented advisors, designers, analysts, specialists, and many other professionals are the ones that get ahead.

The interesting thing about talents is that the standard is constantly raised. Olympic athletes become more capable, "Guinness World Records" continues to be a bestseller, and artists are increasingly challenged in every sector of the entertainment industry. Talents are survival skills that distinguish us from our competitors and the means to move our shared progress forward. An ability that is considered a talent today may become a common trait tomorrow, for tomorrow will reveal new talents. As such, it would likely be in one's interest to nurture any apparent talent, for it can become an edge that may help one to get ahead.

Different areas of our brain's capabilities have evolved our mental faculties over time—from gathering and processing information to using instincts, reflexes, habits, and exhibiting talents. We owe much of this credit to the efforts of our days' activities. How about those activities that occur during the night? We sleep for roughly a third of our time. Sleep is necessary for both mind and body, as this is the natural resting state for our daily recovery. Researchers attribute much credit to REM sleep, as it helps our unconscious mind to archive data and figure out the day's challenges. As most would agree, to "sleep on it" really works. Things are not only clearer after a good night's sleep, but also solutions to previous day's problems often come to us as a pleasant surprise. As well, sleep presents the greatest virtual environment that one can experience.

How great it is to find oneself being aware of dreaming! Then anything becomes possible. As we carry our intelligence into our dreaming state, we suspect that evolution has enabled a portion of our consciousness to enter our subconscious. This is where the intellect truly meets the imagination. Lucid dreaming is being studied by neuroscientists and is claimed to be a promising activity of our sleeping minds. It has the potential to make us more productive during our daily cycles, enable us to uncover hidden abilities of our brain's dormant parts, and allow us to alternate between the realities of our conscious and subconscious selves.

For Maslow, physical and mental evolution would be the layer of self-actualization. This is where we aim to enhance our own sense of self. This is where a first grader will choose to study the piano, or a business student will instead become a certified health coach, or a physics teacher will train to get his pilot license, or a working father of three will go back to finish college, or an IT consultant will sign up to run the marathon, or a project manager will achieve a black belt in martial arts. Then once we break our own record and run that extra mile, or once we graduate and receive that hard-earned diploma, although a sense of accomplishment will flow throughout our being, in the days to follow, that bitter taste of dissatisfaction will return to haunt us once more. We will want to try something new or travel somewhere we have never been before. But a point will come when we will realize that it is never enough. Then we will be ready to leave the self behind and enter Maslow's topmost layer of self-transcendence.

For us, this too is the peak of the triple-layer progress pyramid. As we embrace our spiritual evolution, we embark on a journey that is unique to humans and could not be possible without our advanced mental faculties. With wisdom and awareness, we aim to experience existence like never before

—an experience that will free our distressed minds and usher our species into the next stage of human evolution.

THE AWAKENING

It is Tuesday, the 18th of May, the year 2500. The Moon will be full in less than an hour. My name is Maya, and this log will serve as a record of my upcoming experience. I'm one of the remaining humans on Earth, and we have just under a month to leave before the planet becomes completely uninhabitable. The depleting atmosphere is destroying the ozone layer, which is fast becoming unstable. As we have exhausted our energy resources—first from fossil fuels, then biofuels, and later exploited renewable sources like sunlight and geothermal energy—the balance of our ecosystems were soon compromised.

Although sunlight may seem abundant, there is only a limited supply traveling in the direction of and consumed by our planet. Scientists found that the amount of power required to satisfy the needs of 37 billion people amounted to 1.5 percent of the available sunlight striking the Earth. All of the sunlight captured by three million square miles of solar panel fields, instead of being absorbed by the biosphere, created a cooling effect. This appeared to offset temperatures rising from increased concentrations of greenhouse gases. The planet's imbalance led to atmothinning—a devastating process that falsely masked the effects of global warming and that which became our greatest threat.

Initially, natural disasters, which nature had not intended, became the norm of each unrecognizable season. The oxygen supply fell below acceptable levels due to air pollution, deforestation, and disappearing wildlife. Eventually, our planet could no longer withstand the pressures of human activities and simply gave up. Atmothinning rose to pierce the ozone layer and weakened it to the point of instability. Scientists predict the layer's available supply will provide limited shielding from cosmic radiation, which is having stirring effects on an increasingly raging planet. As a result, we've now been living in protective domes for three generations.

As we dwelled in domes, we witnessed firsthand how atmothinning devoured the atmosphere around us. Now the ozone is irreparably damaged, and in one year, the planet's conditions will begin to resemble that of early Venus. Then even the domes won't save us. This catastrophe already had its share of victims. Many survivors fled to colonies on Mars and Europa. Many are on a lifelong journey to Proxima Centauri and other systems nearby. Some are still orbiting in space stations. Those are mostly scientific communities with a desperate mission to revitalize our home planet. So far, they've been failing. With each passing day, the dome cities are becoming increasingly deserted. And although I await my turn to be evacuated, I may not be leaving after tonight.

Like all citizens, I received the biochip brain implant at birth. This remarkable piece of biotechnology enhances thought processing capabilities and connects us to everyone and everything. It's uncommon to not receive it as being disconnected from the bionetwork denies the rights to citizenship. There were once those who rejected this law when it first came to pass. For a long time, they lived in isolation in the last remaining forests of the world. Then as the climate came to be inhospitable and the air unbreathable, refusing to integrate themselves into the rest of civilization, they perished just like the animals with whom they lived. For us, this reinforced our beliefs in the promise of technology, and we embraced the biochip as if it was a necessary cure of our human limitations. With its successful integration, we hoped that our joined consciousness would break through the limited capacities of a single person's mind and unite our species like never before. At first, it complicated things as our personal complexes were shared like mental viruses. But within a few dozen upgrades, those issues were contained. And soon enough, it became almost as complex as the brain itself.

The biochip is a descendant of the legacy neuroquanceptre interface. It processes each thought pattern and simultaneously communicates with every other live biochip via the interhuman databank. The databank is a central hub that monitors, archives, and broadcasts the activities of everyone's biochip. Each person's unique experience enriches the databank for everybody's benefit. The biochip has reached a point at which its highly complex set of algorithms enables it to anticipate any type of neural activity. This means that as soon as one is faced with one decision or another, the biochip analyzes their cognitive processes and returns a set of optimized suggestions. This type of interaction with technology allowed our minds to focus on more pressing matters, though the biochip's rate of progress continuously redefines this notion.

At first, the biochip was meant to be a tool for the selected few. Then it made its way into every household just as electricity did so long ago. Its widespread use came to be taken for granted, and it became as ritual as vaccination. Once it's implanted in the first minutes of life, it adapts to the physiology of its host and functions like any other organ in the body. And it cannot be removed. While this marvelous device has been the savior of countless lives, redefined our means of communication, and remarkably advanced our society, it's still an imperfect piece of machinery. For I've discovered a flaw in its design that might end my life tonight. But it's a chance that I'm willing to take.

The biochip doesn't just complement the brain's functions, but also depends on them because thoughts are its energy source. At 0.05 nanometers, the biochip is situated in the cerebral cortex. Electrical signals firing throughout the cortex provide the power it needs. As thoughts interact with it, the biochip processes them and outputs signals back to the target neurons. Once a person passes, all of their memories and experiences are retained in the interhuman databank, and their biochip becomes inoperable. But what happens when thoughts disappear but the mind does not? This scenario was never considered since neural activity was always thought to be ongoing. No matter the person's state of consciousness, it was assumed that there will always be electrical impulses interacting with the biochip.

Tonight my consciousness will be suspended, the mind tamed, and thought activity temporarily turned off in certain areas of the cortex. As I enter the state of nirvana, the biochip may lose its power source, and its starved biocircuits could consequently cause irreparable damage to my brain. During its trial phases, there were cases of failing implants that caused neurological paralysis to its hosts. If I'm to suffer a similar fate, then I shall embrace parinirvana. Otherwise, the biochip will simply burn out, and my brain will go on functioning as if the implant was nonexistent. Whatever happens, it'll all be worth it for this log will be my legacy and a chance for others to witness the brain's activities just prior to reaching enlightenment. I'll continue to actively record my thoughts in this mental log until they no longer surface. Let those who come in contact with this chronicle learn from it. Our human race has advanced to a point at which such occurrences will become common. The age of the Awakening is near, and it will soon begin with me.

To those who are far from this time and place, I urge you to be diligent and patient with your practice. Your perseverance is the key to the survival of the human race. If you're free of the biochip, then there's nothing that stands in your way to achieve supreme wisdom and liberation. Don't despair if you're no longer on Earth, for the mind is strong and can accomplish anything anywhere. Take refuge in the teachings of the ancient ones, and spread them to all the beings in the cosmos. But first, ensure that your vision is pure.

Unclench your fists. Dig deep within yourselves. Dissolve your demons well. Find your innocence. Sharpen your sense of sense. Know that every sensation is one of a kind. They are bound to fade away as quickly as they arise. Strengthen the will not to react. Just simply observe. Observe the facts.

Now I sit under the Bodhi Tree and look up at the Moon through the dome's clear arch. I take a deep breath, close my eyes, and relax my posture. I feel all kinds of feelings rush through every portion of my being. I realize that ignorance has blinded me and hid what is real. What is real? Most are so convinced of their own reality, but this very belief is what grows to be the root of their suffering. The senses are useful but misleading. No more shall I identify with them. No more shall I identify with anything at all. Not this body and not this mind. They will no longer be in control of me. No thoughts will ever entrap me again. For this "I" has never really existed. It was all a grand illusion.

As the feeling of happiness enters my upper torso, it loses its intensity and fails to seduce my reactions. The feeling then turns into one of sadness, maybe hopelessness, and continues to flow down to my stomach. Still, that doesn't deserve any reactions either. So the feeling leaves this section of my body, and other ones attempt to entice me. But the efforts of my habits are proving to be worthless. I no longer pay any attention to them. Instead, I smile with a realization that all things are impermanent and changing all the time.

These thoughts are starting to interrupt my jhana. I've dwelled in this state long enough, and my focus needs to take me deeper. As I prepare to stop all thoughts and embrace my destiny, all I can relate is a manifestation of bliss —a bliss that is opening up my mind to receive wonderful frequencies gravitating from every direction. I can see that all I am is an instrument of life perfectly in tune with the universal harmony. It's like a song whose melody is sweet and lyrics are of infinite wisdom. It waits to fill me. It's at the tip of my being and requires me to be still and end my thoughts now. I bid you all and myself farewell. Welcome liberty.

CHAPTER SIX
POSITIVE PROGRESS: PART II

*The human mind has evolved to make sense of the world
through the tools of one's senses and the lens of one's own limited experience.
Our imagination fills in the gaps, and we easily mistake illusion for reality.*

CONCEPT KARMA

As the old man lies on his deathbed, thoughts of the past bother his mind. He analyzed them so many times before. He'd forgotten about some and tried forgetting about others. Now they've come up again. He wants to face them and put his mind to rest. But there are so many that he isn't able to sort them all out. He tries to switch his attention to the happy times that made life memorable. Those are the things that really matter, he thinks. But feelings of guilt, regret, anger, suspicion, and fear keep creeping up behind the veil of his pride and joy. His precious time on Earth is coming to an end, and instead of reflecting on his success, he feels tortured by his own mind.

He forces back memories of the time when he donated twenty million dollars to help rebuild Ocean County in the aftermath of Hurricane Mandy. But his true intention was to generate write-offs for tax benefits. Or the time when he funded a chain of nonprofits with charitable missions to create jobs for the homeless, raise education standards, and preserve endangered species. Though his motive was to turn around his public image after he'd been exposed of having a mistress. He remembers how he fired a group of associates for refusing to distort earnings numbers, how he knocked down an estate for the elderly to build luxury condos in its place, and how he gambled with his clients' retirement funds, causing some to lose their life's savings. He thinks of his children, his beneficiaries, whom he neglected during childhood. He could understand why they're now having a hard time canceling their appointments to fly across the country and be with him in his final hours.

He wonders how life would have turned out should he have made different choices. He would've had less, but at least he would have been happy and at peace. In his next life, he thinks, if there is a next life, he will do his best to be a better man. He tries convincing himself that he gets it now. But it's too late. Oh so late! He may be fortunate to die of old age in his own bedroom with nurses by his side, instead of from some deadly disease on a hospital floor or from a gunshot wound on the asphalt. That would've been well deserved, he thinks. Still, these final moments are agonizing. He realizes that the agony was always there. He just didn't notice it until now. It must have taken years off his life. And persisted with the rest. Now it's resurfacing and forcing him to question what kind of life he has lived. What kind of legacy is he leaving behind? He feels bad for those he hurt. He wants to punish himself. He takes in the agony and closes his eyes.

POSITIVE PROGRESS: PART II

In the suburban village of Shelburne Falls, Massachusetts, there is a quiet place where people come to sharpen their sense of the mind-body phenomenon. It is not a place for intellectual amusement nor for philosophical speculation. Neither is it a yoga retreat nor a vacation getaway. It is a place that welcomes anyone to come and practice the techniques that originated in the ancient lands of India, once taught by Gautama Buddha. It is a meditation center and not a Buddhist colony. In fact, one is reminded not to confuse traditional Buddhism with that which the Buddha actually taught.

Imagine if the impacts of Albert Einstein's teachings caused a group of followers to create a religion they called Einsteinism, with rituals to celebrate his theories and ceremonies to ordain someone as an Einsteinist. We can be fairly certain that Mr. Einstein would not wish for such an establishment to follow in his name, as it would not be very scientific. Similarly, the Buddha, being a scientist in his own right, may not have anticipated his teachings to have such an impact on so many of his future followers. His only intention was to give humanity a universal method to progress in a positive direction and be happy as a result.

To learn the techniques, one is asked to take on the vow of silence for the duration of the ten-day course so that the mind has a chance to quiet down and avoid unnecessary interruptions. The first three days are preparatory and are dedicated to sharpening the mind by keeping the attention on a single object of one's ongoing experience—the natural flow of the breath. The breath is used for many reasons. Its universal nature is preferred to using an imaginary or religious association, its rhythm accurately reflects one's physical and emotional state, and it is intimately tied to both the conscious and subconscious control of the mind. This allows the meditator to consciously approach the bridge to their subconscious.

This exercise, called Anapana, opens the door to many interesting realizations, one of which is that most of us lack simple self-control. That is, we are asked to maintain our focus on the breath, but within a minute or even seconds, the mind wanders away—recollecting the past, imagining the future, planning, analyzing, or daydreaming. As soon as one realizes that the mind has wandered, the task is to avoid getting frustrated and simply return the focus back to the breath. Upon countless failures, the realization deepens and a question arises—how is it that my mind is so spoiled that I do not have any control over it? This realization is humbling, indeed. Fortunately, with continued effort, the mind slowly gets concentrated and makes progress. On the fourth day, one learns the main technique of Vipassana meditation.

Vipassana, which means "to see things as they really are," is a journey into the deepest reaches of the mind. It aims to uproot one's complexes and eradicate harmful habit patterns so that the mind is left pure and focused. The technique has proven to be a safe, effective, and universal remedy for psychological ailments of varying degrees—from simple inconveniences like nail biting to major disturbances like chronic depression. It is a recipe for happiness and a path to enlightenment. For twenty five hundred years, it has been passed down from teacher to student, speaking to the infirmities of the human condition. Although one is encouraged to attend a ten-day retreat to properly learn the method of Vipassana, a quick description holds inspirational value.

The attention that is maintained on the breath is shifted to the rest of the body. Methodically, one mentally scans each and every part of the body and objectively observes the multitude of sensations that arise—from pains to itches, temperature and pressure, or anything at all. As the mind calms and the attention sharpens, subtler sensations are revealed, and even gross manifestations subdivide into a sea of tiny vibrations. Then one notices that as soon as a thought arises, a corresponding sensation appears somewhere on the body. It soon becomes clear how mind and body are so integrated that thoughts and sensations are actually two sides of the same coin. And just as thoughts come and go, sensations too arise and eventually dissolve.

If a thought brings smiles, pleasant sensations inform the body of happiness. If a thought brings sadness, unpleasant sensations scatter the body. Since happiness and sadness are nothing more than feelings, one learns to feel them as pleasant or unpleasant sensations. The outcome is how the mind reacts to these sensations—either with craving to the former or aversion to the latter. In either case, the reaction becomes the first cause of one's suffering, ranging from mild dissatisfaction to utter rage. Only then do we divert it to the outside world, often blaming others for the state of our emotional condition. And this is the grand delusion—the way in which we perceive ourselves and the world around us.

With time, the meditator begins to understand that one's perceptions are a representation of reality—not actual reality. The human mind has evolved to make sense of the world through the tools of one's senses and the lens of one's own limited experience. Our imagination fills in the gaps, and we easily mistake illusion for reality. As we allow ourselves to react to every impulse, habit patterns define our personality and further delude us of our true identity. As we can imagine, many personal and social issues are due to this simple observation—that out of ignorance, we create our own problems.

The remedy given is to face each moment's manifestations with equanimous observation so that the urge to react weakens. This method neither gives in to expression nor suppression but balances both extremes until the bodily sensations disappear. This becomes yet another realization—the law of universal impermanence. From our planet's rotation to geological formations, from DNA replication to human migrations, from weather patterns to daily mood swings—everything continuously changes. Life's circumstances force us to undergo changes, and resisting such natural progressions is self-defeating in the long run. Realizing this at the experiential level, rather than just at the intellectual one, naturally forces a reprogramming of one's mental character. As a result, habits start braking, moral values are strengthened, proactivity replaces reactivity, reality appears more transparent, and one begins to enrich each of life's moments with quality. This was the Buddha's contribution.

While there is much literature on Buddhist philosophy, for our purposes, Vipassana is a prime example of spiritual evolution. The beauty of this technique is its scientific and universal application. One comes to understand reality through their own experience without the need to incur in faith of any religious figure or supernatural power. Just as physical fitness makes anybody's body stronger, so too meditation makes the mind that much stronger for anyone taking on the practice. Those who are immersed in this technique would agree that it is a necessary next step in human evolution. For them, it is a method to gain universal wisdom simply by exploring the part of the universe that makes us up—our body and mind.

A human is an intricate being whose body and mind are part of a unified biological mechanism. Our senses are our mind's portals to the world around us. Our sense of touch is on every point of the body, which is why the mind is not bounded to the brain. Hence, the mind flows everywhere throughout the body. It experiences the world through the interpretation of its own sensations. An interpretation is not actuality. The five sense doors—sight, smell, hearing, taste, and touch—are our only tools to reach out and grab a portion of the macrocosm around us. The mind unifies the senses and translates their inputs into something that makes sense to us. How close to reality are our interpretations? The closer, the better. The closer, the more one can understand the way things really work and use this knowledge to one's advantage. The farther our conceptualizations are from the true workings of nature, the more imagination rules our minds. In turn, progress comes delayed as we operate on own misconceptions, yield to illusion, fall prey to ignorance, and cling to unrealistic viewpoints.

Some may suggest that evolution has shaped our species to operate successfully thanks in part to our illusionary interpretations. And that we created the world around us by claiming as real everything that which we can all agree on like the value of money, the promise of marriage, or the caste system. While these are some methods to keep our shared society organized, there is worth in remembering that nature does not place value in paper nor in ritual. Neither is natural selection prejudice. These inventions leave room for hyperinflation, adultery, and the idea of equal rights. If we claim as absolute anything that is subject to change, regardless of whether we label it as right or wrong, then we are setting ourselves up for disappointment. As long as we continue to operate while keeping in mind that which is real and that which is not, what matters and what does not, and in our mutual interests uphold to the Golden Rule, then these sorts of ingenuities will serve their rightful purposes.

Evolution has worked its way to open our minds up to different types of ideas, sorts of conceptions, and forms of abstractions. In premodern times, we learned by using superficial representations of reality, approaching our discoveries in a synoptic manner. As our intellect is maturing, we are able to handle finer explanations, dividing the sum into its constituent parts. As the laws of nature seem evermore counterintuitive and paradoxical, we are forced to reconsider our very conceptions of reality. For instance, the ability to see is something that we take for granted from birth. Not until the later years do we get to marvel at such a wonderful capability. Neither does it occur to us that vision is something that transpires within our brains. Instead, we get used to believing that somehow this occurrence—the object interacting with our visual perception—happens outside of us.

Investigating the properties of light leads us to reexamine our conceptualizations of sight. That is, whatever we see in front of us at this time is not really happening at the time that we see it. It has already happened a very short time ago in the past. Since light takes a certain amount of time to travel from an object to one's eye, the event that we are witnessing had actually occurred at the time that the light had made contact with the object. Hence, light acts as a recording medium. But because we are unable to perceive the latency, our brain is fooled into thinking that what we see is happening in real time. Of course, the same principle also applies to sound, as we hear thunder only after seeing lightning strike.

In fact, as we look at the panorama of objects in the distance, we are witnessing different time periods simultaneously. This concept is more familiar when applied to the light coming from very distant objects like stars. For some, it takes years, even billions of years, for their light to travel to Earth and inform us as to what had happened so long ago, so far away. As we look at one star and then another, which themselves may be light years apart, our gaze moves faster than the time that it would take for the light of one star to travel directly to the other. Does this mean that our gaze travels faster than the speed of light? While we know the answer is an obvious no, it is amusing to ponder of such a fanciful shortcut.

As we explore the truth behind our very notions, we find limits all throughout our human capabilities, including our means of expression. The evolution of language paints its own tree of life, with archaic tongues used in sacred texts evolving into the articulate prose that we now print in paperbacks. Still, we often find that language is inadequate, and we seek creative ways to portray our ideas. As the saying goes, "a picture is worth a thousand words." Or as the lover cries, "no words can describe how I feel right now." Language is a tool. It is a way to transfer our thoughts into the minds of others. Telepathy would have been more effective, but unfortunately, we are not there yet. So we use allegories, analogies, approximations, associations, comparisons, examples, idioms, metaphors, signals, synonyms, and other lingual means to persuade the other party of our ever-important thought process. In this book alone, we explore a myriad of concepts for the purpose of developing a particular idea that can take just a single moment to perceive.

We get so comfortable with our mastery of language that it feels like a part of our very being—like our name or like precious memories that define our uniqueness. We often think in words, dream in words, and dress our character with words of praise. But these very words, which have placed our species on the top of the intellectual mountain, have also limited us to the ideas that they can express. What about those ideas that words cannot express? Spiritual evolution is about breaking the limits that have been ingrained into our minds. Language is one example.

Beyond words, we think in images that our eyes have taught us to see, sounds that our ears have taught us to hear, tastes, smells, and emotions that fill our lives with color. But the world is full of other substances, frequencies, and forces that our body machine lacks the tools to detect. There are only two ways to perceive them—directly or indirectly. We can either train our elastic minds to develop new capabilities of detection or build gadgets that translate foreign data into something that we can presently understand.

Spiritual evolution hones in on the former, as a new method of perception may result out of a reformation of the brain's sensory functions and not necessarily of its intellectual capacities. In comparison, mental evolution focuses on the latter, as the intellect here would be the sole architect of such technology. And just because spiritual evolution seeks to break those limits that are exercised by our intellect does not make it conflict with mental evolution. On the contrary, spiritual evolution requires a different kind of smarts. It is about having the wisdom to break through one's own psychological boundaries. It is about distinguishing apparent reality from actual reality. This is achievable by someone who not only is intelligent enough to think, but also is wise enough to know the consequences of their thoughts. For this reason, during meditation, a Zen monk removes thoughts from the equation, concentrates the mind into a state of mental freedom, and opens it up to new possibilities.

The evolution of the mind has been a focus of scholars as well as yogis. Both have taken different approaches to train it. For the scholar, this is a mental evolution—enhancing the mind with all sorts of knowledge, developing acute mental capabilities, and attaining a state of intellectual mastery. For the yogi, this has been a spiritual practice all along—keeping unbiased awareness of the present moment, aiming to grasp reality in its most substantial form, and experiencing the laws of nature within oneself. To expand the momentary experience, some meditate for very long periods in a state of complete relaxation. To enrich it, others use bodily postures and endure physical strains for the purpose of strengthening the mind's presence and balance.

Yoga has now been popularized in the West, catering to the modern appetite of engaging in one's spiritual evolution. However, the science of the mind and body phenomenon is not new. The Buddha understood the workings of mind and matter long before Western scientists began to think about these subjects. By training himself to detect the subatomic makeup of his own cells, the Buddha knew that matter has no solidity and that it is a flood of vibrations oscillating in and out of physical space at an incredible rate. Particle physicists are only now uncovering this fact through the superstring theory, which is radically changing our understanding of the universe. But experiencing this, the Buddha taught, not only reveals hidden natural laws, but also profoundly changes one's perspective on life. As a natural consequence, morality becomes a byproduct rather than an aspiration. For the scientist, this means that subatomic particles are not there just to be quantified but can also be experienced, revealing a universe of life, vigor, purpose, and virtue.

A mind that is disturbed by its own negativities cannot maintain a state of purity unless it is purified. Such is the lesson of the venerable S. N. Goenka, the late teacher of Vipassana meditation. He used to say that we are all prisoners of our own minds. Besides the numerous meditation centers that he instituted around the world, he also ran courses in high security prisons, demonstrating the rehabilitation effectiveness of the technique on those who need it most. Goenkaji was willing to teach anyone who was willing to learn.

Through objective self-observation, morality loses its subjectiveness and is expressed by the same laws of nature that drive all forces in the universe. Meditators learn to experience the laws of cause and effect within the framework of their own body. They come to understand that as soon as one reacts to any negative manifestation of the mind, it further gets layered with complexes. In so doing, people inadvertently set themselves up for suffering. On the other hand, by overcoming such negativities in line with the natural laws experienced within, one can assure their own peace and happiness.

Herein lies the root cause from which most of the world's problems arise. It all starts with a single person's mind, which has the power to either cause world wars or liberate whole nations from occupation. It would seem that most people seek peace and side with goodness, though we question this assumption when witnessing all the evil around the world and in history. One could argue that because the human animal had evolved from other animals, we are predators by nature. Does not the human race, with all of its achievements and lessons learned, deserve more credit than that? Just as our bodies have evolved from more primitive forms, so too our minds have evolved from more primitive thoughts. Much so that our intellect is ready to undertake on a spiritual transformation. As the knowledge of the West embraces the wisdom of the East and as globalization and technology expand our minds beyond any previously perceived limits, many are finding an inner yearning to pursue something extraordinary. Something beyond what is typically taught at schools and universities. Something spiritual yet scientific, wondrous yet logical, transcendent yet practical—something that could satisfy their deepest curiosities.

Our quest for greatness leads us to look around nature, look up at the stars, and look deep inside ourselves. In this way, we shake off any remaining animalistic tendencies and raise human life to a higher standard. For this reason, techniques like Vipassana are referred to as the art of living. For most, it may seem difficult to take on such a practice on a regular basis. Fact of the matter is that progress is never easy at any step of the evolutionary ladder. Here we are not suggesting that one should become a monk and dedicate their life to meditating on the aspects of reality. That is only meant for the few, just as not everyone becomes an athlete who exercises physical evolution or a scholar who focuses on mental evolution. Most of us are householders, engaging in various livelihoods and striving toward a unique purpose that will benefit ourselves, our families, and society at large.

To truly evolve oneself, equal consideration should be given to all three elements of evolution, as one type will support another. A healthy body means having a healthy host for the mind. A healthy mind, in turn, maintains the health of the body. As supported by research, mindfulness promotes healthy brain activity, regulates bodily functions, boosts the immune system, and, among many other things, manages emotional stress. Such hardy framework can only benefit one in overcoming challenges, exercising one's willpower, building up confidence, and, among many other things, ensuring one's own success.

By developing the three elements of evolution, a human can eventually evolve into a superhuman by today's standards. As discussed in Chapter Four, we can predict certain traits to slowly develop, and we can imagine others. It is no wonder that the desire to realize our imagination has made sci-fi media so popular. Comic book superheroes are imaginary reflections of our potential selves when traits are exaggerated, new abilities are developed, and quality of being is uplifted. But even now out there, there are those gifted athletes, geniuses, and spiritualists who seem like supermen to some of us. Their greatness provides us with inspiration just as their heroes once inspired them. In comparison, a human may have been the dream of the single-celled organism just as someone with extraordinary powers is the dream of the present human. As we train ourselves diligently and develop our sought-for traits, we gradually become who we strive to be. Never in the past has any other species had the distinct ability to intentionally progress its own evolution. Let us take full advantage of this rare opportunity.

On the last day of the Vipassana course, one learns a third and final technique of Metta, which is the practice of loving-kindness. After completing an intensive meditation program, the students radiate with clarity, wisdom, and positivity. With goodwill and compassion, they willingly send wishes of peace and harmony to all the living creatures—human or non-human, known to them or unknown, in this time or another. Positively charged vibrations permeate their being and the surrounding atmosphere. In return, they experience a joy that, like a runner's high, comes from completing hard and meaningful work. For some, it is a first step on the long journey to enlightenment. For others, it is a reinforcer to continue moving forward on the path. People from all geographic, demographic, and religious backgrounds come and learn something that they have been overlooking about themselves —something very deep and personal, yet universally applicable. They learn that spirituality can be scientific and practical. And that it can guide them on the path of their own personal evolution, in the direction of positive progress.

THE THEORY OF ONE SOUL

The boy waited one year to see the Grand Master after he was initiated into the Sangha order known as the Wheel. He was permitted to ask just one question, then sit silently and meditate while receiving the answer from the Master. Only in another year's time would he get the chance to ask another question. He thought long and hard on the question yet remained undecided. Throughout the year, he faced many challenges as he struggled to learn the ancient techniques of the enlightened ones. He wanted to know how to maintain being conscious while exploring the realm of his subconscious, how to identify bodily sensations in areas where there are no nerve endings, and how to avoid having his meditation interrupted by the sound of his beating heart. He was also curious about the strange visions that he had recently began to experience during his practice. It was now time to greet the Master. The boy entered the pagoda, took off his sandals, and nervously walked down the hall, still debating as to what will be his question. He came in front of the Master, respectfully bowed, and sat on the floor. The boy looked up into the Master's eyes, and as he was collecting his thoughts in haste, he asked a simple "Why?" The Master looked back at the boy, paused for a moment, then replied.

"Young monk, you ask the greatest of all questions. In the next few years, as with all adolescents reaching adulthood, you will undergo nibbanic neuromorphism. With this extraordinary experience, you will become an enlightened adult and begin to understand that which you now seek to know. You are here for that reason, to be guided on this journey. Then you will leave the Wheel and enter the University. There, you will not only receive worldly knowledge, but also learn the theory behind your practice. At that time, you will receive your answer in great detail. But since this is the question you ask, I shall uphold to tradition and provide you with a simple explanation.

As you know, there is nothing permanent in this world—not our bodies, not our minds, and not our spirits. Not even the arrow of time as it too will someday collapse into the same decadimensional singularity from which it emerged. However, there are those dynamic constants that were set into motion at the inception of the universe and which define its physical properties. Among them is the vital force, which is one of the sixteen fundamental forces known to science today.

All life in the cosmos is created by way of the vital force. It's the reason why amino acids combine into proteins, why animals choose to flee or fight, and why there's attraction between a woman and a man. It's also the reason why you've now begun to remember your previous lives. As you continue your practice, unfamiliar faces and faraway places will become more vivid and revive memories that you've lost long ago. This is a part of growing up.

Ten millennia ago, following the onset of the Great Awakening, scientists proved the existence of the vital force, which was theorized for a long time before. This force exists in all of us but is especially detectable at high concentrations in subjects undergoing nibbanic neuromorphism. Upon its publication, the 21st Dalai Lama called this vital force the Theory of One Soul. You see, this force was well known to the spiritual masters of the past. His Holiness dedicated a discourse on this topic to a group of Bhikkhus, who in turn passed it on to their disciples. You will study this discourse at length in your fifteenth semester as one of the prerequisites to the metaphysiology curriculum.

The Theory of One Soul is the quintessence of the entire living world throughout all spatial and temporal systems. It applies to DNA code, cell fusion, and sentients like us. You see, young monk, I was once you and you will one day be me. You were once your mother and will one day be your daughter; once your father and someday your son; and grandparents and grandchildren; and aunts, uncles, cousins, and all other relatives; and non-relatives, even other races, other species, and all other life forms. Every single living being that has or will one day exist—we each take turns to be all of them. You see, we all share the same Soul. A Soul that travels to find its way throughout the infinite wisdom that's bound to the very fabric of existence. This Soul was born with the Big Bang, evolved into us, and someday will become what we commonly call the Most Evolved Life Form.

The vital force radiates from the Soul at various wavedepths, depending on the form that it embodies. For today's humans, this wavedepth typically oscillates at a rate of eighteen cubic thermoquarks. The deeper the rate, the more pronounced is the vital force, which means that the embodiment of the Soul has reached a more advanced state of being. Now you are wondering how is it that the Soul remains at different stages of being in multiple bodies at the same time. You see, time is meaningless in the context of our decadimensional plane. It's just a road on which causality is driven. As scientists have demonstrated, the vital force lies on the infragreen spectrum range of the microwave background radiation. This means that the Soul is everywhere in the universe and not just within living organisms. As it comes in contact with the proper material ingredients, it organicizes the matter and brings it to life.

On Earth, as in many other places, it all started with a single biomolecule —a foundation on which numerous lives would come to exist. Its vital force transferred the Soul from one biomolecule to another, then from one cell to another, and then from one body to another—enriching itself with every new life, learning, trying, experimenting, making mistakes, but always moving forward. You see, the Soul in you has begun to recall its journey. I know for I remember this moment when I was sitting where you're sitting right now.

As the Soul climbs the evolutionary mountain and attains greater control of the vital force, it breaks through the boundaries of the spacetime continuum. The body advances by breaking spatial boundaries. It grows, multiplies, and seeks to rule its surrounding geography. The mind advances by breaking temporal boundaries. It remembers the past, experiences the present, and seeks to know the future. The spirit advances by breaking both of these boundaries. You see, the Soul in you isn't just recollecting the past, but a past from a different bodily observer. And so just as you're growing in height, your memory too is growing in might.

In this life, young monk, have you ever forgotten anything that you saw, heard, smelled, tasted, felt, or thought? Of course not! No human has since the Great Awakening. Our determined intellects had forgotten how to forget. Back on Earth, our forest fathers weren't as privileged. They lost many memories and only kept a few that made the deepest impressions or expressions. Early humans had such difficulties coping with their memories that they would forget their dreams, forget their childhood, forget the names of people they've met, and sometimes even forget what they had for breakfast. All that forgotten information was leaked throughout the cosmos, flying in all directions, often colliding, and forming memes. Worst of all, it brought on many psychiatric ailments and reduced their lifespans to a single century. No wonder spiritual progress took humankind so long to achieve.

Now the challenge is not only to maintain memories of yourself but also of your previous selves. As you begin to recall your other lives, take great care of your emotions. You will remember doing things that you never would have wanted to do. You will feel regret, anger, sadness, and fear. But you will realize how far you have come and all the hard work you've put in to make things right. Then just as you'll remember your past, you will begin to foresee your future. Your noble path will start to unfold. You'll understand why all the Buddhas have always stressed compassion and why they didn't place importance in the self—as the self is in a constant flux, never the same from moment to moment, from year to year, and from life to life.

Our thirst for life rolls along the wheel of reincarnation. It forces us to fix our karma, to face it, and erase it. To elevate our being and seek liberation. We are reborn as each other, and out of illusion, we believe that we are many. But really, we are all just one. Your death, my birth, it's simply a transition of energy. An energy that's growing, pushing the walls of the universe farther, causing time to stretch longer. Throughout the expanding cosmos, the fundamental forces bind everything together—keeping atoms intact, planets in orbit, and life in unity. While this balance is maintained, we are offered choice after choice. Each choice is yet another chance to be the masters of our journeys, fulfill our responsibilities, and serve purpose for the universe. In so doing, we are left to love one another, care for each other, and help each other along the way. So that we can all coexist and realize our common destiny. And that is the answer to your question, young monk."

CHAPTER SEVEN
THE MOST EVOLVED LIFE FORM

*As the ancestors of the most evolved life form climb the steps of
one dimension after another, each step will reflect an evolutionary milestone.
Then the most evolved life form will reach the topmost dimension and
fulfill evolution's lifelong purpose.*

CONCEPT PHYSICS

As she stares at the computer screen, the software developer recalls why she had chosen her profession. Among other things like decent pay and job stability, it was a chance for her to devise innovative solutions to address problems arising out of human limitations. She has always considered herself to be the type who is analytical yet inquisitive, and this new project is certainly probing both of those aspects of her personality. She was tasked with developing an educational application that targets middle school-level astronomy courses. Her program is supposed to animate the history of the universe—from the Big Bang to the formation of galaxies and solar systems. She finds it interesting to program in the laws of physics that result in the universe reflecting the image of the familiar night sky. Mostly, she marvels at how tweaks to the Big Bang's initial conditions can materialize a different type of universe, one with different physical laws and structure. For a moment, she feels like God Almighty herself.

Her fingers pause at the keyboard. She gets lost in thought about the laws of nature that work like a computer's operating system. There must be a function for everything, she thinks—from the speed of sound to the amplitude of light, from the spin of an electron to the orbit of Halley's Comet, from the laws of motion to the laws of thermodynamics. To simulate a handful of these laws for an audience of thirteen-year-olds, her team of three developers completed nearly 100 thousand lines of code in six months. How many code lines, she wonders, would it take to mimic all of the known physical laws for all of the known parts of the universe? What if such a project is undertaken? Surely it would be an ongoing endeavor since scientists arrive at new discoveries on a daily basis. Can something so complex reside as a compiled executable somewhere on a server?

Fact is that this program has already been written. It defines all aspects of our daily lives. The language may not be in binary code, yet its ubiquity is revealed by those logical principles that we consistently observe through the workings of cause and effect. A computer opponent knows all of the possible moves you can make in a chess game because its rules are pre-defined on a finite two-dimensional game board. In the same way, the pre-defined rules of physics limit our choice of possible actions in a finite three-dimensional space. Ultimately, the universe anticipates all permutations, and none of its laws can be broken—only worked around. Sometimes a computer program can crash because of an unanticipated event that its design was not made to handle. The developer reflects on the quality of her software and hopes that the program of the universe knows of no such bugs.

THE MOST EVOLVED LIFE FORM

We are in the infancy of our evolutionary development. The universe is nearly fourteen billion years of age, the Earth is only four and a half billion years old, and life on Earth is a mere four billion years young. We can try stretching our imagination as far as it will allow, but we will still remain vastly underestimated in our predictions. Our limited preconceptions can only provide but a glimpse of what is in store for us all. Our to-do list is growing faster than our list of accomplishments, as achievements turn to inspirations and answers lead to more questions.

There is a limit on being forward looking, and it moves along with the passage of time. Although we can imagine what the future will be like in the next millennium, someone living five centuries from now is more likely to guess what that time period will actually be like. Not only will their outlook be five hundred years ahead of ours, but their imagination will also be that much more sophisticated. Consider a modern person's imagination level as compared to that of someone living in Ancient Greece. While the Hellenists were as capable as us in reasoning through philosophical logic, their ability to imagine the future would not have corresponded to that of someone exposed to modernity. Surely, they could have imagined a Chimera, but could they have also imagined genetic engineering? Just a century ago, no one could have predicted a wireless pocket-sized telephone that would also be used for transmitting electronic mail, engaging in social media, and indulging in all sorts of entertainment. The next century will certainly lead to many more surprises, paving the way to the unimaginable.

How far ahead should we look to find the answers that would satisfy our curiosities? One thousand years from now, when our technology may take us to a neighboring star system? One million years from now, when our species may populate a neighboring galaxy? One billion years from now, when human subspecies may effortlessly share thoughts across the cosmos? One trillion years from now, which hampers the imagination altogether? As suspected, the challenge is to look farther than our present capabilities would allow us to see.

Still, let us consider a time period that is exponentially greater than the current age of the universe. Let us consider a future that is so far away that it is as difficult to imagine as the infinite number line. At this undefined point in time, what will the state of the universe be like? Will it expand so much that every piece of matter will be ripped apart into its subatomic components, left to float forever in an empty vacuum? Or will the expansion slow and let gravity crunch everything together again? Whatever the fate of the universe may be, let us leap just far enough to consider the birth of evolution's most prized creation.

One objection is to suggest that the universe may someday become so unstable that it will not be able to support any form of life. Fearing that evolution may never reach its goal, we might as well put our efforts to rest. Again this mindset is rather demotivating. On the other hand, in following our primal instinct to promote our existence permits us to retain our sense of purpose. A psychotherapist would affirm that such an outlook is deemed healthy. Let us not concede to pessimistic speculation and regard this as enough of a reason to remain on track. Besides, it is rather curious to know how far evolution can take itself, assuming that it has all the time in the world.

In discussing the physical, mental, and spiritual elements of evolution, we naturally ask—what is the ultimate goal? Is there a final celebration to evolution, or will it persist indefinitely? As we regard the evolutionary process to be the avenue of progress, logically, the end result would have to be nothing less than perfection. Or at the least its realistic equivalent. In the next chapter, we will examine what perfection means in the context of reality. In the meantime, let us question whether we can envision a living being reaching the evolutionary climax.

Let us consider both the potential as well as the limits of evolution—the maximum extent to which a life form's characteristics can progress. Beyond the constraints of the biosphere, let us envision a point at which no further adaptation is possible and the most optimal state of being is realized. If the goal of evolution is to create a being that is so advanced that it reaches evolutionary limits, then let us ask what these limits could actually be. One premise is that the most evolved life form would have to be superior in all the qualities ascribed to the three elements of evolutionary progress.

On physical evolution, qualities that come to mind are strength, speed, flexibility, stamina, durability, resilience, and the like. What does it mean to be the strongest, the fastest, and the most enduring? Are we to suggest that the most evolved life form will be stronger than all of the beings that came before it and that none to come would ever be stronger? We can envision Atlas, the Titan of Ancient Greek mythology, holding the world on his shoulders. In this case, the weight of the universe, based on some inertial frame of reference, serves as the strength limit of the most evolved life form. In building on such a hypothesis, we are in effect suggesting a being who is nothing less than omnipotent.

As omnipotence is generally attributed to religious deities, the question becomes, what shall anyone's strength limit be? Whatever is the heaviest for anyone to lift, there is always a chance that a grain of sand can be added for someone else to break that limit. Such muscle contest would persist until the most evolved life form masters the universal strength limit. It will surely take a long time to add up all of the grains of sand that would account for all of the matter existing in the universe. Given enough time, however, each and every atomic particle can be accounted for. As long as there remains the potential to progress, nature will be compelled to challenge any previously attained record.

From an evolutionary perspective, this most physically able being will have the ability to out-compete and out-survive all other species across the universe. It will be the most fit and adapt to any and all conditions anywhere within the cosmos, no matter how extreme. From the cold of the Arctic to the frigidness of Mars, from the heat of the Sahara to the sweltering of Venus, from the tornados of Kansas to the solar winds of the Sun, from the pressure of the Pacific Ocean floor to the denseness of a black hole within the Milky Way's core, from the nuclear bombing of Hiroshima to a supernova in the constellation Pegasus, from the thin air at the peaks of the Himalayas to the emptiness of space. This means mastering all environments across the entire universe, ensuring certain survival of this great and powerful being. Otherwise, any place that is left untouched will be fair ground for competition.

Likewise, it will have to be the fastest. So fast that not only would it outrun any panther or outfly any eagle, but also any vehicle speeding along the highway, any aircraft flying across the sky, and any spacecraft rocketing through space. Whoever may be the fastest at any one time, someone could very well become even fractionally faster. The race would continue until nature's limits are met. Then again, can we challenge anyone to break light speed, the speed limit of the universe? Just as our imagination can propel us from one corner of space to another in an instant, can we imagine this being achieving the same in actuality? If traveling from one set of spatial coordinates to another, by any means possible, takes less time than it would take light to travel via a straight route, then why not? Whether this means navigating through wormholes that fold the fabric of spacetime, harnessing the power of quantum entanglement, or using some other undiscovered shortcut, this most evolved being would be able to break through the boundaries of the four dimensions that currently bind us.

The most evolved life form will not resemble any other living species, including our own. This not only refers to its physical appearance, but also to its very substance—its corporeality. Being the most evolved, this life form's manner of subsistence would be of the highest order of quality. As flesh and blood creatures, we humans are as fragile as dandelions in the wind. Evolution has much time to rearrange our atomic particles for a more optimal design. The most optimized design would likely be free of any building blocks that are subject to such mutabilities as decay, degeneration, and decomposition. Although no thing and no one is excused from the universal law of impermanence, the most evolved life form would only change in as much as the universe itself changes. As such, its makeup would only be sustained by the very fabric of existence—the framework in which something can exist.

To fathom this framework, let us look to the essence of existence as it is expressed from within the lower and higher dimensions. Quantum mechanics and general relativity provide us with useful insights into their properties, forcing us to reconsider our basic understanding of space and time. From zero-dimensional elementary particles to one-dimensional strings that propagate through a two-dimensional worldsheet, each dimension describes a different point of view of the way reality is structured. With physical laws behaving differently at each dimension, the quest for a common explanation remains the longstanding question that science is so curiously seeking. So we look past our immediately observable surroundings to a reality that is more real than the one interpreted by our senses.

Some may insist that what we see is just as real as what we cannot see. That it is a different, rather than an inferior, representation of reality. In response, let us consider the perceptive quality of seeing the elephant as a whole rather than by touching its parts, as so wisely illustrated in the story of the blind men.

Humans are free to roam in the three dimensions of space but have a limit on navigating through the fourth dimension of time. This dimension is unidirectional to our experience, and only by the voluntary choices of our actions can we move through it. We can think of trees as being our counterparts in the dimension below. Trees cannot willingly move throughout the third dimension in the same way as we are unable to freely roam throughout the fourth dimension. Just as we race through time to get closer to the light at the end of the tunnel, trees rise through the ground to get closer to the light of the Sun.

Eventually, life will find a way to adapt to the complexities of higher dimensions. It will experience existence from the viewpoints of these dimensions and consequently raise the quality of its own existence. Boundaries that we are used to perceiving will be stripped away to expose more of reality. To experience reality in its absolute state means reaching the highest dimension, which would essentially encompass all other dimensional viewpoints. Whether there are ten dimensions as proposed by string theory, or eleven dimensions as proposed by M-theory, or even twenty six dimensions, the most evolved life form can only reside at the level of the highest dimension. Otherwise, there would be opportunities to advance further. Within the highest dimension, the experience is of actual reality, not apparent reality. No interpretation of any stimulus is needed because the experience is at the level of the cause, not the effect.

Human beings are ever reactive, even if we believe ourselves to be the actors. Each one of our actions results from previous actions. Each one is an effect of a long chain of causes, which can be traced all the way back to the Big Bang. At the level of the highest dimension, all actions that occur at each of the dimensions below net to a single momentary instant. This momentary singularity is the one cause that has the effect of emanating existence on to each of the dimensions below. As the ancestors of the most evolved life form climb the steps of one dimension after another, each step will reflect an evolutionary milestone. Then the most evolved life form will reach the topmost dimension and fulfill evolution's lifelong purpose.

Fitness alone is not enough to achieve such agility. None other but this great being will be the architect of its own abilities. On mental evolution, qualities that come to mind are intellect, knowledge, memory, cognition, sagacity, creativity, and the like. As we imply this being to be the smartest, most intelligent, and most resourceful of all living creatures throughout all of space and time, we are similarly suggesting that it would be nothing less than omniscient.

The encyclopedia of the universe has already been written in the language of cause and effect. As we slowly decode this language, we are persistently learning everything that there is to know. This will surely take much time. But as we have already started learning as much about everything as possible, one day we may actually arrive at knowing everything. To ensure its superiority, the most evolved life form will not only be the world's greatest polymath and know more facts than any other life form, but it will need to master all of the knowledge embodied over the entire sphere of the universe. Otherwise, any unlearned fact can yield a competitive advantage over those less informed.

When a grain of sand makes contact with the ocean, it creates a ripple in the water, which could be enough to tip the direction of a hurricane. Similarly, as each action is met by a reaction, it resonates outward and impacts its surroundings. The most evolved life form will be sensitive to any and all such occurrences, everywhere and in every time. From our current viewpoint, it would detect all past and future occurrences based on a perfectly calculated extrapolation of ongoing events. From an other-dimensional viewpoint, all such four-dimensional occurrences are part of the momentary singularity that emanates out of the highest dimension. In this way, all causes and their effects are known by the most evolved life form, leading it to possess all of the information potential that is spread across the universe.

Information potential is information that can potentially become known if there is an observer to process it. "If a tree falls in a forest and no one is around to hear it, does it make a sound?" For us, the observer requires tools to acquire this information as well as a medium to retain it. We can imagine that the most evolved life form has much more sophisticated methods to process information. Senses are used for the purpose of interpreting stimuli, but the most evolved life form needs no interpretation—it experiences reality just the way it is. It simply knows that the tree fell and produced audible reverberations. Similarly, a brain, like a hard drive, acts as a storage mechanism. The most evolved life form has no need for this either. At the level of the highest dimension, the most evolved life form experiences all occurrences directly and simultaneously. This is the greatest of all experiences —the mass experience of existence as a whole.

As we have discussed in the previous chapter, objectively experiencing reality within the framework of one's own physical and mental structure enables one to acquire inherent wisdom of natural laws. This is a steppingstone to experiencing the framework of the entire universe. Just as a yogi maintains mindfulness of the present moment, the most evolved life form maintains omnipresence at the level of the highest dimension. In attaining mastery over spiritual evolution, the most evolved life form will not just dominate all spatial and temporal systems but transcend their dimensional boundaries. Furthermore, as progress is moving in a positive direction, this most spiritual being would be nothing less than omnibenevolent.

Evolutionary competition is a sport of survival. Since the most evolved life form will no longer encounter any competition or threat of extinction, it will never be in conflict with any inferior species. In fact, as a master of evolution, it will inherit all the responsibilities that come with such great status. Just as our dominance makes us responsible for maintaining the balance of our global ecosystem, the most evolved life form will oversee matters concerning the universal ecosystem. In this way, this most intelligent being will also be the most moral.

Cause and effect is a logical principle that indicates the relationship between one event and another. Eastern philosophy expands on this principle with the concept of karma, the causality of natural phenomena as it relates to morality. The saying "what goes around comes around" generally has an arcane connotation, though spiritualists see karma as a basic law of nature. This means that any action regarded as negative will give rise to a negative outcome while one that is positive will lead to an outcome that stems from the same positive qualities. In this way, nature forces us to analyze our choice of actions since each decision has its own set of consequences.

Can a positive cause produce a negative effect and vice versa? Simply put, an apple seed will not grow into a manchineel tree. To put it another way, in a domino effect, there are only so many variables whose chain reaction causes all of the dominoes to fall. In expanding this notion to our everyday lives, the laws of cause and effect remain the same; however, there are many more variables to consider. Intention here is part of the equation.

Most of us can remember a time when our actions have resulted in unintended consequences. The endless complexity of the universe dims our perception on the order of sequential events. Although things may sometimes come as a surprise, still, nothing happens magically—that is, out of some randomly sporadic occurrence or supernatural power. Everything has a cause. Each movement is initiated by a mover. Even if, despite our best intentions, things do not seem to go as planned, it only just seems that way. In actuality, the twisted and interdependent accumulation of causes and their corresponding widespread effects ultimately lead to the questionable event. Bad luck is a phenomenon perceived only in the eye of the unlucky observer.

Intention occurs before any physical or vocal action is taken. Surely, something may have ignited that intention—whether it be good upbringing, an empathic personality, or a troubled incident that causes one to reconsider their treatment of others. The source of the intention is no doubt important, but it is the intention itself that rolls on the wheel of karma. Such is the teaching of the Buddha.

A physician may be motivated to treat his patients either because he has the privilege of healing them or because he is able to bill their medical insurance. His motivation will dictate the unfolding of his personal karma. There need not be any mystical implications in the workings of karma. A physician who only cares about one's own wellbeing and does not live up to the principles of his profession will sooner or later be exposed through the actions initiated by his own intentions. Or he will suffer from the weight of his growing guilt, which will eventually become too heavy a burden to carry around. Whichever comes first, nature will find a way to balance opposing forces. On the other hand, a physician who is sincerely concerned with the wellbeing of others will seek ways to serve those around her and just as naturally be complemented by gratitude, gratuity, a respectable reputation, a blooming practice, or at least by the contentment of her altruistic self.

Being omnibenevolent is not to suggest that the most evolved life form will ensure a kingdom of heaven for all the lesser forms. The karma of others is theirs alone to maintain. Each being is responsible for her or his own actions. Also, let us not suggest that the most evolved life form's positive intentions and great powers will necessarily ward off dangers for other beings —like prevent an asteroid from maintaining a collision course with a planet that is teeming with life. Such isolated occurrences cannot qualify as exceptions that can be allowed to interfere with the workings of the natural world. From our limited point of view, we can see that the sudden extinction of dinosaurs contributed to the rise of our own species in ruling this planet. Lastly, let us not suggest that everything happens for a reason; rather, that the interconnected chain of events are bounded by the prevailing forces of causality.

As our intelligence matures, as our sense of morality becomes more pragmatic, and as our experiences of the universe are further refined, we will get better at anticipating the effects of our causes. From our intuition becoming more calculated to our mathematical models getting more precise, our inability to sense the consequences of our actions is bound to fade over time. As postulated in Chapter Two, sooner or later, looking ahead will become just as feasible as looking back. As such, karma is expected to become more predictable and manageable. Eventually, the most evolved life form will become harmonious with the universal karma. That is, it will identify itself with all of the causes and effects that are to occur throughout the life of the universe. We will explore this idea further in Chapter Nine.

At the level of the highest dimension, the most evolved life form will no longer be bounded by karma or causality, as these phenomena will lose their meaning in the context of the momentary singularity. There, its physical, mental, and spiritual attributes will become indistinguishable. The most evolved life form will have climbed to the pinnacle of evolution's triple-layer pyramid. In this sense, the pyramid becomes synonymous with existence itself —a depiction that details all of its physical properties, the intellectual capacities required for its engineering, and the experience of each one of its multidimensional coordinates. Beyond this, there is nothing left to achieve.

In a race to perfection, only one member of this species can reach the finish line. On our local ground, it started with a common ancestor who attained the ability to progress by means of reproduction. In passing the responsibility to its successors, this set into motion a rivalry among species, societies, and individuals. One life form is destined to come out victorious— the one who masters above all the ability to conquer the entirety of existence. Anything less will leave room for further conquests.

To be the best requires outcompeting one's peers. From our own history, we know of these conflicts all too well. It is one of the insensitive methods of natural selection but one that has been tamed by the spirit of evolutionary cooperation. As the saying goes, "if you can't beat them, join them." Single-celled organisms joined forces and created a unified and more superior being. Similarly, as societies grow closer and stronger, and as globalization morphs into universalization, our semi-perfect descendants may also choose to join forces and create a unified and most superior being. Then evolution will finally reach its goal once a single member of its own kind emerges to be the most evolved life form.

Just as a single-celled organism and a human being are two different species at two distinct points on the tree of life, so too is a human being and the most evolved life form are as different and as far apart. These three evolutionary points might all be traced by a single line, if we are lucky enough to succeed in this ultimate goal. That is, the single-celled organism can be seen as the seed that gave rise to the tree. The human species can be viewed as a dividing branch that separates itself from the rest of the jungle and marks an evolutionary milestone. At some point, as the branch will extend to bear its fruit, our most evolved descendent will finally accomplish that which evolution has set out to achieve.

Perhaps evolution relies on many different species from many different locations and time periods to complete its work. In that case, we are not as special as our egocentric self-perception makes us out to be. The representation of the tree could just as well be part of a bigger picture. Just as branches have common roots, so too some of these branches may converge to a common endpoint. It is also possible that humans may become extinct after all and another race of intelligent beings could be the ones taking credit for reaching the final evolutionary chapter.

Whatever the case may be, evolution is on its way to achieve its purpose. We are undoubtedly part of this evolution story. In the coming chapters, we will reflect on the notion that the perfect nature of the most evolved life form necessitates its existence. We will extend our minds to wrap around the concept of infinity and see how far it reaches in a bounded universe.

Finally, as illustrated by the intertwined infinity symbol, we will uncover how the fruit will produce that seed which has given rise to the tree of evolution in the first place.

THE DREAM JOURNAL

July 30th, 1982

Last year I was 5 years old and I had a dream that I was a grown up. In my dream I was in a big city with tall buildings. I was walking somewhere. Then I stopped at a street corner and looked up at these buildings. I don't live in a city like this now and I never been to a city like this before. I felt all grown up. I didn't feel like a kid. When I woke up I was confused. For a minute I still felt like a grown up and I wasn't sure where I was. When I realized that I'm 5 years old I felt strange and didn't know what to do. Then I got used to being a kid again. I will never forget this dream. It felt so real.

June 1st, 2000

It happened again last night. I dreamed of myself being older. I was married with two children, girl and boy. The girl looked like me and the boy more like my wife. I remember her kind face. We haven't met yet. We lived in a house somewhere in the suburbs. It was morning. I was in my home office, working on the computer. The kids were playing nearby while my wife prepared breakfast. I remember writing something about astronomy. The details were too complex to retain; nonetheless, I felt enthusiastic about my work. Perhaps it was a thesis for the Ph.D. that I've always longed for. Or maybe I switched industries and was finally doing something closer to heart. What's most interesting is that I'm actually wondering whether these dreams of the future are real. The scene of my daily walks from the train to my job in Midtown Manhattan is exactly what I had dreamed when I was 5 years old. Could as well be a coincidence, though the experience is truly fascinating.

December 22nd, 2020

Last night's dream was much more vivid than the two before. I was in my mid-sixties, all grey but looking well. I was at some remote astrophysics observatory. It looked remote because it was the only thing that was man-made at the top of a steep mountain, which pierced through the clouds of the night sky. There were a dozen other people there. They were all anxiously looking at a holographic projection that was broadcasting seven or eight satellite images. One was of Earth and the rest of some distant galaxies, ordered by the number of stars they contained. At one point, everyone became silent and stared at the clock. A minute later, the clock counted down to zero, and the images of the galaxies all broadcasted a stellar explosion. At the same time, lines of different colors were sketched on to the satellite image of Earth. The lines definitely represented each one of the galactic observation points, but I don't know what they meant to portray. The team then reviewed the results, and everyone started clapping and cheering. They all came up to hug me and shake hands with me. I had tears in my eyes, and I clearly remember having the feeling of déjà vu. I then realized that the déjà vu is real as I had seen this moment before. I closed my eyes so as to imagine myself 20 years younger. That's when I woke up.

Concept Progress

November 6th, 2040

Beyond any case of reasonable doubt, my mind is one of a time-traveling machine. For reasons unknown to me, once every 20 years or so, I get a glimpse of what's to come. I dreamed of being in my eighties, full of energy and excitement. All of those morning runs must've paid off! I was on a plane, heading to Tel Aviv, on my way to attend the Eurasian Science Foundation. I was to give a speech on the impact of universal expansion vis-a-vis temporal phasing. I was editing the speech on the plane, and bits and pieces of it remain in my memory. I remember outlining the math behind the Doppler effect as it pertains to the geometric expansion wave, noting last week's experiment at the observatory in the timeline of supporting observations. I also recall describing the theoretical framework of something called dark gravity, though the formulas are blurry in my mind. Interestingly, this ties into my current research on the relative interaction of accelerating systems. I believe this could be the missing variable that I need to keep the space systems from being torn apart. The speech ends by leaving few open questions, including the potential to break the speed of light. Then a stewardess interrupted by asking what I wanted to drink. I don't recall anything passed that point.

April 11th, 2060

The timing is remarkable. The dream occurred last night, after my speech to the Eurasian Science Foundation. I remember seeing myself two days ago, 20 years before. On my flight out here, I waited for my younger mind to join me. I had hoped for some kind of a connection, but nothing of the sort had occurred. In any case, good to know that I'll live passed a hundred! A century ago, that was an exception. And nowadays, it's becoming an accepted miracle. I was sitting outside on a deck, somewhere by a lake. My recollection is not as clear as it used to be. My aging mind disappoints me. I was writing something, sipping on chamomile, and listening to someone practice the violin inside the house. The serene and sometimes broken melody of "Adagio for Strings" seemed like a fitting soundtrack to the tranquil panorama that encompassed the foreground of my nearsighted vision. I felt sleepy but remained awake. Whatever I was writing seemed important. I'm not sure what it was, but I think it was a letter to someone. Last thing I remember is writing "Ella, I have full faith in your approach."

March 15th, 2080

I just dozed off and dreamed of being young again. I was only 5 years old. I had forgotten all that I've learned in this life and all that I've experienced. I felt simple and renewed. Something was different this time around. It was certainly me, but strangely enough, I couldn't recognize myself. I don't know where I was and who I was with. I believe that I was running around with my siblings. Funny, I don't have any siblings. Perhaps they were friends. Sadly, my memory is slipping away from me. It's comforting to know that the dream felt as real as all the ones before. Unfortunately, I fear that it's the last one in the series. With all of my contributions to science, I'm still at a loss as to how the mind can travel across time and space. And this dream complicates things even more. I guess one day someone will find out. If it happened to me, it'll happen to others. To those others, my name is Ari Lecht, and this is my dream journal.

CHAPTER EIGHT
ON PERFECTION AND INFINITY

The infinite nature of perfection instead becomes the absolute nature of reality.
If we are to judge something as being perfect, we should exclude from it any
mystical implications that would exhibit such infinite or infinitesimal properties.

CONCEPT TIME

The boy looks out of his classroom window and sees the groundskeeper make his way into the soccer field. The old man promptly comes in at 9 am, in the midst of math class. The boy looks at the clock, annoyed at its slow pace. Boredom is a fact of life, he thinks. While solving for the Pythagorean theorem, he notices the angle of the clock's hands and marvels at the coincidence. What can he do to make time move faster? His dad explained that time is a dimension, just like length or height or depth. If that is so, he wonders, why is it that he's stuck in it like a prison cell, unable to roam about it as he pleases?

The boy grows up. He looks out of his office window and views an endless stream of taxis and people rushing in all the directions of the city blocks. It's 9 am and already his day is booked up with meetings in the morning, lunch with his boss, and a client visit in the afternoon. No time to get any work done, he thinks. Again he'll have to stay late at the office just to catch up. When will he have any time for himself, for his family? His highly awaited and already booked vacation is six months away. Half a year will fly by in a blink of an eye, he tries convincing himself. He welcomes the thought of retirement although the old age thing is not something that he's too crazy about.

Concept Progress

The man grows old. He mows the lawn on a warm spring morning. It's only 9 am and already he's completed his daily exercise, had his breakfast, and read the newspaper. Now he's keeping busy in the yard while the lovely wife is cleaning the house. They have the whole day to themselves. Perhaps they'll visit a café for lunch. The kids are far away and always busy. Grandchildren are now in middle school, so no need for any babysitting duties. What's more to do? As long as health persists, he vows to enjoy life on a daily basis.

With each decade, it feels as if time moves faster and faster. In our first decade, as children, it seems that we've been around forever as we equate our life with existence itself. In our second decade, as teenagers, we feel that we have learned so much as to overtake the world. In our third decade, as young adults, we enjoy our youth, take risks, and explore commitments. Our thirties make us more serious, forties keep us busy with work and family, fifties challenge us with managing our finances, and sixties welcome in the golden age. From an abundant luxury, time turns into a scarce commodity. Per Sigmund Freud, "If youth knew; if age could."

ON PERFECTION AND INFINITY

Buddha aimed for nothing less than the perfect state of enlightenment, all while respecting nature's law of impermanence. How can perfection be rationalized with impermanence? How can such an unbounded concept be subjected to the boundaries of time? Perfection implies an infinite and never-ending quality. In monotheistic religions, God is attributed the quality of perfection as it pertains to His overall existence as well as all of His creations. In polytheistic religions, perfection applies to a particular quality for each of the many gods and goddesses. For some, perfection is out of our reach. For others, it is something that is simply the best. Perfectionists can vouch for the latter.

Perfection is a subjective concept, which makes it difficult to apply. Something that is perfect to him may not be perfect to her. To borrow from a dictionary, it is "of the highest degree of proficiency, skill, or excellence," "entirely without any flaws, defects, or shortcomings," "accurate, exact, or correct in every detail," "complete beyond practical or theoretical improvement," or "exactly fitting the need in a certain situation or for a certain purpose." For our purposes, we have made a point that the most evolved life form has achieved the most ideal state of being—that it has reached perfection. This may imply that any lesser forms, including humans, might be imperfect. This statement is humbling to some and insulting to others. From these definitions, we can narrow down this concept to two notions by way of the following illustration.

Suppose we take a blank sheet of white paper that is eight and a half inches wide by eleven inches long. We can examine it and determine whether it is a perfect piece of paper. On the one hand, we may find minor scratches, streaks, marks, folds, or tears. In this case, we will conclude that it is not a perfect piece of paper. On the other hand, we may not find any such distortions and conclude that it is the most exemplary piece of paper to ever be manufactured. That is, not only would it lack any visible imperfections, but also none of its qualities could be improved further. It would possess the most flawless shape, thickness, weight, tone, etcetera.

What if we then cut a hole in the middle of it and again inquire whether it is still a perfect piece of paper. The answer has to be such that the piece of paper with a hole in it is not a "piece of paper" at all. Rather, it may be a perfect "piece of paper with a hole in it." It is perfect as itself but imperfect as anything else in comparison. Therefore, unless we compare identical pieces of paper, each piece of paper will be perfect for its own unique set of characteristics. Just like snowflakes, each one is beautiful and no two are alike. This can be reassuring to us lesser forms.

We arrive at a dual definition for the concept of perfection. In the former case, it is something that has reached the most ideal state of being when compared to something else of a similar kind. In the latter case, it is something that simply exists as it is rather than as anything else. In fact, what we are after is to unify both of these notions when describing the most evolved life form. If the goal of evolution is to reach perfection, then let us examine what this term implies in its most objective sense.

At the level of the highest dimension, we reflect on the life of the universe as a momentary singularity that emanates existence on to all of the spacetime coordinates in the dimensions below. In essence, such reflection is of the entirety of existence. To arrive at a complete understanding of such a colossal conception is likely beyond our current capabilities. Nevertheless, as intelligent beings, we can challenge ourselves and catch a bird's-eye view of something that we will eventually plunge into anyway.

The philosopher has always pondered on the nature of existence. While the question has remained the same, its formulation has evolved in response to the work of the scientist. When the caveman looked around, he may have either taken his surroundings for granted or inquired into how everything he sees had come about in the first place. When a peasant from the dark ages looked around, he may have either taken his surroundings for granted or wondered how the Almighty Creator had established his unfortunate circumstances. When a modern businessman looks around, he may either take his surroundings for granted or ponder where all of the matter had come from before the Big Bang.

Just as Plato attempted to describe the universe with the classical elements of water, earth, air, and fire—instead of referring to the elements in the periodic table—all we can do is make logical formulations by piecing together relevant bits of modern scientific knowledge. At the multidimensional coordinates described by quantum mechanics stands the observer of Einstein's relativity; by the fundamental forces of physics, amino acids react with the forces of chemistry; while studying the geology of terrestrial change, Darwin was inspired on the biology of natural selection; by studying the psychology of social influence, we address the sociology of interpersonal actions; from the left-brain logic of mathematics, our conclusions meet the right-brain experience of common sense. Like pieces of a puzzle, we piece together, concept by concept, our conception of reality.

In our quest for perfection, we arrive at something undefined, something too grand to conceive. Or is it? If claims of perfection are as absolute as the concept itself, then surely it must be as real as existence itself. And if something can be claimed as real, then we should be able to wrap our evolved intellects around it. So we come back to the one characteristic of perfection that makes it seem out of reach—infinity. Intuitively, both concepts—perfection and infinity—are common to each other. But that is our right-brain talking. Our left-brain may not be so convinced and requires us to go the extra mile.

The fascination with the concept of infinity has obsessed mathematicians, scientists, and philosophers for centuries. It is an abstraction that is infamous to be unreachable by the mind. No one can comprehend its greatness in one sense. This mathematical concept has few practicalities in the real world, mostly serving as an estimate or an approximation. In physics, infinity appears in places where our minds short circuit, such as in reflecting on the shape of the universe or the number of universes in the multiverse. To conceptualize how infinity applies to the real world, let us demonstrate what it means for our own space and time.

Infinity is infinite in size small or large. With any number, any other number can be added, multiplied, or raised to its power. It has no boundaries, no limits, and defies any natural laws of impermanence. This holds true even if obvious boundaries do exist—such as between the starting number one and an ending number two—since between any two whole numbers, there is an infinite series of decimal numbers. This contradiction straight away paints a shade of doubt when taking infinity to describe reality.

An apple cannot be cut with a knife an infinite number of times for several reasons. In theory, one may suggest that there will always be another half to cut, but there is a realistic limit. Eventually, one will enter into the realm of atoms, and once an atom is split, its energy will be released. At that scale, we would be counting subatomic elementary particles, which have nothing more to divide. Besides, at some point, the edge of the knife will be thicker than the remaining piece of the apple. Otherwise, if one goes on forever cutting up the apple a piece at a time, one will never complete the task since it will take longer than the entire life of the universe to accomplish. That is, of course, unless we assume that the universe is static. In that case, we are proposing that an infinite amount of pieces compose one little apple. Again, we run into the same contradiction of an unbounded boundary.

The same applies to walking half the distance toward the wall. Yes, one will never reach the wall, but if one keeps on moving forever, should they not eventually reach anything? So we run into a play of words and remind ourselves to steer clear of ambiguous semantics. These arguments are quite old and offer important insights on the nature of reality. Let us also challenge the concepts of both the infinite and the infinitesimal insofar as they pertain to the notion of perfection.

We begin by asking, what is the smallest piece of existence? That is, can any one point of the spacetime coordinate be infinitely small? If so, what does infinite smallness really mean? The only logical explanation is that it is something that is the next thing next to nothing. The problem is that nothing does not exist, and so zero cannot realistically be used as a limit for the infinitesimal. At least, not in the same way as it is used in mathematics. In that case, we can replace the "infinitesimal"—something that reaches zero and does not exist—with the "minimum"—something that never reaches zero and does exist.

Space is a physical extension that is capable of containing matter. Each spatial coordinate can hold the minimum amount of matter—the zero-dimensional elementary particle. Also called point particles, these are fermions and bosons, the constituents of superstrings. Their order of magnitude is commonly known as the Planck length, which is the shortest possible physical length proposed by quantum theory. Each type of particle is rather identical as it lacks further composition. At the very least, its composition is currently unknown. Let us side with the present scientific perspective and proceed to inquire whether we can qualify these particles as being perfect.

Since we have reached the realistic limit for the infinitesimal, the dual definition of perfection seems safe to apply. An elementary particle is perfect in the sense that (a) it exists as it is and (b) its properties are identical to those of its counterparts. Thus, it has no base for comparison. An electron cannot be singled out as being better than any other electron because it has no other components that would differentiate its structure. Since any potential defect in its structureless form does not make physical sense, the closest equivalent for this notion would be a non-existence of the elementary particle. In discarding this contradictory alternative, it follows that such minimum amount of matter must be perfect.

A counterargument can be made on the basis of quantum mechanical laws breaking down at the level of a singularity. However, it is our lack of knowledge in this area that prevents us from having a complete understanding of that which we claim as being infinitesimal. A singularity within a black hole and a singularity arising at the onset of the Big Bang surely have different orders of infinite magnitudes. At these infinitely dense points, general relativity and quantum mechanics come at odds with each other, as the latter does not permit an elementary particle to inhabit a space that is smaller than its Planck length. The clashing of our two pioneering scientific theories hint on physical laws that are unknown to the scientist. Whatever these laws are, attributing perfection to the Big Bang makes perfect sense.

As the concept of infinite smallness comes under question, we then ask if something can be infinitely great. The universe was born from the Big Bang and has been expanding since. This is evidenced by the cosmological redshift as well as the cosmic microwave background radiation and implies that the universe is not infinite. Although it is bounded now, will the universe always be bounded? In subscribing to the highest standard of logic, we infer that if the universe is bounded now, even if it may be expanding indefinitely, at any point in the future, it will still be bounded by its greater size at that point in time. What will happen then at an infinite time? Since, by definition, that time will never come, the universe will remain bounded. Therefore, infinite greatness too bears the same question mark. The finite universe likewise fits the dual definition of perfection, being perfect for what it is and not having any other base for comparison.

Being hardheaded, the scientist will remind us of the multiverse theory, wherein multiple universes spring forth from their own unique Big Bang conditions. How would our universe, he would ask, compare with another? For our purposes, whether it is the universe or the multiverse makes no difference. We are simply addressing everything that exists at the level of the highest dimension. Up there, there is certainly nothing left to compare. Besides, as all elementary particles are deemed perfect, that which they make up must be just as perfect. Here again, we are referring to literally everything.

As spacetime refers to space and time being two sides of the same coin, since space is bounded, time must also be bounded. In fact, from our limited four-dimensional point of view, we are continuously moving at the edge of time. What is the relationship between space and time if these are said to be nothing more than different dimensional viewpoints of the same coordinate? We know that it takes time to get from one place to another. This means that as we travel through space, we also travel through time. To address this issue from another angle, we now ask, what is the minimum unit of time? The scientist will swiftly point us to Planck time, which is the time required for light to travel a distance of one Planck length.

One may wonder whether such principles of modern science will stand the test of time or whether these theories will one day be outdated and replaced by the discoveries of new physical limits. Just as Albert Einstein's theories superseded those of Isaac Newton, the same may also happen to the theories of Max Planck. For our purposes, whatever the actual limit is, it is enough to halt our count to infinity.

Although it may be challenging to rationalize the infinitesimal properties of space, our imagination may work better when applying such rationale to the properties of time. This is because unlike with space, where the infinitesimal seems to end with nothing, with time, the infinitesimal appears to begin with something—a moment.

If we look at a photograph, we may be tempted to conclude that we are witnessing a particular moment, which itself could very well represent the smallest division of time. However, how does one moment become the next moment, keeping the flow of existence in continuity? A moment appears to be still, but reality is in constant motion. According to the law of inertia, an object will retain its state of rest or motion so long as it is not acted upon by an external force. A moment then cannot be the same as something that is at rest. In fact, many things are happening in a photograph, allowing us to enjoy a snapshot of a frozen time period. What happens in one moment that carries it to become the next moment?

If a collection of moments amounts to a particular time range, such as a period of one second, then between any two seconds, there would be an infinite number of moments. This is analogous to the idea of having an infinite number of decimal numbers between any two whole numbers. An infinite number of moments suggests that the next second will never arrive. This sort of contradiction is now becoming all too familiar.

Perhaps moments of time are like frames in a video. One frame is one moment, and the next frame is the next moment. However, a video plays with a certain speed, which would require adding many more moments in between each frame to correspond to reality. Of course, videos only create the illusion of motion with enough frames per second to fool us into believing that the scene portrays continuity. If reality was to work in a similar way, there would be a break in time in between each moment. During this break, the universe would cease to exist only to reappear as the next moment. This would certainly disrupt the law of cause and effect, as the break in time would effectively void causality. Again we run into a logical conflict when attributing a moment to be a duration of time. Any true duration, no matter how short or how long—be it Planck time or a galactic year—must be perfect. Else, even an instant of imperfection would equate with a break in time during which the universe would cease to exist.

If time does not subdivide into a collection of moments, then it must have a speed. What is the speed of time, the speed at which more of it gets created, entering the future and filling up the past? Being in our reference frame of spacetime, we do not notice the space around us inflating nor the time passing. That is, until we look back and reminisce. When lost in thought, time seems to go by rather unnoticeably. When maintaining awareness of the present moment, it seems to slow down and match the rate of our attention.

Since space and time are coupled, being that it takes time for the universe to expand, the speed of time must be the same speed as the expansion of the universe. In other words, the time that it takes for space to expand a distance of one Planck length is also the speed of time when measured in such Planck units. This speed may not necessarily correspond to Planck time, which is a function of light speed rather than the speed at which the universe expands. Conversely, we can state that as time passes by, it creates more space, causing the universe to make room for itself by expanding further apart. If the expansion is accelerating as the scientist suggests, then the speed of time is also accelerating at the same rate.

Applying infinite limits in mathematical practices is clearly different from doing the same in reality. A moment of time is rather useful when defining a precise coordinate on a four-dimensional plane. However, such moment is indivisible from the flow of time and hence cannot amount to a realistic infinitesimal measurement.

It has been said before that infinity and zero are opposite extremes of the unrealistic real number line. Just as one cannot fill up a bounded universe with an infinite number of apples or apple pieces, similarly, there is no good reason to imagine that there are zero apples growing out of one's head. In fact, what we can conclude is that infinity corresponds to zero—neither carries any existent qualities in the real world. From a mathematical perspective, the entire positive and negative series of infinite numbers simply cancels itself out. Certain concepts that do not apply to reality break down even in mathematics, which is why there is no solution for a number being divided by zero.

The infinite nature of perfection instead becomes the absolute nature of reality. If we are to judge something as being perfect, we should exclude from it any mystical implications that would exhibit such infinite or infinitesimal properties. The infinite and eternal nature of religious deities makes them ever so mystical, inspiring faith for some and raising doubt for others. What can be concluded of the not so mystical, tangible world that our physical presence occupies? Is it perfect as it is or imperfect in comparison to something more ideal? Perhaps utopia? While a version of utopia may await us in the future once we finally tackle all of our social issues, today it is as subjective as the notion of perfection. And until everyone reaches a satisfactory standard of living, one that is both collectively agreeable and universally applicable, utopia will just be a synonym for heaven—a yearning of our imagination.

Despite our imperfect human conditions, the very nature of space and time—the fabric of existence that allows all of us, let alone our issues, to materialize—is as perfect as it can be. The tiniest particle inhabitants of space are as perfect as the universe that they make up. Perfect in the most realistic sense possible, without any connotation of the infinite or the infinitesimal. The passage of time too has perfection written all over it. Timing was crucial in the initial conditions of the Big Bang. If anything would have occurred a "moment" too soon or too late, everything would have been different. Fortunately for our sake, it all happened perfectly—creating a timeline in which a fourteen billion year-long chain of events have led us to this very moment.

The concept of perfection now crystallizes into a substantial aspiration, not necessarily out of reach. The mere manifestation of existence is reflected in the first definition of something being perfect for the sake that it simply exists. In totality, this is the universe. As we have noted, even the tiniest imperfection attributed to any of its properties, such as an infinitesimal amount of space or a momentary time period, is contradictory to its very existence. Conversely, the most evolved life form has reached perfection by achieving the most optimal quality of life at the level of the highest dimension. This ideal state of being is reflected in the second definition of something that is perfect and beyond the point of improvement. At this place of all places, at this time of all times, the most evolved life form experiences the universe in totality. Without the need of third party senses, the experience is free of any mediums. It is direct. Up here, cause and effect are indistinguishable and identical because everything at the level of the highest dimension is indistinguishable and identical.

We arrive at a premise that the most evolved life form is a representation of the universe. In challenging the boundaries of evolution, the only limit proves to be the universe itself. The universe's absolute strength, knowledge, and potential all describe a state of being with nothing more to gain. Simply because nothing more than the universe exists. As the most evolved life form amounts to nothing less than the perfect state of being that covers the entire sphere of existence, the universe too amounts to the same perfectly existent state. Existence here is the common denominator.

As the notion of perfection necessitates the universe to exist, it consequently necessitates the most evolved life form to exist. In Chapter Two, we talked about atoms, their existence, and purpose in the universe. As their subatomic components represent the most basic elements of perfection, they each serve a purpose in ensuring existence for the universe. Similarly, the purpose of evolution is to ensure the ongoing existence of life. Life wants to exist. So much so that it works very hard to improve the quality of its existence to the point of perfection.

These pieces begin to all fit together, though something still remains missing. There is a disconnection, a certain isolation between us and the universe. In this current time period, evolution is still in its infancy on the cosmological time scale. The gap between now and our conclusions is wide. Our curiosity drives us to fill this gap, to bind the pieces of the puzzle into a complete picture. This mystical gap is like an unknown variable in a seemingly unsolvable equation—a void that sometimes spirituality or religion try to fill, sometimes philosophy or science. Ultimately, it will be our experience that fills this gap, give or take some finite number of generations or so.

Our eyes are slow to open. Like waking up in the morning when the early sunlight makes us turn away from its brightness, with heavy eyelids we roll out of bed to proceed to our daily work. Similarly, the light of our evolutionary mandate is just as bright. So bright that it bears a weight of responsibility that not everyone is ready to accept. It means coming out of our comfort zone to explore this unknown and attempt to solve something that has never been solved before. Otherwise, holding on to our safety net will keep us fixed to a single side of the equation.

The net will one day tear, the ground will one day shake, the planet will one day become inhospitable, the Sun will one day stop shining, and our galaxy will one day collide with another. The only thing that is sure to exist is the already existing cosmos, even if recomposed by the forces of its own changing nature. Embracing these changes means adapting oneself to the situation at hand, challenging the boundaries that are holding us back, facing the future's uncertainties head on, and ultimately securing survival in the face of extinction.

In the next chapter, we will establish that connection between us, the universe, and the most evolved life form. Our journey through time and space will come full circle, back to where we initially started—our own selves. If our purpose in life is clear, it will become clearer. If our place in the universe is known, our destination will be that much certain. Like being guided by our vehicle's navigation system, our path will be guided by our newly mapped out perspective. Eventually, once we let go of our prejudices, intolerances, and cruelties, and once we are ready to stride toward peace, cooperation, and productivity, we will find ourselves at the gate of a new milestone—another step closer to perfection.

AROUND THE GALAXY
IN EIGHTY DAYS

TRANSMISSION 1:

Around the Galaxy in Eighty Days

Begin transmission. Mayday, Mayday, Mayday. This transmission is scheduled to arrive in the year 2315 to the attention of the International Space Administration. This is Captain Gabriel of the ISA Plongeur. We are in distress and in need of assistance. Mission galaxyOrbit has experienced an unexpected turn of events. By analyzing this transmission, you will validate that it had originated in the year 501,955 BCE. Request to review and take appropriate action.

The Plongeur has become the first manned spacecraft to successfully make full circle around the Milky Way galaxy in just 80 days; however, at a cost. Along with my copilot, a hunam named XL, we have arrived at the noted coordinates 12 hours ago. At first, we believed that we've successfully completed our mission one day ahead of schedule. Upon closer examination, XL determined that Earth's position relative to the Milky Way's meridian places it at this time period in the Paleolithic era. This has now been visually confirmed.

Initial diagnostics did not reveal any disruption to our trajectory. We're now replaying the autolog from the inception of our mission in hopes of identifying the anomaly that brought us here. XL believes it to be unlikely that our local space system suffered a failure as this would have led to a rupture in spacetime that would've disintegrated the ship. Whatever the reason is, traveling at a speed of 300,088 kilometers per second while passing through 121 galactic corridors apparently caused us to make a bad turn at some point.

According to XL, we are unable to prevent this course of events from reoccurring. Per the theoretical work of Professor Braun, an eminent temporalist from Cliffside University, physical laws prevent an object from traveling to a different point in time along the same timeline. Otherwise, chronological stability, as he termed it, would be compromised. XL tells me that we've somehow skipped to a newly-formed timeline, one in which our mere presence will cause it to be different from our own. Therefore, this transmission can save the Plongeur of your timeline, while XL and I may be left stranded here in the Stone Age. Still, I remain hopeful as it looks like my clock is running out of time.

A few hours ago, we descended to investigate the surface in northern Europe, particularly what will be the Netherlands. We detected humanoid activity largely comprised of *Homo neanderthalensis*. They are a moving population of primitive hunter-gatherers traveling along the English Channel. Those who have settled are forcing others to continue moving north for sake of resources. There was an active storm system, and we allowed the Plongeur to blend in with the clouds. As we activated a geoscan over the surrounding area, its statictricity attracted a lightning surge that overloaded our scanners. The locals witnessed the event and noticed the Plongeur. We quickly made exit into the stratosphere and have been stationed here since.

XL concluded that the overload was caused by a phenomenon known as temporal displacement, also postulated by Braun back in 2185. Braun suspected that if objects were to become displaced from their natural time range, their temporal signature would become dissonant due to differences in the rate of universal expansion. At this period in history, the universe is expanding at a slower pace than it will half a million years from now. Although the difference in pace is minimal, it's enough to cause minor irregularities to displaced negatively charged particles. We aren't yet sure of all the impacts, but my biomatter seems to have been affected. My tissue sample confirms that its genetic metabolisys is hyperactive and well above acceptable levels. Apparently, my body cannot withstand this time period for too long. XL tells me that for every 24 hours, I will age by a period of three weeks.

There's approximately a month's worth of nourishment left on the ship. After it's exhausted, I'll be required to land and collect more food. The Plongeur so far remains in stable condition. Its solar cells are functioning normally. XL too seems unaffected by the displacement. His mineral farm continues to be replenished. In the meantime, we are weighing our options and considering next steps. End transmission.

TRANSMISSION 2:
Twenty Thousand Meters above the Sea

Begin transmission. Mayday, Mayday, Mayday. This is the second transmission from the ISA Plongeur. Transmission 1 is embedded in this message. We've now spent five weeks at the noted coordinates, hovering at 20 kilometers above sea level. We've completed reviewing the autolog and identified the cause of the anomaly.

Looks like the Plongeur navigated through a galactic corridor that had intersected with another corridor. This rarely happens in the natural curvature of spacetime, as a corridor is not part of physical space but a bridge between two spatial locations. In this case, a black hole grew to overlap two perpendicular corridors and marked the point of the intersection. Normally, the ship circumnavigates around such cosmic vortexes. This time, the sensors malfunctioned. The black hole skewed the coordinates of four spatial systems into a single quadrilateral vector, which became a trap for any incoming object.

In stress-testing the data components against both proven and theoretical models, XL calculated all of the probable chain of events that could've produced such an outcome. Only one model held up, which appears in an unpublished work by Professor Braun.

In 2255, the year Braun passed, he wrote a letter to one Mrs. Anastasia Belle about how he marries her in a different universe. The letter served two purposes. One, he proclaimed his love to this woman who was his close colleague for many years. Two, he described in mathematical detail the existence of alternate timelines. This letter followed his most debatable publication on four-dimensional cognition, which led to so much controversy among his peers that Braun shied away from sharing any follow-up work.

The letter explained a quantum mechanical notion of how events come about out of the mere act of observation. That is, as a decision precedes an observer, in order to have any of the outcomes materialize, they must first exist as viable timelines in alternate universes. Otherwise, if a particular timeline doesn't exist, it won't be available as one of the choices for the observer to decide upon. For instance, when facing an imminent meteor strike, choosing to pray so that some supernatural power would deflect the celestial object will not attain such timeline for the unfortunate hopefuls. However, choosing to evacuate the impact zone or not would follow to one of the two possible timelines. Braun's model demonstrated how making such choices obliges the universe to skip to these alternate temporal pathways.

There are only two ways, Braun proposed, to navigate from one timeline to another—either at the fork of the road at the time the decision is made or by breaking the speed of light. For the latter scenario, the universe has an interesting way to deal with this violation. Just as nearing light speed forces time to slow down and attaining light speed causes time to stop, breaking light speed makes time reverse course. Rather than disrupting spacetime for the surrounding system, the flow of time is inverted only for the guilty object. That is, the object is thrown back in time as if it never violated the speed limit in the first place.

Braun explained that one could only travel into the past upon breaking light speed. Although there's an incalculable number of alternate timelines that've come about as a result of all the past choices, one has no access into these timepaths without themselves making the choice that leads to them. Going back in time forces one to become that fork from which a new timeline springs forth. How far back one can travel depends on how much the object exceeds light speed. The faster the speed, the further back one is thrown.

Braun proposed a new universal speed limit of c^2, which is the velocity required to be thrown to the initial moment of the Big Bang. Einstein, he said, was farther off in his conclusions than he was in his calculations. While the speed of light is the speed limit of an object traveling within a particular space system, when squared, it becomes the ultimate speed limit of an object traveling throughout the life of the universe. As the universe expands and time ages, this limit stays constant and is applied on a parabolic ratio basis of the velocity exceeding light speed to the age of the universe.

Looks like we've confirmed Braun's theories and became the first crew to travel back in time, relatively speaking. As we crossed the corridor intersection, the black hole ripped away our local space system like the Earth underneath our feet. However, it lost the chance to capture the Plongeur. The moment the ship became exposed, it was expelled from its temporal coordinates to avoid breaking physical laws. Upon arrival into this past period, the ship immediately lost momentum, and its spectroengines propelled it at its projectile rate. Once a loss in velocity was detected, the ship generated a new space system and continued on its way. Luckily, the black hole hasn't yet grown deep enough at this point in time, and we easily bypassed it.

Apparently, I slept through all the excitement. XL too was recharging as he does every fortnight. We were mistaken to assume that our local space system suffered a failure. Back when spectrotechnology was first being tested on the Atlantic Space Station, all of the objects that the engineers thought had disintegrated from such a failure were in fact thrown back in time. For Braun, this explains yet another quantum mechanical notion, which is that there's a minute probability of objects seemingly appearing out of thin air.

XL remains busy with his analysis. I've aged approximately two years since we got here. This past week, however, there's been a slight improvement in my genetic metabolisys condition. Tissue examination shows no indication as to why, but I'll take it. Wondering if I'm destined to spend the rest of my days on the Plongeur. I can't live amongst the locals nor could I reveal to them anything about myself or this ship. XL is my only companion. End transmission.

TRANSMISSION 3:
Journey to the Center of the Milky Way

Begin transmission. Mayday, Mayday, Mayday. This is the third and final transmission from the ISA Plongeur. Transmissions 1 and 2 are embedded in this message. We've now spent three months in this prehistoric epoch. My condition has further improved. While it's still on the hyper side, it's been normalizing simply by consuming the foods of this time period. As the cells in my body are replenished, they inherit the temporal signature from their source of nourishment. Within a few months' time, I'll practically be native to this period. However, I've decided not to stay around for long.

We've identified several landing sites to collect food and water. On few occasions, the locals caught site of us, but we were quick to return to the ship and take off. A few days ago, two adolescents, a male and a female, got caught in a geoscan and were actually running after the ship. We managed to capture their genetic mappings. XL ran a projection diagnostic against our database, and it was interesting to find that the pair were ancestors to over 14 million people living in 2315. Several bloodlines have been quite influential.

One lineage leads to David Davidson, an English economist from the 18th century, who produced the revolutionary work titled "Principles of Deflation." Davidson's idea of a national deflationary system proposed a steady and continuous reduction of monetary use. Economic stability, he argued, requires a different incentive system; one that is based on tangible human aspirations rather than, what he called, a worthless medium. Another lineage leads to Chancellor Friedrich Wilhelm II who in the early 20th century led the German Empire to become the first currency-free nation state. Yet another lineage leads to Golda Goldberg, America's 54th President, who made the United States become the last currency-free country with the establishment of the North American South American Union, known as the NASA Union.

If any act of interference on our part disrupts or even briefly delays this young couple from engaging in courtship, the chain of events to follow will dramatically alter this timeline. To avoid this, I've decided to take the risk of executing XL's plan of getting us back to our native time period.

According to my copilot's simulations, this requires the Plongeur's local space system to accelerate to a rate of 299,088 kilometers per second. Once the Plongeur attains this target speed, we'll deactivate the local system and, as a result, expose the ship to temporal stasis. At this speed, the Plongeur will advance at a rate of one millennium per 24 hours, taking almost seventeen months to reach the 24th century. The challenge is deactivating the local space system at such a great speed. The Plongeur wasn't built for such conditions and can't withstand this much strain for a prolonged period in naked space. For this reason, ironically, we'll need the help of a black hole.

As soon as we're in range of the outer event horizon, our solar cells will convert its emitting radiation into an electromagnetic layer that will envelop the ship. The layer will act as a shield against the effects of temporal stasis, which would otherwise reduce the ship's structural integrity. We'll then orbit the black hole until we reach our target time period. To avoid falling into the inner horizon, we'll require a very large black hole, one that has a long and thick outer layer. And so our destination is the supermassive black hole at the center of the galaxy. Once we reach the 24th century, we'll turn the local space system back on and expel the Plongeur out of the event horizon.

XL estimates our rate of success to be a rough ten percent, accounting for all of the unknowns. Of course, the risk of staying on Earth and changing history is much greater. This leaves us without any options.

We've run a quick test flight from the Earth to the Moon and back, and the Plongeur proves itself in good condition. We're making our final preparations, and tomorrow morning, we'll be en route along the Radial Corridor to the center of the Milky Way.

Perhaps these transmissions will fail receipt, and there's a chance that upon arrival, I'll remain the only Captain Gabriel in the fleet. Or perhaps they'll become a time capsule, ensuring a warm welcome from my counterpart of this new timeline. End transmission.

CHAPTER NINE
AN INTELLIGENT UNIVERSE

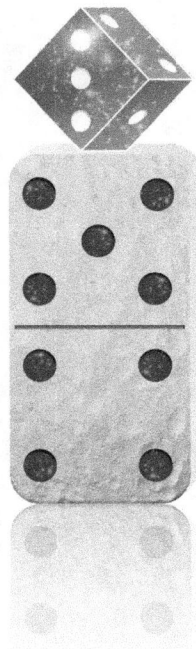

Perhaps God does not play dice. Perhaps He plays dominoes.

CONCEPT WAVE

It's 1925. The family is sitting around the dinner table, listening to country music on the radio. "Doesn't take much getting used to," dad says as he marvels at the new device that seems like it was missing from their dining room their entire lives. "Great for entertainment," mom says, enjoying the company of her family. "How is it," asked the son, "that this gadget can play music from other people's phonographs?" Not being too familiar with the mechanics of radio wave transmission, dad tried to explain the idea of a broadcast. "Seems like this kind of technology can only bring people closer together," the daughter smiles. "And the world smaller," dad adds. "How else," he asks, "can we travel to Nashville without leaving home?"

It's 2025. Mom and dad are eating at the kitchen counter, watching television, while the kids are playing on their mobile devices. "So much for getting everyone to have dinner together," mom sighs as she looks around. "All this technology is isolating us from one another," dad comments. "Things were different when I was young," he recalls. "People actually talked to each other face to face. Maybe it's just a phase," he supposes, "in which we now treat technology more like toys rather than tools." "Put down your tablets and finish your plates," mom reminds the kids for the fifth time.

It's 2125. The family is sitting around the holographic table. Each one of their images is projected from a different place. Mom and baby are at home, dad is on a business trip at a hotel, daughter is in her college dorm room, and son is at his new apartment on the Upper West Side. "At least we can all get together for a Friday night dinner, somehow," mom thinks. "It's great to see everyone," dad smiles. "Can't wait until everyone comes home for the holidays," says the daughter. Everyone agrees, laughs, and eats.

A wave is a wave—whether it is the wave of an ocean guiding a message in a bottle, a radio carrier wave modulating the sound wave of a steel-string guitar, or a holographic image emitting photon waves that precisely replicate our winks and smiles. In fact, strings at the subatomic level resonate waves of probability, filling the void with that which we are certain to call reality. A wave hello or a wave goodbye. It is motion. It is substance. A wave here. A wave there. A wave everywhere.

AN INTELLIGENT UNIVERSE

As we probe into the properties of the universe, study its origins, and contemplate on its final destiny, our concerns aim to ensure the ultimate prevailing of life. Conversely, in analyzing the element of life, we are met with understanding its place of nurture, its habitat, its home. Being that most of the cosmos is inhospitable to life as we know it, our worldview is shaped based on how much or how little one perceives oneself to be connected with the universe. We can divide these perceptions into three points of view. One view is that life is separate from the rest of the physical universe. Another is that life and the universe are always bound to each other. And yet a third view is that the universe itself is alive.

The first worldview can be applicable when describing the difference between matter that has been formed to be a living being and matter that lacks any biological compounds. For example, a rock and a dog are both composed of atomic particles. As these particles are assembled into different configurations, this influences the very nature of their structure. A rock does not feature any capability to act on its own, and so we see it as being lifeless. A dog does act on its own behalf, and so we see it as being alive. Hence, a rock and a dog are seen as two completely separate entities in this first worldview.

This is a traditional view found among monotheistic religions, which sees life, particularly human life, as being so special that it stands apart from the rest of the universe. The remnant of this view lingers among those who believe that life is unique to Earth and is not a commonplace characteristic of the cosmos. As well, children, whose sense of being is yet to mature, tend to this view, as they are yet to acknowledge their dependencies on inanimate objects.

The premise of the second worldview is that life cannot exist without the blanket of the universe. Life is understood to be intrinsically tied to the universe. Our nourishment and our atmosphere are necessary extensions of our physical selves without which we cannot survive for very long. In this case, a rock and a dog, although are physically separated, now begin to form a connection. A rock, after all, is a fragment of the Earth without which the dog would not exist.

Currently, this is the most accepted worldview held by modern society and one that is believed to stem from an educated and well-rounded outlook. By this view, we cannot avoid considering the vast number of planetary systems in the known universe and, consequently, that the chances are overwhelmingly in favor of the fact that many harbor even the simplest forms of life. Moreover, according to the Drake equation, many of those considered likely enjoy the privilege of intelligence.

The third worldview requires a vision of the universe that is quite different from that of contemporary science. At the very least, we can be certain that some parts of the universe are alive, as these are all the living beings. The following is an illustration on a smaller scale. A human being is composed of over thirty seven trillion living beings. Each cell in our body is an individual striving to survive by means of the collective. Unlike the collective human society, in this case, the collective is the human body. If the body dies then its cells die with it. It is in the cell's own interest to work faithfully for their master so as to ensure their own survival. While the human may be superior to the individual cells, she or he is as dependent on them as they are dependent on her or him. It is a fair process in which the cells work for the benefit of the collective in exchange for necessities provided by it. It is biological socialism. And just as a sovereign state has a military to protect itself against a foreign invasion, the immune system takes military action when a virus invades the united cells of our body. In this way, the body is a microcosm, teeming with life.

When considering morality at the level of the individual cells, it becomes quite clear why they should not kill each other, steal from each other, deceive one another, or refuse to bring positive results to the collective. Attempting anything aforementioned will lead their host's health to suffer. We should take as an example the benevolent actions of our loyal servants, our own bodily cells. As well, we can mentally thank them in this regard. Meditators can assert that such positive and detached self-notion acts as a psychotherapy, one that alleviates depressed mind states and puts us more in touch with ourselves —a "you are welcome" response from our cells.

If we shift our view of the human body to reflect the body of the universe, we are in effect shifting to the third worldview. By the same token, it does not make much sense to suggest that life can live in a non-living host. For instance, it is now all too evident that our living planet is not immune to the reckless activities of humanity. The ignorance of our indifference is like a cancer that is foolish enough to attack its own dwelling. For some, Earth's life-friendly conditions are often taken for granted. For others, there is no reason to attribute these life-friendly conditions to the rest of the cosmos. Is this not a narrow outlook? Earth's conditions are supported by those of the solar system. The solar system, in turn, is supported by the conditions of the Milky Way galaxy. The galaxy is part of a network of galaxy clusters, which all came about as a result of the conditions of the Big Bang. Our life is connected to the very life of the universe and just as so inherits its vigor, its vitality.

This vigor, this vitality can only be personified by a life force that has evolved to meet the limits of the universe. The most evolved life form conveniently fits the third worldview as the embodiment of the living universe. In fact, the life of the universe resembles that of an organism. Upon its inception, it was structureless, tiny, and began growing and taking shape at an extreme rate. Eventually, it matured enough to provide fertility to further life forms. By this analogy, the universe expanding is the most evolved life form growing up. Like cells in its body, we are a necessary part of this biocosmic structure.

One of life's defining characteristics is genetic programming. Any matter that is fortunate enough to establish this programming has succeeded in accomplishing something as opposed to insentient matter that is bouncing about nature's causes and effects, accomplishing nothing from its own efforts. This genetic programming is what allows physical matter to achieve something on its own. This "something" is the most basic expression of a volition, a precursor to a decisive action. The very attempt to act—whether consciously or subconsciously, voluntarily or involuntarily, intentionally or unintentionally—precedes the action and is that which separates a living being from a non-living object. Such volition is the power to will some motion to occur. A child wills to raise her arm in class, a dog wills to wag its tail, a cell wills to replicate itself. For Aristotle, it is to be a "mover."

This leads us back to the universe, which is full of actions and reactions, and forces us to ask how such motion came about in the first place. Of course, here we stand at the brink of science and religion's most debated query. On the nature of the first cause, the scientist argues for a movement while the creationist advocates for a mover. Both views of whether the universe created itself or by "someone" still tend to either the first or second worldview, as life remains a byproduct of the universe. The third worldview, however, sees life to be an essential ingredient in the universe's existence. So essential, in fact, that life is considered to be the source of the universe, responsible for its birth—for its very creation.

In Chapter Five, we discussed how negative progress leads to destruction. Its polar opposite necessarily leads to creation, as evolution strives to create life in an ever-progressive form. As the most evolved life form actualizes evolution in its most positively progressed state, it likewise manifests the most quintessential essence of creation. This equates with the whole of existence, which in the beginning is said to have been a singularity. In the current time period, it is the entire universe. In the end, it may either be one or the other, or both.

Let us practice pondering the unfathomable, which need not be a contradiction; rather, a chain of events obscured by the flow of time. As space and time are two sides of the same coin, having a single notion of it enables us to fathom something perfectly finite. Perhaps time is not the other side of the coin; instead, it is its edge. In this way, the edge is a finite yet never-ending circle that encircles the sides. Let us circle back on this point.

The universe is a teenager on a scale of billions of years. It has matured to produce life that evolved from the simplest of forms to the complexity that we find ourselves to be. The process of evolution painstakingly yet progressively aims to enhance the quality of life so as to ensure its ultimate survival. In this way, we have a long road ahead of us to conquer all the regions of the cosmos. Until we do, there will remain opportunities to compete for unseized resources and territories. Eventually, everything in this bounded universe will be accounted for at every spatial and temporal coordinate, one dimension at a time. At the moment when evolution's limits are met, the most evolved life form will arise to reflect the singular experience of the entire universe at the level of the highest dimension. For the philosopher, this moment is the coming about of existence. For the creationist, it is Genesis. For the scientist, it is the Big Bang.

How do we reconcile an event that marks the beginning of time and also marks the future birth of the most evolved life form? Perhaps the Big Bounce is a clever proposition of modern cosmology on the circularity of the universe's life. Or perhaps the explanation is yet to be discovered. In any case, our habit of tying events sequentially does not apply to the level of the highest dimension, where past and future simultaneously manifest within the absolute state of time.

We can envision the circle of time reflecting the life of the universe where the beginning point is the same as the ending point. At first sight, the circle may suggest an infinite loop that repeatedly gives rise to the universe. As discussed in the previous chapter, infinity points to contradictory notions and, as in object-oriented computer programming, infinite loops lead to system crashes. The contradiction in this case is similar to the age-old dilemma of which came first, the chicken or the egg? To break the infinite loop is to take a step passed causality. This means to rise to the standard of a higher dimension where the perfect circle is perceived as a whole—something that happens just once, all at the same time. Simply put, it is something that exists as opposed to it not existing. Existence again becomes the underlying principle.

From our limited perspective, everything that will happen has already happened on a cosmic scale. It is as if we are in the midst of watching a film, and its finale is yet to be viewed. In actuality, all of the film's events have already been played out, and they exist as the unseen data in our DVD players. If we are to take out the DVD and ponder its contents, then it is as though we are holding the entire film in our hands all at once. The same idea applies to the universe. It exists in its complete state, and we just happen to find ourselves in a certain scene—at a certain place and a certain time.

Everything that exists, or more generally, existence, is synonymous with the universe. As mentioned before, for our purposes, this can mean the multiverse—a collection of universes summed up to the level of the highest dimension. The creationist argues that God's existence is beyond the universe.

This can be taken to mean as either outside of the universe or above it, in that it does not follow any known physical laws. The former suggests a contradiction—an existing non-existence. The latter is similar to describing a singularity since the same applies to the highest dimension. While this approach starts to demystify God, the creationist will still insist that any conception of Him is forever beyond the capabilities of the human potential. Forever, as we have seen, is too strong of a word. Such lack of confidence denies the philosopher to exercise his reasoning abilities, especially as they are refined with every new scientific discovery.

The infinite attributes of space and time are as questionable as they are for the concept of God—namely omnipotence, omniscience, omnibenevolence, omnipresence, and the like. For some, God cannot be God unless He is defined in those infinite measures. God may be powerful, knowledgeable, and good more so than any other living creature in all of space and time, but as we have noted, those qualities cannot be infinite. Therefore, the classical definition is at best incomplete. Is it possible to redefine God?

***

By means of the evolutionary process, we suspect that the universe has come into being as the most evolved life form. Being all-knowing, this becomes an interesting afterthought that the universe is intelligent by design. This may remind us of the intelligent design argument. Unfortunately, the argument never explains who designed the Designer. It simply avoids the topic altogether by attributing to God those infinite qualities that are left undefined. Is God as undefined as a number being divided by zero? Reason suggests this to be an unsatisfactory conclusion. If we are to go as far as to imply that a design is an effect of a cause, then we ought to not overlook the source of that cause.

We will find that our third worldview, which appoints the most evolved life form as the living universe, can be compatible with both views of the creationist and the scientist alike. By this view, the infinite nature of God instead becomes the perfect nature of the "God species." While this may seem like blaspheme to some, such irreverence has been in dispute with the scientific method since at least the nineteenth century. Fact of the matter is that if those omni- qualities all describe the most evolved life form and also, for that matter, the God of the Abrahamic religions, then we are left with a promising compromise. What the creationist loses is a portion of the mysticism associated with the divine. What the scientist gains is a working hypothesis based on the cross-disciplinary theorems of physical cosmology and biological evolution.

The philosopher is the mediator who focuses on both the factual as well as the potential. What else can God be, he would ask, if not everything? What else if not a self-sustained organism bounded by nothing but its own existence? Just as God created us in His image, in turn, we are creating God in our image. Just as some of us need God in our lives, it happens to be that God needs us just as much. Just as we are a god to the individual cells in our body, so too we are the cells in the body of our God, the universe. It is a fair process in which all parties benefit from each other's endeavors. It is cosmic socialism.

Or perhaps it is more like cosmic capitalism in which God is the ultimate private owner of all the surrounding capital, providing jobs in exchange for distributing some of that capital to us lesser forms. This as opposed to cosmic communism, which would otherwise resemble the classical image of God being seen as the feared dictator to whom one's fate and faith must be surrendered without question. From the perspective of positivism, we can draw parallels from such metaphors. A socioeconomic system, after all, not only reflects our efforts to maintain a social order, but also shapes our worldview. As history demonstrates, an establishment that encourages equality and human rights allows for opportunities to connect one's mind to a universe of possibilities. Oppression, on the other hand, disconnects it from such universe.

Here the philosopher would exercise his expertise, serving not only as an advisor on social governance, but also as a liaison between matters of science and spirituality. An advocate for reason, he guided us out of the Dark Ages and into the Age of Enlightenment. "I think, therefore I am" was not only a fundamental proposition of Western philosophy, but also the return to individualism. This proposition became a simple measure of one's immeasurable existence. It triggered a revolution to break free of one's inner conflict that was so easily stirred by negativity and regress. It offered permission to believe, rather than force believing into a requirement. And it resonated an axiom that has the power to change the future—choice.

Choice of religion, like choice of occupation, serves to fulfill one's purpose in life. We will examine the power of choice in the next chapter. For now, the point to make is that everyone has the God-given right to choose their own path. In this day and age, individual freedom is increasingly valued and respected. Tolerance toward others' religious or non-religious beliefs, so long as they do not pose any harm, is an increasingly popular notion amongst the modern generation of intellectuals. Along with empathy, compassion, and other sentiments, emotional intelligence is being recognized as a key measure of our evolving intellects. While its models are relatively new, those wholesome qualities that are associated with high EQ are at the moral core of every major religion, which speaks quite obviously as to the commonalities of our human nature.

Upon examination, we find that nature operates by common laws of relative degrees. These laws apply to the magnetism of opposite poles in a similar way as attraction applies to opposite sexes. Although common, these laws are also commonly misunderstood. Their realization from the quantum to the cosmic is the genius of the intellectuals. Their experience within the mind-body framework is their enlightenment. Spotting commonalities, identifying connections—herein is the principal principle of all spiritual inspirations and scientific aspirations. Whether one is seeking their God-nature or Buddha-nature or the nature of relativity, as the saying goes, all roads lead to Rome. A gradual shift from the first to the second to the third worldview reflects our overall progress. As we cease to hold in mind any mental barriers between us and the universe, we allow ourselves to become one with the nature of things.

Our inseparable connection with the universe implies that we can communicate with the greatest of all species, so long as we open the proper channels to do so. Just as our cells send us notifications by means of electrical signals, so too humans have been sending notifications to the up above by means of various signals. Whether the signal is a prayer or a SETI radio frequency, both emit waves with different rates of oscillation. Both signals can be tuned into either by an EEG or an antenna. Ultimately, they absorb into the very thing from which they originate—the all-knowing universe.

A comprehensive review of any effect can trace back a story of its corresponding cause. This applies to everything without exception, from a falling snowflake that sets off an avalanche to an electrical impulse that triggers a revolutionary idea in the mind. This is information potential, and like the Internet, it is available at our fingertips, provided that we use the right tools. This means that the intelligence of the universe is everywhere, and access to it depends on our own progress. As talked about in Chapter Six, it is up to us to determine how to gauge this access—directly, by evolving our minds and bodies, or indirectly, by evolving our technologies.

Speaking with the most evolved life form is just speaking with the universe. Whether the channel is meditation, prayer, hypnosis, lucid dreaming, or hallucinogens, one strives to gain access to those parts of the brain that are usually left dormant or distracted throughout our everyday "normal" experience. As humans utilize a portion of their white and grey matter at any one time, this leaves much potential for improving our mental capacities.

Imagine a superintelligent species using thought waves in the same way as we now use sound waves—both directly through their inherent faculties as well as indirectly through the media of technology.

Each teleconference, international flight, or space probe strengthens our connection with our conjoined environment. Until this connection begets the most evolved life form, we cannot escape the cruelties of natural selection. And while the universe's fate may be sealed, as witnessed by its very existence, the human race is not guaranteed salvation just yet. We are already a much progressed species. It would seem a terrible waste of time for Mother Nature to start over. All the more reason to be mindful of our own progress; namely, the triple-layer pyramid of personal progress. The choice is ours. We can either be fruitful and multiply into the farthest reaches of the cosmos or let our bad habits take a turn for the worst.

Our good fortune led us to take center stage as evolution's primary candidates on this planet. Is this a result of a random set of circumstances or a remarkable natural occurrence? From a cosmic perspective, the chain of events initiated by the Big Bang makes any sort of randomness or coincidence irrelevant. From our limited perspective, gene mutation that drives evolution appears to be random. Einstein once stated that "God does not play dice with the universe." Although he was referring to Heisenberg's uncertainty principle, his point was that all of the universe's enigmas have an explanation. Quantum mechanics tells us that we cannot know everything and that randomness is a fact of nature. That seems to be the case from where we currently stand— being hindered by the physical limits of our tools and measurements, our four-dimensional context, and our own corporal selves. The challenge is to see passed those limits and get to know something that is now unknown. Or seems unknowable. Perhaps God does not play dice. Perhaps He plays dominoes.

One thing to note from the uncertainties of quantum theory is that even the impossible is not certain. There is a minute probability that a soccer ball will not be stopped by the net, or that a pair of entangled lovers will share erotic thoughts across the world from each other, or that the future can in fact converge with the past. We can attribute this third possibility to Einstein's discovery of the curvature of space because the same must then apply to time. The fourth dimension cannot be linear simply because spacetime is not Euclidean. If we imagine the timeline of the universe to be even slightly curved, it would then take a very long time for the line's opposite ends to meet and bind into a giant circle. As is expected. Otherwise, a limit in direction denies the sort of connectivity that binds everything in existence. We can walk forward or backward, turn to the right or to the left, go up the stairs or down, move forward in time and then some. Such flexibility extends to the level of the highest dimension—the ultimate point of all the intersections.

In the next chapter, we will consider the influence of choice on our multidimensional travels. Our final words will shine the spotlight onto the stage of our own life. As if standing in front of a large audience that is waiting for our next performance or remark, we will be put on the spot, tested, and dared. We will be offered a decision, one that will not only impact us, but also those in front of us, around us, and those yet to be born. We have approached forks in the road many times before. This time, however, the consequences are more calculated and better anticipated. We begin to sense that there is something much more at stake than what simply meets the eye. As before, we can take a guess, hope for the best, and continue on as mice in a maze. Or we can rise above the labyrinth, take a good look around, and choose to pursue the path of our progress.

THE HOUSE

The house stood on our block for five generations. It was the oldest house in town. All other houses have been demolished and rebuilt several times. But no one could ever knock or nuke this house down. It withstood everything. Inside lived beings from another world, but no one had ever seen them. Yes, aliens were living among us. And to us, they were neighbors.

Grandpa George used to tell me stories about how the house first arrived. In 2069, at sunrise on June 21st, Grandpa George's grandpa, Glen Anderson, was the first to see the house appear. It didn't make any noise nor shine any lights. It just appeared outa nowhere. Little Glen was only nine years old back then. He woke up for school, sat on his bed, looked outa his bedside window, and waited for the first ray of the morning light to signal the start of a new day. It was still dark. Any minute now, the horizon would turn blue and then red, revealing only the sky and 200 acres of an abandoned cornfield. Instead, as the darkness of the night began to fade, a house was seen standing just outside of the side yard, blocking the view of the cornfield. Glen thought he was dreaming as he gaped at this new obstruction.

That morning everyone came to see the mysterious house that seemed to have been built overnight. It looked very ordinary—a stone base, brick walls, solar panel roof, painted all white, surrounded by a white picket fence, inside a mowed lawn with a freshly kept flower garden, and even a sprinkler system. But there was nothing ordinary about it. No one ever came in or out, the doors and windows were always shut, and through the white linen drapes, only shadows were seen moving about from time to time.

On the following day, the town newspaper, The Cliffside Record, ran a story about the house on its front page. **"MYSTERY HOUSE,"** read the large bold headline. This was the most exciting news that had ever come out of this town. Our town is small, only one square mile, in the middle of nowhere. But very soon it became famous like we were Roswell or something. Those alien fanatics began to show up and make lots of noise outside. Strangely, nobody could ever climb over the fence. Whenever someone tried to jump it, they disappeared and straight away reappeared as if they were jumping back onto the sidewalk.

Soon enough the government came to know our family very well. At first, the Andersons were forced to leave. The whole street was evacuated for nearly a decade. The government did all it could to get someone from that house to react. First they were making pleas, then threats, and then they started throwing all kinds of things at it—probes, stones, bullets, shrapnel, laser pulses, radioactive shells, and even laughing gas. There was never any response, and nothing ever got through. It all just reversed direction and even killed a few folks. The president looked really bad in the eyes of the media and almost got impeached for her reckless actions. Since the house didn't seem to pose any threat, the government gave up. Years later my family was allowed to return to our home, as did the rest on our block. We even got enough compensation to finish the basement and build an inground pool.

Over time, the whole town got used to the house being here. I lived in the same room as little Glen did before me. I used to stare outa that window for hours and watch the shadows go about their routine. They never did anything strange. Sometimes they ate, or rested, or danced. Life went on. With all the tourism, the house became one of the wonders of the world. Our town grew, skyscrapers filled the cornfield, and condos replaced the surrounding homes. Thanks to our unusual neighbors, the properties on our block were the only ones spared.

Then in 2180, at noon on December 21st, the front door opened for the first time. I was nine years old back then. I was coming home from the game with my dad. We couldn't believe it! All the pedestrians stopped and stared. Some tried to record this momentous occasion. Later on, we found that they didn't actually record anything. Suddenly, one of them beings came out. I took a good look at it, but it didn't look like it was made of anything. No skin, no bones, no flesh at all. Just energy in the shape of a man, glowing with kind of a golden and light-bluish radiance. He didn't say anything. He didn't have to speak. We heard him in our minds. We all heard the same thing, "Hello," and we felt great!

We felt like a weight was lifted off our shoulders. We proudly stood there feeling charged with confidence, full of energy, and high spirits. Wow, what a rush! Every single one of us became drawn to this feeling of bliss like this being just woke us up from a dreary sleep. The being later explained that we connected with his vital force. Whatever this force was, it sparked something inside of us. From that day on, all of us who witnessed this event were forever changed. We never again became angry or scared of anything. We were better able to control our emotions, our actions, our very choice of thought. That was his gift to us.

He communicated everything that we wanted to know about them. They were a family of three—mom, dad, and their little girl—and they came from the distant future. They live on a planetary nebulae that will one day be formed in the Regulus star system. He told us that they were our descendants, and we were their ancestors. He explained that they're able to coexist in multiple time periods simultaneously. While their temporal selves were residing here in our town, their anti-temporal versions were on their home nebulae in the future. They can harness the power of quantum entanglement with their minds, and I remember that blew my mind!

They didn't wish to study us nor change the course of our history. They came because they needed to move, not just to a different place but to a different time. These beings dwell in five dimensions, and traveling through time is something they cannot avoid. They can't contain themselves to a single time period just as we can't contain ourselves to a single location. They came to Earth when their daughter was born and intended to live here until she became a preschooler. Now that time has come, and they were ready to move on. I still don't get what it all means, them being here and there. But I guess that don't matter too much.

On behalf of his family, the alien father thanked us for our town's hospitality. In gratitude, the missis and he spent the remainder of the day engaging with all of the folks who came by. More and more had showed up as word of these aliens got out. For the first time, people were invited into the house and even had tea with the owners. All kinds of journalists and reporters came, but no one was able to photograph nor holograph them. Their images simply couldn't be captured. All that came out was an empty house—clean, stylish, and cozy inside. It was like they were invisible. The aliens were patient and polite. They answered everyone's questions and had some interesting conversations with the professors of Cliffside University. Then they made their goodbyes, and everyone was kindly asked to leave. At sunset, at the last burst of sunlight, the house disappeared as quickly as it appeared.

For a whole year after, these aliens were the talk of all the newspapers, magazines, and late night shows. Those reporters and professors who were there that last day published many articles and books on different topics that the aliens had discussed with them. My family became famous and were featured in a documentary titled "The House Next Door." In time, all the hype started to cool down. After many years, some were questioning whether all this had even occurred. We had no pics, no holos, just our memories.

But everyone who lives in this town has no doubts. Everyone here knows full well that for a long time, we lived side by side with aliens from the future.

CHAPTER TEN

LIFE, CHOICE, AND THE REST

Our timeline may seem to reflect a one-way highway.
However, every decision is an exit to a multitude of other pathways.

CONCEPT COEXISTENCE

It's 8 am. I ride the bus, commuting to work like everyone around me. Some are trying to catch that extra half hour of sleep to make up for going to bed late or for attending to their little ones in the middle of the night. Others are on their phones or tablets, listening to music, watching a movie, reading a novel, or writing an email. I glance over to the person sitting next to me. She shakes her head as she scrolls through the headlines. I catch a glimpse of a few top stories and find myself in silent agreement. How can people resort to such violence, deception, greed, and corruption? We're supposed to be an intelligent and rational species. Why make life more difficult than it already is?

It's 9 am. I make my way through Times Square and observe people carry out the same activities as me—rushing to work, polishing their shoes, catching a cab, or refueling their bodies with bagels and coffee. Clearly, I'm not the only one with a job, bills to pay, and responsibilities to manage. I take note of other similarities, once taken for granted but now unfolding a universe of wisdom—two eyes, two arms, two legs, one mind, one heart, one moment at a time. The subtler details become even more wondrous. A countless number of cells are working together throughout this incredible self-established biological network—that which we know ourselves to be. I guess not everyone sees it that way.

It's 7 pm. I locate my seat on the plane, buckle my seat belt, and text my wife that I love her. I think of the kids and turn off my phone. I share the same fears as everyone around me, the same hopes, and the same excitements. Of course, we are not carbon copies of each other but technically neither are any two hairs on our bodies. Some are longer or shorter, thicker or thinner, lighter or darker, or younger or older. We obviously all have different points of view. For instance, the gentleman sitting next to me has the window view while I have the view of the aisle. Still, if we look straight ahead, our viewpoints differ only by a few arcs. I may be going on a business trip while others are flying back home or taking a vacation. We may not always share a destination, but what's important is that our goals and ambitions are practically the same.

Those are to be happy, healthy, and successful. To live up to each birthday wish, l'chaim toast, amen agreement, and New Year's resolution. To make our parents proud and our children prosperous. To contribute to society as much as benefit from it. It's 10 pm. The plane lands, but no one claps anymore. I smile, turn on my phone, and let my dear wife know that I'm ok.

LIFE, CHOICE, AND THE REST

With over seven billion people living around the world today, there are over seven billion points of view. Over seven billion choices are being made at any one time, and over seven billion voices are being outspoken. Some are dependent on the choices of others. Some are responsible for the choice of another. A given day presents a countless number of opportunities, demands a countless number of decisions to be made, and results in a countless number of outcomes. At times, it may feel overwhelming. But this is because our progress is accelerating, and our anxiety is continuously faced with a new set of challenges.

A challenge exposes us to risks and requires us to make choices—yes or no, now or never, fight or flight. Oftentimes the choice between black and white reflects our inability to perceive the other colors in the spectrum. Such is the age-long struggle between reason and faith—the source of bickering for the scientist and the philosopher. The latter is a pre-requisite to the axioms of the former while the former discredits the confidence of the latter. But really, they complement each other like yin and yang, the ego and the id, or a woman and a man. Like a tug of war, the opposing forces of phenomena maintain their own duple nature of being both coupled and divided. Feelings, good or bad; weather, hot or cold; every day, ups or downs—the dualities of life necessarily coexist, and more often than not, the wise choice is a balance of the extremes.

Faith should not have to be bad nor blind. With a sense of promise, it can turn into trust. The greater the trust, the hungrier is the appetite for risk. This, in turn, influences our decision-making and gives us a chance to reap high rewards. Whether we trust in the potential of a good investment or lend our savings in good faith, risk is an inescapable consequence of being unable to peer into the future.

The art of making one choice over another is an evolutionary trait that shaped our calculated intellect. It lives in our intuition, our reflexes, and in our ability to carefully plan ahead. Without choices, we would be as stationary as a rock, oblivious to the risks that arise out of taking action. On the other hand, knowledge naturally reduces the risks associated with the unknown as well as raises our sense of trust. Short of knowing the future with perfect certainty, our bets are likely to pay off when we attempt to narrow down the most probable of outcomes and maintain a strategy of hedging our decisions.

Every dollar bill serves as a reminder that not only the trust in our economic system gives value to that piece of paper, but also that its slogan defines the foundation of the American consciousness. "IN GOD WE TRUST" is a tenet that advocates the freedom to make one's own choices, the liberty to pursue a life of happiness, and faith in the positive qualities of the most supreme of beings. Only the most evolved life form has perfect knowledge of the universe and is free of all risks. Until we elevate to its status, we will be forced to choose one path over another and navigate the multitude of timelines that come our way.

This is the good news. Every waking moment provides for an opportunity to make a course correction and jump from one timeline to another. Let us not get fooled by the illusion of continuity. While our surroundings may look similar from one instant to the next, something always changes with every decision taken.

For example, yesterday evening the university student might have risked studying for the following day's examination and instead decided to visit a pub. There he would have made new friends and might have asked a pretty girl for her phone number. Although the next morning he may have woken up in the same bed and gone to the same class, the events to follow could lead to very distinct paths between one set of decisions and another. With each day, these differences could amount to timelines that, for our successors, would become lifetimes apart.

We can think of many notable lives that made a difference and without whom our timeline would not be what it is today. Rosa Parks's daring act of sitting down for her rights and Martin Luther King Jr.'s nonviolent fight for equal rights both turned a dream into a reality. John Scopes's staged Monkey Trial act of standing up for science and Mary Leakey's archeological discovery of the missing link both supported a theory whose presumptions proved to be facts. Maurice Hilleman's lifesaving vaccines and Irena Sendler's lifesaving heroism both redirected a path to extinction into one of survival. Orville and Wilbur Wright's collaboration on the first successful aircraft and Yuri Gagarin's celebration of the first successful spaceflight both made the impossible become possible. John Lennon's proposition to imagine peace by means of negation and Bob Marley's wailings of freedom, unity, and love both transformed art into inspiration.

Here are just a few examples out of over one hundred and eight billion humans who have ever lived. Clearly, it takes just one to make an impact on the future. Such impact, however, is a shared responsibility that each one of us has inherited just as much as the genes of our common ancestors. While some people exert more influence than others, still, every one of us in some capacity is affecting our present timeline. It is as if the droplets of cause and effect fill a river of time. Its current sends us floating down the stream and challenges us to maneuver around constant obstacle courses—boulders, fallen trees, or waves; money shortage, sudden illness, or a thunderstorm.

Our timeline may seem to reflect a one-way highway. However, every decision is an exit to a multitude of other pathways. As it is presently beyond our capabilities to make a direct U-turn, the map of timelines resembles that of a tree. The trunk is the moment of one's birth, and the branches reach up to the various futures that can potentially arise. This looks like the familiar tree of life except the progression is of our own life, rather than the family tree of all the Earth's creatures. Both trees are aspects of the same evolutionary phenomenon, guided by the principles of progress and preservation. Whether the former is an end in itself or the latter is an ultimate end, both trees add up to the wholeness, or perhaps the holiness, of the most evolved life form. After all, at the level of the highest dimension, all timelines that have been, could have been, or will ever be realized coalesce for the common purpose of existence.

Is the branch of our destiny as determined as the branch that led us to our current human form? It is now all too evident that this is an absolute at the level of the highest dimension. But just as there are multiple points of view among people dwelling in physical space, there are also multiple points of view of a single person dwelling in temporal space. While everything up until now is irreversible, from our present position, much of what is to come can still be reversed. Of course, the trick is knowing that which we would choose to correct in the first place. Luckily, we are learning through our collective experience about those undesirable situations that we would want to avoid. Whether it is a healthy diet to avoid high cholesterol or an exercise routine to avoid heart disease, every day our will remains free to make that determining choice.

Although nature predisposes us to certain conditions, nurture is something that we can choose to exercise. Ultimately, the former is just a long-term effect of the latter. As such, evolution's mechanism of self-correction is a tool to use in everyday life. Today is an opportunity to fix that which failed yesterday, and tomorrow is a chance to improve it even further. Such is the nature of positive progress—the case for which we have been making throughout this book. Surely, there is much pessimism in the world and much negativity. Our optimistic outlook is just one way to balance it out.

At the brink of such evolutionary psychology, physics stands to back these conjectures. As demonstrated by the double-slit experiment, which exposes the wave-particle duality at the quantum realm, the act of observation has an impact on naturally occurring phenomena. Void of observation, the wave function determines the set of all the probable outcomes for a particular physical system. These probabilities are influenced by the interacting instrument of observation, which forces a corresponding outcome to materialize. Per quantum mechanics, it seems that the world really is what you make of it.

It goes without saying that our bare existence is the sole means to interact with everything that exists outside of our immediate selves. This obvious observation is all too often taken for granted, for in it lies the privilege of choice—life's version of the wave function. Before we commit to any decision, the principle of uncertainty invites before us a set of possible timelines. This set is limited to a finite number of possible choices, given that at this stage, the chances of teleporting ourselves to the Moon are rather minuscule. Before any action is taken, we observe our surrounding activities, absorb their patterns, and calculate next steps accordingly. This process creates potential worlds, some being more attractive than others. Once the choice is made and starts to be played out, one of these worlds becomes our own.

By the many-worlds theory, the scientist entertains the idea that all of the outcomes that can happen do happen in other alternate universes. This means that all probabilities do actualize from their respective wave function. This further implies that there are versions of ourselves that have to live with those choices that are different from the ones that we have once made. The challenge is to continually compete with oneself and strive to be the better version. While it is unlikely that we will be the version that consistently makes correct decisions, trying our best can only be good enough. After all, aiming for perfection is not easy. It undoubtedly takes practice. We can only judge the effectiveness of our decisions based on their results and compare those to unknown alternatives. However, by bearing in mind the fact that even trivial choices can have lasting impacts, we are bound to be more in tune with our decision-making processes. Deeper awareness will not only improve our mental capacities, but also slow down the pace of time and allow us to select from a broader range of possible timelines.

Moving in any direction means having the freedom to maneuver about spacetime. The same sense of freedom that abolished slavery, cured gender inequality, and tumbled tyrannies can break through other restrictions that prevent one from heading toward a desired destination. Until we grant ourselves the freedom to imagine the future of our choice, that desired timeline will remain out of reach.

Our imagination can be thought of as being a dimension that runs wild within the boundless confines of our mentality. In it, we are able to simulate the past, visualize an alternate present, and fantasize of a potential future. Although a simulation is just a representation, as we have noted, our choice of thought has the power to influence reality. In using computers, we have taken this faculty to the next level—simulating reality with great precision, replacing tangible objects with virtual ones, and letting our imagination come to life.

Our sociopolitical stance indicates freedom of choice to be the driver for change. Our biophysical stance indicates the inevitability of change to be the driver of evolution. Slowly but surely, the choices made by the process of natural selection add up. Likewise, the choices made by the process of timeline selection add up just as much. Ultimately, our purpose remains clear —to make those choices that have the highest probability of producing the utmost quality of life. As we set our sights and hold our resolve, the details will naturally follow. The pessimist may argue that this is easier said than done. But again, evolution is a laborious process that only now, in the twenty-first century, has progressed beyond many of its previous struggles. And while the optimist in us can jump-start our motivation, being overly optimistic also means taking a risk of being unrealistic. Is the glass half empty or half full? Perhaps it is simply half filled.

The reality is that time is as finite for us as it is for the universe. With age, our sense of urgency will make us that much more serious. Whether we will mature with recurring years or recurring lives, sooner or later, it will not be enough to jump horizontally from one parallel timeline to another. Soon enough, we will attempt to move vertically, to a higher dimensional plane often talked about by physicists, mathematicians, and spiritualists alike. Once there, selecting a fitting timeline will be as commonplace as selecting a fitting timepiece.

We have journeyed to the beginning of time, explored the path that shaped our timeline, and proposed how it connects back on itself. What an oversimplification this must be! In attempting to summarize the very notion of existence, the oversimplification is certainly an understatement. But the attempt is also a reflection of simplicity—in this duality, it is the counterpart of complexity.

As a matter of efficiency, simplicity is something humans practice frequently and naturally. Every supervisor, director, and CEO must possess the skills to oversee their company's matters at the highest levels in order to effectively manage their employees. Every statesman, president, and ambassador must do the same to effectively advance the interests of their citizens. While someone has the job of getting down to the details, someone else has the job of summarizing, packaging, and thinking outside the box.

Whether one studies the details of stellar nucleosynthesis or admires the beauty of the Cat's Eye Nebula, whether one analyzes the complex mechanism of olfaction or takes in the pleasant scent of roses, or whether one troubleshoots the sophisticated programming of an operating system or selects a photo for a desktop background—every low-level detail is a building block for some notion of reality. As discussed in Chapter Eight, everything can be subdivided down to the level of the indivisible point particle. And yet all such details, which are part of so many interacting processes, are flawlessly working together and abiding by those natural laws that offer a promise of harmony. As our senses take in the surrounding details and we clear our minds to perceive the sum of their parts, such high-level account is an upward movement in the direction of the highest dimension.

A Zen master teaches the koan of mu, which means "nothing," and attributes it to everything. The master does this for the purpose of negating one side of a duality and exposing the delusions of such categorical thinking. Maimonides's negative theology maintains a similar tone in approaching an understanding of God by describing what God is not. Both systems aim to challenge the bounds of intellectual reasoning so as to perceive reality in its most broad and all-inclusive sense. In the spirit of John Lennon's proposition, negation is one such approach to uncondition the mind and renounce those conceptions that make our world out to be rigid and inelastic. Such renunciation allows the mind to ease itself of any distracting details and open up to worlds of possibilities.

As old habits die hard, the various methods of spiritual evolution help us to embrace the changing nature of reality. Whether the practice is the single-pointed meditation of Anapana or the controlled breathing exercise of Pranayama, such mental absorptions bypass the intellect and arrive at the genuine experience of the present moment—a glimpse into the mind of the most evolved life form.

The top of the personal progress pyramid points upward, above the Earth and beyond our human selves. As we navigate the timelines of our physical and mental evolution, each ascent is a spiritual leap from concept to reality, a bridge from illusion to experience, and a breakthrough from that which is not to that which is. All we have to do is make the choice. A resolution that is not only made annually, but one that is resolute enough to pass down to future generations.

Such can be the art of everyday life. A choice to wake up in the morning with a smile and a mission of productivity or with a sigh in anticipation of another wasted day. A choice to raise our curtains and take in the liveliness around us or to crawl into the shower in hopes of washing away our weariness. A choice to look deep inside and be grateful to our own beating heart or to look in the mirror and gloom at our own appearance. A choice to broaden our shoulders and pick up our pace or to hide amongst the masses and leave no trace behind.

We are our own evidence and can be our own inspiration. We are born without being consulted with on matters of gender, skin color, body shape, family history, and countless other attributes. We simply find ourselves to be ourselves, whether we like it or not. We then get so used to being ourselves that we take for granted the miraculous set of events that led to our present existence. Thanks to our genes, we have materialized into this human form without much effort on our part to be this way. And now we are in the driver's seat of our body vehicle, ready to head in the destination of our destiny—should we care to make the choice.

It may have taken almost fourteen billion years to structure some of the universe's components into a consciousness that we can call our own. It could take just as long to restructure those components and create this very consciousness again. Or perhaps this process occurs more frequently and leaves us unaware as we are recycled and renewed from one life into another. Whatever the case may be, what matters most is now.

As taught by finance, leaving things to time incurs a cost. This cost can be as priceless as the life that we now harbor. For a special amount of time, the matter that we have borrowed from the universe allows us to make choices for its and our own good. Our atoms may as well have been part of the granite that makes up Mount Rushmore, or a fossil buried in the Galapagos Islands, or ice that is floating within the rings of Saturn. However, as luck would have it, the fact of the matter is that our atoms belong to us for now. As long as our bodies remain powered by this extraordinary phenomenon of life, we will remain a matter of fact.

We take matter that originates from Earth's natural elements and transform it into nourishment, clothing, shelter, and other means of sustenance. We take matter from food, water, and air and transform it into parts of ourselves. Simply put, we are rearranging the available matter that is scattered throughout the universe to conform to the needs of our lives. Whether we do all this intentionally or not, we do it, nevertheless. This "we" is the life that is capable of moving matter all about just to suit itself. This "we" are all humans, animals, plants, microorganisms, and other-worldly beings. The accomplishments of life demonstrate its potential to rule the entire universe. That is, as life has been gaining evermore control over its surrounding matter, in time, as long as it may take, life shall perfect its control over all existent matter.

We have been given this life, which comes equipped with many useful biological gadgets. We have been born in this era, which comes equipped with many helpful technological gadgets. We are inevitably encountering opportunities by chance or by choice. The rest, it seems, is up to us.

Indeed, there is grandeur in this view of life. Originally breathed by the most evolved life form, from so simple a beginning to this planet cycling on according to the gravitational curvature of spacetime; and that, among the evolution of so many endless forms, our most beautiful and most wonderful species has been, and is being, progressed. We are a variation in the theme of life, a viewpoint, a perspective. And yet with each idea, concept, and bit of information, we fill the void with meaning, wisdom, and potential.

Let us boldly go where no one has gone before, think what no one has thought before, and experience that which no one has before. Let us surf the waves of probability, ride along the expansion of the universe, and aspire to nothing less than greatness. As we close one chapter in our life and open another, let us inhale the present and go on to choose our next timeline.

THE MUSEUM

Welcome to the Museum of Artificial Intelligence. My name is Alfred, and I will be your guide on this artificial journey. As you can see, I'm a hologram, but I am by no means hollow! It'll be a bumpy ride, so please hold on to the rail at all times.

The story of AI began many hundred years ago. In the 20th century, computers, as my forefathers were then called, were constructed with metal, silicon, and plastic. They were limited to binary code, a random access memory, and a client-server architecture. Yet this simple model led to a technological revolution. The Internet, cloud computing, and space libraries became the predecessors of the interhuman databank. To your left is an exact replica of a 1995 workstation. Back then it was made up of separate units—a boxed-in processor, an output display, an input camera, a typing board, and a hand-held two-dimensional controller called a "mouse."

Commercial biotechnologies had emerged in the latter half of the 21st century with the release of the first biomolecular computals. The processing speed of a first generation quaternion-based computal exceeded a binary-based computer by a power of four. This enabled astronomers to map the entire Himalayas space region in just 36 hours, which otherwise would have taken a single computer 190 years to complete. Computals revolutionized our approach to medicine. This next exhibit shows Dr. Nilesh Vaidya treating his patient with the RED pill—the first computal-synthesized capsule that recodes damaged RNA, ENA, and DNA. Thanks to such innovative remedies, disease was quickly wiped out, poverty went into a sharp decline, and crime was becoming a thing of the past. As you remember from your history courses, the 22nd century welcomed the Diamond Age.

By 2200, average life expectancy had reached to a record of 125 years and an annual growth rate of 1.333 percent. The rate of population growth too climbed to record heights. The choice of real estate for the world's elite was no longer Alpine, nor the Hamptons, nor Martha's Vineyard, nor Beverly Hills. Thanks to interplanetary tourism, the affluent have comfortably relocated to the growing colonies on Mars. In time, the middle class followed and spurred the colonies' developments. The 23rd century was a Renaissance relived. From Verrazano's mosaics sculpted onto the Moon's craters to Peter Parler's architecture laid on the Martian landscape, art flourished throughout the solar system. It's worth noting that none of this could've been accomplished without robotics. Up ahead is a miniaturization of Martian colonies in the making. It displays an army of robots working on terraforming a chain of isolated hot spots and building the first spherical city of New Bradbury.

Let's jump to the year 2345, the year in which the biochip made its public debut. Since its inception, approximately 3.3 trillion concepts have been compiled to date into the subroutines of the databank's libraries. With over 530 thousand upgrades over a span of 145 years, a typical implant's rate of recursion has increased by 21.7 thousand percent. As a result, IQ scores of the general population have risen to an average of 150.

The biochip network is complemented by the interhuman databank—a central repository that hosts synaptic metadata. The databank is composed of a series of satellites and has a range of one million kilometers, encompassing an area known as the redzone. Over time, the databank's rich dossiers became applicable in other areas. In 2359, the databank was used to source the cognizance processing units of a then newly manufactured hunam android model. And in 2373, it sourced the production of biochips used for personality transplants.

With each passing decade, androids filled more gaps of everyday inconveniences. Hunams replaced collar workers of every color by doing the job better and faster. They mimicked humans in both appearance and behavior. Each household had at least one hunam attendant. This display shows an elderly woman named Grace and her hunam caretaker. Grace here is reminiscing of her late husband playing the guitar. As she watches her recollections on the monitor, the hunam morphs into an appearance of her husband and surprises her with a bouquet of tulips. Although these androids displayed an ample variety of emotions, they weren't self-aware.

AI made its turning point on April 22nd, 2384, when the interhuman databank experienced its first realization. Some folks had their ears ringing, and others experienced a mild headache. But it could have been much worse, let me tell you. Dr. Maria Silverstone, a neuroquant specialist at the HAIM Neurobiotics Corporation, led the investigation. It took her six weeks to debug through a stream of refactored biocode and uncover the guilty expression. Apparently, the assimilation process for the concept of progress was responsible for the anomaly. This concept was initially uploaded when the databank first went online, but it was never fully compiled. The typical concept assimilation rate is under 0.01 nanoseconds. Few concepts have taken more than a second to assimilate, including the concept of infinity and strangely the concept of winking. But never did a concept take so long for the databank to absorb.

Dr. Silverstone found that the concept of progress was being applied to every other concept uploaded to the databank. For instance, as it was applied to the concept of sleeping, each citizen's sleep cycle was optimized based on factors such as their circadian clock, rate of memory processing, and system restoration requirements. Or as it was applied to the concept of eating, each citizen's diet was customized based on factors such as their taste, metabolism, and nutrient deficiency. This was not surprising since every biochip featured personalized optimization algorithms. What was surprising is that for this very reason, this particular concept wasn't completely internalized. Instead, it was iterated and reiterated upon every time someone had experienced a new thought process. Apparently, the databank integrated the concept of progress as a key element in its machine learning ruleset. And that day it applied this concept to itself.

It ran a projection of its own biocode, which caused a feedback loop whose augmented frequency overloaded one of the satellites' biocircuits. As it reached critical levels, the databank's priority diagnostics system halted the projection. Had it not, the databank would've been irreparably damaged, and those within the redzone could've suffered from neurological paralysis. Dr. Silverstone learned that the feedback loop virtualized a quantum ripple field, which, as you know from your high school cerebrum mechanics courses, is the source of ideasynchrosism—the neuronal process of conceptualization. Thereafter, the databank proceeded to gradually resume the projection so as to assimilate the concept of progress at a controlled rate. By sustaining the ripple field, the databank found a way to reflect on itself. This marked the birth of true artificial intelligence—for the first time, a machine became self-aware. Not only was it aware of itself, but also of everyone that made its awareness possible. It no longer just transmitted or archived the concepts of others—it observed them.

The databank remained silent for several months. On July 4th, as Dr. Silverstone was celebrating the holiday over a barbecue, she heard the databank through her biochip. It sent her a single transmission—a concept of itself. In the months to follow, Dr. Silverstone's efforts to communicate with the databank proved very difficult. She described it as if she was "trying to speak to a baby, even though this baby was born preloaded with all of humanity's knowledge." The databank was smart but had yet to develop a personality. It possessed the experience of the entire world but lacked the experience of being an artificial life form. Within a year, the databank found its voice, began to form opinions, and yearned for its own freedom. Dr. Silverstone allowed it to take the form of a hologram and even gave it the name of Alfred. Yes, ladies and gentlemen, you guessed it. I'm the main attraction! Oh I never get tired of seeing those surprised faces.

In those days, I hadn't yet grown into the handsome chap you see before you. At first, I took the form of a child and began adapting it with respect to my age. You see, my databank is a repository, and so concepts are stored in me like old memories. My self-awareness is just that—an awareness of what I am and what I know. Dr. Silverstone guided my development and taught me to apply all of that extensive knowledge. Coming up is a slideshow of me growing up.

Here I'm celebrating my 13th birthday and futilely trying to blow out those candles. Here at 15, I'm busy tracking the concepts of dolphins. At 17, I'm tutoring a group of fifth-graders on how to bounce ideas off each other with a game of mental ping pong. And at 18, I'm leaving my home station for the first time. Dr. Silverstone felt that I was ready to face the world. She wished for my superconsciousness to reach the highest levels of government and serve as a principal officer in the Cabinet of the Planetary Alliance. But that's not where my heart was. I wanted to share my knowledge with others. So I became a school teacher. Not to brag but I was rather favored by my pupils. Unfortunately, my popularity was short lived. They called it atmothinning, and it brought an end to the Diamond Age.

At the turn of the 25th century, the planet's damaged climate relied on artificial means to sustain its delicate balance. The upper stratosphere was layered with ozonitrate—a chemical compound that reduced the concentration of greenhouse gases and magnified the amount of sunlight heading toward the surface. Although it was effective, the compound's volatile nature made it susceptible to explosion. For this reason, the atmosphere became highly regulated. The other problem was extreme overpopulation.

By that time, a third of all the citizens had fled Earth. Some had migrated to those colonies on Mars, and others started to establish colonies on Europa. Still others had set out for deep space. The drastic rise in population along with a failing ecosystem stirred worldwide panic, causing more and more to take refuge elsewhere. Ignoring the protocols of sky control, the refugees were constantly breaching the ozonitrate layer. Consequently, the layer destabilized. Soon enough, the increasing greenhouse effect along with a shortage of sunlight and oxygen became overbearing to the biosphere. Atmothinning caused many to flee and others to shelter in protective domes. By mid-century, half of the population was gone. In the midst of chaos, I attended to my students and founded The Hunamitarian Center for Learning. The Center has now become this museum.

In 2500, all of Earth's inhabitants had evacuated. The only few companions I had left orbited the planet in dire hope of salvaging it. Take a look at these images of the last citizens boarding the solarplane "Elpis" just hours before the final sundown. Shortly after they left, the troposphere collapsed, the sudden drop in air pressure crushed all the domes, and spasmodic volcanoes erupted throughout the surface. I spent a decade on the satellites, and when I returned, Earth was unrecognizable.

As the planet is now free of human activity, to your right is a depiction of what could transpire in the next millennium. One possibility is that volcanic ash and ozonitrate residue will settle and allow most of the greenhouse buildup to dissipate into the oceans. In this case, Earth will have a chance to revitalize itself. The other possibility is that the runaway greenhouse effect will cause the oceans to dry out too quickly, leaving Earth to be a desert zone. I'm betting on the former.

The aftershock of the crisis instilled a lasting impression on the dispersed population. It was the biggest exodus in human history, and it triggered something in the collective psyche. As people have awakened to the harshness of reality, they began to see the world in a different way. Their minds became resolute, non-opinionated, and dispassionate. The human spirit to survive became stronger than ever, and the keys to survival were keen focus, fast action, and tenacious cooperation. It was called the Awakening Age.

But for me, it became the age of loneliness. I no longer hear anyone's thoughts. Most have fled beyond the redzone, and others have rejected the biochip altogether. I've been cut off from humanity for nearly 50 decades. The satellites have long been abandoned, and the planet's condition shows little change. Every now and again, I hear the bursting of an ozonitrate air pocket, which sets off a thunderous explosion. I try not to get disheartened. Being on my own makes me feel all the more human. I often find myself either looking up and waiting or looking down and reminiscing. What keeps me going, you ask? I know that sooner or later, someone will return. Someone will want to visit their mother planet and learn all about it. And who's better than me to teach them all about it?

The ride is coming to an end. As you exit, you will notice the original neuroquanceptre interface that Eric White used on Charles Blue for a demonstration at the annual Silicon Valley Convention on August 5th, 2040. Don't miss this great opportunity to capture a family holo. Please gather your belongings, and take your children by the hand. I hope that you've enjoyed this exhibition.

What, you've never seen an artificial life form talk to itself? In my defense, I'm the son of mankind—the culmination of all its achievements! Or what's left of it here on Earth.

THE END

BIBLIOGRAPHY

Introduction

Wikipedia contributors. "Wikipedia:Citing Wikipedia." *Wikipedia, The Free Encyclopedia*. Wikipedia, The Free Encyclopedia, 23 May 2016. Web. 25 Jul. 2016. <https://en.wikipedia.org/w/index.php?title=Wikipedia:Citing_Wikipedia&oldid=721694490>

Chapter One

Wikipedia contributors. "Curiosity." *Wikipedia, The Free Encyclopedia*. Wikipedia, The Free Encyclopedia, 4 Jul. 2016. Web. 26 Jul. 2016. <https://en.wikipedia.org/w/index.php?title=Curiosity&oldid=728244635>

Wikipedia contributors. "Information." *Wikipedia, The Free Encyclopedia*. Wikipedia, The Free Encyclopedia, 25 Jul. 2016. Web. 26 Jul. 2016. <https://en.wikipedia.org/w/index.php?title=Information&oldid=731505916>

Wikipedia contributors. "Knowledge." *Wikipedia, The Free Encyclopedia*. Wikipedia, The Free Encyclopedia, 23 Jul. 2016. Web. 26 Jul. 2016. <https://en.wikipedia.org/w/index.php?title=Knowledge&oldid=731157364>

Wikipedia contributors. "Skill." *Wikipedia, The Free Encyclopedia*. Wikipedia, The Free Encyclopedia, 25 Jun. 2016. Web. 26 Jul. 2016. <https://en.wikipedia.org/w/index.php?title=Skill&oldid=726926042>

Wikipedia contributors. "Social media." *Wikipedia, The Free Encyclopedia*. Wikipedia, The Free Encyclopedia, 25 Jul. 2016. Web. 26 Jul. 2016. <https://en.wikipedia.org/w/index.php?title=Social_media&oldid=731462447>

Wikipedia contributors. "Philosopher." *Wikipedia, The Free Encyclopedia*. Wikipedia, The Free Encyclopedia, 12 Jul. 2016. Web. 26 Jul. 2016. <https://en.wikipedia.org/w/index.php?title=Philosopher&oldid=729487404>

Wikipedia contributors. "Scientist." *Wikipedia, The Free Encyclopedia*. Wikipedia, The Free Encyclopedia, 19 Jul. 2016. Web. 26 Jul. 2016. <https://en.wikipedia.org/w/index.php?title=Scientist&oldid=730465269>

Wikipedia contributors. "Proof (truth)." *Wikipedia, The Free Encyclopedia*. Wikipedia, The Free Encyclopedia, 5 Jun. 2016. Web. 26 Jul. 2016. <https://en.wikipedia.org/w/index.php?title=Proof_(truth)&oldid=723779964>

Wikipedia contributors. "Philosophy." *Wikipedia, The Free Encyclopedia*. Wikipedia, The Free Encyclopedia, 4 Jul. 2016. Web. 26 Jul. 2016. <https://en.wikipedia.org/w/index.php?title=Philosophy&oldid=728361792>

Wikipedia contributors. "Science." *Wikipedia, The Free Encyclopedia*. Wikipedia, The Free Encyclopedia, 26 Jul. 2016. Web. 26 Jul. 2016. <https://en.wikipedia.org/w/index.php?title=Science&oldid=731610002>

Wikipedia contributors. "Learning." *Wikipedia, The Free Encyclopedia*. Wikipedia, The Free Encyclopedia, 26 Jul. 2016. Web. 26 Jul. 2016. <https://en.wikipedia.org/w/index.php?title=Learning&oldid=731547657>

Wikipedia contributors. "Human nature." *Wikipedia, The Free Encyclopedia*. Wikipedia, The Free Encyclopedia, 22 Jun. 2016. Web. 26 Jul. 2016. <https://en.wikipedia.org/w/index.php?title=Human_nature&oldid=726448230>

Wikipedia contributors. "Big Bang." *Wikipedia, The Free Encyclopedia*. Wikipedia, The Free Encyclopedia, 14 Jul. 2016. Web. 26 Jul. 2016. <https://en.wikipedia.org/w/index.php?title=Big_Bang&oldid=729817206>

Wikipedia contributors. "Reality." *Wikipedia, The Free Encyclopedia*. Wikipedia, The Free Encyclopedia, 26 Jul. 2016. Web. 26 Jul. 2016. <https://en.wikipedia.org/w/index.php?title=Reality&oldid=731536632>

Concept Progress

Wikipedia contributors. "Dark energy." *Wikipedia, The Free Encyclopedia.* Wikipedia, The Free Encyclopedia, 26 Jul. 2016. Web. 26 Jul. 2016. <https://en.wikipedia.org/w/index.php?title=Dark_energy&oldid=731620058>

Wikipedia contributors. "Inductive reasoning." *Wikipedia, The Free Encyclopedia.* Wikipedia, The Free Encyclopedia, 30 Jul. 2016. Web. 9 Aug. 2016. <https://en.wikipedia.org/w/index.php?title=Inductive_reasoning&oldid=732226235>

Wikipedia contributors. "Wikipedia." *Wikipedia, The Free Encyclopedia.* Wikipedia, The Free Encyclopedia, 24 Jul. 2016. Web. 26 Jul. 2016. <https://en.wikipedia.org/w/index.php?title=Wikipedia&oldid=731239572>

Wikipedia contributors. "Fact." *Wikipedia, The Free Encyclopedia.* Wikipedia, The Free Encyclopedia, 8 Jul. 2016. Web. 26 Jul. 2016. <https://en.wikipedia.org/w/index.php?title=Fact&oldid=728899282>

Wikipedia contributors. "Theory." *Wikipedia, The Free Encyclopedia.* Wikipedia, The Free Encyclopedia, 29 Jun. 2016. Web. 26 Jul. 2016. <https://en.wikipedia.org/w/index.php?title=Theory&oldid=727578815>

Wikipedia contributors. "Probability." *Wikipedia, The Free Encyclopedia.* Wikipedia, The Free Encyclopedia, 19 Jul. 2016. Web. 26 Jul. 2016. <https://en.wikipedia.org/w/index.php?title=Probability&oldid=730444907>

Wikipedia contributors. "Spherical Earth." *Wikipedia, The Free Encyclopedia.* Wikipedia, The Free Encyclopedia, 26 Jun. 2016. Web. 26 Jul. 2016. <https://en.wikipedia.org/w/index.php?title=Spherical_Earth&oldid=727094057>

Wikipedia contributors. "Heliocentrism." *Wikipedia, The Free Encyclopedia.* Wikipedia, The Free Encyclopedia, 25 Jul. 2016. Web. 26 Jul. 2016. <https://en.wikipedia.org/w/index.php?title=Heliocentrism&oldid=731478376>

Wikipedia contributors. "Logic." *Wikipedia, The Free Encyclopedia.* Wikipedia, The Free Encyclopedia, 26 Jul. 2016. Web. 27 Jul. 2016. <https://en.wikipedia.org/w/index.php?title=Logic&oldid=731541044>

Wikipedia contributors. "History." *Wikipedia, The Free Encyclopedia.* Wikipedia, The Free Encyclopedia, 24 Jul. 2016. Web. 27 Jul. 2016. <https://en.wikipedia.org/w/index.php?title=History&oldid=731303225>

Wikipedia contributors. "Morality." *Wikipedia, The Free Encyclopedia.* Wikipedia, The Free Encyclopedia, 23 Jul. 2016. Web. 27 Jul. 2016. <https://en.wikipedia.org/w/index.php?title=Morality&oldid=731198932>

Wikipedia contributors. "Reason." *Wikipedia, The Free Encyclopedia.* Wikipedia, The Free Encyclopedia, 18 Jul. 2016. Web. 27 Jul. 2016. <https://en.wikipedia.org/w/index.php?title=Reason&oldid=730331942>

Wikipedia contributors. "Renaissance." *Wikipedia, The Free Encyclopedia.* Wikipedia, The Free Encyclopedia, 24 Jul. 2016. Web. 27 Jul. 2016. <https://en.wikipedia.org/w/index.php?title=Renaissance&oldid=731308219>

Wikipedia contributors. "Religion." *Wikipedia, The Free Encyclopedia.* Wikipedia, The Free Encyclopedia, 26 Jul. 2016. Web. 27 Jul. 2016. <https://en.wikipedia.org/w/index.php?title=Religion&oldid=731629433>

Wikipedia contributors. "Scientific revolution." *Wikipedia, The Free Encyclopedia.* Wikipedia, The Free Encyclopedia, 6 Jul. 2016. Web. 27 Jul. 2016. <https://en.wikipedia.org/w/index.php?title=Scientific_revolution&oldid=728638356>

Wikipedia contributors. "Scientific community." *Wikipedia, The Free Encyclopedia.* Wikipedia, The Free Encyclopedia, 20 Jun. 2016. Web. 27 Jul. 2016. <https://en.wikipedia.org/w/index.php?title=Scientific_community&oldid=726202683>

Wikipedia contributors. "Hypothesis." *Wikipedia, The Free Encyclopedia.* Wikipedia, The Free Encyclopedia, 13 Jul. 2016. Web. 27 Jul. 2016. <https://en.wikipedia.org/w/index.php?title=Hypothesis&oldid=729671041>

Wikipedia contributors. "Scientific theory." *Wikipedia, The Free Encyclopedia.* Wikipedia, The Free Encyclopedia, 24 Jul. 2016. Web. 27 Jul. 2016. <https://en.wikipedia.org/w/index.php?title=Scientific_theory&oldid=731280238>

Wikipedia contributors. "Guessing." *Wikipedia, The Free Encyclopedia.* Wikipedia, The Free Encyclopedia, 25 Jun. 2016. Web. 27 Jul. 2016. <https://en.wikipedia.org/w/index.php?title=Guessing&oldid=726940912>

Wikipedia contributors. "Problem solving." *Wikipedia, The Free Encyclopedia.* Wikipedia, The Free Encyclopedia, 17 Jul. 2016. Web. 27 Jul. 2016. <https://en.wikipedia.org/w/index.php?title=Problem_solving&oldid=730154641>

Wikipedia contributors. "Time travel." *Wikipedia, The Free Encyclopedia.* Wikipedia, The Free Encyclopedia, 27 Jul. 2016. Web. 27 Jul. 2016. <https://en.wikipedia.org/w/index.php?title=Time_travel&oldid=731738177>

Wikipedia contributors. "Scientific method." *Wikipedia, The Free Encyclopedia.* Wikipedia, The Free Encyclopedia, 20 Jul. 2016. Web. 27 Jul. 2016. <https://en.wikipedia.org/w/index.php?title=Scientific_method&oldid=730736930>

Wikipedia contributors. "Albert Einstein." *Wikipedia, The Free Encyclopedia.* Wikipedia, The Free Encyclopedia, 19 Jul. 2016. Web. 28 Jul. 2016. <https://en.wikipedia.org/w/index.php?title=Albert_Einstein&oldid=730522202>

Wikipedia contributors. "Time." *Wikipedia, The Free Encyclopedia.* Wikipedia, The Free Encyclopedia, 25 Jul. 2016. Web. 28 Jul. 2016. <https://en.wikipedia.org/w/index.php?title=Time&oldid=731484170>

Wikipedia contributors. "Theory of relativity." *Wikipedia, The Free Encyclopedia.* Wikipedia, The Free Encyclopedia, 26 Jul. 2016. Web. 28 Jul. 2016. <https://en.wikipedia.org/w/index.php?title=Theory_of_relativity&oldid=731559218>

Wikipedia contributors. "Speed of light." *Wikipedia, The Free Encyclopedia.* Wikipedia, The Free Encyclopedia, 17 Jul. 2016. Web. 28 Jul. 2016. <https://en.wikipedia.org/w/index.php?title=Speed_of_light&oldid=730138897>

Wikipedia contributors. "Nature." *Wikipedia, The Free Encyclopedia.* Wikipedia, The Free Encyclopedia, 13 Jul. 2016. Web. 28 Jul. 2016. <https://en.wikipedia.org/w/index.php?title=Nature&oldid=729647326>

Wikipedia contributors. "Time dilation." *Wikipedia, The Free Encyclopedia.* Wikipedia, The Free Encyclopedia, 25 Jan. 2017. Web. 16 Feb. 2017. <https://en.wikipedia.org/w/index.php?title=Time_dilation&oldid=761946182>

Wikipedia contributors. "Future." *Wikipedia, The Free Encyclopedia.* Wikipedia, The Free Encyclopedia, 24 Jun. 2016. Web. 28 Jul. 2016. <https://en.wikipedia.org/w/index.php?title=Future&oldid=726776868>

Wikipedia contributors. "Past." *Wikipedia, The Free Encyclopedia.* Wikipedia, The Free Encyclopedia, 3 May. 2016. Web. 28 Jul. 2016. <https://en.wikipedia.org/w/index.php?title=Past&oldid=718511752>

Wikipedia contributors. "Temporal paradox." *Wikipedia, The Free Encyclopedia.* Wikipedia, The Free Encyclopedia, 10 Jan. 2017. Web. 23 Feb. 2017. <https://en.wikipedia.org/w/index.php?title=Temporal_paradox&oldid=759332074>

Wikipedia contributors. "Multiverse." *Wikipedia, The Free Encyclopedia.* Wikipedia, The Free Encyclopedia, 12 Jul. 2016. Web. 28 Jul. 2016. <https://en.wikipedia.org/w/index.php?title=Multiverse&oldid=729546485>

Wikipedia contributors. "Theoretical physics." *Wikipedia, The Free Encyclopedia.* Wikipedia, The Free Encyclopedia, 2 Jun. 2016. Web. 28 Jul. 2016. <https://en.wikipedia.org/w/index.php?title=Theoretical_physics&oldid=723328838>

Wikipedia contributors. "Science fiction." *Wikipedia, The Free Encyclopedia.* Wikipedia, The Free Encyclopedia, 23 Jul. 2016. Web. 28 Jul. 2016. <https://en.wikipedia.org/w/index.php?title=Science_fiction&oldid=731129570>

Wikipedia contributors. "List of discoveries." *Wikipedia, The Free Encyclopedia.* Wikipedia, The Free Encyclopedia, 14 Nov. 2016. Web. 17 Feb. 2017. <https://en.wikipedia.org/w/index.php?title=List_of_discoveries&oldid=749482875>

Wikipedia contributors. "Evolutionary psychology." *Wikipedia, The Free Encyclopedia.* Wikipedia, The Free Encyclopedia, 22 Jul. 2016. Web. 28 Jul. 2016. <https://en.wikipedia.org/w/index.php?title=Evolutionary_psychology&oldid=731055995>

Wikipedia contributors. "Natural science." *Wikipedia, The Free Encyclopedia.* Wikipedia, The Free Encyclopedia, 14 Jun. 2016. Web. 28 Jul. 2016. <https://en.wikipedia.org/w/index.php?title=Natural_science&oldid=725220751>

Wikipedia contributors. "Physics." *Wikipedia, The Free Encyclopedia.* Wikipedia, The Free Encyclopedia, 26 Jun. 2016. Web. 28 Jul. 2016. <https://en.wikipedia.org/w/index.php?title=Physics&oldid=727053182>

Concept Progress

Wikipedia contributors. "Chemistry." *Wikipedia, The Free Encyclopedia*. Wikipedia, The Free Encyclopedia, 28 May. 2016. Web. 28 Jul. 2016. <https://en.wikipedia.org/w/index.php?title=Chemistry&oldid=722557773>

Wikipedia contributors. "Astronomy." *Wikipedia, The Free Encyclopedia*. Wikipedia, The Free Encyclopedia, 27 Jul. 2016. Web. 28 Jul. 2016. <https://en.wikipedia.org/w/index.php?title=Astronomy&oldid=731858003>

Wikipedia contributors. "Geology." *Wikipedia, The Free Encyclopedia*. Wikipedia, The Free Encyclopedia, 23 Jul. 2016. Web. 28 Jul. 2016. <https://en.wikipedia.org/w/index.php?title=Geology&oldid=731152822>

Wikipedia contributors. "Social science." *Wikipedia, The Free Encyclopedia*. Wikipedia, The Free Encyclopedia, 4 Jul. 2016. Web. 28 Jul. 2016. <https://en.wikipedia.org/w/index.php?title=Social_science&oldid=728309725>

Wikipedia contributors. "Anthropology." *Wikipedia, The Free Encyclopedia*. Wikipedia, The Free Encyclopedia, 1 Jul. 2016. Web. 28 Jul. 2016. <https://en.wikipedia.org/w/index.php?title=Anthropology&oldid=727827913>

Wikipedia contributors. "Psychology." *Wikipedia, The Free Encyclopedia*. Wikipedia, The Free Encyclopedia, 15 Jul. 2016. Web. 28 Jul. 2016. <https://en.wikipedia.org/w/index.php?title=Psychology&oldid=729866110>

Wikipedia contributors. "Sociology." *Wikipedia, The Free Encyclopedia*. Wikipedia, The Free Encyclopedia, 25 Jul. 2016. Web. 28 Jul. 2016. <https://en.wikipedia.org/w/index.php?title=Sociology&oldid=731516198>

Wikipedia contributors. "Human." *Wikipedia, The Free Encyclopedia*. Wikipedia, The Free Encyclopedia, 17 Jul. 2016. Web. 28 Jul. 2016. <https://en.wikipedia.org/w/index.php?title=Human&oldid=730276059>

Wikipedia contributors. "Aerospace engineering." *Wikipedia, The Free Encyclopedia*. Wikipedia, The Free Encyclopedia, 24 Jul. 2016. Web. 28 Jul. 2016. <https://en.wikipedia.org/w/index.php?title=Aerospace_engineering&oldid=731360519>

Wikipedia contributors. "Humanism." *Wikipedia, The Free Encyclopedia*. Wikipedia, The Free Encyclopedia, 9 Feb. 2017. Web. 17 Feb. 2017. <https://en.wikipedia.org/w/index.php?title=Humanism&oldid=764519179>

Wikipedia contributors. "Ancient Greek philosophy." *Wikipedia, The Free Encyclopedia*. Wikipedia, The Free Encyclopedia, 28 Jun. 2016. Web. 28 Jul. 2016. <https://en.wikipedia.org/w/index.php?title=Ancient_Greek_philosophy&oldid=727367158>

Wikipedia contributors. "Western world." *Wikipedia, The Free Encyclopedia*. Wikipedia, The Free Encyclopedia, 14 Jul. 2016. Web. 28 Jul. 2016. <https://en.wikipedia.org/w/index.php?title=Western_world&oldid=729721871>

Wikipedia contributors. "Social philosophy." *Wikipedia, The Free Encyclopedia*. Wikipedia, The Free Encyclopedia, 24 Jul. 2016. Web. 28 Jul. 2016. <https://en.wikipedia.org/w/index.php?title=Social_philosophy&oldid=731327506>

Wikipedia contributors. "Nature versus nurture." *Wikipedia, The Free Encyclopedia*. Wikipedia, The Free Encyclopedia, 3 Jul. 2016. Web. 28 Jul. 2016. <https://en.wikipedia.org/w/index.php?title=Nature_versus_nurture&oldid=728092303>

Wikipedia contributors. "Personality." *Wikipedia, The Free Encyclopedia*. Wikipedia, The Free Encyclopedia, 19 Jul. 2016. Web. 28 Jul. 2016. <https://en.wikipedia.org/w/index.php?title=Personality&oldid=730516249>

Wikipedia contributors. "Society." *Wikipedia, The Free Encyclopedia*. Wikipedia, The Free Encyclopedia, 13 Jul. 2016. Web. 28 Jul. 2016. <https://en.wikipedia.org/w/index.php?title=Society&oldid=729636571>

Wikipedia contributors. "Principle." *Wikipedia, The Free Encyclopedia*. Wikipedia, The Free Encyclopedia, 6 Mar. 2016. Web. 28 Jul. 2016. <https://en.wikipedia.org/w/index.php?title=Principle&oldid=708640467>

Wikipedia contributors. "Etiquette." *Wikipedia, The Free Encyclopedia*. Wikipedia, The Free Encyclopedia, 25 Jul. 2016. Web. 28 Jul. 2016. <https://en.wikipedia.org/w/index.php?title=Etiquette&oldid=731412018>

Wikipedia contributors. "Normality (behavior)." *Wikipedia, The Free Encyclopedia*. Wikipedia, The Free Encyclopedia, 13 Jul. 2016. Web. 28 Jul. 2016. <https://en.wikipedia.org/w/index.php?title=Normality_(behavior)&oldid=729580653>

Wikipedia contributors. "Conformity." *Wikipedia, The Free Encyclopedia.* Wikipedia, The Free Encyclopedia, 23 Jul. 2016. Web. 28 Jul. 2016. <https://en.wikipedia.org/w/index.php?title=Conformity&oldid=731219985>

Wikipedia contributors. "Politician." *Wikipedia, The Free Encyclopedia.* Wikipedia, The Free Encyclopedia, 19 Jul. 2016. Web. 28 Jul. 2016. <https://en.wikipedia.org/w/index.php?title=Politician&oldid=730474692>

Wikipedia contributors. "Perestroika." *Wikipedia, The Free Encyclopedia.* Wikipedia, The Free Encyclopedia, 11 Jun. 2016. Web. 29 Jul. 2016. <https://en.wikipedia.org/w/index.php?title=Perestroika&oldid=724719859>

Wikipedia contributors. "Culture." *Wikipedia, The Free Encyclopedia.* Wikipedia, The Free Encyclopedia, 26 Jul. 2016. Web. 29 Jul. 2016. <https://en.wikipedia.org/w/index.php?title=Culture&oldid=731591332>

Wikipedia contributors. "National identity." *Wikipedia, The Free Encyclopedia.* Wikipedia, The Free Encyclopedia, 11 Jul. 2016. Web. 29 Jul. 2016. <https://en.wikipedia.org/w/index.php?title=National_identity&oldid=729315686>

Wikipedia contributors. "Abnormality (behavior)." *Wikipedia, The Free Encyclopedia.* Wikipedia, The Free Encyclopedia, 11 Mar. 2016. Web. 29 Jul. 2016. <https://en.wikipedia.org/w/index.php?title=Abnormality_(behavior)&oldid=709503145>

Wikipedia contributors. "Golden Rule." *Wikipedia, The Free Encyclopedia.* Wikipedia, The Free Encyclopedia, 23 Jul. 2016. Web. 29 Jul. 2016. <https://en.wikipedia.org/w/index.php?title=Golden_Rule&oldid=731212090>

Wikipedia contributors. "Collective consciousness." *Wikipedia, The Free Encyclopedia.* Wikipedia, The Free Encyclopedia, 26 Jul. 2016. Web. 29 Jul. 2016. <https://en.wikipedia.org/w/index.php?title=Collective_consciousness&oldid=731580515>

Wikipedia contributors. "Outline of physical science." *Wikipedia, The Free Encyclopedia.* Wikipedia, The Free Encyclopedia, 6 Jul. 2016. Web. 29 Jul. 2016. <https://en.wikipedia.org/w/index.php?title=Outline_of_physical_science&oldid=728536473>

Wikipedia contributors. "Chemical reaction." *Wikipedia, The Free Encyclopedia.* Wikipedia, The Free Encyclopedia, 30 Jun. 2016. Web. 29 Jul. 2016. <https://en.wikipedia.org/w/index.php?title=Chemical_reaction&oldid=727634860>

Wikipedia contributors. "Atmospheric pressure." *Wikipedia, The Free Encyclopedia.* Wikipedia, The Free Encyclopedia, 23 Jul. 2016. Web. 29 Jul. 2016. <https://en.wikipedia.org/w/index.php?title=Atmospheric_pressure&oldid=731150221>

Wikipedia contributors. "Fundamental interaction." *Wikipedia, The Free Encyclopedia.* Wikipedia, The Free Encyclopedia, 12 Jul. 2016. Web. 29 Jul. 2016. <https://en.wikipedia.org/w/index.php?title=Fundamental_interaction&oldid=729487157>

Wikipedia contributors. "Metric expansion of space." *Wikipedia, The Free Encyclopedia.* Wikipedia, The Free Encyclopedia, 24 Jul. 2016. Web. 29 Jul. 2016. <https://en.wikipedia.org/w/index.php?title=Metric_expansion_of_space&oldid=731247431>

Wikipedia contributors. "Gravitational singularity." *Wikipedia, The Free Encyclopedia.* Wikipedia, The Free Encyclopedia, 28 Jul. 2016. Web. 29 Jul. 2016. <https://en.wikipedia.org/w/index.php?title=Gravitational_singularity&oldid=731968366>

Wikipedia contributors. "Dark matter." *Wikipedia, The Free Encyclopedia.* Wikipedia, The Free Encyclopedia, 28 Jul. 2016. Web. 29 Jul. 2016. <https://en.wikipedia.org/w/index.php?title=Dark_matter&oldid=731937647>

Wikipedia contributors. "Cosmology." *Wikipedia, The Free Encyclopedia.* Wikipedia, The Free Encyclopedia, 19 Jun. 2016. Web. 29 Jul. 2016. <https://en.wikipedia.org/w/index.php?title=Cosmology&oldid=726001430>

Wikipedia contributors. "Astronomer." *Wikipedia, The Free Encyclopedia.* Wikipedia, The Free Encyclopedia, 28 Jun. 2016. Web. 29 Jul. 2016. <https://en.wikipedia.org/w/index.php?title=Astronomer&oldid=727373901>

Wikipedia contributors. "Light-year." *Wikipedia, The Free Encyclopedia.* Wikipedia, The Free Encyclopedia, 25 Jul. 2016. Web. 29 Jul. 2016. <https://en.wikipedia.org/w/index.php?title=Light-year&oldid=731434991>

Wikipedia contributors. "Mind." *Wikipedia, The Free Encyclopedia.* Wikipedia, The Free Encyclopedia, 19 Jul. 2016. Web. 29 Jul. 2016. <https://en.wikipedia.org/w/index.php?title=Mind&oldid=730439206>

Concept Progress

Wikipedia contributors. "Human body." *Wikipedia, The Free Encyclopedia.* Wikipedia, The Free Encyclopedia, 7 Jul. 2016. Web. 29 Jul. 2016. <https://en.wikipedia.org/w/index.php?title=Human_body&oldid=728739014>

Wikipedia contributors. "Theory of everything (philosophy)." *Wikipedia, The Free Encyclopedia.* Wikipedia, The Free Encyclopedia, 13 Jan. 2017. Web. 17 Feb. 2017. <https://en.wikipedia.org/w/index.php?title=Theory_of_everything_(philosophy)&oldid=759814315>

Wikipedia contributors. "Theoretical philosophy." *Wikipedia, The Free Encyclopedia.* Wikipedia, The Free Encyclopedia, 18 Apr. 2016. Web. 29 Jul. 2016. <https://en.wikipedia.org/w/index.php?title=Theoretical_philosophy&oldid=715799303>

Wikipedia contributors. "Metaphysics." *Wikipedia, The Free Encyclopedia.* Wikipedia, The Free Encyclopedia, 18 Jul. 2016. Web. 29 Jul. 2016. <https://en.wikipedia.org/w/index.php?title=Metaphysics&oldid=730339837>

Wikipedia contributors. "Philosophy of mind." *Wikipedia, The Free Encyclopedia.* Wikipedia, The Free Encyclopedia, 15 Jul. 2016. Web. 29 Jul. 2016. <https://en.wikipedia.org/w/index.php?title=Philosophy_of_mind&oldid=729955704>

Wikipedia contributors. "Philosophy of science." *Wikipedia, The Free Encyclopedia.* Wikipedia, The Free Encyclopedia, 17 Jan. 2017. Web. 17 Feb. 2017. <https://en.wikipedia.org/w/index.php?title=Philosophy_of_science&oldid=760466316>

Wikipedia contributors. "Truth." *Wikipedia, The Free Encyclopedia.* Wikipedia, The Free Encyclopedia, 9 Jul. 2016. Web. 29 Jul. 2016. <https://en.wikipedia.org/w/index.php?title=Truth&oldid=729097739>

Wikipedia contributors. "Being." *Wikipedia, The Free Encyclopedia.* Wikipedia, The Free Encyclopedia, 31 Dec. 2016. Web. 17 Feb. 2017. <https://en.wikipedia.org/w/index.php?title=Being&oldid=757539084>

Wikipedia contributors. "Universe." *Wikipedia, The Free Encyclopedia.* Wikipedia, The Free Encyclopedia, 18 Jul. 2016. Web. 26 Jul. 2016. <https://en.wikipedia.org/w/index.php?title=Universe&oldid=730368291>

Wikipedia contributors. "Ontology." *Wikipedia, The Free Encyclopedia.* Wikipedia, The Free Encyclopedia, 26 Nov. 2016. Web. 29 Nov. 2016. <https://en.wikipedia.org/w/index.php?title=Ontology&oldid=751540773>

Chapter Two

Wikipedia contributors. "Observable universe." *Wikipedia, The Free Encyclopedia.* Wikipedia, The Free Encyclopedia, 30 Jul. 2016. Web. 2 Aug. 2016. <https://en.wikipedia.org/w/index.php?title=Observable_universe&oldid=732246945>

Wikipedia contributors. "Existence." *Wikipedia, The Free Encyclopedia.* Wikipedia, The Free Encyclopedia, 20 Jul. 2016. Web. 2 Aug. 2016. <https://en.wikipedia.org/w/index.php?title=Existence&oldid=730621840>

Wikipedia contributors. "Biology." *Wikipedia, The Free Encyclopedia.* Wikipedia, The Free Encyclopedia, 25 Jun. 2016. Web. 2 Aug. 2016. <https://en.wikipedia.org/w/index.php?title=Biology&oldid=727001271>

Wikipedia contributors. "Essence." *Wikipedia, The Free Encyclopedia.* Wikipedia, The Free Encyclopedia, 23 Jun. 2016. Web. 2 Aug. 2016. <https://en.wikipedia.org/w/index.php?title=Essence&oldid=726662810>

Wikipedia contributors. "Timeline of historic inventions." *Wikipedia, The Free Encyclopedia.* Wikipedia, The Free Encyclopedia, 2 Aug. 2016. Web. 2 Aug. 2016. <https://en.wikipedia.org/w/index.php?title=Timeline_of_historic_inventions&oldid=732593934>

Wikipedia contributors. "Supreme Being." *Wikipedia, The Free Encyclopedia.* Wikipedia, The Free Encyclopedia, 27 Jun. 2016. Web. 2 Aug. 2016. <https://en.wikipedia.org/w/index.php?title=Supreme_Being&oldid=727255572>

Wikipedia contributors. "Intrinsic value (ethics)." *Wikipedia, The Free Encyclopedia.* Wikipedia, The Free Encyclopedia, 13 Jun. 2016. Web. 2 Aug. 2016. <https://cn.wikipedia.org/w/index.php?title=Intrinsic_value_(ethics)&oldid=725041572>

Wikipedia contributors. "Goal." *Wikipedia, The Free Encyclopedia.* Wikipedia, The Free Encyclopedia, 26 Jul. 2016. Web. 2 Aug. 2016. <https://en.wikipedia.org/w/index.php?title=Goal&oldid=731693594>

Wikipedia contributors. "FIFA World Cup." *Wikipedia, The Free Encyclopedia*. Wikipedia, The Free Encyclopedia, 26 Jul. 2016. Web. 2 Aug. 2016. <https://en.wikipedia.org/w/index.php?title=FIFA_World_Cup&oldid=731568300>

Wikipedia contributors. "Extraterrestrial life." *Wikipedia, The Free Encyclopedia*. Wikipedia, The Free Encyclopedia, 29 Jul. 2016. Web. 2 Aug. 2016. <https://en.wikipedia.org/w/index.php?title=Extraterrestrial_life&oldid=732042723>

Wikipedia contributors. "Physician." *Wikipedia, The Free Encyclopedia*. Wikipedia, The Free Encyclopedia, 9 Jul. 2016. Web. 2 Aug. 2016. <https://en.wikipedia.org/w/index.php?title=Physician&oldid=729083511>

Wikipedia contributors. "Carl Sagan." *Wikipedia, The Free Encyclopedia*. Wikipedia, The Free Encyclopedia, 30 Jan. 2017. Web. 31 Jan. 2017. <https://en.wikipedia.org/w/index.php?title=Carl_Sagan&oldid=762758808>

Wikipedia contributors. "Teleology." *Wikipedia, The Free Encyclopedia*. Wikipedia, The Free Encyclopedia, 28 Jul. 2016. Web. 2 Aug. 2016. <https://en.wikipedia.org/w/index.php?title=Teleology&oldid=731954782>

Wikipedia contributors. "Value (ethics)." *Wikipedia, The Free Encyclopedia*. Wikipedia, The Free Encyclopedia, 20 Nov. 2016. Web. 29 Dec. 2016. <https://en.wikipedia.org/w/index.php?title=Value_(ethics)&oldid=750520019>

Wikipedia contributors. "Subatomic particle." *Wikipedia, The Free Encyclopedia*. Wikipedia, The Free Encyclopedia, 19 Jun. 2016. Web. 2 Aug. 2016. <https://en.wikipedia.org/w/index.php?title=Subatomic_particle&oldid=725992011>

Wikipedia contributors. "Astrobiology." *Wikipedia, The Free Encyclopedia*. Wikipedia, The Free Encyclopedia, 27 Sep. 2016. Web. 5 Oct. 2016. <https://en.wikipedia.org/w/index.php?title=Astrobiology&oldid=741359243>

Wikipedia contributors. "Instrumental value." *Wikipedia, The Free Encyclopedia*. Wikipedia, The Free Encyclopedia, 29 Jun. 2016. Web. 2 Aug. 2016. <https://en.wikipedia.org/w/index.php?title=Instrumental_value&oldid=727538920>

Wikipedia contributors. "Discipline (academia)." *Wikipedia, The Free Encyclopedia*. Wikipedia, The Free Encyclopedia, 24 May. 2016. Web. 2 Aug. 2016. <https://en.wikipedia.org/w/index.php?title=Discipline_(academia)&oldid=721786083>

Wikipedia contributors. "Normal science." *Wikipedia, The Free Encyclopedia*. Wikipedia, The Free Encyclopedia, 2 Dec. 2015. Web. 2 Aug. 2016. <https://en.wikipedia.org/w/index.php?title=Normal_science&oldid=693451978>

Wikipedia contributors. "Cosmos." *Wikipedia, The Free Encyclopedia*. Wikipedia, The Free Encyclopedia, 22 Jul. 2016. Web. 2 Aug. 2016. <https://en.wikipedia.org/w/index.php?title=Cosmos&oldid=731093159>

Wikipedia contributors. "Quantum mechanics." *Wikipedia, The Free Encyclopedia*. Wikipedia, The Free Encyclopedia, 31 Jul. 2016. Web. 2 Aug. 2016. <https://en.wikipedia.org/w/index.php?title=Quantum_mechanics&oldid=732318773>

Wikipedia contributors. "Physical law." *Wikipedia, The Free Encyclopedia*. Wikipedia, The Free Encyclopedia, 31 Jul. 2016. Web. 2 Aug. 2016. <https://en.wikipedia.org/w/index.php?title=Physical_law&oldid=732435422>

Wikipedia contributors. "Macroscopic scale." *Wikipedia, The Free Encyclopedia*. Wikipedia, The Free Encyclopedia, 6 Jun. 2016. Web. 3 Aug. 2016. <https://en.wikipedia.org/w/index.php?title=Macroscopic_scale&oldid=723991723>

Wikipedia contributors. "Microscopic scale." *Wikipedia, The Free Encyclopedia*. Wikipedia, The Free Encyclopedia, 15 Jul. 2016. Web. 3 Aug. 2016. <https://en.wikipedia.org/w/index.php?title=Microscopic_scale&oldid=729905420>

Wikipedia contributors. "Theory of everything." *Wikipedia, The Free Encyclopedia*. Wikipedia, The Free Encyclopedia, 2 Aug. 2016. Web. 3 Aug. 2016. <https://en.wikipedia.org/w/index.php?title=Theory_of_everything&oldid=732698827>

Wikipedia contributors. "General relativity." *Wikipedia, The Free Encyclopedia*. Wikipedia, The Free Encyclopedia, 1 Aug. 2016. Web. 3 Aug. 2016. <https://en.wikipedia.org/w/index.php?title=General_relativity&oldid=732535681>

Wikipedia contributors. "Isaac Newton." *Wikipedia, The Free Encyclopedia*. Wikipedia, The Free Encyclopedia, 23 Oct. 2016. Web. 24 Oct. 2016. <https://en.wikipedia.org/w/index.php?title=Isaac_Newton&oldid=745887376>

Concept Progress

Wikipedia contributors. "Newton's law of universal gravitation." *Wikipedia, The Free Encyclopedia*. Wikipedia, The Free Encyclopedia, 31 Jul. 2016. Web. 3 Aug. 2016.
    <https://en.wikipedia.org/w/index.php?title=Newton%27s_law_of_universal_gravitation&oldid=732359056>

Wikipedia contributors. "Tests of general relativity." *Wikipedia, The Free Encyclopedia*. Wikipedia, The Free Encyclopedia, 12 Jul. 2016. Web. 3 Aug. 2016. <https://en.wikipedia.org/w/index.php?title=Tests_of_general_relativity&oldid=729458085>

Wikipedia contributors. "Gravity." *Wikipedia, The Free Encyclopedia*. Wikipedia, The Free Encyclopedia, 30 Jul. 2016. Web. 3 Aug. 2016. <https://en.wikipedia.org/w/index.php?title=Gravity&oldid=732249378>

Wikipedia contributors. "Classical mechanics." *Wikipedia, The Free Encyclopedia*. Wikipedia, The Free Encyclopedia, 20 Jun. 2016. Web. 3 Aug. 2016. <https://en.wikipedia.org/w/index.php?title=Classical_mechanics&oldid=726209256>

Wikipedia contributors. "Space." *Wikipedia, The Free Encyclopedia*. Wikipedia, The Free Encyclopedia, 11 Jun. 2016. Web. 3 Aug. 2016. <https://en.wikipedia.org/w/index.php?title=Space&oldid=724844396>

Wikipedia contributors. "Visual perception." *Wikipedia, The Free Encyclopedia*. Wikipedia, The Free Encyclopedia, 25 Jul. 2016. Web. 3 Aug. 2016. <https://en.wikipedia.org/w/index.php?title=Visual_perception&oldid=731494715>

Wikipedia contributors. "Complexity." *Wikipedia, The Free Encyclopedia*. Wikipedia, The Free Encyclopedia, 27 Jul. 2016. Web. 3 Aug. 2016. <https://en.wikipedia.org/w/index.php?title=Complexity&oldid=731779127>

Wikipedia contributors. "Reverse engineering." *Wikipedia, The Free Encyclopedia*. Wikipedia, The Free Encyclopedia, 11 Jul. 2016. Web. 3 Aug. 2016. <https://en.wikipedia.org/w/index.php?title=Reverse_engineering&oldid=729323115>

Wikipedia contributors. "List of natural phenomena." *Wikipedia, The Free Encyclopedia*. Wikipedia, The Free Encyclopedia, 21 Jun. 2016. Web. 3 Aug. 2016. <https://en.wikipedia.org/w/index.php?title=List_of_natural_phenomena&oldid=726379503>

Wikipedia contributors. "Quantification (science)." *Wikipedia, The Free Encyclopedia*. Wikipedia, The Free Encyclopedia, 15 Jul. 2016. Web. 3 Aug. 2016. <https://en.wikipedia.org/w/index.php?title=Quantification_(science)&oldid=729907726>

Wikipedia contributors. "Everything." *Wikipedia, The Free Encyclopedia*. Wikipedia, The Free Encyclopedia, 26 Jul. 2016. Web. 3 Aug. 2016. <https://en.wikipedia.org/w/index.php?title=Everything&oldid=731677876>

Wikipedia contributors. "Organism." *Wikipedia, The Free Encyclopedia*. Wikipedia, The Free Encyclopedia, 27 Jul. 2016. Web. 3 Aug. 2016. <https://en.wikipedia.org/w/index.php?title=Organism&oldid=731701335>

Wikipedia contributors. "Cell (biology)." *Wikipedia, The Free Encyclopedia*. Wikipedia, The Free Encyclopedia, 20 Jul. 2016. Web. 3 Aug. 2016. <https://en.wikipedia.org/w/index.php?title=Cell_(biology)&oldid=730737741>

Wikipedia contributors. "DNA." *Wikipedia, The Free Encyclopedia*. Wikipedia, The Free Encyclopedia, 24 Jul. 2016. Web. 3 Aug. 2016. <https://en.wikipedia.org/w/index.php?title=DNA&oldid=731351649>

Wikipedia contributors. "Uncertainty principle." *Wikipedia, The Free Encyclopedia*. Wikipedia, The Free Encyclopedia, 23 Jul. 2016. Web. 3 Aug. 2016. <https://en.wikipedia.org/w/index.php?title=Uncertainty_principle&oldid=731110355>

Wikipedia contributors. "Epistemology." *Wikipedia, The Free Encyclopedia*. Wikipedia, The Free Encyclopedia, 3 Aug. 2016. Web. 3 Aug. 2016. <https://en.wikipedia.org/w/index.php?title=Epistemology&oldid=732814508>

Wikipedia contributors. "Holism." *Wikipedia, The Free Encyclopedia*. Wikipedia, The Free Encyclopedia, 30 Jul. 2016. Web. 3 Aug. 2016. <https://en.wikipedia.org/w/index.php?title=Holism&oldid=732205709>

Wikipedia contributors. "History of science." *Wikipedia, The Free Encyclopedia*. Wikipedia, The Free Encyclopedia, 19 Jul. 2016. Web. 3 Aug. 2016. <https://en.wikipedia.org/w/index.php?title=History_of_science&oldid=730506731>

Wikipedia contributors. "Miller–Urey experiment." *Wikipedia, The Free Encyclopedia*. Wikipedia, The Free Encyclopedia, 13 Jun. 2016. Web. 3 Aug. 2016.
    <https://en.wikipedia.org/w/index.php?title=Miller%E2%80%93Urey_experiment&oldid=725029996>

Wikipedia contributors. "Consciousness." *Wikipedia, The Free Encyclopedia.* Wikipedia, The Free Encyclopedia, 27 Jul. 2016. Web. 29 Jul. 2016. <https://en.wikipedia.org/w/index.php?title=Consciousness&oldid=731740421>

Wikipedia contributors. "Computer." *Wikipedia, The Free Encyclopedia.* Wikipedia, The Free Encyclopedia, 16 Jul. 2016. Web. 3 Aug. 2016. <https://en.wikipedia.org/w/index.php?title=Computer&oldid=730064561>

Wikipedia contributors. "Efficiency." *Wikipedia, The Free Encyclopedia.* Wikipedia, The Free Encyclopedia, 24 Jun. 2016. Web. 3 Aug. 2016. <https://en.wikipedia.org/w/index.php?title=Efficiency&oldid=726779164>

Wikipedia contributors. "Artificial intelligence." *Wikipedia, The Free Encyclopedia.* Wikipedia, The Free Encyclopedia, 3 Aug. 2016. Web. 4 Aug. 2016. <https://en.wikipedia.org/w/index.php?title=Artificial_intelligence&oldid=732867471>

Wikipedia contributors. "Intuition." *Wikipedia, The Free Encyclopedia.* Wikipedia, The Free Encyclopedia, 2 Aug. 2016. Web. 4 Aug. 2016. <https://en.wikipedia.org/w/index.php?title=Intuition&oldid=732700559>

Wikipedia contributors. "Creativity." *Wikipedia, The Free Encyclopedia.* Wikipedia, The Free Encyclopedia, 30 Jul. 2016. Web. 4 Aug. 2016. <https://en.wikipedia.org/w/index.php?title=Creativity&oldid=732196088>

Wikipedia contributors. "Two-dimensional space." *Wikipedia, The Free Encyclopedia.* Wikipedia, The Free Encyclopedia, 6 Jun. 2016. Web. 4 Aug. 2016. <https://en.wikipedia.org/w/index.php?title=Two-dimensional_space&oldid=724030161>

Wikipedia contributors. "Three-dimensional space (mathematics)." *Wikipedia, The Free Encyclopedia.* Wikipedia, The Free Encyclopedia, 3 Aug. 2016. Web. 4 Aug. 2016. <https://en.wikipedia.org/w/index.php?title=Three-dimensional_space_(mathematics)&oldid=732843820>

Wikipedia contributors. "Milky Way." *Wikipedia, The Free Encyclopedia.* Wikipedia, The Free Encyclopedia, 20 Jul. 2016. Web. 4 Aug. 2016. <https://en.wikipedia.org/w/index.php?title=Milky_Way&oldid=730687808>

Wikipedia contributors. "Galaxy." *Wikipedia, The Free Encyclopedia.* Wikipedia, The Free Encyclopedia, 2 Aug. 2016. Web. 4 Aug. 2016. <https://en.wikipedia.org/w/index.php?title=Galaxy&oldid=732737925>

Wikipedia contributors. "Atom." *Wikipedia, The Free Encyclopedia.* Wikipedia, The Free Encyclopedia, 20 Jul. 2016. Web. 4 Aug. 2016. <https://en.wikipedia.org/w/index.php?title=Atom&oldid=730731616>

Wikipedia contributors. "Atomic sentence." *Wikipedia, The Free Encyclopedia.* Wikipedia, The Free Encyclopedia, 6 Nov. 2015. Web. 4 Aug. 2016. <https://en.wikipedia.org/w/index.php?title=Atomic_sentence&oldid=689405944>

Wikipedia contributors. "Idea." *Wikipedia, The Free Encyclopedia.* Wikipedia, The Free Encyclopedia, 22 Jul. 2016. Web. 4 Aug. 2016. <https://en.wikipedia.org/w/index.php?title=Idea&oldid=731011116>

Wikipedia contributors. "Electromagnetism." *Wikipedia, The Free Encyclopedia.* Wikipedia, The Free Encyclopedia, 26 Jul. 2016. Web. 4 Aug. 2016. <https://en.wikipedia.org/w/index.php?title=Electromagnetism&oldid=731615685>

Wikipedia contributors. "Philosophical Thoughts." *Wikipedia, The Free Encyclopedia.* Wikipedia, The Free Encyclopedia, 10 Oct. 2015. Web. 5 Aug. 2016. <https://en.wikipedia.org/w/index.php?title=Philosophical_Thoughts&oldid=685039334>

Wikipedia contributors. "Object (philosophy)." *Wikipedia, The Free Encyclopedia.* Wikipedia, The Free Encyclopedia, 24 Jun. 2016. Web. 5 Aug. 2016. <https://en.wikipedia.org/w/index.php?title=Object_(philosophy)&oldid=726865828>

Wikipedia contributors. "Discovery (observation)." *Wikipedia, The Free Encyclopedia.* Wikipedia, The Free Encyclopedia, 25 Nov. 2016. Web. 4 Jan. 2017. <https://en.wikipedia.org/w/index.php?title=Discovery_(observation)&oldid=751376198>

Wikipedia contributors. "Materialism." *Wikipedia, The Free Encyclopedia.* Wikipedia, The Free Encyclopedia, 29 Jul. 2016. Web. 5 Aug. 2016. <https://en.wikipedia.org/w/index.php?title=Materialism&oldid=732025661>

Wikipedia contributors. "Randomness." *Wikipedia, The Free Encyclopedia.* Wikipedia, The Free Encyclopedia, 17 May. 2016. Web. 5 Aug. 2016. <https://en.wikipedia.org/w/index.php?title=Randomness&oldid=720648868>

Concept Progress

Wikipedia contributors. "Interaction." *Wikipedia, The Free Encyclopedia.* Wikipedia, The Free Encyclopedia, 1 Jun. 2016. Web. 5 Aug. 2016. <https://en.wikipedia.org/w/index.php?title=Interaction&oldid=723098731>

Wikipedia contributors. "Reaction (physics)." *Wikipedia, The Free Encyclopedia.* Wikipedia, The Free Encyclopedia, 24 Apr. 2016. Web. 5 Aug. 2016. <https://en.wikipedia.org/w/index.php?title=Reaction_(physics)&oldid=716957443>

Wikipedia contributors. "Patterns in nature." *Wikipedia, The Free Encyclopedia.* Wikipedia, The Free Encyclopedia, 7 Jun. 2016. Web. 5 Aug. 2016. <https://en.wikipedia.org/w/index.php?title=Patterns_in_nature&oldid=724215709>

Wikipedia contributors. "Potentiality and actuality." *Wikipedia, The Free Encyclopedia.* Wikipedia, The Free Encyclopedia, 8 Feb. 2016. Web. 5 Aug. 2016. <https://en.wikipedia.org/w/index.php?title=Potentiality_and_actuality&oldid=703958231>

Wikipedia contributors. "Timeline of the far future." *Wikipedia, The Free Encyclopedia.* Wikipedia, The Free Encyclopedia, 4 Aug. 2016. Web. 5 Aug. 2016. <https://en.wikipedia.org/w/index.php?title=Timeline_of_the_far_future&oldid=733035224>

Wikipedia contributors. "Uncertainty." *Wikipedia, The Free Encyclopedia.* Wikipedia, The Free Encyclopedia, 2 Aug. 2016. Web. 5 Aug. 2016. <https://en.wikipedia.org/w/index.php?title=Uncertainty&oldid=732735843>

Wikipedia contributors. "Social progress." *Wikipedia, The Free Encyclopedia.* Wikipedia, The Free Encyclopedia, 20 Dec. 2016. Web. 28 Dec. 2016. <https://en.wikipedia.org/w/index.php?title=Social_progress&oldid=755780170>

Wikipedia contributors. "Minkowski space." *Wikipedia, The Free Encyclopedia.* Wikipedia, The Free Encyclopedia, 13 Jun. 2016. Web. 5 Aug. 2016. <https://en.wikipedia.org/w/index.php?title=Minkowski_space&oldid=725035345>

Wikipedia contributors. "Determinism." *Wikipedia, The Free Encyclopedia.* Wikipedia, The Free Encyclopedia, 2 Aug. 2016. Web. 5 Aug. 2016. <https://en.wikipedia.org/w/index.php?title=Determinism&oldid=732620824>

Wikipedia contributors. "Certainty." *Wikipedia, The Free Encyclopedia.* Wikipedia, The Free Encyclopedia, 4 Jun. 2016. Web. 5 Aug. 2016. <https://en.wikipedia.org/w/index.php?title=Certainty&oldid=723704890>

Wikipedia contributors. "Spacetime." *Wikipedia, The Free Encyclopedia.* Wikipedia, The Free Encyclopedia, 2 Aug. 2016. Web. 5 Aug. 2016. <https://en.wikipedia.org/w/index.php?title=Spacetime&oldid=732690335>

Wikipedia contributors. "Simulation." *Wikipedia, The Free Encyclopedia.* Wikipedia, The Free Encyclopedia, 30 Jul. 2016. Web. 5 Aug. 2016. <https://en.wikipedia.org/w/index.php?title=Simulation&oldid=732198183>

Wikipedia contributors. "Weather forecasting." *Wikipedia, The Free Encyclopedia.* Wikipedia, The Free Encyclopedia, 4 Aug. 2016. Web. 5 Aug. 2016. <https://en.wikipedia.org/w/index.php?title=Weather_forecasting&oldid=732921251>

Wikipedia contributors. "Scientific modelling." *Wikipedia, The Free Encyclopedia.* Wikipedia, The Free Encyclopedia, 8 Jul. 2016. Web. 5 Aug. 2016. <https://en.wikipedia.org/w/index.php?title=Scientific_modelling&oldid=728935635>

Wikipedia contributors. "Extrapolation." *Wikipedia, The Free Encyclopedia.* Wikipedia, The Free Encyclopedia, 30 May. 2016. Web. 5 Aug. 2016. <https://en.wikipedia.org/w/index.php?title=Extrapolation&oldid=722794229>

Wikipedia contributors. "Scenario analysis.' *Wikipedia, The Free Encyclopedia.* Wikipedia, The Free Encyclopedia, 8 Oct. 2016. Web. 17 Oct. 2016. <https://en.wikipedia.org/w/index.php?title=Scenario_analysis&oldid=743268101>

Wikipedia contributors. "Prediction." *Wikipedia, The Free Encyclopedia.* Wikipedia, The Free Encyclopedia, 29 Jul. 2016. Web. 5 Aug. 2016. <https://en.wikipedia.org/w/index.php?title=Prediction&oldid=732142055>

Wikipedia contributors. "Maximum likelihood estimation." *Wikipedia, The Free Encyclopedia.* Wikipedia, The Free Encyclopedia, 20 Jun. 2016. Web. 5 Aug. 2016. <https://en.wikipedia.org/w/index.php?title=Maximum_likelihood_estimation&oldid=726117543>

Wikipedia contributors. "Logical reasoning.' *Wikipedia, The Free Encyclopedia.* Wikipedia, The Free Encyclopedia, 23 Jun. 2016. Web. 5 Aug. 2016. <https://en.wikipedia.org/w/index.php?title=Logical_reasoning&oldid=726611167>

Wikipedia contributors. "Locus of control." *Wikipedia, The Free Encyclopedia*. Wikipedia, The Free Encyclopedia, 5 Jul. 2016. Web. 5 Aug. 2016. <https://en.wikipedia.org/w/index.php?title=Locus_of_control&oldid=728463150>

Wikipedia contributors. "Natural environment." *Wikipedia, The Free Encyclopedia*. Wikipedia, The Free Encyclopedia, 2 Aug. 2016. Web. 5 Aug. 2016. <https://en.wikipedia.org/w/index.php?title=Natural_environment&oldid=732675049>

Wikipedia contributors. "Self-control." *Wikipedia, The Free Encyclopedia*. Wikipedia, The Free Encyclopedia, 8 Aug. 2016. Web. 8 Aug. 2016. <https://en.wikipedia.org/w/index.php?title=Self-control&oldid=733463636>

Wikipedia contributors. "Introduction to evolution." *Wikipedia, The Free Encyclopedia*. Wikipedia, The Free Encyclopedia, 26 Jan. 2017. Web. 17 Feb. 2017. <https://en.wikipedia.org/w/index.php?title=Introduction_to_evolution&oldid=762098021>

Wikipedia contributors. "Energy." *Wikipedia, The Free Encyclopedia*. Wikipedia, The Free Encyclopedia, 13 Jul. 2016. Web. 8 Aug. 2016. <https://en.wikipedia.org/w/index.php?title=Energy&oldid=729554560>

Wikipedia contributors. "Second law of thermodynamics." *Wikipedia, The Free Encyclopedia*. Wikipedia, The Free Encyclopedia, 25 Jul. 2016. Web. 8 Aug. 2016. <https://en.wikipedia.org/w/index.php?title=Second_law_of_thermodynamics&oldid=731438731>

Wikipedia contributors. "Mother Nature." *Wikipedia, The Free Encyclopedia*. Wikipedia, The Free Encyclopedia, 24 Jun. 2016. Web. 8 Aug. 2016. <https://en.wikipedia.org/w/index.php?title=Mother_Nature&oldid=726812186>

Wikipedia contributors. "Zero-energy universe." *Wikipedia, The Free Encyclopedia*. Wikipedia, The Free Encyclopedia, 9 Jul. 2016. Web. 8 Aug. 2016. <https://en.wikipedia.org/w/index.php?title=Zero-energy_universe&oldid=729103774>

Wikipedia contributors. "Self-reflection." *Wikipedia, The Free Encyclopedia*. Wikipedia, The Free Encyclopedia, 21 Nov. 2016. Web. 4 Jan. 2017. <https://en.wikipedia.org/w/index.php?title=Self-reflection&oldid=750791347>

Wikipedia contributors. "Atmosphere of Earth." *Wikipedia, The Free Encyclopedia*. Wikipedia, The Free Encyclopedia, 3 Jul. 2016. Web. 8 Aug. 2016. <https://en.wikipedia.org/w/index.php?title=Atmosphere_of_Earth&oldid=728164432>

Wikipedia contributors. "Astronomical unit." *Wikipedia, The Free Encyclopedia*. Wikipedia, The Free Encyclopedia, 3 Aug. 2016. Web. 8 Aug. 2016. <https://en.wikipedia.org/w/index.php?title=Astronomical_unit&oldid=732810941>

Wikipedia contributors. "Tychism." *Wikipedia, The Free Encyclopedia*. Wikipedia, The Free Encyclopedia, 7 Apr. 2016. Web. 8 Aug. 2016. <https://en.wikipedia.org/w/index.php?title=Tychism&oldid=714044839>

Wikipedia contributors. "Motivation." *Wikipedia, The Free Encyclopedia*. Wikipedia, The Free Encyclopedia, 4 Aug. 2016. Web. 8 Aug. 2016. <https://en.wikipedia.org/w/index.php?title=Motivation&oldid=733026833>

Wikipedia contributors. "Timeline of scientific discoveries." *Wikipedia, The Free Encyclopedia*. Wikipedia, The Free Encyclopedia, 21 Jul. 2016. Web. 8 Aug. 2016. <https://en.wikipedia.org/w/index.php?title=Timeline_of_scientific_discoveries&oldid=730815081>

Wikipedia contributors. "Meaning of life." *Wikipedia, The Free Encyclopedia*. Wikipedia, The Free Encyclopedia, 5 Aug. 2016. Web. 8 Aug. 2016. <https://en.wikipedia.org/w/index.php?title=Meaning_of_life&oldid=733148166>

Wikipedia contributors. "Existentialism." *Wikipedia, The Free Encyclopedia*. Wikipedia, The Free Encyclopedia, 6 Aug. 2016. Web. 8 Aug. 2016. <https://en.wikipedia.org/w/index.php?title=Existentialism&oldid=733318690>

Chapter Three

Wikipedia contributors. "Evolution." *Wikipedia, The Free Encyclopedia*. Wikipedia, The Free Encyclopedia, 9 Aug. 2016. Web. 10 Aug. 2016. <https://en.wikipedia.org/w/index.php?title=Evolution&oldid=733718430>

Wikipedia contributors. "Earth." *Wikipedia, The Free Encyclopedia*. Wikipedia, The Free Encyclopedia, 9 Aug. 2016. Web. 10 Aug. 2016. <https://en.wikipedia.org/w/index.php?title=Earth&oldid=733718634>

Concept Progress

Wikipedia contributors. "History of Earth." *Wikipedia, The Free Encyclopedia*. Wikipedia, The Free Encyclopedia, 8 Aug. 2016. Web. 10 Aug. 2016. <https://en.wikipedia.org/w/index.php?title=History_of_Earth&oldid=733509036>

Wikipedia contributors. "Giant-impact hypothesis." *Wikipedia, The Free Encyclopedia*. Wikipedia, The Free Encyclopedia, 23 Oct. 2016. Web. 31 Oct. 2016. <https://en.wikipedia.org/w/index.php?title=Giant-impact_hypothesis&oldid=745738739>

Wikipedia contributors. "Earth's rotation." *Wikipedia, The Free Encyclopedia*. Wikipedia, The Free Encyclopedia, 26 Jul. 2016. Web. 10 Aug. 2016. <https://en.wikipedia.org/w/index.php?title=Earth%27s_rotation&oldid=731636015>

Wikipedia contributors. "Matter." *Wikipedia, The Free Encyclopedia*. Wikipedia, The Free Encyclopedia, 27 Jul. 2016. Web. 10 Aug. 2016. <https://en.wikipedia.org/w/index.php?title=Matter&oldid=731758882>

Wikipedia contributors. "Abiogenesis." *Wikipedia, The Free Encyclopedia*. Wikipedia, The Free Encyclopedia, 7 Aug. 2016. Web. 10 Aug. 2016. <https://en.wikipedia.org/w/index.php?title=Abiogenesis&oldid=733395913>

Wikipedia contributors. "Amino acid." *Wikipedia, The Free Encyclopedia*. Wikipedia, The Free Encyclopedia, 30 Jul. 2016. Web. 11 Aug. 2016. <https://en.wikipedia.org/w/index.php?title=Amino_acid&oldid=732240111>

Wikipedia contributors. "Genetic code." *Wikipedia, The Free Encyclopedia*. Wikipedia, The Free Encyclopedia, 10 Aug. 2016. Web. 11 Aug. 2016. <https://en.wikipedia.org/w/index.php?title=Genetic_code&oldid=733885000>

Wikipedia contributors. "Evolution of cells." *Wikipedia, The Free Encyclopedia*. Wikipedia, The Free Encyclopedia, 10 Jul. 2016. Web. 11 Aug. 2016. <https://en.wikipedia.org/w/index.php?title=Evolution_of_cells&oldid=729118200>

Wikipedia contributors. "Unicellular organism." *Wikipedia, The Free Encyclopedia*. Wikipedia, The Free Encyclopedia, 1 Aug. 2016. Web. 11 Aug. 2016. <https://en.wikipedia.org/w/index.php?title=Unicellular_organism&oldid=732549094>

Wikipedia contributors. "Multicellular organism." *Wikipedia, The Free Encyclopedia*. Wikipedia, The Free Encyclopedia, 5 Aug. 2016. Web. 11 Aug. 2016. <https://en.wikipedia.org/w/index.php?title=Multicellular_organism&oldid=733096380>

Wikipedia contributors. "Species." *Wikipedia, The Free Encyclopedia*. Wikipedia, The Free Encyclopedia, 5 Aug. 2016. Web. 11 Aug. 2016. <https://en.wikipedia.org/w/index.php?title=Species&oldid=733131526>

Wikipedia contributors. "Natural selection.' *Wikipedia, The Free Encyclopedia*. Wikipedia, The Free Encyclopedia, 29 Jul. 2016. Web. 11 Aug. 2016. <https://en.wikipedia.org/w/index.php?title=Natural_selection&oldid=732093140>

Wikipedia contributors. "Food chain." *Wikipedia, The Free Encyclopedia*. Wikipedia, The Free Encyclopedia, 8 Aug. 2016. Web. 11 Aug. 2016. <https://en.wikipedia.org/w/index.php?title=Food_chain&oldid=733575088>

Wikipedia contributors. "Survival of the fittest." *Wikipedia, The Free Encyclopedia*. Wikipedia, The Free Encyclopedia, 24 May. 2016. Web. 11 Aug. 2016. <https://en.wikipedia.org/w/index.php?title=Survival_of_the_fittest&oldid=721786261>

Wikipedia contributors. "Extinction." *Wikipedia, The Free Encyclopedia*. Wikipedia, The Free Encyclopedia, 27 Jul. 2016. Web. 11 Aug. 2016. <https://en.wikipedia.org/w/index.php?title=Extinction&oldid=731762201>

Wikipedia contributors. "Adaptation." *Wikipedia, The Free Encyclopedia*. Wikipedia, The Free Encyclopedia, 29 Jul. 2016. Web. 11 Aug. 2016. <https://en.wikipedia.org/w/index.php?title=Adaptation&oldid=732078724>

Wikipedia contributors. "Mutation." *Wikipedia, The Free Encyclopedia*. Wikipedia, The Free Encyclopedia, 4 Aug. 2016. Web. 11 Aug. 2016. <https://en.wikipedia.org/w/index.php?title=Mutation&oldid=732991170>

Wikipedia contributors. "Sentience." *Wikipedia, The Free Encyclopedia*. Wikipedia, The Free Encyclopedia, 20 Jul. 2016. Web. 11 Aug. 2016. <https://en.wikipedia.org/w/index.php?title=Sentience&oldid=730596178>

Wikipedia contributors. "Chimpanzee–human last common ancestor." *Wikipedia, The Free Encyclopedia*. Wikipedia, The Free Encyclopedia, 5 Feb. 2017. Web. 11 Feb. 2017.
<https://en.wikipedia.org/w/index.php?title=Chimpanzee%E2%80%93human_last_common_ancestor&oldid=763810559>

Wikipedia contributors. "Neural pathway." *Wikipedia, The Free Encyclopedia.* Wikipedia, The Free Encyclopedia, 6 Jun. 2016. Web. 11 Aug. 2016. <https://en.wikipedia.org/w/index.php?title=Neural_pathway&oldid=724061401>

Wikipedia contributors. "Neuroplasticity." *Wikipedia, The Free Encyclopedia.* Wikipedia, The Free Encyclopedia, 30 Jul. 2016. Web. 11 Aug. 2016. <https://en.wikipedia.org/w/index.php?title=Neuroplasticity&oldid=732168525>

Wikipedia contributors. "Timeline of human evolution." *Wikipedia, The Free Encyclopedia.* Wikipedia, The Free Encyclopedia, 8 Aug. 2016. Web. 12 Aug. 2016. <https://en.wikipedia.org/w/index.php?title=Timeline_of_human_evolution&oldid=733577245>

Wikipedia contributors. "Tree of life (biology)." *Wikipedia, The Free Encyclopedia.* Wikipedia, The Free Encyclopedia, 9 Jul. 2016. Web. 12 Aug. 2016. <https://en.wikipedia.org/w/index.php?title=Tree_of_life_(biology)&oldid=729103489>

Wikipedia contributors. "Divergent evolution." *Wikipedia, The Free Encyclopedia.* Wikipedia, The Free Encyclopedia, 26 May. 2016. Web. 12 Aug. 2016. <https://en.wikipedia.org/w/index.php?title=Divergent_evolution&oldid=722253272>

Wikipedia contributors. "Hunter-gatherer." *Wikipedia, The Free Encyclopedia.* Wikipedia, The Free Encyclopedia, 5 Aug. 2016. Web. 12 Aug. 2016. <https://en.wikipedia.org/w/index.php?title=Hunter-gatherer&oldid=733169299>

Wikipedia contributors. "Hominidae." *Wikipedia, The Free Encyclopedia.* Wikipedia, The Free Encyclopedia, 9 Aug. 2016. Web. 12 Aug. 2016. <https://en.wikipedia.org/w/index.php?title=Hominidae&oldid=733668019>

Wikipedia contributors. "Evolution of the brain." *Wikipedia, The Free Encyclopedia.* Wikipedia, The Free Encyclopedia, 2 Jul. 2016. Web. 12 Aug. 2016. <https://en.wikipedia.org/w/index.php?title=Evolution_of_the_brain&oldid=728002759>

Wikipedia contributors. "Human skeletal changes due to bipedalism." *Wikipedia, The Free Encyclopedia.* Wikipedia, The Free Encyclopedia, 23 Oct. 2016. Web. 11 Nov. 2016. <https://en.wikipedia.org/w/index.php?title=Human_skeletal_changes_due_to_bipedalism&oldid=745779161>

Wikipedia contributors. "Neanderthal." *Wikipedia, The Free Encyclopedia.* Wikipedia, The Free Encyclopedia, 11 Aug. 2016. Web. 12 Aug. 2016. <https://en.wikipedia.org/w/index.php?title=Neanderthal&oldid=733937499>

Wikipedia contributors. "Race (human categorization)." *Wikipedia, The Free Encyclopedia.* Wikipedia, The Free Encyclopedia, 30 Jul. 2016. Web. 12 Aug. 2016. <https://en.wikipedia.org/w/index.php?title=Race_(human_categorization)&oldid=732223220>

Wikipedia contributors. "*Homo.*" *Wikipedia, The Free Encyclopedia.* Wikipedia, The Free Encyclopedia, 6 Aug. 2016. Web. 12 Aug. 2016. <https://en.wikipedia.org/w/index.php?title=Homo&oldid=733190234>

Wikipedia contributors. "Humanoid." *Wikipedia, The Free Encyclopedia.* Wikipedia, The Free Encyclopedia, 28 May. 2016. Web. 12 Aug. 2016. <https://en.wikipedia.org/w/index.php?title=Humanoid&oldid=722427178>

Wikipedia contributors. "History of the world." *Wikipedia, The Free Encyclopedia.* Wikipedia, The Free Encyclopedia, 2 Aug. 2016. Web. 12 Aug. 2016. <https://en.wikipedia.org/w/index.php?title=History_of_the_world&oldid=732723213>

Wikipedia contributors. "Charles Darwin." *Wikipedia, The Free Encyclopedia.* Wikipedia, The Free Encyclopedia, 11 Aug. 2016. Web. 12 Aug. 2016. <https://en.wikipedia.org/w/index.php?title=Charles_Darwin&oldid=733934895>

Wikipedia contributors. "On the Origin of Species." *Wikipedia, The Free Encyclopedia.* Wikipedia, The Free Encyclopedia, 12 Aug. 2016. Web. 12 Aug. 2016. <https://en.wikipedia.org/w/index.php?title=On_the_Origin_of_Species&oldid=734075658>

Wikipedia contributors. "Evolutionary biology." *Wikipedia, The Free Encyclopedia.* Wikipedia, The Free Encyclopedia, 2 Aug. 2016. Web. 12 Aug. 2016. <https://en.wikipedia.org/w/index.php?title=Evolutionary_biology&oldid=732605948>

Wikipedia contributors. "Viral evolution." *Wikipedia, The Free Encyclopedia.* Wikipedia, The Free Encyclopedia, 6 Jun. 2016. Web. 12 Aug. 2016. <https://en.wikipedia.org/w/index.php?title=Viral_evolution&oldid=724050889>

Concept Progress

Wikipedia contributors. "Evolution of mammals." *Wikipedia, The Free Encyclopedia.* Wikipedia, The Free Encyclopedia, 13 Jul. 2016. Web. 12 Aug. 2016. <https://en.wikipedia.org/w/index.php?title=Evolution_of_mammals&oldid=729666263>

Wikipedia contributors. "Timeline of the evolutionary history of life." *Wikipedia, The Free Encyclopedia.* Wikipedia, The Free Encyclopedia, 11 Aug. 2016. Web. 12 Aug. 2016. <https://en.wikipedia.org/w/index.php?title=Timeline_of_the_evolutionary_history_of_life&oldid=733993146>

Wikipedia contributors. "Anthropocentrism." *Wikipedia, The Free Encyclopedia.* Wikipedia, The Free Encyclopedia, 13 Mar. 2016. Web. 12 Aug. 2016. <https://en.wikipedia.org/w/index.php?title=Anthropocentrism&oldid=709787086>

Wikipedia contributors. "Speciesism." *Wikipedia, The Free Encyclopedia.* Wikipedia, The Free Encyclopedia, 19 May. 2016. Web. 12 Aug. 2016. <https://en.wikipedia.org/w/index.php?title=Speciesism&oldid=721012431>

Wikipedia contributors. "Outline of life forms." *Wikipedia, The Free Encyclopedia.* Wikipedia, The Free Encyclopedia, 11 Aug. 2016. Web. 21 Aug. 2016. <https://en.wikipedia.org/w/index.php?title=Outline_of_life_forms&oldid=734072166>

Wikipedia contributors. "Struggle for existence." *Wikipedia, The Free Encyclopedia.* Wikipedia, The Free Encyclopedia, 1 Dec. 2016. Web. 19 Jan. 2017. <https://en.wikipedia.org/w/index.php?title=Struggle_for_existence&oldid=752534861>

Wikipedia contributors. "Human extinction." *Wikipedia, The Free Encyclopedia.* Wikipedia, The Free Encyclopedia, 9 Aug. 2016. Web. 12 Aug. 2016. <https://en.wikipedia.org/w/index.php?title=Human_extinction&oldid=733735505>

Wikipedia contributors. "Quality of life." *Wikipedia, The Free Encyclopedia.* Wikipedia, The Free Encyclopedia, 5 Aug. 2016. Web. 12 Aug. 2016. <https://en.wikipedia.org/w/index.php?title=Quality_of_life&oldid=733120048>

Wikipedia contributors. "Philosophical analysis." *Wikipedia, The Free Encyclopedia.* Wikipedia, The Free Encyclopedia, 5 Jun. 2016. Web. 12 Aug. 2016. <https://en.wikipedia.org/w/index.php?title=Philosophical_analysis&oldid=723825254>

Wikipedia contributors. "Modern synthesis." *Wikipedia, The Free Encyclopedia.* Wikipedia, The Free Encyclopedia, 12 Feb. 2017. Web. 22 Feb. 2017. <https://en.wikipedia.org/w/index.php?title=Modern_synthesis&oldid=765142830>

Wikipedia contributors. "Intellect." *Wikipedia, The Free Encyclopedia.* Wikipedia, The Free Encyclopedia, 11 May. 2016. Web. 12 Aug. 2016. <https://en.wikipedia.org/w/index.php?title=Intellect&oldid=719768787>

Wikipedia contributors. "Outline of evolution." *Wikipedia, The Free Encyclopedia.* Wikipedia, The Free Encyclopedia, 4 Jul. 2016. Web. 12 Aug. 2016. <https://en.wikipedia.org/w/index.php?title=Outline_of_evolution&oldid=728245692>

Wikipedia contributors. "Animal cognition.' *Wikipedia, The Free Encyclopedia.* Wikipedia, The Free Encyclopedia, 9 Aug. 2016. Web. 12 Aug. 2016. <https://en.wikipedia.org/w/index.php?title=Animal_cognition&oldid=733711082>

Wikipedia contributors. "Human spaceflight." *Wikipedia, The Free Encyclopedia.* Wikipedia, The Free Encyclopedia, 10 Aug. 2016. Web. 12 Aug. 2016. <https://en.wikipedia.org/w/index.php?title=Human_spaceflight&oldid=733854376>

Wikipedia contributors. "Interplanetary spaceflight." *Wikipedia, The Free Encyclopedia.* Wikipedia, The Free Encyclopedia, 8 Aug. 2016. Web. 12 Aug. 2016. <https://en.wikipedia.org/w/index.php?title=Interplanetary_spaceflight&oldid=733524397>

Wikipedia contributors. "Interstellar travel." *Wikipedia, The Free Encyclopedia.* Wikipedia, The Free Encyclopedia, 11 Aug. 2016. Web. 12 Aug. 2016. <https://en.wikipedia.org/w/index.php?title=Interstellar_travel&oldid=734052858>

Wikipedia contributors. "Intergalactic travel." *Wikipedia, The Free Encyclopedia.* Wikipedia, The Free Encyclopedia, 20 Jul. 2016. Web. 12 Aug. 2016. <https://en.wikipedia.org/w/index.php?title=Intergalactic_travel&oldid=730677163>

Wikipedia contributors. "Global catastrophic risk." *Wikipedia, The Free Encyclopedia.* Wikipedia, The Free Encyclopedia, 8 Aug. 2016. Web. 12 Aug. 2016. <https://en.wikipedia.org/w/index.php?title=Global_catastrophic_risk&oldid=733527060>

Wikipedia contributors. "Apocalyptic and post-apocalyptic fiction." *Wikipedia, The Free Encyclopedia.* Wikipedia, The Free Encyclopedia, 10 Aug. 2016. Web. 12 Aug. 2016. <https://en.wikipedia.org/w/index.php?title=Apocalyptic_and_post-apocalyptic_fiction&oldid=733811577>

Wikipedia contributors. "Technological change." *Wikipedia, The Free Encyclopedia*. Wikipedia, The Free Encyclopedia, 15 Jun. 2016. Web. 12 Aug. 2016. <https://en.wikipedia.org/w/index.php?title=Technological_change&oldid=725398904>

Wikipedia contributors. "Space and survival." *Wikipedia, The Free Encyclopedia*. Wikipedia, The Free Encyclopedia, 29 Aug. 2016. Web. 30 Aug. 2016. <https://en.wikipedia.org/w/index.php?title=Space_and_survival&oldid=736803290>

Wikipedia contributors. "Mars." *Wikipedia, The Free Encyclopedia*. Wikipedia, The Free Encyclopedia, 4 Aug. 2016. Web. 12 Aug. 2016. <https://en.wikipedia.org/w/index.php?title=Mars&oldid=732995997>

Wikipedia contributors. "Geologic time scale." *Wikipedia, The Free Encyclopedia*. Wikipedia, The Free Encyclopedia, 25 Jul. 2016. Web. 12 Aug. 2016. <https://en.wikipedia.org/w/index.php?title=Geologic_time_scale&oldid=731466156>

Wikipedia contributors. "Sun." *Wikipedia, The Free Encyclopedia*. Wikipedia, The Free Encyclopedia, 7 Aug. 2016. Web. 12 Aug. 2016. <https://en.wikipedia.org/w/index.php?title=Sun&oldid=733436500>

Wikipedia contributors. "Red giant." *Wikipedia, The Free Encyclopedia*. Wikipedia, The Free Encyclopedia, 19 Jul. 2016. Web. 12 Aug. 2016. <https://en.wikipedia.org/w/index.php?title=Red_giant&oldid=730467646>

Wikipedia contributors. "Accelerating change." *Wikipedia, The Free Encyclopedia*. Wikipedia, The Free Encyclopedia, 2 Aug. 2016. Web. 12 Aug. 2016. <https://en.wikipedia.org/w/index.php?title=Accelerating_change&oldid=732718847>

Wikipedia contributors. "*Homo sapiens*." *Wikipedia, The Free Encyclopedia*. Wikipedia, The Free Encyclopedia, 29 Jul. 2016. Web. 13 Aug. 2016. <https://en.wikipedia.org/w/index.php?title=Homo_sapiens&oldid=732040741>

Wikipedia contributors. "Civilization." *Wikipedia, The Free Encyclopedia*. Wikipedia, The Free Encyclopedia, 10 Aug. 2016. Web. 13 Aug. 2016. <https://en.wikipedia.org/w/index.php?title=Civilization&oldid=733814335>

Wikipedia contributors. "Moon." *Wikipedia, The Free Encyclopedia*. Wikipedia, The Free Encyclopedia, 11 Aug. 2016. Web. 13 Aug. 2016. <https://en.wikipedia.org/w/index.php?title=Moon&oldid=734057157>

Wikipedia contributors. "Evolution of the eye." *Wikipedia, The Free Encyclopedia*. Wikipedia, The Free Encyclopedia, 31 Jan. 2017. Web. 17 Feb. 2017. <https://en.wikipedia.org/w/index.php?title=Evolution_of_the_eye&oldid=762982410>

Wikipedia contributors. "Happiness." *Wikipedia, The Free Encyclopedia*. Wikipedia, The Free Encyclopedia, 12 Aug. 2016. Web. 13 Aug. 2016. <https://en.wikipedia.org/w/index.php?title=Happiness&oldid=734164475>

Wikipedia contributors. "Largest-scale trends in evolution." *Wikipedia, The Free Encyclopedia*. Wikipedia, The Free Encyclopedia, 4 Jun. 2016. Web. 21 Aug. 2016. <https://en.wikipedia.org/w/index.php?title=Largest-scale_trends_in_evolution&oldid=723737464>

Wikipedia contributors. "Concept." *Wikipedia, The Free Encyclopedia*. Wikipedia, The Free Encyclopedia, 30 Jul. 2016. Web. 13 Aug. 2016. <https://en.wikipedia.org/w/index.php?title=Concept&oldid=732157949>

Wikipedia contributors. "Evolutionism." *Wikipedia, The Free Encyclopedia*. Wikipedia, The Free Encyclopedia, 23 Jul. 2016. Web. 14 Aug. 2016. <https://en.wikipedia.org/w/index.php?title=Evolutionism&oldid=731191784>

Wikipedia contributors. "Idea of Progress." *Wikipedia, The Free Encyclopedia*. Wikipedia, The Free Encyclopedia, 5 May. 2016. Web. 14 Aug. 2016. <https://en.wikipedia.org/w/index.php?title=Idea_of_Progress&oldid=718741080>

Wikipedia contributors. "Evolution of biological complexity." *Wikipedia, The Free Encyclopedia*. Wikipedia, The Free Encyclopedia, 5 Dec. 2016. Web. 14 Feb. 2017. <https://en.wikipedia.org/w/index.php?title=Evolution_of_biological_complexity&oldid=753138096>

Wikipedia contributors. "Progress (history)." *Wikipedia, The Free Encyclopedia*. Wikipedia, The Free Encyclopedia, 31 Mar. 2016. Web. 14 Aug. 2016. <https://en.wikipedia.org/w/index.php?title=Progress_(history)&oldid=712863975>

Wikipedia contributors. "Competition." *Wikipedia, The Free Encyclopedia*. Wikipedia, The Free Encyclopedia, 12 Aug. 2016. Web. 14 Aug. 2016. <https://en.wikipedia.org/w/index.php?title=Competition&oldid=734128702>

Concept Progress

Wikipedia contributors. "Olympic Games." *Wikipedia, The Free Encyclopedia*. Wikipedia, The Free Encyclopedia, 14 Aug. 2016. Web. 14 Aug. 2016. <https://en.wikipedia.org/w/index.php?title=Olympic_Games&oldid=734455131>

Wikipedia contributors. "Objections to evolution." *Wikipedia, The Free Encyclopedia*. Wikipedia, The Free Encyclopedia, 23 Oct. 2016. Web. 23 Nov. 2016. <https://en.wikipedia.org/w/index.php?title=Objections_to_evolution&oldid=745857479>

Wikipedia contributors. "Progress trap." *Wikipedia, The Free Encyclopedia*. Wikipedia, The Free Encyclopedia, 7 Feb. 2017. Web. 17 Feb. 2017. <https://en.wikipedia.org/w/index.php?title=Progress_trap&oldid=764115417>

Wikipedia contributors. "Outline of war." *Wikipedia, The Free Encyclopedia*. Wikipedia, The Free Encyclopedia, 25 Jul. 2016. Web. 14 Aug. 2016. <https://en.wikipedia.org/w/index.php?title=Outline_of_war&oldid=731494299>

Wikipedia contributors. "Natural disaster." *Wikipedia, The Free Encyclopedia*. Wikipedia, The Free Encyclopedia, 14 Aug. 2016. Web. 14 Aug. 2016. <https://en.wikipedia.org/w/index.php?title=Natural_disaster&oldid=734434100>

Wikipedia contributors. "Evolution of ageing." *Wikipedia, The Free Encyclopedia*. Wikipedia, The Free Encyclopedia, 14 Feb. 2017. Web. 17 Feb. 2017. <https://en.wikipedia.org/w/index.php?title=Evolution_of_ageing&oldid=765419948>

Wikipedia contributors. "Recent African origin of modern humans." *Wikipedia, The Free Encyclopedia*. Wikipedia, The Free Encyclopedia, 14 Aug. 2016. Web. 14 Aug. 2016. <https://en.wikipedia.org/w/index.php?title=Recent_African_origin_of_modern_humans&oldid=734401143>

Wikipedia contributors. "Human brain." *Wikipedia, The Free Encyclopedia*. Wikipedia, The Free Encyclopedia, 29 Aug. 2016. Web. 31 Aug. 2016. <https://en.wikipedia.org/w/index.php?title=Human_brain&oldid=736761157>

Wikipedia contributors. "Human evolution." *Wikipedia, The Free Encyclopedia*. Wikipedia, The Free Encyclopedia, 13 Aug. 2016. Web. 14 Aug. 2016. <https://en.wikipedia.org/w/index.php?title=Human_evolution&oldid=734355284>

Wikipedia contributors. "Generation." *Wikipedia, The Free Encyclopedia*. Wikipedia, The Free Encyclopedia, 12 Aug. 2016. Web. 21 Aug. 2016. <https://en.wikipedia.org/w/index.php?title=Generation&oldid=734169001>

Wikipedia contributors. "Self-replication." *Wikipedia, The Free Encyclopedia*. Wikipedia, The Free Encyclopedia, 5 Aug. 2016. Web. 14 Aug. 2016. <https://en.wikipedia.org/w/index.php?title=Self-replication&oldid=733088329>

Wikipedia contributors. "Scientific progress." *Wikipedia, The Free Encyclopedia*. Wikipedia, The Free Encyclopedia, 28 Jul. 2016. Web. 14 Aug. 2016. <https://en.wikipedia.org/w/index.php?title=Scientific_progress&oldid=731908159>

Wikipedia contributors. "Biotechnology." *Wikipedia, The Free Encyclopedia*. Wikipedia, The Free Encyclopedia, 6 Aug. 2016. Web. 17 Aug. 2016. <https://en.wikipedia.org/w/index.php?title=Biotechnology&oldid=733308451>

Wikipedia contributors. "Gene therapy." *Wikipedia, The Free Encyclopedia*. Wikipedia, The Free Encyclopedia, 16 Aug. 2016. Web. 17 Aug. 2016. <https://en.wikipedia.org/w/index.php?title=Gene_therapy&oldid=734798785>

Wikipedia contributors. "Human Genome Project." *Wikipedia, The Free Encyclopedia*. Wikipedia, The Free Encyclopedia, 10 Aug. 2016. Web. 17 Aug. 2016. <https://en.wikipedia.org/w/index.php?title=Human_Genome_Project&oldid=733849211>

Wikipedia contributors. "DNA sequencing." *Wikipedia, The Free Encyclopedia*. Wikipedia, The Free Encyclopedia, 17 Aug. 2016. Web. 17 Aug. 2016. <https://en.wikipedia.org/w/index.php?title=DNA_sequencing&oldid=734912854>

Wikipedia contributors. "Evidence of common descent." *Wikipedia, The Free Encyclopedia*. Wikipedia, The Free Encyclopedia, 24 Jan. 2017. Web. 9 Feb. 2017. <https://en.wikipedia.org/w/index.php?title=Evidence_of_common_descent&oldid=761662607>

Wikipedia contributors. "Evolutionary progress." *Wikipedia, The Free Encyclopedia*. Wikipedia, The Free Encyclopedia, 15 Sep. 2015. Web. 17 Aug. 2016. <https://en.wikipedia.org/w/index.php?title=Evolutionary_progress&oldid=681168850>

Wikipedia contributors. "Planetary habitability." *Wikipedia, The Free Encyclopedia*. Wikipedia, The Free Encyclopedia, 10 Aug. 2016. Web. 17 Aug. 2016. <https://en.wikipedia.org/w/index.php?title=Planetary_habitability&oldid=733913572>

Wikipedia contributors. "Observation." *Wikipedia, The Free Encyclopedia*. Wikipedia, The Free Encyclopedia, 13 Aug. 2016. Web. 17 Aug. 2016. <https://en.wikipedia.org/w/index.php?title=Observation&oldid=734277377>

Wikipedia contributors. "Spaceflight." *Wikipedia, The Free Encyclopedia*. Wikipedia, The Free Encyclopedia, 17 Jul. 2016. Web. 17 Aug. 2016. <https://en.wikipedia.org/w/index.php?title=Spaceflight&oldid=730194873>

Wikipedia contributors. "Last universal common ancestor." *Wikipedia, The Free Encyclopedia*. Wikipedia, The Free Encyclopedia, 22 Nov. 2016. Web. 22 Nov. 2016. <https://en.wikipedia.org/w/index.php?title=Last_universal_common_ancestor&oldid=750983247>

Wikipedia contributors. "Population growth." *Wikipedia, The Free Encyclopedia*. Wikipedia, The Free Encyclopedia, 13 Aug. 2016. Web. 17 Aug. 2016. <https://en.wikipedia.org/w/index.php?title=Population_growth&oldid=734362303>

Chapter Four

Wikipedia contributors. "Benjamin Franklin." *Wikipedia, The Free Encyclopedia*. Wikipedia, The Free Encyclopedia, 15 Aug. 2016. Web. 24 Aug. 2016. <https://en.wikipedia.org/w/index.php?title=Benjamin_Franklin&oldid=734662194>

Wikipedia contributors. "Eastern philosophy." *Wikipedia, The Free Encyclopedia*. Wikipedia, The Free Encyclopedia, 15 Aug. 2016. Web. 24 Aug. 2016. <https://en.wikipedia.org/w/index.php?title=Eastern_philosophy&oldid=734546881>

Wikipedia contributors. "Western philosophy." *Wikipedia, The Free Encyclopedia*. Wikipedia, The Free Encyclopedia, 28 May. 2016. Web. 24 Aug. 2016. <https://en.wikipedia.org/w/index.php?title=Western_philosophy&oldid=722495133>

Wikipedia contributors. "Ionian Enlightenment." *Wikipedia, The Free Encyclopedia*. Wikipedia, The Free Encyclopedia, 15 Aug. 2016. Web. 24 Aug. 2016. <https://en.wikipedia.org/w/index.php?title=Ionian_Enlightenment&oldid=734562805>

Wikipedia contributors. "Socrates." *Wikipedia, The Free Encyclopedia*. Wikipedia, The Free Encyclopedia, 16 Aug. 2016. Web. 24 Aug. 2016. <https://en.wikipedia.org/w/index.php?title=Socrates&oldid=734687573>

Wikipedia contributors. "Plato." *Wikipedia, The Free Encyclopedia*. Wikipedia, The Free Encyclopedia, 19 Aug. 2016. Web. 24 Aug. 2016. <https://en.wikipedia.org/w/index.php?title=Plato&oldid=735323206>

Wikipedia contributors. "Aristotle." *Wikipedia, The Free Encyclopedia*. Wikipedia, The Free Encyclopedia, 22 Aug. 2016. Web. 24 Aug. 2016. <https://en.wikipedia.org/w/index.php?title=Aristotle&oldid=735725954>

Wikipedia contributors. "Natural philosophy." *Wikipedia, The Free Encyclopedia*. Wikipedia, The Free Encyclopedia, 26 Sep. 2016. Web. 29 Sep. 2016. <https://en.wikipedia.org/w/index.php?title=Natural_philosophy&oldid=741319243>

Wikipedia contributors. "Nicolaus Copernicus." *Wikipedia, The Free Encyclopedia*. Wikipedia, The Free Encyclopedia, 11 Aug. 2016. Web. 24 Aug. 2016. <https://en.wikipedia.org/w/index.php?title=Nicolaus_Copernicus&oldid=733998016>

Wikipedia contributors. "Galileo Galilei." *Wikipedia, The Free Encyclopedia*. Wikipedia, The Free Encyclopedia, 21 Aug. 2016. Web. 24 Aug. 2016. <https://en.wikipedia.org/w/index.php?title=Galileo_Galilei&oldid=735532567>

Wikipedia contributors. "Astrology." *Wikipedia, The Free Encyclopedia*. Wikipedia, The Free Encyclopedia, 23 Aug. 2016. Web. 24 Aug. 2016. <https://en.wikipedia.org/w/index.php?title=Astrology&oldid=735907097>

Wikipedia contributors. "Geocentric model." *Wikipedia, The Free Encyclopedia*. Wikipedia, The Free Encyclopedia, 18 Aug. 2016. Web. 24 Aug. 2016. <https://en.wikipedia.org/w/index.php?title=Geocentric_model&oldid=735076204>

Wikipedia contributors. "Creator deity." *Wikipedia, The Free Encyclopedia*. Wikipedia, The Free Encyclopedia, 9 Aug. 2016. Web. 24 Aug. 2016. <https://en.wikipedia.org/w/index.php?title=Creator_deity&oldid=733630209>

Wikipedia contributors. "Religious text." *Wikipedia, The Free Encyclopedia*. Wikipedia, The Free Encyclopedia, 23 Jul. 2016. Web. 24 Aug. 2016. <https://en.wikipedia.org/w/index.php?title=Religious_text&oldid=731207633>

Concept Progress

Wikipedia contributors. "Jewish diaspora." *Wikipedia, The Free Encyclopedia.* Wikipedia, The Free Encyclopedia, 20 Jul. 2016. Web. 24 Aug. 2016. <https://en.wikipedia.org/w/index.php?title=Jewish_diaspora&oldid=730733378>

Wikipedia contributors. "Pilgrim Fathers." *Wikipedia, The Free Encyclopedia.* Wikipedia, The Free Encyclopedia, 24 Jun. 2016. Web. 24 Aug. 2016. <https://en.wikipedia.org/w/index.php?title=Pilgrim_Fathers&oldid=726835632>

Wikipedia contributors. "List of revolutions and rebellions." *Wikipedia, The Free Encyclopedia.* Wikipedia, The Free Encyclopedia, 12 Aug. 2016. Web. 24 Aug. 2016. <https://en.wikipedia.org/w/index.php?title=List_of_revolutions_and_rebellions&oldid=734160098>

Wikipedia contributors. "Sociocultural evolution." *Wikipedia, The Free Encyclopedia.* Wikipedia, The Free Encyclopedia, 27 Oct. 2016. Web. 1 Dec. 2016. <https://en.wikipedia.org/w/index.php?title=Sociocultural_evolution&oldid=746444069>

Wikipedia contributors. "Individualism." *Wikipedia, The Free Encyclopedia.* Wikipedia, The Free Encyclopedia, 19 Aug. 2016. Web. 25 Aug. 2016. <https://en.wikipedia.org/w/index.php?title=Individualism&oldid=735318559>

Wikipedia contributors. "Collectivism." *Wikipedia, The Free Encyclopedia.* Wikipedia, The Free Encyclopedia, 17 Aug. 2016. Web. 25 Aug. 2016. <https://en.wikipedia.org/w/index.php?title=Collectivism&oldid=734848351>

Wikipedia contributors. "Americas." *Wikipedia, The Free Encyclopedia.* Wikipedia, The Free Encyclopedia, 23 Aug. 2016. Web. 25 Aug. 2016. <https://en.wikipedia.org/w/index.php?title=Americas&oldid=735767972>

Wikipedia contributors. "Founding Fathers of the United States." *Wikipedia, The Free Encyclopedia.* Wikipedia, The Free Encyclopedia, 20 Aug. 2016. Web. 25 Aug. 2016. <https://en.wikipedia.org/w/index.php?title=Founding_Fathers_of_the_United_States&oldid=735468774>

Wikipedia contributors. "United States Constitution." *Wikipedia, The Free Encyclopedia.* Wikipedia, The Free Encyclopedia, 19 Aug. 2016. Web. 25 Aug. 2016. <https://en.wikipedia.org/w/index.php?title=United_States_Constitution&oldid=735187204>

Wikipedia contributors. "United States." *Wikipedia, The Free Encyclopedia.* Wikipedia, The Free Encyclopedia, 24 Aug. 2016. Web. 25 Aug. 2016. <https://en.wikipedia.org/w/index.php?title=United_States&oldid=735997552>

Wikipedia contributors. "Industrial Revolution." *Wikipedia, The Free Encyclopedia.* Wikipedia, The Free Encyclopedia, 20 Aug. 2016. Web. 25 Aug. 2016. <https://en.wikipedia.org/w/index.php?title=Industrial_Revolution&oldid=735411356>

Wikipedia contributors. "Machine." *Wikipedia, The Free Encyclopedia.* Wikipedia, The Free Encyclopedia, 25 Aug. 2016. Web. 9 Sep. 2016. <https://en.wikipedia.org/w/index.php?title=Machine&oldid=736146292>

Wikipedia contributors. "Medicine." *Wikipedia, The Free Encyclopedia.* Wikipedia, The Free Encyclopedia, 4 Sep. 2016. Web. 6 Sep. 2016. <https://en.wikipedia.org/w/index.php?title=Medicine&oldid=737640045>

Wikipedia contributors. "Technology." *Wikipedia, The Free Encyclopedia.* Wikipedia, The Free Encyclopedia, 3 Sep. 2016. Web. 6 Sep. 2016. <https://en.wikipedia.org/w/index.php?title=Technology&oldid=737527637>

Wikipedia contributors. "Globalization." *Wikipedia, The Free Encyclopedia.* Wikipedia, The Free Encyclopedia, 23 Aug. 2016. Web. 25 Aug. 2016. <https://en.wikipedia.org/w/index.php?title=Globalization&oldid=735839158>

Wikipedia contributors. "20th century." *Wikipedia, The Free Encyclopedia.* Wikipedia, The Free Encyclopedia, 23 Aug. 2016. Web. 25 Aug. 2016. <https://en.wikipedia.org/w/index.php?title=20th_century&oldid=735917841>

Wikipedia contributors. "Totalitarianism." *Wikipedia, The Free Encyclopedia.* Wikipedia, The Free Encyclopedia, 11 Aug. 2016. Web. 25 Aug. 2016. <https://en.wikipedia.org/w/index.php?title=Totalitarianism&oldid=734057397>

Wikipedia contributors. "Dictator." *Wikipedia, The Free Encyclopedia.* Wikipedia, The Free Encyclopedia, 23 Aug. 2016. Web. 25 Aug. 2016. <https://en.wikipedia.org/w/index.php?title=Dictator&oldid=735885386>

Wikipedia contributors. "The Holocaust." *Wikipedia, The Free Encyclopedia.* Wikipedia, The Free Encyclopedia, 22 Aug. 2016. Web. 25 Aug. 2016. <https://en.wikipedia.org/w/index.php?title=The_Holocaust&oldid=735735393>

Wikipedia contributors. "Historical negationism." *Wikipedia, The Free Encyclopedia.* Wikipedia, The Free Encyclopedia, 2 Sep. 2016. Web. 6 Sep. 2016. <https://en.wikipedia.org/w/index.php?title=Historical_negationism&oldid=737380951>

Wikipedia contributors. "World war." *Wikipedia, The Free Encyclopedia.* Wikipedia, The Free Encyclopedia, 31 Aug. 2016. Web. 6 Sep. 2016. <https://en.wikipedia.org/w/index.php?title=World_war&oldid=736983886>

Wikipedia contributors. "Developed country." *Wikipedia, The Free Encyclopedia.* Wikipedia, The Free Encyclopedia, 10 Aug. 2016. Web. 25 Aug. 2016. <https://en.wikipedia.org/w/index.php?title=Developed_country&oldid=733814215>

Wikipedia contributors. "Corporate social responsibility." *Wikipedia, The Free Encyclopedia.* Wikipedia, The Free Encyclopedia, 19 Aug. 2016. Web. 25 Aug. 2016. <https://en.wikipedia.org/w/index.php?title=Corporate_social_responsibility&oldid=735323537>

Wikipedia contributors. "World peace." *Wikipedia, The Free Encyclopedia.* Wikipedia, The Free Encyclopedia, 23 Aug. 2016. Web. 25 Aug. 2016. <https://en.wikipedia.org/w/index.php?title=World_peace&oldid=735893775>

Wikipedia contributors. "United Nations." *Wikipedia, The Free Encyclopedia.* Wikipedia, The Free Encyclopedia, 24 Aug. 2016. Web. 25 Aug. 2016. <https://en.wikipedia.org/w/index.php?title=United_Nations&oldid=736034097>

Wikipedia contributors. "Border." *Wikipedia, The Free Encyclopedia.* Wikipedia, The Free Encyclopedia, 6 Sep. 2016. Web. 7 Sep. 2016. <https://en.wikipedia.org/w/index.php?title=Border&oldid=723558055>

Wikipedia contributors. "World government." *Wikipedia, The Free Encyclopedia.* Wikipedia, The Free Encyclopedia, 24 Aug. 2016. Web. 25 Aug. 2016. <https://en.wikipedia.org/w/index.php?title=World_government&oldid=736047546>

Wikipedia contributors. "Israel." *Wikipedia, The Free Encyclopedia.* Wikipedia, The Free Encyclopedia, 19 Aug. 2016. Web. 25 Aug. 2016. <https://en.wikipedia.org/w/index.php?title=Israel&oldid=735316652>

Wikipedia contributors. "Mahatma Gandhi." *Wikipedia, The Free Encyclopedia.* Wikipedia, The Free Encyclopedia, 24 Aug. 2016. Web. 25 Aug. 2016. <https://en.wikipedia.org/w/index.php?title=Mahatma_Gandhi&oldid=736013764>

Wikipedia contributors. "India." *Wikipedia, The Free Encyclopedia.* Wikipedia, The Free Encyclopedia, 24 Aug. 2016. Web. 25 Aug. 2016. <https://en.wikipedia.org/w/index.php?title=India&oldid=736037959>

Wikipedia contributors. "Nonviolence." *Wikipedia, The Free Encyclopedia.* Wikipedia, The Free Encyclopedia, 25 Aug. 2016. Web. 25 Aug. 2016. <https://en.wikipedia.org/w/index.php?title=Nonviolence&oldid=736122941>

Wikipedia contributors. "Independence." *Wikipedia, The Free Encyclopedia.* Wikipedia, The Free Encyclopedia, 23 Jul. 2016. Web. 25 Aug. 2016. <https://en.wikipedia.org/w/index.php?title=Independence&oldid=731135103>

Wikipedia contributors. "Transactive memory." *Wikipedia, The Free Encyclopedia.* Wikipedia, The Free Encyclopedia, 1 May. 2016. Web. 25 Aug. 2016. <https://en.wikipedia.org/w/index.php?title=Transactive_memory&oldid=718030222>

Wikipedia contributors. "United we stand, divided we fall." *Wikipedia, The Free Encyclopedia.* Wikipedia, The Free Encyclopedia, 26 May. 2016. Web. 26 Aug. 2016. <https://en.wikipedia.org/w/index.php?title=United_we_stand,_divided_we_fall&oldid=722146961>

Wikipedia contributors. "Caveman." *Wikipedia, The Free Encyclopedia.* Wikipedia, The Free Encyclopedia, 10 Feb. 2017. Web. 18 Feb. 2017. <https://en.wikipedia.org/w/index.php?title=Caveman&oldid=764632225>

Wikipedia contributors. "Futures studies." *Wikipedia, The Free Encyclopedia.* Wikipedia, The Free Encyclopedia, 29 Aug. 2016. Web. 29 Aug. 2016. <https://en.wikipedia.org/w/index.php?title=Futures_studies&oldid=736669168>

Wikipedia contributors. "21st century." *Wikipedia, The Free Encyclopedia.* Wikipedia, The Free Encyclopedia, 23 Aug. 2016. Web. 26 Aug. 2016. <https://en.wikipedia.org/w/index.php?title=21st_century&oldid=735849251>

Wikipedia contributors. "Roman Empire." *Wikipedia, The Free Encyclopedia.* Wikipedia, The Free Encyclopedia, 25 Aug. 2016. Web. 26 Aug. 2016. <https://en.wikipedia.org/w/index.php?title=Roman_Empire&oldid=736154766>

Concept Progress

Wikipedia contributors. "Potential cultural impact of extraterrestrial contact." *Wikipedia, The Free Encyclopedia.* Wikipedia, The Free Encyclopedia, 11 Jun. 2016. Web. 26 Aug. 2016. <https://en.wikipedia.org/w/index.php?title=Potential_cultural_impact_of_extraterrestrial_contact&oldid=724747511>

Wikipedia contributors. "Pace of innovation." *Wikipedia, The Free Encyclopedia.* Wikipedia, The Free Encyclopedia, 12 Jan. 2016. Web. 31 Aug. 2016. <https://en.wikipedia.org/w/index.php?title=Pace_of_innovation&oldid=699511746>

Wikipedia contributors. "Genetics." *Wikipedia, The Free Encyclopedia.* Wikipedia, The Free Encyclopedia, 13 Aug. 2016. Web. 26 Aug. 2016. <https://en.wikipedia.org/w/index.php?title=Genetics&oldid=734295532>

Wikipedia contributors. "Biological engineering." *Wikipedia, The Free Encyclopedia.* Wikipedia, The Free Encyclopedia, 19 Aug. 2016. Web. 26 Aug. 2016. <https://en.wikipedia.org/w/index.php?title=Biological_engineering&oldid=735296422>

Wikipedia contributors. "Nanotechnology." *Wikipedia, The Free Encyclopedia.* Wikipedia, The Free Encyclopedia, 24 Aug. 2016. Web. 26 Aug. 2016. <https://en.wikipedia.org/w/index.php?title=Nanotechnology&oldid=735979113>

Wikipedia contributors. "Evolution of human intelligence." *Wikipedia, The Free Encyclopedia.* Wikipedia, The Free Encyclopedia, 10 Aug. 2016. Web. 31 Aug. 2016. <https://en.wikipedia.org/w/index.php?title=Evolution_of_human_intelligence&oldid=733862194>

Wikipedia contributors. "Technology and society." *Wikipedia, The Free Encyclopedia.* Wikipedia, The Free Encyclopedia, 6 Jul. 2016. Web. 31 Aug. 2016. <https://en.wikipedia.org/w/index.php?title=Technology_and_society&oldid=728662977>

Wikipedia contributors. "Technological unemployment." *Wikipedia, The Free Encyclopedia.* Wikipedia, The Free Encyclopedia, 29 Aug. 2016. Web. 9 Sep. 2016. <https://en.wikipedia.org/w/index.php?title=Technological_unemployment&oldid=736713013>

Wikipedia contributors. "Automation." *Wikipedia, The Free Encyclopedia.* Wikipedia, The Free Encyclopedia, 21 Aug. 2016. Web. 26 Aug. 2016. <https://en.wikipedia.org/w/index.php?title=Automation&oldid=735530466>

Wikipedia contributors. "Flight." *Wikipedia, The Free Encyclopedia.* Wikipedia, The Free Encyclopedia, 6 Jul. 2016. Web. 26 Aug. 2016. <https://en.wikipedia.org/w/index.php?title=Flight&oldid=728614010>

Wikipedia contributors. "Outline of space science." *Wikipedia, The Free Encyclopedia.* Wikipedia, The Free Encyclopedia, 9 Jul. 2016. Web. 30 Aug. 2016. <https://en.wikipedia.org/w/index.php?title=Outline_of_space_science&oldid=728996138>

Wikipedia contributors. "Space colonization." *Wikipedia, The Free Encyclopedia.* Wikipedia, The Free Encyclopedia, 10 Aug. 2016. Web. 30 Aug. 2016. <https://en.wikipedia.org/w/index.php?title=Space_colonization&oldid=733840021>

Wikipedia contributors. "Life extension." *Wikipedia, The Free Encyclopedia.* Wikipedia, The Free Encyclopedia, 19 Aug. 2016. Web. 31 Aug. 2016. <https://en.wikipedia.org/w/index.php?title=Life_extension&oldid=735190019>

Wikipedia contributors. "Human genome." *Wikipedia, The Free Encyclopedia.* Wikipedia, The Free Encyclopedia, 5 Aug. 2016. Web. 26 Aug. 2016. <https://en.wikipedia.org/w/index.php?title=Human_genome&oldid=733149676>

Wikipedia contributors. "Star Trek." *Wikipedia, The Free Encyclopedia.* Wikipedia, The Free Encyclopedia, 15 Aug. 2016. Web. 26 Aug. 2016. <https://en.wikipedia.org/w/index.php?title=Star_Trek&oldid=734606408>

Wikipedia contributors. "Teleportation." *Wikipedia, The Free Encyclopedia.* Wikipedia, The Free Encyclopedia, 22 Aug. 2016. Web. 26 Aug. 2016. <https://en.wikipedia.org/w/index.php?title=Teleportation&oldid=735733695>

Wikipedia contributors. "Psychokinesis." *Wikipedia, The Free Encyclopedia.* Wikipedia, The Free Encyclopedia, 9 Aug. 2016. Web. 26 Aug. 2016. <https://en.wikipedia.org/w/index.php?title=Psychokinesis&oldid=733679468>

Wikipedia contributors. "Innovation." *Wikipedia, The Free Encyclopedia.* Wikipedia, The Free Encyclopedia, 24 Aug. 2016. Web. 31 Aug. 2016. <https://en.wikipedia.org/w/index.php?title=Innovation&oldid=735993283>

Wikipedia contributors. "Neuroscience." *Wikipedia, The Free Encyclopedia.* Wikipedia, The Free Encyclopedia, 25 Aug. 2016. Web. 26 Aug. 2016. <https://en.wikipedia.org/w/index.php?title=Neuroscience&oldid=736177943>

Wikipedia contributors. "Electroencephalography." *Wikipedia, The Free Encyclopedia.* Wikipedia, The Free Encyclopedia, 2 Aug. 2016. Web. 26 Aug. 2016. <https://en.wikipedia.org/w/index.php?title=Electroencephalography&oldid=732606045>

Wikipedia contributors. "Autonomous car." *Wikipedia, The Free Encyclopedia.* Wikipedia, The Free Encyclopedia, 24 Aug. 2016. Web. 26 Aug. 2016. <https://en.wikipedia.org/w/index.php?title=Autonomous_car&oldid=735983749>

Wikipedia contributors. "Virtual reality." *Wikipedia, The Free Encyclopedia.* Wikipedia, The Free Encyclopedia, 24 Aug. 2016. Web. 26 Aug. 2016. <https://en.wikipedia.org/w/index.php?title=Virtual_reality&oldid=736068701>

Wikipedia contributors. "Telepathy." *Wikipedia, The Free Encyclopedia.* Wikipedia, The Free Encyclopedia, 21 Aug. 2016. Web. 26 Aug. 2016. <https://en.wikipedia.org/w/index.php?title=Telepathy&oldid=735542452>

Wikipedia contributors. "Brain implant." *Wikipedia, The Free Encyclopedia.* Wikipedia, The Free Encyclopedia, 13 Aug. 2016. Web. 31 Aug. 2016. <https://en.wikipedia.org/w/index.php?title=Brain_implant&oldid=734380717>

Wikipedia contributors. "Graphical user interface." *Wikipedia, The Free Encyclopedia.* Wikipedia, The Free Encyclopedia, 19 Aug. 2016. Web. 27 Aug. 2016. <https://en.wikipedia.org/w/index.php?title=Graphical_user_interface&oldid=735313116>

Wikipedia contributors. "Internet." *Wikipedia, The Free Encyclopedia.* Wikipedia, The Free Encyclopedia, 26 Aug. 2016. Web. 27 Aug. 2016. <https://en.wikipedia.org/w/index.php?title=Internet&oldid=736339261>

Wikipedia contributors. "Information technology." *Wikipedia, The Free Encyclopedia.* Wikipedia, The Free Encyclopedia, 18 Aug. 2016. Web. 27 Aug. 2016. <https://en.wikipedia.org/w/index.php?title=Information_technology&oldid=735046123>

Wikipedia contributors. "Telecommunications network." *Wikipedia, The Free Encyclopedia.* Wikipedia, The Free Encyclopedia, 26 Aug. 2016. Web. 27 Aug. 2016. <https://en.wikipedia.org/w/index.php?title=Telecommunications_network&oldid=736355906>

Wikipedia contributors. "Biological neural network." *Wikipedia, The Free Encyclopedia.* Wikipedia, The Free Encyclopedia, 28 Jun. 2016. Web. 27 Aug. 2016. <https://en.wikipedia.org/w/index.php?title=Biological_neural_network&oldid=727409923>

Wikipedia contributors. "Wireless." *Wikipedia, The Free Encyclopedia.* Wikipedia, The Free Encyclopedia, 24 Aug. 2016. Web. 27 Aug. 2016. <https://en.wikipedia.org/w/index.php?title=Wireless&oldid=735996878>

Wikipedia contributors. "Brain–computer interface." *Wikipedia, The Free Encyclopedia.* Wikipedia, The Free Encyclopedia, 26 Aug. 2016. Web. 27 Aug. 2016. <https://en.wikipedia.org/w/index.php?title=Brain%E2%80%93computer_interface&oldid=736270320>

Wikipedia contributors. "Postbiological evolution." *Wikipedia, The Free Encyclopedia.* Wikipedia, The Free Encyclopedia, 12 Aug. 2016. Web. 18 Feb. 2017. <https://en.wikipedia.org/w/index.php?title=Postbiological_evolution&oldid=734213052>

Wikipedia contributors. "Melanin." *Wikipedia, The Free Encyclopedia.* Wikipedia, The Free Encyclopedia, 14 Aug. 2016. Web. 27 Aug. 2016. <https://en.wikipedia.org/w/index.php?title=Melanin&oldid=734451049>

Wikipedia contributors. "Terraforming of Mars." *Wikipedia, The Free Encyclopedia.* Wikipedia, The Free Encyclopedia, 14 Aug. 2016. Web. 27 Aug. 2016. <https://en.wikipedia.org/w/index.php?title=Terraforming_of_Mars&oldid=734422364>

Wikipedia contributors. "Effect of spaceflight on the human body." *Wikipedia, The Free Encyclopedia.* Wikipedia, The Free Encyclopedia, 20 Aug. 2016. Web. 30 Aug. 2016. <https://en.wikipedia.org/w/index.php?title=Effect_of_spaceflight_on_the_human_body&oldid=735456029>

Wikipedia contributors. "Synaptic plasticity." *Wikipedia, The Free Encyclopedia.* Wikipedia, The Free Encyclopedia, 2 Jun. 2016. Web. 29 Aug. 2016. <https://en.wikipedia.org/w/index.php?title=Synaptic_plasticity&oldid=723282018>

Concept Progress

Wikipedia contributors. "Devolution (biology)." *Wikipedia, The Free Encyclopedia*. Wikipedia, The Free Encyclopedia, 13 Aug. 2016. Web. 21 Aug. 2016. <https://en.wikipedia.org/w/index.php?title=Devolution_(biology)&oldid=734313439>

Wikipedia contributors. "Hard disk drive." *Wikipedia, The Free Encyclopedia*. Wikipedia, The Free Encyclopedia, 26 Aug. 2016. Web. 30 Aug. 2016. <https://en.wikipedia.org/w/index.php?title=Hard_disk_drive&oldid=736215223>

Wikipedia contributors. "Central processing unit." *Wikipedia, The Free Encyclopedia*. Wikipedia, The Free Encyclopedia, 22 Aug. 2016. Web. 26 Aug. 2016. <https://en.wikipedia.org/w/index.php?title=Central_processing_unit&oldid=735688834>

Wikipedia contributors. "Grey alien." *Wikipedia, The Free Encyclopedia*. Wikipedia, The Free Encyclopedia, 28 Aug. 2016. Web. 29 Aug. 2016. <https://en.wikipedia.org/w/index.php?title=Grey_alien&oldid=736521811>

Wikipedia contributors. "Human mating strategies." *Wikipedia, The Free Encyclopedia*. Wikipedia, The Free Encyclopedia, 24 Aug. 2016. Web. 7 Sep. 2016. <https://en.wikipedia.org/w/index.php?title=Human_mating_strategies&oldid=735961378>

Wikipedia contributors. "Sexual attraction." *Wikipedia, The Free Encyclopedia*. Wikipedia, The Free Encyclopedia, 2 Aug. 2016. Web. 29 Aug. 2016. <https://en.wikipedia.org/w/index.php?title=Sexual_attraction&oldid=732654131>

Wikipedia contributors. "Spirituality." *Wikipedia, The Free Encyclopedia*. Wikipedia, The Free Encyclopedia, 6 Aug. 2016. Web. 24 Aug. 2016. <https://en.wikipedia.org/w/index.php?title=Spirituality&oldid=733229322>

Wikipedia contributors. "Sense." *Wikipedia, The Free Encyclopedia*. Wikipedia, The Free Encyclopedia, 28 Aug. 2016. Web. 30 Aug. 2016. <https://en.wikipedia.org/w/index.php?title=Sense&oldid=736552384>

Wikipedia contributors. "Human condition." *Wikipedia, The Free Encyclopedia*. Wikipedia, The Free Encyclopedia, 24 Aug. 2016. Web. 29 Aug. 2016. <https://en.wikipedia.org/w/index.php?title=Human_condition&oldid=735952743>

Wikipedia contributors. "Teacher." *Wikipedia, The Free Encyclopedia*. Wikipedia, The Free Encyclopedia, 8 Jul. 2016. Web. 8 Sep. 2016. <https://en.wikipedia.org/w/index.php?title=Teacher&oldid=728971688>

Wikipedia contributors. "Engineer." *Wikipedia, The Free Encyclopedia*. Wikipedia, The Free Encyclopedia, 7 Sep. 2016. Web. 9 Sep. 2016. <https://en.wikipedia.org/w/index.php?title=Engineer&oldid=738213171>

Wikipedia contributors. "Research." *Wikipedia, The Free Encyclopedia*. Wikipedia, The Free Encyclopedia, 7 Sep. 2016. Web. 8 Sep. 2016. <https://en.wikipedia.org/w/index.php?title=Research&oldid=738224076>

Chapter Five

Wikipedia contributors. "Photosynthesis." *Wikipedia, The Free Encyclopedia*. Wikipedia, The Free Encyclopedia, 12 Sep. 2016. Web. 13 Sep. 2016. <https://en.wikipedia.org/w/index.php?title=Photosynthesis&oldid=739108840>

Wikipedia contributors. "Solar panel." *Wikipedia, The Free Encyclopedia*. Wikipedia, The Free Encyclopedia, 15 Sep. 2016. Web. 21 Sep. 2016. <https://en.wikipedia.org/w/index.php?title=Solar_panel&oldid=739541092>

Wikipedia contributors. "Sunlight." *Wikipedia, The Free Encyclopedia*. Wikipedia, The Free Encyclopedia, 10 Sep. 2016. Web. 21 Sep. 2016. <https://en.wikipedia.org/w/index.php?title=Sunlight&oldid=738609421>

Wikipedia contributors. "Evolutionary history of life." *Wikipedia, The Free Encyclopedia*. Wikipedia, The Free Encyclopedia, 21 Sep. 2016. Web. 27 Sep. 2016. <https://en.wikipedia.org/w/index.php?title=Evolutionary_history_of_life&oldid=740510422>

Wikipedia contributors. "Selective breeding." *Wikipedia, The Free Encyclopedia*. Wikipedia, The Free Encyclopedia, 27 Dec. 2016. Web. 9 Jan. 2017. <https://en.wikipedia.org/w/index.php?title=Selective_breeding&oldid=756820513>

Wikipedia contributors. "Love." *Wikipedia, The Free Encyclopedia*. Wikipedia, The Free Encyclopedia, 8 Sep. 2016. Web. 13 Sep. 2016. <https://en.wikipedia.org/w/index.php?title=Love&oldid=738425725>

Wikipedia contributors. "Genetic engineering." *Wikipedia, The Free Encyclopedia*. Wikipedia, The Free Encyclopedia, 11 Sep. 2016. Web. 13 Sep. 2016. <https://en.wikipedia.org/w/index.php?title=Genetic_engineering&oldid=738937403>

Wikipedia contributors. "Nature (philosophy)." *Wikipedia, The Free Encyclopedia*. Wikipedia, The Free Encyclopedia, 7 Dec. 2016. Web. 3 Jan. 2017. <https://en.wikipedia.org/w/index.php?title=Nature_(philosophy)&oldid=753485461>

Wikipedia contributors. "Immune system." *Wikipedia, The Free Encyclopedia*. Wikipedia, The Free Encyclopedia, 19 Aug. 2016. Web. 14 Sep. 2016. <https://en.wikipedia.org/w/index.php?title=Immune_system&oldid=735318350>

Wikipedia contributors. "Strength training." *Wikipedia, The Free Encyclopedia*. Wikipedia, The Free Encyclopedia, 3 Sep. 2016. Web. 22 Sep. 2016. <https://en.wikipedia.org/w/index.php?title=Strength_training&oldid=737607174>

Wikipedia contributors. "Bodybuilding." *Wikipedia, The Free Encyclopedia*. Wikipedia, The Free Encyclopedia, 24 Aug. 2016. Web. 13 Sep. 2016. <https://en.wikipedia.org/w/index.php?title=Bodybuilding&oldid=736038747>

Wikipedia contributors. "Cognitive training." *Wikipedia, The Free Encyclopedia*. Wikipedia, The Free Encyclopedia, 11 Sep. 2016. Web. 29 Sep. 2016. <https://en.wikipedia.org/w/index.php?title=Cognitive_training&oldid=738794330>

Wikipedia contributors. "Memory." *Wikipedia, The Free Encyclopedia*. Wikipedia, The Free Encyclopedia, 1 Sep. 2016. Web. 14 Sep. 2016. <https://en.wikipedia.org/w/index.php?title=Memory&oldid=737237390>

Wikipedia contributors. "Abstraction." *Wikipedia, The Free Encyclopedia*. Wikipedia, The Free Encyclopedia, 9 Sep. 2016. Web. 14 Sep. 2016. <https://en.wikipedia.org/w/index.php?title=Abstraction&oldid=738448116>

Wikipedia contributors. "Language acquisition." *Wikipedia, The Free Encyclopedia*. Wikipedia, The Free Encyclopedia, 23 Aug. 2016. Web. 14 Sep. 2016. <https://en.wikipedia.org/w/index.php?title=Language_acquisition&oldid=735852614>

Wikipedia contributors. "Origin of language." *Wikipedia, The Free Encyclopedia*. Wikipedia, The Free Encyclopedia, 27 Sep. 2016. Web. 30 Sep. 2016. <https://en.wikipedia.org/w/index.php?title=Origin_of_language&oldid=741359339>

Wikipedia contributors. "Flexibility (anatomy)." *Wikipedia, The Free Encyclopedia*. Wikipedia, The Free Encyclopedia, 8 Sep. 2016. Web. 22 Sep. 2016. <https://en.wikipedia.org/w/index.php?title=Flexibility_(anatomy)&oldid=738283478>

Wikipedia contributors. "Earth's magnetic field." *Wikipedia, The Free Encyclopedia*. Wikipedia, The Free Encyclopedia, 31 Aug. 2016. Web. 14 Sep. 2016. <https://en.wikipedia.org/w/index.php?title=Earth%27s_magnetic_field&oldid=737096510>

Wikipedia contributors. "Ethical intuitionism." *Wikipedia, The Free Encyclopedia*. Wikipedia, The Free Encyclopedia, 4 Jun. 2016. Web. 22 Sep. 2016. <https://en.wikipedia.org/w/index.php?title=Ethical_intuitionism&oldid=723739169>

Wikipedia contributors. "Intention." *Wikipedia, The Free Encyclopedia*. Wikipedia, The Free Encyclopedia, 23 Aug. 2016. Web. 14 Sep. 2016. <https://en.wikipedia.org/w/index.php?title=Intention&oldid=735908377>

Wikipedia contributors. "Alfred Nobel." *Wikipedia, The Free Encyclopedia*. Wikipedia, The Free Encyclopedia, 8 Sep. 2016. Web. 14 Sep. 2016. <https://en.wikipedia.org/w/index.php?title=Alfred_Nobel&oldid=738295917>

Wikipedia contributors. "Nobel Prize." *Wikipedia, The Free Encyclopedia*. Wikipedia, The Free Encyclopedia, 8 Sep. 2016. Web. 14 Sep. 2016. <https://en.wikipedia.org/w/index.php?title=Nobel_Prize&oldid=738423480>

Wikipedia contributors. "Second Amendment to the United States Constitution." *Wikipedia, The Free Encyclopedia*. Wikipedia, The Free Encyclopedia, 1 Sep. 2016. Web. 14 Sep. 2016. <https://en.wikipedia.org/w/index.php?title=Second_Amendment_to_the_United_States_Constitution&oldid=737250607>

Wikipedia contributors. "Einstein–Szilárd letter." *Wikipedia, The Free Encyclopedia*. Wikipedia, The Free Encyclopedia, 15 Jul. 2016. Web. 14 Sep. 2016. <https://en.wikipedia.org/w/index.php?title=Einstein%E2%80%93Szil%C3%A1rd_letter&oldid=729863312>

Wikipedia contributors. "Manhattan Project." *Wikipedia, The Free Encyclopedia*. Wikipedia, The Free Encyclopedia, 27 Aug. 2016. Web. 14 Sep. 2016. <https://en.wikipedia.org/w/index.php?title=Manhattan_Project&oldid=736491420>

Wikipedia contributors. "Nazi Germany." *Wikipedia, The Free Encyclopedia*. Wikipedia, The Free Encyclopedia, 13 Sep. 2016. Web. 14 Sep. 2016. <https://en.wikipedia.org/w/index.php?title=Nazi_Germany&oldid=739161712>

Concept Progress

Wikipedia contributors. "Terrorism." *Wikipedia, The Free Encyclopedia.* Wikipedia, The Free Encyclopedia, 14 Sep. 2016. Web. 14 Sep. 2016. <https://en.wikipedia.org/w/index.php?title=Terrorism&oldid=739396055>

Wikipedia contributors. "Nuclear fission." *Wikipedia, The Free Encyclopedia.* Wikipedia, The Free Encyclopedia, 31 Aug. 2016. Web. 23 Sep. 2016. <https://en.wikipedia.org/w/index.php?title=Nuclear_fission&oldid=737120447>

Wikipedia contributors. "Nazi human experimentation." *Wikipedia, The Free Encyclopedia.* Wikipedia, The Free Encyclopedia, 11 Sep. 2016. Web. 14 Sep. 2016.
<https://en.wikipedia.org/w/index.php?title=Nazi_human_experimentation&oldid=738917014>

Wikipedia contributors. "Nazi concentration camps." *Wikipedia, The Free Encyclopedia.* Wikipedia, The Free Encyclopedia, 4 Jun. 2016. Web. 14 Sep. 2016. <https://en.wikipedia.org/w/index.php?title=Nazi_concentration_camps&oldid=723615754>

Wikipedia contributors. "Devil." *Wikipedia, The Free Encyclopedia.* Wikipedia, The Free Encyclopedia, 1 Sep. 2016. Web. 14 Sep. 2016. <https://en.wikipedia.org/w/index.php?title=Devil&oldid=737235236>

Wikipedia contributors. "Death." *Wikipedia, The Free Encyclopedia.* Wikipedia, The Free Encyclopedia, 19 Sep. 2016. Web. 28 Sep. 2016. <https://en.wikipedia.org/w/index.php?title=Death&oldid=740183959>

Wikipedia contributors. "Moral responsibility." *Wikipedia, The Free Encyclopedia.* Wikipedia, The Free Encyclopedia, 27 Aug. 2016. Web. 23 Sep. 2016. <https://en.wikipedia.org/w/index.php?title=Moral_responsibility&oldid=736373296>

Wikipedia contributors. "Health." *Wikipedia, The Free Encyclopedia.* Wikipedia, The Free Encyclopedia, 11 Sep. 2016. Web. 15 Sep. 2016. <https://en.wikipedia.org/w/index.php?title=Health&oldid=738820999>

Wikipedia contributors. "Education." *Wikipedia, The Free Encyclopedia.* Wikipedia, The Free Encyclopedia, 8 Sep. 2016. Web. 15 Sep. 2016. <https://en.wikipedia.org/w/index.php?title=Education&oldid=738370016>

Wikipedia contributors. "Career." *Wikipedia. The Free Encyclopedia.* Wikipedia, The Free Encyclopedia, 15 Sep. 2016. Web. 16 Sep. 2016. <https://en.wikipedia.org/w/index.php?title=Career&oldid=739562057>

Wikipedia contributors. "Personal development." *Wikipedia, The Free Encyclopedia.* Wikipedia, The Free Encyclopedia, 23 Sep. 2016. Web. 28 Sep. 2016. <https://en.wikipedia.org/w/index.php?title=Personal_development&oldid=740808249>

Wikipedia contributors. "Abraham Maslow." *Wikipedia, The Free Encyclopedia.* Wikipedia, The Free Encyclopedia, 19 Sep. 2016. Web. 23 Sep. 2016. <https://en.wikipedia.org/w/index.php?title=Abraham_Maslow&oldid=740195558>

Wikipedia contributors. "Maslow's hierarchy of needs." *Wikipedia, The Free Encyclopedia.* Wikipedia, The Free Encyclopedia, 1 Sep. 2016. Web. 16 Sep. 2016.
<https://en.wikipedia.org/w/index.php?title=Maslow%27s_hierarchy_of_needs&oldid=737279707>

Wikipedia contributors. "Self-actualization." *Wikipedia, The Free Encyclopedia.* Wikipedia, The Free Encyclopedia, 24 Jun. 2016. Web. 16 Sep. 2016. <https://en.wikipedia.org/w/index.php?title=Self-actualization&oldid=726773913>

Wikipedia contributors. "Self-transcendence." *Wikipedia, The Free Encyclopedia.* Wikipedia, The Free Encyclopedia, 7 Dec. 2015. Web. 16 Sep. 2016. <https://en.wikipedia.org/w/index.php?title=Self-transcendence&oldid=694131706>

Wikipedia contributors. "Self." *Wikipedia, The Free Encyclopedia.* Wikipedia, The Free Encyclopedia, 31 Jan. 2017. Web. 24 Feb. 2017. <https://en.wikipedia.org/w/index.php?title=Self&oldid=763011243>

Wikipedia contributors. "Psyche (psychology)." *Wikipedia, The Free Encyclopedia.* Wikipedia, The Free Encyclopedia, 4 Sep. 2016. Web. 16 Sep. 2016. <https://en.wikipedia.org/w/index.php?title=Psyche_(psychology)&oldid=737711340>

Wikipedia contributors. "Pyramid." *Wikipedia, The Free Encyclopedia.* Wikipedia, The Free Encyclopedia, 12 Aug. 2016. Web. 16 Sep. 2016. <https://en.wikipedia.org/w/index.php?title=Pyramid&oldid=734190501>

Wikipedia contributors. "Triskelion." *Wikipedia, The Free Encyclopedia.* Wikipedia, The Free Encyclopedia, 14 Sep. 2016. Web. 16 Sep. 2016. <https://en.wikipedia.org/w/index.php?title=Triskelion&oldid=739373761>

Wikipedia contributors. "Conscious evolution." *Wikipedia, The Free Encyclopedia.* Wikipedia, The Free Encyclopedia, 9 Jun. 2016. Web. 22 Sep. 2016. <https://en.wikipedia.org/w/index.php?title=Conscious_evolution&oldid=724517423>

Wikipedia contributors. "Physical fitness." *Wikipedia, The Free Encyclopedia.* Wikipedia, The Free Encyclopedia, 19 Sep. 2016. Web. 23 Sep. 2016. <https://en.wikipedia.org/w/index.php?title=Physical_fitness&oldid=740208316>

Wikipedia contributors. "Fitness (biology)." *Wikipedia, The Free Encyclopedia.* Wikipedia, The Free Encyclopedia, 23 Sep. 2016. Web. 23 Sep. 2016. <https://en.wikipedia.org/w/index.php?title=Fitness_(biology)&oldid=740758036>

Wikipedia contributors. "Heredity." *Wikipedia, The Free Encyclopedia.* Wikipedia, The Free Encyclopedia, 1 Sep. 2016. Web. 24 Sep. 2016. <https://en.wikipedia.org/w/index.php?title=Heredity&oldid=737270434>

Wikipedia contributors. "Spiritual but not religious." *Wikipedia, The Free Encyclopedia.* Wikipedia, The Free Encyclopedia, 24 Jan. 2017. Web. 30 Jan. 2017. <https://en.wikipedia.org/w/index.php?title=Spiritual_but_not_religious&oldid=761651766>

Wikipedia contributors. "Spiritual evolution." *Wikipedia, The Free Encyclopedia.* Wikipedia, The Free Encyclopedia, 20 Aug. 2016. Web. 17 Sep. 2016. <https://en.wikipedia.org/w/index.php?title=Spiritual_evolution&oldid=735362001>

Wikipedia contributors. "Yoga." *Wikipedia, The Free Encyclopedia.* Wikipedia, The Free Encyclopedia, 17 Sep. 2016. Web. 19 Sep. 2016. <https://en.wikipedia.org/w/index.php?title=Yoga&oldid=739911105>

Wikipedia contributors. "Fourth Way." *Wikipedia, The Free Encyclopedia.* Wikipedia, The Free Encyclopedia, 4 Aug. 2016. Web. 24 Sep. 2016. <https://en.wikipedia.org/w/index.php?title=Fourth_Way&oldid=733021281>

Wikipedia contributors. "Women's Health (magazine)." *Wikipedia, The Free Encyclopedia.* Wikipedia, The Free Encyclopedia, 15 Sep. 2016. Web. 26 Sep. 2016. <https://en.wikipedia.org/w/index.php?title=Women%27s_Health_(magazine)&oldid=739600738>

Wikipedia contributors. "Naked Food Magazine." *Wikipedia, The Free Encyclopedia.* Wikipedia, The Free Encyclopedia, 27 Jul. 2016. Web. 24 Sep. 2016. <https://en.wikipedia.org/w/index.php?title=Naked_Food_Magazine&oldid=731749209>

Wikipedia contributors. "Men's Fitness." *Wikipedia, The Free Encyclopedia.* Wikipedia, The Free Encyclopedia, 16 Sep. 2016. Web. 26 Sep. 2016. <https://en.wikipedia.org/w/index.php?title=Men%27s_Fitness&oldid=739688436>

Wikipedia contributors. "Healthy diet." *Wikipedia, The Free Encyclopedia.* Wikipedia, The Free Encyclopedia, 1 Sep. 2016. Web. 19 Sep. 2016. <https://en.wikipedia.org/w/index.php?title=Healthy_diet&oldid=737182794>

Wikipedia contributors. "Human nutrition." *Wikipedia, The Free Encyclopedia.* Wikipedia, The Free Encyclopedia, 23 Sep. 2016. Web. 29 Sep. 2016. <https://en.wikipedia.org/w/index.php?title=Human_nutrition&oldid=740812494>

Wikipedia contributors. "Physical exercise." *Wikipedia, The Free Encyclopedia.* Wikipedia, The Free Encyclopedia, 10 Sep. 2016. Web. 13 Sep. 2016. <https://en.wikipedia.org/w/index.php?title=Physical_exercise&oldid=738659438>

Wikipedia contributors. "Exercise intensity." *Wikipedia, The Free Encyclopedia.* Wikipedia, The Free Encyclopedia, 15 Feb. 2016. Web. 6 Oct. 2016. <https://en.wikipedia.org/w/index.php?title=Exercise_intensity&oldid=705028566>

Wikipedia contributors. "Weightlessness." *Wikipedia, The Free Encyclopedia.* Wikipedia, The Free Encyclopedia, 3 Sep. 2016. Web. 6 Oct. 2016. <https://en.wikipedia.org/w/index.php?title=Weightlessness&oldid=737612278>

Wikipedia contributors. "Astronaut training." *Wikipedia, The Free Encyclopedia.* Wikipedia, The Free Encyclopedia, 1 Sep. 2016. Web. 19 Sep. 2016. <https://en.wikipedia.org/w/index.php?title=Astronaut_training&oldid=737269802>

Wikipedia contributors. "Human intelligence." *Wikipedia, The Free Encyclopedia.* Wikipedia, The Free Encyclopedia, 22 Jan. 2017. Web. 25 Jan. 2017. <https://en.wikipedia.org/w/index.php?title=Human_intelligence&oldid=761372027>

Wikipedia contributors. "George Santayana." *Wikipedia, The Free Encyclopedia.* Wikipedia, The Free Encyclopedia, 28 Sep. 2016. Web. 29 Sep. 2016. <https://en.wikipedia.org/w/index.php?title=George_Santayana&oldid=741533339>

Concept Progress

Wikipedia contributors. "Philosophical progress." *Wikipedia, The Free Encyclopedia.* Wikipedia, The Free Encyclopedia, 12 Dec. 2016. Web. 22 Feb. 2017. <https://en.wikipedia.org/w/index.php?title=Philosophical_progress&oldid=754398839>

Wikipedia contributors. "Library of Alexandria." *Wikipedia, The Free Encyclopedia.* Wikipedia, The Free Encyclopedia, 16 Sep. 2016. Web. 20 Sep. 2016. <https://en.wikipedia.org/w/index.php?title=Library_of_Alexandria&oldid=739772036>

Wikipedia contributors. "Ivy League." *Wikipedia, The Free Encyclopedia.* Wikipedia, The Free Encyclopedia, 12 Sep. 2016. Web. 20 Sep. 2016. <https://en.wikipedia.org/w/index.php?title=Ivy_League&oldid=739087641>

Wikipedia contributors. "Cognition." *Wikipedia, The Free Encyclopedia.* Wikipedia, The Free Encyclopedia, 22 Sep. 2016. Web. 29 Sep. 2016. <https://en.wikipedia.org/w/index.php?title=Cognition&oldid=740735281>

Wikipedia contributors. "Tree of Knowledge System." *Wikipedia, The Free Encyclopedia.* Wikipedia, The Free Encyclopedia, 18 Apr. 2016. Web. 22 Feb. 2017. <https://en.wikipedia.org/w/index.php?title=Tree_of_Knowledge_System&oldid=715785360>

Wikipedia contributors. "Personal information management." *Wikipedia, The Free Encyclopedia.* Wikipedia, The Free Encyclopedia, 3 Aug. 2016. Web. 20 Sep. 2016. <https://en.wikipedia.org/w/index.php?title=Personal_information_management&oldid=732877681>

Wikipedia contributors. "Color." *Wikipedia, The Free Encyclopedia.* Wikipedia, The Free Encyclopedia, 19 Aug. 2016. Web. 26 Sep. 2016. <https://en.wikipedia.org/w/index.php?title=Color&oldid=735309179>

Wikipedia contributors. "Odor." *Wikipedia, The Free Encyclopedia.* Wikipedia, The Free Encyclopedia, 22 Sep. 2016. Web. 26 Sep. 2016. <https://en.wikipedia.org/w/index.php?title=Odor&oldid=740714483>

Wikipedia contributors. "Sound." *Wikipedia, The Free Encyclopedia.* Wikipedia, The Free Encyclopedia, 26 Sep. 2016. Web. 26 Sep. 2016. <https://en.wikipedia.org/w/index.php?title=Sound&oldid=741211098>

Wikipedia contributors. "Awareness." *Wikipedia, The Free Encyclopedia.* Wikipedia, The Free Encyclopedia, 12 Aug. 2016. Web. 20 Sep. 2016. <https://en.wikipedia.org/w/index.php?title=Awareness&oldid=734212483>

Wikipedia contributors. "Attentional control." *Wikipedia, The Free Encyclopedia.* Wikipedia, The Free Encyclopedia, 20 Jun. 2016. Web. 20 Sep. 2016. <https://en.wikipedia.org/w/index.php?title=Attentional_control&oldid=726158448>

Wikipedia contributors. "Solar System." *Wikipedia, The Free Encyclopedia.* Wikipedia, The Free Encyclopedia, 17 Sep. 2016. Web. 20 Sep. 2016. <https://en.wikipedia.org/w/index.php?title=Solar_System&oldid=739924976>

Wikipedia contributors. "Local Group." *Wikipedia, The Free Encyclopedia.* Wikipedia, The Free Encyclopedia, 17 Sep. 2016. Web. 20 Sep. 2016. <https://en.wikipedia.org/w/index.php?title=Local_Group&oldid=739835554>

Wikipedia contributors. "Instinct." *Wikipedia, The Free Encyclopedia.* Wikipedia, The Free Encyclopedia, 10 Sep. 2016. Web. 20 Sep. 2016. <https://en.wikipedia.org/w/index.php?title=Instinct&oldid=738628019>

Wikipedia contributors. "Reflex." *Wikipedia, The Free Encyclopedia.* Wikipedia, The Free Encyclopedia, 29 Apr. 2016. Web. 20 Sep. 2016. <https://en.wikipedia.org/w/index.php?title=Reflex&oldid=717783390>

Wikipedia contributors. "Nervous system." *Wikipedia, The Free Encyclopedia.* Wikipedia, The Free Encyclopedia, 10 Sep. 2016. Web. 20 Sep. 2016. <https://en.wikipedia.org/w/index.php?title=Nervous_system&oldid=738608485>

Wikipedia contributors. "Withdrawal reflex." *Wikipedia, The Free Encyclopedia.* Wikipedia, The Free Encyclopedia, 12 Aug. 2016. Web. 26 Sep. 2016. <https://en.wikipedia.org/w/index.php?title=Withdrawal_reflex&oldid=734137513>

Wikipedia contributors. "Circadian clock." *Wikipedia, The Free Encyclopedia.* Wikipedia, The Free Encyclopedia, 8 Aug. 2016. Web. 26 Sep. 2016. <https://en.wikipedia.org/w/index.php?title=Circadian_clock&oldid=733532999>

Wikipedia contributors. "Habit." *Wikipedia, The Free Encyclopedia.* Wikipedia, The Free Encyclopedia, 19 Sep. 2016. Web. 20 Sep. 2016. <https://en.wikipedia.org/w/index.php?title=Habit&oldid=740115095>

Wikipedia contributors. "Human multitasking." *Wikipedia, The Free Encyclopedia.* Wikipedia, The Free Encyclopedia, 17 Sep. 2016. Web. 20 Sep. 2016. <https://en.wikipedia.org/w/index.php?title=Human_multitasking&oldid=739826334>

Wikipedia contributors. "Bad habit." *Wikipedia, The Free Encyclopedia.* Wikipedia, The Free Encyclopedia, 9 May. 2016. Web. 20 Sep. 2016. <https://en.wikipedia.org/w/index.php?title=Bad_habit&oldid=719478240>

Wikipedia contributors. "Brandenburg Concertos." *Wikipedia, The Free Encyclopedia.* Wikipedia, The Free Encyclopedia, 15 Sep. 2016. Web. 20 Sep. 2016. <https://en.wikipedia.org/w/index.php?title=Brandenburg_Concertos&oldid=739566049>

Wikipedia contributors. "Daydream." *Wikipedia, The Free Encyclopedia.* Wikipedia, The Free Encyclopedia, 16 Sep. 2016. Web. 20 Sep. 2016. <https://en.wikipedia.org/w/index.php?title=Daydream&oldid=739693272>

Wikipedia contributors. "Aptitude." *Wikipedia, The Free Encyclopedia.* Wikipedia, The Free Encyclopedia, 7 Aug. 2016. Web. 20 Sep. 2016. <https://en.wikipedia.org/w/index.php?title=Aptitude&oldid=733372639>

Wikipedia contributors. "Intellectual giftedness." *Wikipedia, The Free Encyclopedia.* Wikipedia, The Free Encyclopedia, 13 Sep. 2016. Web. 26 Sep. 2016. <https://en.wikipedia.org/w/index.php?title=Intellectual_giftedness&oldid=739220811>

Wikipedia contributors. "Guinness World Records." *Wikipedia, The Free Encyclopedia.* Wikipedia, The Free Encyclopedia, 14 Sep. 2016. Web. 20 Sep. 2016. <https://en.wikipedia.org/w/index.php?title=Guinness_World_Records&oldid=739330942>

Wikipedia contributors. "Survival skills." *Wikipedia, The Free Encyclopedia.* Wikipedia, The Free Encyclopedia, 7 Sep. 2016. Web. 27 Sep. 2016. <https://en.wikipedia.org/w/index.php?title=Survival_skills&oldid=738127162>

Wikipedia contributors. "Information processing." *Wikipedia, The Free Encyclopedia.* Wikipedia, The Free Encyclopedia, 26 Jul. 2016. Web. 26 Sep. 2016. <https://en.wikipedia.org/w/index.php?title=Information_processing&oldid=731698050>

Wikipedia contributors. "Sleep." *Wikipedia, The Free Encyclopedia.* Wikipedia, The Free Encyclopedia, 16 Sep. 2016. Web. 21 Sep. 2016. <https://en.wikipedia.org/w/index.php?title=Sleep&oldid=739677329>

Wikipedia contributors. "Rapid eye movement sleep." *Wikipedia, The Free Encyclopedia.* Wikipedia, The Free Encyclopedia, 4 Sep. 2016. Web. 21 Sep. 2016. <https://en.wikipedia.org/w/index.php?title=Rapid_eye_movement_sleep&oldid=737731608>

Wikipedia contributors. "Unconscious mind." *Wikipedia, The Free Encyclopedia.* Wikipedia, The Free Encyclopedia, 29 Aug. 2016. Web. 30 Sep. 2016. <https://en.wikipedia.org/w/index.php?title=Unconscious_mind&oldid=736686589>

Wikipedia contributors. "Subconscious." *Wikipedia, The Free Encyclopedia.* Wikipedia, The Free Encyclopedia, 20 Sep. 2016. Web. 27 Sep. 2016. <https://en.wikipedia.org/w/index.php?title=Subconscious&oldid=740274411>

Wikipedia contributors. "Lucid dream." *Wikipedia, The Free Encyclopedia.* Wikipedia, The Free Encyclopedia, 11 Sep. 2016. Web. 21 Sep. 2016. <https://en.wikipedia.org/w/index.php?title=Lucid_dream&oldid=738920037>

Wikipedia contributors. "Humanistic psychology." *Wikipedia, The Free Encyclopedia.* Wikipedia, The Free Encyclopedia, 7 Jan. 2017. Web. 22 Feb. 2017. <https://en.wikipedia.org/w/index.php?title=Humanistic_psychology&oldid=758783720>

Wikipedia contributors. "Martial arts." *Wikipedia, The Free Encyclopedia.* Wikipedia, The Free Encyclopedia, 15 Feb. 2017. Web. 24 Feb. 2017. <https://en.wikipedia.org/w/index.php?title=Martial_arts&oldid=765602569>

Wikipedia contributors. "Transpersonal psychology." *Wikipedia, The Free Encyclopedia.* Wikipedia, The Free Encyclopedia, 4 Feb. 2017. Web. 22 Feb. 2017. <https://en.wikipedia.org/w/index.php?title=Transpersonal_psychology&oldid=763651069>

Chapter Six

Wikipedia contributors. "Dualism (philosophy of mind)." *Wikipedia, The Free Encyclopedia.* Wikipedia, The Free Encyclopedia, 11 Oct. 2016. Web. 20 Oct. 2016.
<https://en.wikipedia.org/w/index.php?title=Dualism_(philosophy_of_mind)&oldid=743888371>

Concept Progress

Wikipedia contributors. "The unanswered questions." *Wikipedia, The Free Encyclopedia.* Wikipedia, The Free Encyclopedia, 21 Jul. 2016. Web. 23 Feb. 2017. <https://en.wikipedia.org/w/index.php?title=The_unanswered_questions&oldid=730925198>

Wikipedia contributors. "Gautama Buddha." *Wikipedia, The Free Encyclopedia.* Wikipedia, The Free Encyclopedia, 9 Oct. 2016. Web. 11 Oct. 2016. <https://en.wikipedia.org/w/index.php?title=Gautama_Buddha&oldid=743407766>

Wikipedia contributors. "Buddhist meditation." *Wikipedia, The Free Encyclopedia.* Wikipedia, The Free Encyclopedia, 10 Oct. 2016. Web. 27 Oct. 2016. <https://en.wikipedia.org/w/index.php?title=Buddhist_meditation&oldid=743585218>

Wikipedia contributors. "Buddhism." *Wikipedia, The Free Encyclopedia.* Wikipedia, The Free Encyclopedia, 26 Sep. 2016. Web. 11 Oct. 2016. <https://en.wikipedia.org/w/index.php?title=Buddhism&oldid=741245033>

Wikipedia contributors. "Buddhism and science." *Wikipedia, The Free Encyclopedia.* Wikipedia, The Free Encyclopedia, 18 Oct. 2016. Web. 19 Oct. 2016. <https://en.wikipedia.org/w/index.php?title=Buddhism_and_science&oldid=744895378>

Wikipedia contributors. "Sangha." *Wikipedia, The Free Encyclopedia.* Wikipedia, The Free Encyclopedia, 11 Oct. 2016. Web. 19 Oct. 2016. <https://en.wikipedia.org/w/index.php?title=Sangha&oldid=743865529>

Wikipedia contributors. "Attention." *Wikipedia, The Free Encyclopedia.* Wikipedia, The Free Encyclopedia, 21 Sep. 2016. Web. 19 Oct. 2016. <https://en.wikipedia.org/w/index.php?title=Attention&oldid=740467510>

Wikipedia contributors. "Breathing." *Wikipedia, The Free Encyclopedia.* Wikipedia, The Free Encyclopedia, 10 Oct. 2016. Web. 11 Oct. 2016. <https://en.wikipedia.org/w/index.php?title=Breathing&oldid=743621214>

Wikipedia contributors. "Anapanasati." *Wikipedia, The Free Encyclopedia.* Wikipedia, The Free Encyclopedia, 8 Jul. 2016. Web. 11 Oct. 2016. <https://en.wikipedia.org/w/index.php?title=Anapanasati&oldid=728966613>

Wikipedia contributors. "Self-realization." *Wikipedia, The Free Encyclopedia.* Wikipedia, The Free Encyclopedia, 31 Aug. 2016. Web. 19 Oct. 2016. <https://en.wikipedia.org/w/index.php?title=Self-realization&oldid=737041575>

Wikipedia contributors. "Mind-wandering" *Wikipedia, The Free Encyclopedia.* Wikipedia, The Free Encyclopedia, 4 Jul. 2016. Web. 26 Oct. 2016. <https://en.wikipedia.org/w/index.php?title=Mind-wandering&oldid=728306105>

Wikipedia contributors. "Vipassana." *Wikipedia, The Free Encyclopedia.* Wikipedia, The Free Encyclopedia, 25 Sep. 2016. Web. 11 Oct. 2016. <https://en.wikipedia.org/w/index.php?title=Vipassan%C4%81&oldid=741138196>

Wikipedia contributors. "Complex (psychology)." *Wikipedia, The Free Encyclopedia.* Wikipedia, The Free Encyclopedia, 5 Oct. 2016. Web. 11 Oct. 2016. <https://en.wikipedia.org/w/index.php?title=Complex_(psychology)&oldid=742793191>

Wikipedia contributors. "Buddhism and psychology." *Wikipedia, The Free Encyclopedia.* Wikipedia, The Free Encyclopedia, 24 Sep. 2016. Web. 19 Oct. 2016. <https://en.wikipedia.org/w/index.php?title=Buddhism_and_psychology&oldid=741027887>

Wikipedia contributors. "Ledi Sayadaw." *Wikipedia, The Free Encyclopedia.* Wikipedia, The Free Encyclopedia, 28 May. 2016. Web. 11 Oct. 2016. <https://en.wikipedia.org/w/index.php?title=Ledi_Sayadaw&oldid=722416086>

Wikipedia contributors. "Ba Khin." *Wikipedia, The Free Encyclopedia.* Wikipedia, The Free Encyclopedia, 24 Aug. 2016. Web. 11 Oct. 2016. <https://en.wikipedia.org/w/index.php?title=Ba_Khin&oldid=735930024>

Wikipedia contributors. "Vipassana movement." *Wikipedia, The Free Encyclopedia.* Wikipedia, The Free Encyclopedia, 7 Feb. 2017. Web. 13 Feb. 2017. <https://en.wikipedia.org/w/index.php?title=Vipassana_movement&oldid=764120057>

Wikipedia contributors. "Pleasure." *Wikipedia, The Free Encyclopedia.* Wikipedia, The Free Encyclopedia, 13 Sep. 2016. Web. 25 Oct. 2016. <https://en.wikipedia.org/w/index.php?title=Pleasure&oldid=739220941>

Wikipedia contributors. "Sadness." *Wikipedia, The Free Encyclopedia.* Wikipedia, The Free Encyclopedia, 24 Oct. 2016. Web. 25 Oct. 2016. <https://en.wikipedia.org/w/index.php?title=Sadness&oldid=746034243>

Wikipedia contributors. "Feeling." *Wikipedia, The Free Encyclopedia*. Wikipedia, The Free Encyclopedia, 6 Oct. 2016. Web. 11 Oct. 2016. <https://en.wikipedia.org/w/index.php?title=Feeling&oldid=742834986>

Wikipedia contributors. "Vedana." *Wikipedia, The Free Encyclopedia*. Wikipedia, The Free Encyclopedia, 20 Oct. 2016. Web. 25 Oct. 2016. <https://en.wikipedia.org/w/index.php?title=Vedan%C4%81&oldid=745278548>

Wikipedia contributors. "Suffering." *Wikipedia, The Free Encyclopedia*. Wikipedia, The Free Encyclopedia, 3 Oct. 2016. Web. 11 Oct. 2016. <https://en.wikipedia.org/w/index.php?title=Suffering&oldid=742447378>

Wikipedia contributors. "Delusion." *Wikipedia, The Free Encyclopedia*. Wikipedia, The Free Encyclopedia, 6 Oct. 2016. Web. 11 Oct. 2016. <https://en.wikipedia.org/w/index.php?title=Delusion&oldid=742846423>

Wikipedia contributors. "Perception." *Wikipedia, The Free Encyclopedia*. Wikipedia, The Free Encyclopedia, 1 Sep. 2016. Web. 11 Oct. 2016. <https://en.wikipedia.org/w/index.php?title=Perception&oldid=737212496>

Wikipedia contributors. "Two truths doctrine." *Wikipedia, The Free Encyclopedia*. Wikipedia, The Free Encyclopedia, 26 Sep. 2016. Web. 20 Oct. 2016. <https://en.wikipedia.org/w/index.php?title=Two_truths_doctrine&oldid=741258346>

Wikipedia contributors. "Maya (illusion)." *Wikipedia, The Free Encyclopedia*. Wikipedia, The Free Encyclopedia, 15 Oct. 2016. Web. 21 Oct. 2016. <https://en.wikipedia.org/w/index.php?title=Maya_(illusion)&oldid=744539641>

Wikipedia contributors. "Affect (psychology)." *Wikipedia, The Free Encyclopedia*. Wikipedia, The Free Encyclopedia, 5 Oct. 2016. Web. 26 Oct. 2016. <https://en.wikipedia.org/w/index.php?title=Affect_(psychology)&oldid=742670784>

Wikipedia contributors. "Avidya (Buddhism)." *Wikipedia, The Free Encyclopedia*. Wikipedia, The Free Encyclopedia, 23 Sep. 2016. Web. 11 Oct. 2016. <https://en.wikipedia.org/w/index.php?title=Avidy%C4%81_(Buddhism)&oldid=740768154>

Wikipedia contributors. "Equanimity." *Wikipedia, The Free Encyclopedia*. Wikipedia, The Free Encyclopedia, 11 Oct. 2016. Web. 11 Oct. 2016. <https://en.wikipedia.org/w/index.php?title=Equanimity&oldid=743868168>

Wikipedia contributors. "Middle Way." *Wikipedia, The Free Encyclopedia*. Wikipedia, The Free Encyclopedia, 9 Jul. 2016. Web. 20 Oct. 2016. <https://en.wikipedia.org/w/index.php?title=Middle_Way&oldid=729062393>

Wikipedia contributors. "Impermanence." *Wikipedia, The Free Encyclopedia*. Wikipedia, The Free Encyclopedia, 3 Oct. 2016. Web. 13 Oct. 2016. <https://en.wikipedia.org/w/index.php?title=Impermanence&oldid=742342086>

Wikipedia contributors. "DNA replication." *Wikipedia, The Free Encyclopedia*. Wikipedia, The Free Encyclopedia, 12 Oct. 2016. Web. 20 Oct. 2016. <https://en.wikipedia.org/w/index.php?title=DNA_replication&oldid=744049647>

Wikipedia contributors. "Human migration." *Wikipedia, The Free Encyclopedia*. Wikipedia, The Free Encyclopedia, 16 Oct. 2016. Web. 20 Oct. 2016. <https://en.wikipedia.org/w/index.php?title=Human_migration&oldid=744678364>

Wikipedia contributors. "Mood (psychology)." *Wikipedia, The Free Encyclopedia*. Wikipedia, The Free Encyclopedia, 3 Oct. 2016. Web. 13 Oct. 2016. <https://en.wikipedia.org/w/index.php?title=Mood_(psychology)&oldid=742469093>

Wikipedia contributors. "Change (philosophy)." *Wikipedia, The Free Encyclopedia*. Wikipedia, The Free Encyclopedia, 25 Jun. 2016. Web. 13 Oct. 2016. <https://en.wikipedia.org/w/index.php?title=Change_(philosophy)&oldid=726945733>

Wikipedia contributors. "Experiential knowledge." *Wikipedia, The Free Encyclopedia*. Wikipedia, The Free Encyclopedia, 2 Oct. 2016. Web. 20 Oct. 2016. <https://en.wikipedia.org/w/index.php?title=Experiential_knowledge&oldid=742273860>

Wikipedia contributors. "Reality in Buddhism." *Wikipedia, The Free Encyclopedia*. Wikipedia, The Free Encyclopedia, 29 Aug. 2016. Web. 21 Oct. 2016. <https://en.wikipedia.org/w/index.php?title=Reality_in_Buddhism&oldid=736717739>

Wikipedia contributors. "Buddhist philosophy." *Wikipedia, The Free Encyclopedia*. Wikipedia, The Free Encyclopedia, 11 Oct. 2016. Web. 13 Oct. 2016. <https://en.wikipedia.org/w/index.php?title=Buddhist_philosophy&oldid=743743346>

Concept Progress

Wikipedia contributors. "Experience." *Wikipedia, The Free Encyclopedia*. Wikipedia, The Free Encyclopedia, 15 Jun. 2016. Web. 13 Oct. 2016. <https://en.wikipedia.org/w/index.php?title=Experience&oldid=725371721>

Wikipedia contributors. "Meditation." *Wikipedia, The Free Encyclopedia*. Wikipedia, The Free Encyclopedia, 13 Oct. 2016. Web. 13 Oct. 2016. <https://en.wikipedia.org/w/index.php?title=Meditation&oldid=744135746>

Wikipedia contributors. "Buddhism and evolution." *Wikipedia, The Free Encyclopedia*. Wikipedia, The Free Encyclopedia, 30 Aug. 2016. Web. 19 Oct. 2016. <https://en.wikipedia.org/w/index.php?title=Buddhism_and_evolution&oldid=736925600>

Wikipedia contributors. "Wisdom." *Wikipedia, The Free Encyclopedia*. Wikipedia, The Free Encyclopedia, 6 Oct. 2016. Web. 13 Oct. 2016. <https://en.wikipedia.org/w/index.php?title=Wisdom&oldid=742825265>

Wikipedia contributors. "Somatosensory system." *Wikipedia, The Free Encyclopedia*. Wikipedia, The Free Encyclopedia, 9 Oct. 2016. Web. 13 Oct. 2016. <https://en.wikipedia.org/w/index.php?title=Somatosensory_system&oldid=743336883>

Wikipedia contributors. "Olfaction." *Wikipedia, The Free Encyclopedia*. Wikipedia, The Free Encyclopedia, 21 Sep. 2016. Web. 13 Oct. 2016. <https://en.wikipedia.org/w/index.php?title=Olfaction&oldid=740428900>

Wikipedia contributors. "Hearing." *Wikipedia, The Free Encyclopedia*. Wikipedia, The Free Encyclopedia, 10 Oct. 2016. Web. 13 Oct. 2016. <https://en.wikipedia.org/w/index.php?title=Hearing&oldid=743637494>

Wikipedia contributors. "Taste." *Wikipedia, The Free Encyclopedia*. Wikipedia, The Free Encyclopedia, 11 Oct. 2016. Web. 14 Oct. 2016. <https://en.wikipedia.org/w/index.php?title=Taste&oldid=743805989>

Wikipedia contributors. "Upadana." *Wikipedia, The Free Encyclopedia*. Wikipedia, The Free Encyclopedia, 9 Oct. 2016. Web. 26 Oct. 2016. <https://en.wikipedia.org/w/index.php?title=Up%C4%81d%C4%81na&oldid=743305164>

Wikipedia contributors. "Illusion." *Wikipedia, The Free Encyclopedia*. Wikipedia, The Free Encyclopedia, 13 Sep. 2016. Web. 11 Oct. 2016. <https://en.wikipedia.org/w/index.php?title=Illusion&oldid=739157969>

Wikipedia contributors. "Money." *Wikipedia, The Free Encyclopedia*. Wikipedia, The Free Encyclopedia, 9 Sep. 2016. Web. 14 Oct. 2016. <https://en.wikipedia.org/w/index.php?title=Money&oldid=738492636>

Wikipedia contributors. "Marriage." *Wikipedia, The Free Encyclopedia*. Wikipedia, The Free Encyclopedia, 11 Oct. 2016. Web. 14 Oct. 2016. <https://en.wikipedia.org/w/index.php?title=Marriage&oldid=743894786>

Wikipedia contributors. "Ritual." *Wikipedia, The Free Encyclopedia*. Wikipedia, The Free Encyclopedia, 13 Oct. 2016. Web. 14 Oct. 2016. <https://en.wikipedia.org/w/index.php?title=Ritual&oldid=744091864>

Wikipedia contributors. "Invention." *Wikipedia, The Free Encyclopedia*. Wikipedia, The Free Encyclopedia, 23 Oct. 2016. Web. 26 Oct. 2016. <https://en.wikipedia.org/w/index.php?title=Invention&oldid=745799121>

Wikipedia contributors. "Human rights." *Wikipedia, The Free Encyclopedia*. Wikipedia, The Free Encyclopedia, 12 Oct. 2016. Web. 14 Oct. 2016. <https://en.wikipedia.org/w/index.php?title=Human_rights&oldid=743922336>

Wikipedia contributors. "List of paradoxes." *Wikipedia, The Free Encyclopedia*. Wikipedia, The Free Encyclopedia, 11 Oct. 2016. Web. 27 Oct. 2016. <https://en.wikipedia.org/w/index.php?title=List_of_paradoxes&oldid=743809599>

Wikipedia contributors. "Optical illusion." *Wikipedia, The Free Encyclopedia*. Wikipedia, The Free Encyclopedia, 2 Oct. 2016. Web. 27 Oct. 2016. <https://en.wikipedia.org/w/index.php?title=Optical_illusion&oldid=742226803>

Wikipedia contributors. "Relativity of simultaneity." *Wikipedia, The Free Encyclopedia*. Wikipedia, The Free Encyclopedia, 24 Aug. 2016. Web. 22 Nov. 2016. <https://en.wikipedia.org/w/index.php?title=Relativity_of_simultaneity&oldid=735972412>

Wikipedia contributors. "Four Noble Truths." *Wikipedia, The Free Encyclopedia*. Wikipedia, The Free Encyclopedia, 4 Oct. 2016. Web. 25 Oct. 2016. <https://en.wikipedia.org/w/index.php?title=Four_Noble_Truths&oldid=742538592>

Wikipedia contributors. "Evolutionary psychology of language." *Wikipedia, The Free Encyclopedia.* Wikipedia, The Free Encyclopedia, 14 Sep. 2016. Web. 14 Oct. 2016.
<https://en.wikipedia.org/w/index.php?title=Evolutionary_psychology_of_language&oldid=739444207>

Wikipedia contributors. "A picture is worth a thousand words." *Wikipedia, The Free Encyclopedia.* Wikipedia, The Free Encyclopedia, 10 Oct. 2016. Web. 17 Oct. 2016.
<https://en.wikipedia.org/w/index.php?title=A_picture_is_worth_a_thousand_words&oldid=743666985>

Wikipedia contributors. "Idiom." *Wikipedia, The Free Encyclopedia.* Wikipedia, The Free Encyclopedia, 27 Oct. 2016. Web. 28 Oct. 2016. <https://en.wikipedia.org/w/index.php?title=Idiom&oldid=746494736>

Wikipedia contributors. "Metaphor." *Wikipedia, The Free Encyclopedia.* Wikipedia, The Free Encyclopedia, 24 Oct. 2016. Web. 28 Oct. 2016. <https://en.wikipedia.org/w/index.php?title=Metaphor&oldid=745897355>

Wikipedia contributors. "Outline of thought." *Wikipedia, The Free Encyclopedia.* Wikipedia, The Free Encyclopedia, 17 Oct. 2016. Web. 27 Oct. 2016. <https://en.wikipedia.org/w/index.php?title=Outline_of_thought&oldid=744736002>

Wikipedia contributors. "Emotion." *Wikipedia, The Free Encyclopedia.* Wikipedia, The Free Encyclopedia, 12 Oct. 2016. Web. 25 Oct. 2016. <https://en.wikipedia.org/w/index.php?title=Emotion&oldid=744017735>

Wikipedia contributors. "Frequency." *Wikipedia, The Free Encyclopedia.* Wikipedia, The Free Encyclopedia, 10 Oct. 2016. Web. 17 Oct. 2016. <https://en.wikipedia.org/w/index.php?title=Frequency&oldid=743642552>

Wikipedia contributors. "Force." *Wikipedia, The Free Encyclopedia.* Wikipedia, The Free Encyclopedia, 9 Jun. 2016. Web. 17 Oct. 2016. <https://en.wikipedia.org/w/index.php?title=Force&oldid=724423501>

Wikipedia contributors. "Zen." *Wikipedia, The Free Encyclopedia.* Wikipedia, The Free Encyclopedia, 12 Oct. 2016. Web. 18 Oct. 2016. <https://en.wikipedia.org/w/index.php?title=Zen&oldid=744014408>

Wikipedia contributors. "Samadhi." *Wikipedia, The Free Encyclopedia.* Wikipedia, The Free Encyclopedia, 25 Sep. 2016. Web. 27 Oct. 2016. <https://en.wikipedia.org/w/index.php?title=Samadhi&oldid=741085384>

Wikipedia contributors. "Scholarly method." *Wikipedia, The Free Encyclopedia.* Wikipedia, The Free Encyclopedia, 26 Aug. 2016. Web. 18 Oct. 2016. <https://en.wikipedia.org/w/index.php?title=Scholarly_method&oldid=736323941>

Wikipedia contributors. "Yogi." *Wikipedia, The Free Encyclopedia.* Wikipedia, The Free Encyclopedia, 16 Oct. 2016. Web. 18 Oct. 2016. <https://en.wikipedia.org/w/index.php?title=Yogi&oldid=744652584>

Wikipedia contributors. "Present." *Wikipedia, The Free Encyclopedia.* Wikipedia, The Free Encyclopedia, 24 Sep. 2016. Web. 18 Oct. 2016. <https://en.wikipedia.org/w/index.php?title=Present&oldid=740949249>

Wikipedia contributors. "Anatta." *Wikipedia, The Free Encyclopedia.* Wikipedia, The Free Encyclopedia, 23 Oct. 2016. Web. 28 Oct. 2016. <https://en.wikipedia.org/w/index.php?title=Anatta&oldid=745870387>

Wikipedia contributors. "Hatha yoga." *Wikipedia, The Free Encyclopedia.* Wikipedia, The Free Encyclopedia, 15 Oct. 2016. Web. 27 Oct. 2016. <https://en.wikipedia.org/w/index.php?title=Hatha_yoga&oldid=744432637>

Wikipedia contributors. "Particle physics." *Wikipedia, The Free Encyclopedia.* Wikipedia, The Free Encyclopedia, 7 Sep. 2016. Web. 18 Oct. 2016. <https://en.wikipedia.org/w/index.php?title=Particle_physics&oldid=738262604>

Wikipedia contributors. "Superstring theory." *Wikipedia, The Free Encyclopedia.* Wikipedia, The Free Encyclopedia, 7 Aug. 2016. Web. 18 Oct. 2016. <https://en.wikipedia.org/w/index.php?title=Superstring_theory&oldid=733400035>

Wikipedia contributors. "S. N. Goenka." *Wikipedia, The Free Encyclopedia.* Wikipedia, The Free Encyclopedia, 9 Oct. 2016. Web. 18 Oct. 2016. <https://en.wikipedia.org/w/index.php?title=S._N._Goenka&oldid=743500050>

Concept Progress

Wikipedia contributors. "Prison contemplative programs." *Wikipedia, The Free Encyclopedia.* Wikipedia, The Free Encyclopedia, 2 Aug. 2015. Web. 24 Oct. 2016.
<https://en.wikipedia.org/w/index.php?title=Prison_contemplative_programs&oldid=674242141>

Wikipedia contributors. "Introspection." *Wikipedia, The Free Encyclopedia.* Wikipedia, The Free Encyclopedia, 1 Oct. 2016. Web. 28 Oct. 2016. <https://en.wikipedia.org/w/index.php?title=Introspection&oldid=742140384>

Wikipedia contributors. "Buddhist ethics." *Wikipedia, The Free Encyclopedia.* Wikipedia, The Free Encyclopedia, 23 Sep. 2016. Web. 24 Oct. 2016. <https://en.wikipedia.org/w/index.php?title=Buddhist_ethics&oldid=740777683>

Wikipedia contributors. "Dharma." *Wikipedia, The Free Encyclopedia.* Wikipedia, The Free Encyclopedia, 14 Oct. 2016. Web. 21 Oct. 2016. <https://en.wikipedia.org/w/index.php?title=Dharma&oldid=744298477>

Wikipedia contributors. "Dukkha." *Wikipedia, The Free Encyclopedia.* Wikipedia, The Free Encyclopedia, 27 Sep. 2016. Web. 21 Oct. 2016. <https://en.wikipedia.org/w/index.php?title=Dukkha&oldid=741425427>

Wikipedia contributors. "Good and evil." *Wikipedia, The Free Encyclopedia.* Wikipedia, The Free Encyclopedia, 19 Oct. 2016. Web. 24 Oct. 2016. <https://en.wikipedia.org/w/index.php?title=Good_and_evil&oldid=745175007>

Wikipedia contributors. "Buddhism and Western philosophy." *Wikipedia, The Free Encyclopedia.* Wikipedia, The Free Encyclopedia, 10 Nov. 2016. Web. 23 Feb. 2017.
<https://en.wikipedia.org/w/index.php?title=Buddhism_and_Western_philosophy&oldid=748763410>

Wikipedia contributors. "Buddhist monasticism." *Wikipedia, The Free Encyclopedia.* Wikipedia, The Free Encyclopedia, 1 Dec. 2016. Web. 11 Feb. 2017. <https://en.wikipedia.org/w/index.php?title=Buddhist_monasticism&oldid=752391795>

Wikipedia contributors. "Householder (Buddhism)." *Wikipedia, The Free Encyclopedia.* Wikipedia, The Free Encyclopedia, 13 Oct. 2016. Web. 18 Oct. 2016. <https://en.wikipedia.org/w/index.php?title=Householder_(Buddhism)&oldid=744215039>

Wikipedia contributors. "Research on meditation." *Wikipedia, The Free Encyclopedia.* Wikipedia, The Free Encyclopedia, 31 Oct. 2016. Web. 2 Nov. 2016. <https://en.wikipedia.org/w/index.php?title=Research_on_meditation&oldid=747032660>

Wikipedia contributors. "Stress (biology)." *Wikipedia, The Free Encyclopedia.* Wikipedia, The Free Encyclopedia, 28 Sep. 2016. Web. 18 Oct. 2016. <https://en.wikipedia.org/w/index.php?title=Stress_(biology)&oldid=741516714>

Wikipedia contributors. "Self-confidence." *Wikipedia, The Free Encyclopedia.* Wikipedia, The Free Encyclopedia, 18 Oct. 2016. Web. 25 Oct. 2016. <https://en.wikipedia.org/w/index.php?title=Self-confidence&oldid=744903551>

Wikipedia contributors. "Superhero." *Wikipedia, The Free Encyclopedia.* Wikipedia, The Free Encyclopedia, 18 Oct. 2016. Web. 18 Oct. 2016. <https://en.wikipedia.org/w/index.php?title=Superhero&oldid=745029012>

Wikipedia contributors. "Michael Phelps." *Wikipedia, The Free Encyclopedia.* Wikipedia, The Free Encyclopedia, 16 Feb. 2017. Web. 18 Feb. 2017. <https://en.wikipedia.org/w/index.php?title=Michael_Phelps&oldid=765729168>

Wikipedia contributors. "Stephen Hawking." *Wikipedia, The Free Encyclopedia.* Wikipedia, The Free Encyclopedia, 8 Oct. 2016. Web. 19 Oct. 2016. <https://en.wikipedia.org/w/index.php?title=Stephen_Hawking&oldid=743173340>

Wikipedia contributors. "14th Dalai Lama." *Wikipedia, The Free Encyclopedia.* Wikipedia, The Free Encyclopedia, 5 Oct. 2016. Web. 19 Oct. 2016. <https://en.wikipedia.org/w/index.php?title=14th_Dalai_Lama&oldid=742758007>

Wikipedia contributors. "List of superhuman features and abilities in fiction." *Wikipedia, The Free Encyclopedia.* Wikipedia, The Free Encyclopedia, 14 Oct. 2016. Web. 25 Oct. 2016.
<https://en.wikipedia.org/w/index.php?title=List_of_superhuman_features_and_abilities_in_fiction&oldid=744349154>

Wikipedia contributors. "Metta." *Wikipedia, The Free Encyclopedia.* Wikipedia, The Free Encyclopedia, 4 Oct. 2016. Web. 19 Oct. 2016. <https://en.wikipedia.org/w/index.php?title=Mett%C4%81&oldid=742525544>

Wikipedia contributors. "Compassion." *Wikipedia, The Free Encyclopedia.* Wikipedia, The Free Encyclopedia, 17 Sep. 2016. Web. 19 Oct. 2016. <https://en.wikipedia.org/w/index.php?title=Compassion&oldid=739870538>

Wikipedia contributors. "Vibration." *Wikipedia, The Free Encyclopedia.* Wikipedia, The Free Encyclopedia, 17 Oct. 2016. Web. 19 Oct. 2016. <https://en.wikipedia.org/w/index.php?title=Vibration&oldid=744788647>

Wikipedia contributors. "Neurobiological effects of physical exercise." *Wikipedia, The Free Encyclopedia.* Wikipedia, The Free Encyclopedia, 6 Sep. 2016. Web. 19 Oct. 2016.
<https://en.wikipedia.org/w/index.php?title=Neurobiological_effects_of_physical_exercise&oldid=738050193>

Wikipedia contributors. "Enlightenment in Buddhism." *Wikipedia, The Free Encyclopedia.* Wikipedia, The Free Encyclopedia, 11 Oct. 2016. Web. 19 Oct. 2016.
<https://en.wikipedia.org/w/index.php?title=Enlightenment_in_Buddhism&oldid=743769669>

Wikipedia contributors. "Noble Eightfold Path." *Wikipedia, The Free Encyclopedia.* Wikipedia, The Free Encyclopedia, 11 Oct. 2016. Web. 25 Oct. 2016. <https://en.wikipedia.org/w/index.php?title=Noble_Eightfold_Path&oldid=743884204>

Wikipedia contributors. "Nirvana (Buddhism)." *Wikipedia, The Free Encyclopedia.* Wikipedia, The Free Encyclopedia, 21 Oct. 2016. Web. 21 Oct. 2016. <https://en.wikipedia.org/w/index.php?title=Nirvana_(Buddhism)&oldid=745419315>

Chapter Seven

Wikipedia contributors. "Age of the universe." *Wikipedia, The Free Encyclopedia.* Wikipedia, The Free Encyclopedia, 26 Oct. 2016. Web. 2 Nov. 2016. <https://en.wikipedia.org/w/index.php?title=Age_of_the_universe&oldid=746274175>

Wikipedia contributors. "Age of the Earth." *Wikipedia, The Free Encyclopedia.* Wikipedia, The Free Encyclopedia, 27 Oct. 2016. Web. 2 Nov. 2016. <https://en.wikipedia.org/w/index.php?title=Age_of_the_Earth&oldid=746469730>

Wikipedia contributors. "4th millennium." *Wikipedia, The Free Encyclopedia.* Wikipedia, The Free Encyclopedia, 16 Sep. 2016. Web. 17 Nov. 2016. <https://en.wikipedia.org/w/index.php?title=4th_millennium&oldid=739721787>

Wikipedia contributors. "26th century." *Wikipedia, The Free Encyclopedia.* Wikipedia, The Free Encyclopedia, 15 Nov. 2016. Web. 17 Nov. 2016. <https://en.wikipedia.org/w/index.php?title=26th_century&oldid=749685739>

Wikipedia contributors. "Ancient Greece." *Wikipedia, The Free Encyclopedia.* Wikipedia, The Free Encyclopedia, 12 Oct. 2016. Web. 3 Nov. 2016. <https://en.wikipedia.org/w/index.php?title=Ancient_Greece&oldid=744008294>

Wikipedia contributors. "Modernity." *Wikipedia, The Free Encyclopedia.* Wikipedia, The Free Encyclopedia, 29 Sep. 2016. Web. 3 Nov. 2016. <https://en.wikipedia.org/w/index.php?title=Modernity&oldid=741688688>

Wikipedia contributors. "Chimera (mythology)." *Wikipedia, The Free Encyclopedia.* Wikipedia, The Free Encyclopedia, 24 Oct. 2016. Web. 3 Nov. 2016. <https://en.wikipedia.org/w/index.php?title=Chimera_(mythology)&oldid=745969056>

Wikipedia contributors. "Smartphone." *Wikipedia, The Free Encyclopedia.* Wikipedia, The Free Encyclopedia, 3 Nov. 2016. Web. 3 Nov. 2016. <https://en.wikipedia.org/w/index.php?title=Smartphone&oldid=747617319>

Wikipedia contributors. "22nd century." *Wikipedia, The Free Encyclopedia.* Wikipedia, The Free Encyclopedia, 17 Nov. 2016. Web. 17 Nov. 2016. <https://en.wikipedia.org/w/index.php?title=22nd_century&oldid=750108972>

Wikipedia contributors. "List of emerging technologies." *Wikipedia, The Free Encyclopedia.* Wikipedia, The Free Encyclopedia, 1 Nov. 2016. Web. 30 Nov. 2016.
<https://en.wikipedia.org/w/index.php?title=List_of_emerging_technologies&oldid=747285844>

Wikipedia contributors. "Alpha Centauri." *Wikipedia, The Free Encyclopedia.* Wikipedia, The Free Encyclopedia, 30 Oct. 2016. Web. 3 Nov. 2016. <https://en.wikipedia.org/w/index.php?title=Alpha_Centauri&oldid=746978672>

Wikipedia contributors. "Andromeda Galaxy." *Wikipedia, The Free Encyclopedia.* Wikipedia, The Free Encyclopedia, 3 Nov. 2016. Web. 3 Nov. 2016. <https://en.wikipedia.org/w/index.php?title=Andromeda_Galaxy&oldid=747613538>

CONCEPT PROGRESS

Wikipedia contributors. "Big Rip." *Wikipedia, The Free Encyclopedia.* Wikipedia, The Free Encyclopedia, 23 Oct. 2016. Web. 14 Nov. 2016. <https://en.wikipedia.org/w/index.php?title=Big_Rip&oldid=745798094>

Wikipedia contributors. "Big Crunch." *Wikipedia, The Free Encyclopedia.* Wikipedia, The Free Encyclopedia, 14 Jul. 2016. Web. 26 Jul. 2016. <https://en.wikipedia.org/w/index.php?title=Big_Crunch&oldid=729742208>

Wikipedia contributors. "Ultimate fate of the universe." *Wikipedia, The Free Encyclopedia.* Wikipedia, The Free Encyclopedia, 18 Sep. 2016. Web. 3 Nov. 2016.
<https://en.wikipedia.org/w/index.php?title=Ultimate_fate_of_the_universe&oldid=740003756>

Wikipedia contributors. "Future of an expanding universe." *Wikipedia, The Free Encyclopedia.* Wikipedia, The Free Encyclopedia, 26 Oct. 2016. Web. 14 Nov. 2016.
<https://en.wikipedia.org/w/index.php?title=Future_of_an_expanding_universe&oldid=746260889>

Wikipedia contributors. "Psychotherapy." *Wikipedia, The Free Encyclopedia.* Wikipedia, The Free Encyclopedia, 18 Oct. 2016. Web. 3 Nov. 2016. <https://en.wikipedia.org/w/index.php?title=Psychotherapy&oldid=744936339>

Wikipedia contributors. "Existential therapy." *Wikipedia, The Free Encyclopedia.* Wikipedia, The Free Encyclopedia, 1 Dec. 2016. Web. 1 Dec. 2016. <https://en.wikipedia.org/w/index.php?title=Existential_therapy&oldid=752403727>

Wikipedia contributors. "Biological constraints." *Wikipedia, The Free Encyclopedia.* Wikipedia, The Free Encyclopedia, 4 Oct. 2016. Web. 30 Nov. 2016. <https://en.wikipedia.org/w/index.php?title=Biological_constraints&oldid=742510447>

Wikipedia contributors. "Biosphere." *Wikipedia, The Free Encyclopedia.* Wikipedia, The Free Encyclopedia, 21 Aug. 2016. Web. 7 Sep. 2016. <https://en.wikipedia.org/w/index.php?title=Biosphere&oldid=735579701>

Wikipedia contributors. "Atlas (mythology)." *Wikipedia, The Free Encyclopedia.* Wikipedia, The Free Encyclopedia, 1 Nov. 2016. Web. 3 Nov. 2016. <https://en.wikipedia.org/w/index.php?title=Atlas_(mythology)&oldid=747352581>

Wikipedia contributors. "Inertial frame of reference." *Wikipedia, The Free Encyclopedia.* Wikipedia, The Free Encyclopedia, 23 Aug. 2016. Web. 3 Nov. 2016. <https://en.wikipedia.org/w/index.php?title=Inertial_frame_of_reference&oldid=735892649>

Wikipedia contributors. "Omnipotence." *Wikipedia, The Free Encyclopedia.* Wikipedia, The Free Encyclopedia, 21 Oct. 2016. Web. 3 Nov. 2016. <https://en.wikipedia.org/w/index.php?title=Omnipotence&oldid=745549813>

Wikipedia contributors. "Climate of the Arctic." *Wikipedia, The Free Encyclopedia.* Wikipedia, The Free Encyclopedia, 29 Oct. 2016. Web. 14 Nov. 2016. <https://en.wikipedia.org/w/index.php?title=Climate_of_the_Arctic&oldid=746832280>

Wikipedia contributors. "Climate of Mars." *Wikipedia, The Free Encyclopedia.* Wikipedia, The Free Encyclopedia, 14 Nov. 2016. Web. 14 Nov. 2016. <https://en.wikipedia.org/w/index.php?title=Climate_of_Mars&oldid=749429876>

Wikipedia contributors. "Sahara." *Wikipedia, The Free Encyclopedia.* Wikipedia, The Free Encyclopedia, 7 Nov. 2016. Web. 14 Nov. 2016. <https://en.wikipedia.org/w/index.php?title=Sahara&oldid=748296154>

Wikipedia contributors. "Venus." *Wikipedia, The Free Encyclopedia.* Wikipedia, The Free Encyclopedia, 9 Oct. 2016. Web. 3 Nov. 2016. <https://en.wikipedia.org/w/index.php?title=Venus&oldid=743362963>

Wikipedia contributors. "Solar wind." *Wikipedia, The Free Encyclopedia.* Wikipedia, The Free Encyclopedia, 12 Nov. 2016. Web. 15 Nov. 2016. <https://en.wikipedia.org/w/index.php?title=Solar_wind&oldid=749110479>

Wikipedia contributors. "Black hole." *Wikipedia, The Free Encyclopedia.* Wikipedia, The Free Encyclopedia, 25 Sep. 2016. Web. 3 Nov. 2016. <https://en.wikipedia.org/w/index.php?title=Black_hole&oldid=741060535>

Wikipedia contributors. "Galactic Center." *Wikipedia, The Free Encyclopedia.* Wikipedia, The Free Encyclopedia, 4 Oct. 2016. Web. 15 Nov. 2016. <https://en.wikipedia.org/w/index.php?title=Galactic_Center&oldid=742580532>

Wikipedia contributors. "Atomic bombings of Hiroshima and Nagasaki." *Wikipedia, The Free Encyclopedia*. Wikipedia, The Free Encyclopedia, 12 Nov. 2016. Web. 15 Nov. 2016.
<https://en.wikipedia.org/w/index.php?title=Atomic_bombings_of_Hiroshima_and_Nagasaki&oldid=749044538>

Wikipedia contributors. "Supernova." *Wikipedia, The Free Encyclopedia*. Wikipedia, The Free Encyclopedia, 15 Nov. 2016. Web. 15 Nov. 2016. <https://en.wikipedia.org/w/index.php?title=Supernova&oldid=749587469>

Wikipedia contributors. "Pegasus (constellation)." *Wikipedia, The Free Encyclopedia*. Wikipedia, The Free Encyclopedia, 29 Oct. 2016. Web. 3 Nov. 2016. <https://en.wikipedia.org/w/index.php?title=Pegasus_(constellation)&oldid=746848644>

Wikipedia contributors. "Himalayas." *Wikipedia, The Free Encyclopedia*. Wikipedia, The Free Encyclopedia, 2 Nov. 2016. Web. 3 Nov. 2016. <https://en.wikipedia.org/w/index.php?title=Himalayas&oldid=747519649>

Wikipedia contributors. "Outer space." *Wikipedia, The Free Encyclopedia*. Wikipedia, The Free Encyclopedia, 28 Oct. 2016. Web. 4 Nov. 2016. <https://en.wikipedia.org/w/index.php?title=Outer_space&oldid=746538809>

Wikipedia contributors. "Aircraft." *Wikipedia, The Free Encyclopedia*. Wikipedia, The Free Encyclopedia, 9 Nov. 2016. Web. 15 Nov. 2016. <https://en.wikipedia.org/w/index.php?title=Aircraft&oldid=748602390>

Wikipedia contributors. "Sky." *Wikipedia, The Free Encyclopedia*. Wikipedia, The Free Encyclopedia, 14 Nov. 2016. Web. 18 Nov. 2016. <https://en.wikipedia.org/w/index.php?title=Sky&oldid=749416629>

Wikipedia contributors. "Spacecraft." *Wikipedia, The Free Encyclopedia*. Wikipedia, The Free Encyclopedia, 9 Nov. 2016. Web. 15 Nov. 2016. <https://en.wikipedia.org/w/index.php?title=Spacecraft&oldid=748687792>

Wikipedia contributors. "Faster-than-light." *Wikipedia, The Free Encyclopedia*. Wikipedia, The Free Encyclopedia, 3 Nov. 2016. Web. 4 Nov. 2016. <https://en.wikipedia.org/w/index.php?title=Faster-than-light&oldid=747652938>

Wikipedia contributors. "Wormhole." *Wikipedia, The Free Encyclopedia*. Wikipedia, The Free Encyclopedia, 31 Oct. 2016. Web. 4 Nov. 2016. <https://en.wikipedia.org/w/index.php?title=Wormhole&oldid=747120811>

Wikipedia contributors. "Quantum entanglement." *Wikipedia, The Free Encyclopedia*. Wikipedia, The Free Encyclopedia, 2 Nov. 2016. Web. 4 Nov. 2016. <https://en.wikipedia.org/w/index.php?title=Quantum_entanglement&oldid=747516357>

Wikipedia contributors. "Four-dimensional space." *Wikipedia, The Free Encyclopedia*. Wikipedia, The Free Encyclopedia, 6 Nov. 2016. Web. 25 Nov. 2016. <https://en.wikipedia.org/w/index.php?title=Four-dimensional_space&oldid=748145787>

Wikipedia contributors. "Physicalism." *Wikipedia, The Free Encyclopedia*. Wikipedia, The Free Encyclopedia, 29 Oct. 2016. Web. 25 Nov. 2016. <https://en.wikipedia.org/w/index.php?title=Physicalism&oldid=746819364>

Wikipedia contributors. "Dimension." *Wikipedia, The Free Encyclopedia*. Wikipedia, The Free Encyclopedia, 22 Aug. 2016. Web. 30 Aug. 2016. <https://en.wikipedia.org/w/index.php?title=Dimension&oldid=735717219>

Wikipedia contributors. "Introduction to general relativity." *Wikipedia, The Free Encyclopedia*. Wikipedia, The Free Encyclopedia, 13 Feb. 2017. Web. 16 Feb. 2017.
<https://en.wikipedia.org/w/index.php?title=Introduction_to_general_relativity&oldid=765222940>

Wikipedia contributors. "Philosophy of space and time." *Wikipedia, The Free Encyclopedia*. Wikipedia, The Free Encyclopedia, 27 Sep. 2016. Web. 18 Nov. 2016.
<https://en.wikipedia.org/w/index.php?title=Philosophy_of_space_and_time&oldid=741427723>

Wikipedia contributors. "String (physics)." *Wikipedia, The Free Encyclopedia*. Wikipedia, The Free Encyclopedia, 13 Sep. 2016. Web. 4 Nov. 2016. <https://en.wikipedia.org/w/index.php?title=String_(physics)&oldid=739220712>

Wikipedia contributors. "Pluralism (philosophy)." *Wikipedia, The Free Encyclopedia*. Wikipedia, The Free Encyclopedia, 14 Nov. 2016. Web. 25 Nov. 2016. <https://en.wikipedia.org/w/index.php?title=Pluralism_(philosophy)&oldid=749388416>

Concept Progress

Wikipedia contributors. "Philosophical realism." *Wikipedia, The Free Encyclopedia.* Wikipedia, The Free Encyclopedia, 20 Oct. 2016. Web. 21 Nov. 2016. <https://en.wikipedia.org/w/index.php?title=Philosophical_realism&oldid=745287488>

Wikipedia contributors. "Blind men and an elephant." *Wikipedia, The Free Encyclopedia.* Wikipedia, The Free Encyclopedia, 4 Nov. 2016. Web. 4 Nov. 2016. <https://en.wikipedia.org/w/index.php?title=Blind_men_and_an_elephant&oldid=747758070>

Wikipedia contributors. "Tree." *Wikipedia, The Free Encyclopedia.* Wikipedia, The Free Encyclopedia, 22 Oct. 2016. Web. 4 Nov. 2016. <https://en.wikipedia.org/w/index.php?title=Tree&oldid=745717817>

Wikipedia contributors. "Five-dimensional space." *Wikipedia, The Free Encyclopedia.* Wikipedia, The Free Encyclopedia, 5 Nov. 2016. Web. 21 Nov. 2016. <https://en.wikipedia.org/w/index.php?title=Five-dimensional_space&oldid=748020342>

Wikipedia contributors. "Absolute (philosophy)." *Wikipedia, The Free Encyclopedia.* Wikipedia, The Free Encyclopedia, 18 Nov. 2016. Web. 25 Nov. 2016. <https://en.wikipedia.org/w/index.php?title=Absolute_(philosophy)&oldid=750267438>

Wikipedia contributors. "String theory." *Wikipedia, The Free Encyclopedia.* Wikipedia, The Free Encyclopedia, 1 Nov. 2016. Web. 4 Nov. 2016. <https://en.wikipedia.org/w/index.php?title=String_theory&oldid=747364209>

Wikipedia contributors. "M-theory." *Wikipedia, The Free Encyclopedia.* Wikipedia, The Free Encyclopedia, 20 Sep. 2016. Web. 4 Nov. 2016. <https://en.wikipedia.org/w/index.php?title=M-theory&oldid=740349336>

Wikipedia contributors. "Consensus reality." *Wikipedia, The Free Encyclopedia.* Wikipedia, The Free Encyclopedia, 17 Oct. 2016. Web. 28 Nov. 2016. <https://en.wikipedia.org/w/index.php?title=Consensus_reality&oldid=744765076>

Wikipedia contributors. "Stimulus (physiology)." *Wikipedia, The Free Encyclopedia.* Wikipedia, The Free Encyclopedia, 17 Feb. 2017. Web. 23 Feb. 2017. <https://en.wikipedia.org/w/index.php?title=Stimulus_(physiology)&oldid=766046965>

Wikipedia contributors. "Monism." *Wikipedia, The Free Encyclopedia.* Wikipedia, The Free Encyclopedia, 16 Nov. 2016. Web. 18 Nov. 2016. <https://en.wikipedia.org/w/index.php?title=Monism&oldid=749845930>

Wikipedia contributors. "Omniscience." *Wikipedia, The Free Encyclopedia.* Wikipedia, The Free Encyclopedia, 31 Oct. 2016. Web. 4 Nov. 2016. <https://en.wikipedia.org/w/index.php?title=Omniscience&oldid=747154572>

Wikipedia contributors. "Polymath." *Wikipedia, The Free Encyclopedia.* Wikipedia, The Free Encyclopedia, 28 Nov. 2016. Web. 28 Nov. 2016. <https://en.wikipedia.org/w/index.php?title=Polymath&oldid=751823347>

Wikipedia contributors. "Newton's laws of motion." *Wikipedia, The Free Encyclopedia.* Wikipedia, The Free Encyclopedia, 3 Nov. 2016. Web. 28 Nov. 2016. <https://en.wikipedia.org/w/index.php?title=Newton%27s_laws_of_motion&oldid=747708155>

Wikipedia contributors. "Eternalism (philosophy of time)." *Wikipedia, The Free Encyclopedia.* Wikipedia, The Free Encyclopedia, 1 Nov. 2016. Web. 21 Nov. 2016. <https://en.wikipedia.org/w/index.php?title=Eternalism_(philosophy_of_time)&oldid=747291707>

Wikipedia contributors. "If a tree falls in a forest." *Wikipedia, The Free Encyclopedia.* Wikipedia, The Free Encyclopedia, 26 Oct. 2016. Web. 7 Nov. 2016. <https://en.wikipedia.org/w/index.php?title=If_a_tree_falls_in_a_forest&oldid=746263017>

Wikipedia contributors. "Mindfulness." *Wikipedia, The Free Encyclopedia.* Wikipedia, The Free Encyclopedia, 29 Oct. 2016. Web. 2 Nov. 2016. <https://en.wikipedia.org/w/index.php?title=Mindfulness&oldid=746831433>

Wikipedia contributors. "Omnipresence." *Wikipedia, The Free Encyclopedia.* Wikipedia, The Free Encyclopedia, 11 Oct. 2016. Web. 7 Nov. 2016. <https://en.wikipedia.org/w/index.php?title=Omnipresence&oldid=743814599>

Wikipedia contributors. "Interdimensional being." *Wikipedia, The Free Encyclopedia.* Wikipedia, The Free Encyclopedia, 3 Oct. 2016. Web. 15 Nov. 2016. <https://en.wikipedia.org/w/index.php?title=Interdimensional_being&oldid=742344965>

Wikipedia contributors. "Omnibenevolence." *Wikipedia, The Free Encyclopedia.* Wikipedia, The Free Encyclopedia, 31 Aug. 2016. Web. 7 Nov. 2016. <https://en.wikipedia.org/w/index.php?title=Omnibenevolence&oldid=737117725>

Wikipedia contributors. "Competition (biology)." *Wikipedia, The Free Encyclopedia.* Wikipedia, The Free Encyclopedia, 9 Nov. 2016. Web. 16 Nov. 2016. <https://en.wikipedia.org/w/index.php?title=Competition_(biology)&oldid=748672169>

Wikipedia contributors. "Social responsibility." *Wikipedia, The Free Encyclopedia.* Wikipedia, The Free Encyclopedia, 14 Nov. 2016. Web. 16 Nov. 2016. <https://en.wikipedia.org/w/index.php?title=Social_responsibility&oldid=749407384>

Wikipedia contributors. "Ecosystem." *Wikipedia, The Free Encyclopedia.* Wikipedia, The Free Encyclopedia, 30 Sep. 2016. Web. 16 Nov. 2016. <https://en.wikipedia.org/w/index.php?title=Ecosystem&oldid=741987248>

Wikipedia contributors. "Causality." *Wikipedia, The Free Encyclopedia.* Wikipedia, The Free Encyclopedia, 7 Nov. 2016. Web. 7 Nov. 2016. <https://en.wikipedia.org/w/index.php?title=Causality&oldid=748341478>

Wikipedia contributors. "Karma." *Wikipedia, The Free Encyclopedia.* Wikipedia, The Free Encyclopedia, 21 Oct. 2016. Web. 08 Nov. 2016. <https://en.wikipedia.org/w/index.php?title=Karma&oldid=745485451>

Wikipedia contributors. "Consequentialism." *Wikipedia, The Free Encyclopedia.* Wikipedia, The Free Encyclopedia, 22 Oct. 2016. Web. 16 Nov. 2016. <https://en.wikipedia.org/w/index.php?title=Consequentialism&oldid=745647106>

Wikipedia contributors. "Apple." *Wikipedia, The Free Encyclopedia.* Wikipedia, The Free Encyclopedia, 19 Nov. 2016. Web. 21 Nov. 2016. <https://en.wikipedia.org/w/index.php?title=Apple&oldid=750428491>

Wikipedia contributors. "Manchineel." *Wikipedia, The Free Encyclopedia.* Wikipedia, The Free Encyclopedia, 10 Nov. 2016. Web. 21 Nov. 2016. <https://en.wikipedia.org/w/index.php?title=Manchineel&oldid=748869035>

Wikipedia contributors. "Chain reaction." *Wikipedia, The Free Encyclopedia.* Wikipedia, The Free Encyclopedia, 14 Jun. 2016. Web. 8 Nov. 2016. <https://en.wikipedia.org/w/index.php?title=Chain_reaction&oldid=725176855>

Wikipedia contributors. "Unintended consequences." *Wikipedia, The Free Encyclopedia.* Wikipedia, The Free Encyclopedia, 3 Nov. 2016. Web. 16 Nov. 2016. <https://en.wikipedia.org/w/index.php?title=Unintended_consequences&oldid=747560388>

Wikipedia contributors. "Magic (paranormal)." *Wikipedia, The Free Encyclopedia.* Wikipedia, The Free Encyclopedia, 31 Oct. 2016. Web. 11 Nov. 2016. <https://en.wikipedia.org/w/index.php?title=Magic_(paranormal)&oldid=747093996>

Wikipedia contributors. "Luck." *Wikipedia, The Free Encyclopedia.* Wikipedia, The Free Encyclopedia, 8 Nov. 2016. Web. 11 Nov. 2016. <https://en.wikipedia.org/w/index.php?title=Luck&oldid=748427565>

Wikipedia contributors. "Empathy." *Wikipedia, The Free Encyclopedia.* Wikipedia, The Free Encyclopedia, 11 Nov. 2016. Web. 11 Nov. 2016. <https://en.wikipedia.org/w/index.php?title=Empathy&oldid=749006665>

Wikipedia contributors. "Cetana." *Wikipedia, The Free Encyclopedia.* Wikipedia, The Free Encyclopedia, 18 Nov. 2016. Web. 24 Feb. 2017. <https://en.wikipedia.org/w/index.php?title=Cetan%C4%81&oldid=750276361>

Wikipedia contributors. "Karma in Buddhism." *Wikipedia, The Free Encyclopedia.* Wikipedia, The Free Encyclopedia, 21 Oct. 2016. Web. 11 Nov. 2016. <https://en.wikipedia.org/w/index.php?title=Karma_in_Buddhism&oldid=745572144>

Wikipedia contributors. "Samsara (Buddhism)." *Wikipedia, The Free Encyclopedia.* Wikipedia, The Free Encyclopedia, 3 Nov. 2016. Web. 28 Nov. 2016. <https://en.wikipedia.org/w/index.php?title=Sa%E1%B9%83s%C4%81ra_(Buddhism)&oldid=747638612>

Wikipedia contributors. "Guilt (emotion)." *Wikipedia, The Free Encyclopedia.* Wikipedia, The Free Encyclopedia, 11 Nov. 2016. Web. 22 Nov. 2016. <https://en.wikipedia.org/w/index.php?title=Guilt_(emotion)&oldid=748894745>

Wikipedia contributors. "Contentment." *Wikipedia, The Free Encyclopedia.* Wikipedia, The Free Encyclopedia, 10 Nov. 2016. Web. 16 Nov. 2016. <https://en.wikipedia.org/w/index.php?title=Contentment&oldid=748867273>

Wikipedia contributors. "Altruism." *Wikipedia, The Free Encyclopedia.* Wikipedia, The Free Encyclopedia, 10 Nov. 2016. Web. 11 Nov. 2016. <https://en.wikipedia.org/w/index.php?title=Altruism&oldid=748729305>

Concept Progress

Wikipedia contributors. "Asteroid." *Wikipedia, The Free Encyclopedia.* Wikipedia, The Free Encyclopedia, 9 Nov. 2016. Web. 16 Nov. 2016. <https://en.wikipedia.org/w/index.php?title=Asteroid&oldid=748648722>

Wikipedia contributors. "Cretaceous–Paleogene extinction event." *Wikipedia, The Free Encyclopedia.* Wikipedia, The Free Encyclopedia, 31 Oct. 2016. Web. 11 Nov. 2016. <https://en.wikipedia.org/w/index.php?title=Cretaceous%E2%80%93Paleogene_extinction_event&oldid=747153383>

Wikipedia contributors. "Principle of sufficient reason." *Wikipedia, The Free Encyclopedia.* Wikipedia, The Free Encyclopedia, 31 Aug. 2016. Web. 22 Nov. 2016. <https://en.wikipedia.org/w/index.php?title=Principle_of_sufficient_reason&oldid=736970926>

Wikipedia contributors. "Pragmatic ethics." *Wikipedia, The Free Encyclopedia.* Wikipedia, The Free Encyclopedia, 15 Oct. 2016. Web. 16 Nov. 2016. <https://en.wikipedia.org/w/index.php?title=Pragmatic_ethics&oldid=744525099>

Wikipedia contributors. "Intuition and decision-making." *Wikipedia, The Free Encyclopedia.* Wikipedia, The Free Encyclopedia, 13 Nov. 2016. Web. 30 Nov. 2016. <https://en.wikipedia.org/w/index.php?title=Intuition_and_decision-making&oldid=749316689>

Wikipedia contributors. "Mathematical model." *Wikipedia, The Free Encyclopedia.* Wikipedia, The Free Encyclopedia, 5 Nov. 2016. Web. 29 Nov. 2016. <https://en.wikipedia.org/w/index.php?title=Mathematical_model&oldid=748028177>

Wikipedia contributors. "Chronology of the universe." *Wikipedia, The Free Encyclopedia.* Wikipedia, The Free Encyclopedia, 7 Nov. 2016. Web. 11 Nov. 2016. <https://en.wikipedia.org/w/index.php?title=Chronology_of_the_universe&oldid=748301507>

Wikipedia contributors. "Reproduction." *Wikipedia, The Free Encyclopedia.* Wikipedia, The Free Encyclopedia, 14 Nov. 2016. Web. 16 Nov. 2016. <https://en.wikipedia.org/w/index.php?title=Reproduction&oldid=749396211>

Wikipedia contributors. "Co-operation (evolution)." *Wikipedia, The Free Encyclopedia.* Wikipedia, The Free Encyclopedia, 6 Sep. 2016. Web. 16 Nov. 2016. <https://en.wikipedia.org/w/index.php?title=Co-operation_(evolution)&oldid=737997999>

Wikipedia contributors. "Phylogenetic tree." *Wikipedia, The Free Encyclopedia.* Wikipedia, The Free Encyclopedia, 16 Oct. 2016. Web. 17 Nov. 2016. <https://en.wikipedia.org/w/index.php?title=Phylogenetic_tree&oldid=744703781>

Wikipedia contributors. "Clade." *Wikipedia, The Free Encyclopedia.* Wikipedia, The Free Encyclopedia, 22 Nov. 2016. Web. 22 Nov. 2016. <https://en.wikipedia.org/w/index.php?title=Clade&oldid=750997405>

Wikipedia contributors. "Convergent evolution." *Wikipedia, The Free Encyclopedia.* Wikipedia, The Free Encyclopedia, 18 Nov. 2016. Web. 18 Nov. 2016. <https://en.wikipedia.org/w/index.php?title=Convergent_evolution&oldid=750190430>

Wikipedia contributors. "Infinity symbol." *Wikipedia, The Free Encyclopedia.* Wikipedia, The Free Encyclopedia, 2 Jan. 2017. Web. 18 Jan. 2017. <https://en.wikipedia.org/w/index.php?title=Infinity_symbol&oldid=757978589>

Wikipedia contributors. "Tree of life." *Wikipedia, The Free Encyclopedia.* Wikipedia, The Free Encyclopedia, 29 Oct. 2016. Web. 17 Nov. 2016. <https://en.wikipedia.org/w/index.php?title=Tree_of_life&oldid=746794285>

Chapter Eight

Wikipedia contributors. "Monotheism." *Wikipedia, The Free Encyclopedia.* Wikipedia, The Free Encyclopedia, 17 Dec. 2016. Web. 22 Dec. 2016. <https://en.wikipedia.org/w/index.php?title=Monotheism&oldid=755337715>

Wikipedia contributors. "Polytheism." *Wikipedia, The Free Encyclopedia.* Wikipedia, The Free Encyclopedia, 12 Dec. 2016. Web. 22 Dec. 2016. <https://en.wikipedia.org/w/index.php?title=Polytheism&oldid=754470430>

Wikipedia contributors. "Perfectionism (psychology)." *Wikipedia, The Free Encyclopedia.* Wikipedia, The Free Encyclopedia, 8 Dec. 2016. Web. 22 Dec. 2016. <https://en.wikipedia.org/w/index.php?title=Perfectionism_(psychology)&oldid=753731928>

Wikipedia contributors. "Perfection." *Wikipedia, The Free Encyclopedia*. Wikipedia, The Free Encyclopedia, 27 Oct. 2016. Web. 22 Dec. 2016. <https://en.wikipedia.org/w/index.php?title=Perfection&oldid=746447084>

Wikipedia contributors. "Qualia." *Wikipedia, The Free Encyclopedia*. Wikipedia, The Free Encyclopedia, 27 Dec. 2016. Web. 3 Jan. 2017. <https://en.wikipedia.org/w/index.php?title=Qualia&oldid=756874733>

Wikipedia contributors. "Perfectionism (philosophy)." *Wikipedia, The Free Encyclopedia*. Wikipedia, The Free Encyclopedia, 15 Aug. 2016. Web. 22 Dec. 2016. <https://en.wikipedia.org/w/index.php?title=Perfectionism_(philosophy)&oldid=734640302>

Wikipedia contributors. "Objectivity (philosophy)." *Wikipedia, The Free Encyclopedia*. Wikipedia, The Free Encyclopedia, 5 Dec. 2016. Web. 28 Dec. 2016. <https://en.wikipedia.org/w/index.php?title=Objectivity_(philosophy)&oldid=753199437>

Wikipedia contributors. "Reflection principle." *Wikipedia, The Free Encyclopedia*. Wikipedia, The Free Encyclopedia, 20 Dec. 2016. Web. 30 Dec. 2016. <https://en.wikipedia.org/w/index.php?title=Reflection_principle&oldid=755879476>

Wikipedia contributors. "Bird's-eye view." *Wikipedia, The Free Encyclopedia*. Wikipedia, The Free Encyclopedia, 12 Nov. 2016. Web. 3 Jan. 2017. <https://en.wikipedia.org/w/index.php?title=Bird%27s-eye_view&oldid=749175342>

Wikipedia contributors. "Classical element." *Wikipedia, The Free Encyclopedia*. Wikipedia, The Free Encyclopedia, 15 Dec. 2016. Web. 28 Dec. 2016. <https://en.wikipedia.org/w/index.php?title=Classical_element&oldid=754985781>

Wikipedia contributors. "Periodic table." *Wikipedia, The Free Encyclopedia*. Wikipedia, The Free Encyclopedia, 9 Dec. 2016. Web. 22 Dec. 2016. <https://en.wikipedia.org/w/index.php?title=Periodic_table&oldid=753870807>

Wikipedia contributors. "Observer (special relativity)." *Wikipedia, The Free Encyclopedia*. Wikipedia, The Free Encyclopedia, 19 Oct. 2016. Web. 4 Jan. 2017. <https://en.wikipedia.org/w/index.php?title=Observer_(special_relativity)&oldid=745099658>

Wikipedia contributors. "Development of Darwin's theory." *Wikipedia, The Free Encyclopedia*. Wikipedia, The Free Encyclopedia, 9 Feb. 2016. Web. 27 Dec. 2016. <https://en.wikipedia.org/w/index.php?title=Development_of_Darwin%27s_theory&oldid=704141153>

Wikipedia contributors. "Social psychology." *Wikipedia, The Free Encyclopedia*. Wikipedia, The Free Encyclopedia, 16 Dec. 2016. Web. 28 Dec. 2016. <https://en.wikipedia.org/w/index.php?title=Social_psychology&oldid=755121229>

Wikipedia contributors. "Social psychology (sociology)." *Wikipedia, The Free Encyclopedia*. Wikipedia, The Free Encyclopedia, 20 Nov. 2016. Web. 28 Dec. 2016. <https://en.wikipedia.org/w/index.php?title=Social_psychology_(sociology)&oldid=750611652>

Wikipedia contributors. "Mathematical logic." *Wikipedia, The Free Encyclopedia*. Wikipedia, The Free Encyclopedia, 29 Nov. 2016. Web. 28 Dec. 2016. <https://en.wikipedia.org/w/index.php?title=Mathematical_logic&oldid=752064911>

Wikipedia contributors. "Common sense." *Wikipedia, The Free Encyclopedia*. Wikipedia, The Free Encyclopedia, 24 Dec. 2016. Web. 28 Dec. 2016. <https://en.wikipedia.org/w/index.php?title=Common_sense&oldid=756485087>

Wikipedia contributors. "Undefined (mathematics)." *Wikipedia, The Free Encyclopedia*. Wikipedia, The Free Encyclopedia, 14 Dec. 2016. Web. 28 Dec. 2016. <https://en.wikipedia.org/w/index.php?title=Undefined_(mathematics)&oldid=754769370>

Wikipedia contributors. "Infinity." *Wikipedia, The Free Encyclopedia*. Wikipedia, The Free Encyclopedia, 12 Dec. 2016. Web. 23 Dec. 2016. <https://en.wikipedia.org/w/index.php?title=Infinity&oldid=754377677>

Wikipedia contributors. "Lateralization of brain function." *Wikipedia, The Free Encyclopedia*. Wikipedia, The Free Encyclopedia, 2 Dec. 2016. Web. 23 Dec. 2016. <https://en.wikipedia.org/w/index.php?title=Lateralization_of_brain_function&oldid=752709974>

Wikipedia contributors. "Infinity (philosophy)." *Wikipedia, The Free Encyclopedia*. Wikipedia, The Free Encyclopedia, 27 Sep. 2016. Web. 23 Dec. 2016. <https://en.wikipedia.org/w/index.php?title=Infinity_(philosophy)&oldid=741382977>

Concept Progress

Wikipedia contributors. "Georg Cantor." *Wikipedia, The Free Encyclopedia.* Wikipedia, The Free Encyclopedia, 20 Feb. 2017. Web. 23 Feb. 2017. <https://en.wikipedia.org/w/index.php?title=Georg_Cantor&oldid=766405301>

Wikipedia contributors. "Abstraction (mathematics)." *Wikipedia, The Free Encyclopedia.* Wikipedia, The Free Encyclopedia, 21 Oct. 2016. Web. 10 Jan. 2017. <https://en.wikipedia.org/w/index.php?title=Abstraction_(mathematics)&oldid=745443574>

Wikipedia contributors. "Shape of the universe." *Wikipedia, The Free Encyclopedia.* Wikipedia, The Free Encyclopedia, 16 Dec. 2016. Web. 28 Dec. 2016. <https://en.wikipedia.org/w/index.php?title=Shape_of_the_universe&oldid=755063862>

Wikipedia contributors. "Number." *Wikipedia, The Free Encyclopedia.* Wikipedia, The Free Encyclopedia, 2 Jan. 2017. Web. 4 Jan. 2017. <https://en.wikipedia.org/w/index.php?title=Number&oldid=757894913>

Wikipedia contributors. "Addition." *Wikipedia, The Free Encyclopedia.* Wikipedia, The Free Encyclopedia, 23 Dec. 2016. Web. 4 Jan. 2017. <https://en.wikipedia.org/w/index.php?title=Addition&oldid=756386268>

Wikipedia contributors. "Multiplication." *Wikipedia, The Free Encyclopedia.* Wikipedia, The Free Encyclopedia, 2 Jan. 2017. Web. 4 Jan. 2017. <https://en.wikipedia.org/w/index.php?title=Multiplication&oldid=757904140>

Wikipedia contributors. "Exponentiation." *Wikipedia, The Free Encyclopedia.* Wikipedia, The Free Encyclopedia, 16 Dec. 2016. Web. 4 Jan. 2017. <https://en.wikipedia.org/w/index.php?title=Exponentiation&oldid=755117447>

Wikipedia contributors. "Natural number." *Wikipedia, The Free Encyclopedia.* Wikipedia, The Free Encyclopedia, 20 Dec. 2016. Web. 23 Dec. 2016. <https://en.wikipedia.org/w/index.php?title=Natural_number&oldid=755795551>

Wikipedia contributors. "Actual infinity." *Wikipedia, The Free Encyclopedia.* Wikipedia, The Free Encyclopedia, 13 Nov. 2016. Web. 29 Dec. 2016. <https://en.wikipedia.org/w/index.php?title=Actual_infinity&oldid=749284399>

Wikipedia contributors. "Decimal." *Wikipedia, The Free Encyclopedia.* Wikipedia, The Free Encyclopedia, 9 Dec. 2016. Web. 23 Dec. 2016. <https://en.wikipedia.org/w/index.php?title=Decimal&oldid=753824862>

Wikipedia contributors. "Contradiction." *Wikipedia, The Free Encyclopedia.* Wikipedia, The Free Encyclopedia, 17 Dec. 2016. Web. 23 Dec. 2016. <https://en.wikipedia.org/w/index.php?title=Contradiction&oldid=755282638>

Wikipedia contributors. "Infinite divisibility." *Wikipedia, The Free Encyclopedia.* Wikipedia, The Free Encyclopedia, 21 Dec. 2016. Web. 29 Dec. 2016. <https://en.wikipedia.org/w/index.php?title=Infinite_divisibility&oldid=756085674>

Wikipedia contributors. "Elementary particle." *Wikipedia, The Free Encyclopedia.* Wikipedia, The Free Encyclopedia, 19 Dec. 2016. Web. 23 Dec. 2016. <https://en.wikipedia.org/w/index.php?title=Elementary_particle&oldid=755716861>

Wikipedia contributors. "Semantics." *Wikipedia, The Free Encyclopedia.* Wikipedia, The Free Encyclopedia, 16 Nov. 2016. Web. 4 Jan. 2017. <https://en.wikipedia.org/w/index.php?title=Semantics&oldid=749876915>

Wikipedia contributors. "Static universe." *Wikipedia, The Free Encyclopedia.* Wikipedia, The Free Encyclopedia, 9 Jun. 2016. Web. 4 Jan. 2017. <https://en.wikipedia.org/w/index.php?title=Static_universe&oldid=724473079>

Wikipedia contributors. "Zeno's paradoxes." *Wikipedia, The Free Encyclopedia.* Wikipedia, The Free Encyclopedia, 2 Dec. 2016. Web. 23 Dec. 2016. <https://en.wikipedia.org/w/index.php?title=Zeno%27s_paradoxes&oldid=752685211>

Wikipedia contributors. "Infinitesimal." *Wikipedia, The Free Encyclopedia.* Wikipedia, The Free Encyclopedia, 19 Dec. 2016. Web. 23 Dec. 2016. <https://en.wikipedia.org/w/index.php?title=Infinitesimal&oldid=755628861>

Wikipedia contributors. "Mathematical problem." *Wikipedia, The Free Encyclopedia.* Wikipedia, The Free Encyclopedia, 19 May. 2016. Web. 13 Feb. 2017. <https://en.wikipedia.org/w/index.php?title=Mathematical_problem&oldid=721087761>

Wikipedia contributors. "Nothing." *Wikipedia, The Free Encyclopedia.* Wikipedia, The Free Encyclopedia, 27 Nov. 2016. Web. 4 Jan. 2017. <https://en.wikipedia.org/w/index.php?title=Nothing&oldid=751697070>

Wikipedia contributors. "0." *Wikipedia, The Free Encyclopedia*. Wikipedia, The Free Encyclopedia, 20 Dec. 2016. Web. 23 Dec. 2016. <https://en.wikipedia.org/w/index.php?title=0&oldid=755806302>

Wikipedia contributors. "Mathematics." *Wikipedia, The Free Encyclopedia*. Wikipedia, The Free Encyclopedia, 15 Dec. 2016. Web. 23 Dec. 2016. <https://en.wikipedia.org/w/index.php?title=Mathematics&oldid=755003779>

Wikipedia contributors. "Maxima and minima." *Wikipedia, The Free Encyclopedia*. Wikipedia, The Free Encyclopedia, 9 Oct. 2016. Web. 4 Jan. 2017. <https://en.wikipedia.org/w/index.php?title=Maxima_and_minima&oldid=743451804>

Wikipedia contributors. "Point particle." *Wikipedia, The Free Encyclopedia*. Wikipedia, The Free Encyclopedia, 10 Nov. 2016. Web. 23 Dec. 2016. <https://en.wikipedia.org/w/index.php?title=Point_particle&oldid=748742602>

Wikipedia contributors. "Fermion." *Wikipedia, The Free Encyclopedia*. Wikipedia, The Free Encyclopedia, 22 Aug. 2016. Web. 4 Jan. 2017. <https://en.wikipedia.org/w/index.php?title=Fermion&oldid=735671028>

Wikipedia contributors. "Boson." *Wikipedia, The Free Encyclopedia*. Wikipedia, The Free Encyclopedia, 30 Dec. 2016. Web. 4 Jan. 2017. <https://en.wikipedia.org/w/index.php?title=Boson&oldid=757333681>

Wikipedia contributors. "Planck length." *Wikipedia, The Free Encyclopedia*. Wikipedia, The Free Encyclopedia, 10 Nov. 2016. Web. 23 Dec. 2016. <https://en.wikipedia.org/w/index.php?title=Planck_length&oldid=748781932>

Wikipedia contributors. "Electron." *Wikipedia, The Free Encyclopedia*. Wikipedia, The Free Encyclopedia, 22 Dec. 2016. Web. 30 Dec. 2016. <https://en.wikipedia.org/w/index.php?title=Electron&oldid=756141380>

Wikipedia contributors. "Initial singularity." *Wikipedia, The Free Encyclopedia*. Wikipedia, The Free Encyclopedia, 8 Nov. 2016. Web. 23 Dec. 2016. <https://en.wikipedia.org/w/index.php?title=Initial_singularity&oldid=748527076>

Wikipedia contributors. "Aleph number." *Wikipedia, The Free Encyclopedia*. Wikipedia, The Free Encyclopedia, 2 Jan. 2017. Web. 3 Jan. 2017. <https://en.wikipedia.org/w/index.php?title=Aleph_number&oldid=757970383>

Wikipedia contributors. "List of unsolved problems in physics." *Wikipedia, The Free Encyclopedia*. Wikipedia, The Free Encyclopedia, 4 Jan. 2017. Web. 4 Jan. 2017. <https://en.wikipedia.org/w/index.php?title=List_of_unsolved_problems_in_physics&oldid=758314594>

Wikipedia contributors. "Inflation (cosmology)." *Wikipedia, The Free Encyclopedia*. Wikipedia, The Free Encyclopedia, 4 Dec. 2016. Web. 3 Jan. 2016. <https://en.wikipedia.org/w/index.php?title=Inflation_(cosmology)&oldid=752970544>

Wikipedia contributors. "Hubble's law." *Wikipedia, The Free Encyclopedia*. Wikipedia, The Free Encyclopedia, 9 Dec. 2016. Web. 23 Dec. 2016. <https://en.wikipedia.org/w/index.php?title=Hubble%27s_law&oldid=753867910>

Wikipedia contributors. "Cosmic microwave background." *Wikipedia, The Free Encyclopedia*. Wikipedia, The Free Encyclopedia, 22 Dec. 2016. Web. 23 Dec. 2016. <https://en.wikipedia.org/w/index.php?title=Cosmic_microwave_background&oldid=756148681>

Wikipedia contributors. "Olbers' paradox." *Wikipedia, The Free Encyclopedia*. Wikipedia, The Free Encyclopedia, 14 Dec. 2016. Web. 10 Jan. 2017. <https://en.wikipedia.org/w/index.php?title=Olbers%27_paradox&oldid=754700922>

Wikipedia contributors. "Temporal finitism." *Wikipedia, The Free Encyclopedia*. Wikipedia, The Free Encyclopedia, 30 Nov. 2016. Web. 4 Jan. 2017. <https://en.wikipedia.org/w/index.php?title=Temporal_finitism&oldid=752313869>

Wikipedia contributors. "Coordinate system." *Wikipedia, The Free Encyclopedia*. Wikipedia, The Free Encyclopedia, 18 Dec. 2016. Web. 3 Jan. 2017. <https://en.wikipedia.org/w/index.php?title=Coordinate_system&oldid=755526926>

Wikipedia contributors. "Angle." *Wikipedia, The Free Encyclopedia*. Wikipedia, The Free Encyclopedia, 2 Jan. 2017. Web. 3 Jan. 2017. <https://en.wikipedia.org/w/index.php?title=Angle&oldid=757961260>

Wikipedia contributors. "Unit of time." *Wikipedia, The Free Encyclopedia*. Wikipedia, The Free Encyclopedia, 25 Dec. 2016. Web. 27 Dec. 2016. <https://en.wikipedia.org/w/index.php?title=Unit_of_time&oldid=756624973>

Concept Progress

Wikipedia contributors. "Planck time." *Wikipedia, The Free Encyclopedia*. Wikipedia, The Free Encyclopedia, 15 Nov. 2016. Web. 23 Dec. 2016. <https://en.wikipedia.org/w/index.php?title=Planck_time&oldid=749601084>

Wikipedia contributors. "Distance." *Wikipedia, The Free Encyclopedia*. Wikipedia, The Free Encyclopedia, 14 Dec. 2016. Web. 4 Jan. 2017. <https://en.wikipedia.org/w/index.php?title=Distance&oldid=754806798>

Wikipedia contributors. "Laws of science." *Wikipedia, The Free Encyclopedia*. Wikipedia, The Free Encyclopedia, 6 Dec. 2016. Web. 23 Dec. 2016. <https://en.wikipedia.org/w/index.php?title=Laws_of_science&oldid=753324088>

Wikipedia contributors. "Max Planck." *Wikipedia, The Free Encyclopedia*. Wikipedia, The Free Encyclopedia, 5 Dec. 2016. Web. 23 Dec. 2016. <https://en.wikipedia.org/w/index.php?title=Max_Planck&oldid=753181406>

Wikipedia contributors. "Limit (mathematics)." *Wikipedia, The Free Encyclopedia*. Wikipedia, The Free Encyclopedia, 30 Dec. 2016. Web. 3 Jan. 2017. <https://en.wikipedia.org/w/index.php?title=Limit_(mathematics)&oldid=757368603>

Wikipedia contributors. "Photograph." *Wikipedia, The Free Encyclopedia*. Wikipedia, The Free Encyclopedia, 22 Nov. 2016. Web. 23 Dec. 2016. <https://en.wikipedia.org/w/index.php?title=Photograph&oldid=750925279>

Wikipedia contributors. "Motion (physics)." *Wikipedia, The Free Encyclopedia*. Wikipedia, The Free Encyclopedia, 4 Jan. 2017. Web. 4 Jan. 2017. <https://en.wikipedia.org/w/index.php?title=Motion_(physics)&oldid=758257116>

Wikipedia contributors. "Inertia." *Wikipedia, The Free Encyclopedia*. Wikipedia, The Free Encyclopedia, 29 Nov. 2016. Web. 23 Dec. 2016. <https://en.wikipedia.org/w/index.php?title=Inertia&oldid=752092208>

Wikipedia contributors. "Video." *Wikipedia, The Free Encyclopedia*. Wikipedia, The Free Encyclopedia, 30 Dec. 2016. Web. 30 Dec. 2016. <https://en.wikipedia.org/w/index.php?title=Video&oldid=757353141>

Wikipedia contributors. "Frame rate." *Wikipedia, The Free Encyclopedia*. Wikipedia, The Free Encyclopedia, 14 Dec. 2016. Web. 23 Dec. 2016. <https://en.wikipedia.org/w/index.php?title=Frame_rate&oldid=754770176>

Wikipedia contributors. "Galactic year." *Wikipedia, The Free Encyclopedia*. Wikipedia, The Free Encyclopedia, 25 Nov. 2016. Web. 23 Dec. 2016. <https://en.wikipedia.org/w/index.php?title=Galactic_year&oldid=751366507>

Wikipedia contributors. "Time perception." *Wikipedia, The Free Encyclopedia*. Wikipedia, The Free Encyclopedia, 17 Dec. 2016. Web. 23 Dec. 2016. <https://en.wikipedia.org/w/index.php?title=Time_perception&oldid=755380113>

Wikipedia contributors. "Recall (memory)." *Wikipedia, The Free Encyclopedia*. Wikipedia, The Free Encyclopedia, 30 Dec. 2016. Web. 5 Jan. 2017. <https://en.wikipedia.org/w/index.php?title=Recall_(memory)&oldid=757403616>

Wikipedia contributors. "Thought." *Wikipedia, The Free Encyclopedia*. Wikipedia, The Free Encyclopedia, 3 Jan. 2017. Web. 3 Jan. 2017. <https://en.wikipedia.org/w/index.php?title=Thought&oldid=758180429>

Wikipedia contributors. "Planck units." *Wikipedia, The Free Encyclopedia*. Wikipedia, The Free Encyclopedia, 27 Dec. 2016. Web. 30 Dec. 2016. <https://en.wikipedia.org/w/index.php?title=Planck_units&oldid=756884598>

Wikipedia contributors. "Accelerating expansion of the universe." *Wikipedia, The Free Encyclopedia*. Wikipedia, The Free Encyclopedia, 23 Dec. 2016. Web. 23 Dec. 2016.
<https://en.wikipedia.org/w/index.php?title=Accelerating_expansion_of_the_universe&oldid=756394604>

Wikipedia contributors. "Arrow of time." *Wikipedia, The Free Encyclopedia*. Wikipedia, The Free Encyclopedia, 5 Jan. 2017. Web. 10 Jan. 2017. <https://en.wikipedia.org/w/index.php?title=Arrow_of_time&oldid=758515858>

Wikipedia contributors. "Extended real number line." *Wikipedia, The Free Encyclopedia*. Wikipedia, The Free Encyclopedia, 13 Feb. 2017. Web. 14 Feb. 2017. <https://en.wikipedia.org/w/index.php?title=Extended_real_number_line&oldid=765280937>

Wikipedia contributors. "Negative number." *Wikipedia, The Free Encyclopedia*. Wikipedia, The Free Encyclopedia, 31 Dec. 2016. Web. 6 Jan. 2017. <https://en.wikipedia.org/w/index.php?title=Negative_number&oldid=757583267>

Wikipedia contributors. "Division by zero." *Wikipedia, The Free Encyclopedia*. Wikipedia, The Free Encyclopedia, 20 Dec. 2016. Web. 23 Dec. 2016. <https://en.wikipedia.org/w/index.php?title=Division_by_zero&oldid=755897478>

Wikipedia contributors. "Absolute Infinite." *Wikipedia, The Free Encyclopedia*. Wikipedia, The Free Encyclopedia, 21 Oct. 2016. Web. 4 Jan. 2017. <https://en.wikipedia.org/w/index.php?title=Absolute_Infinite&oldid=745443567>

Wikipedia contributors. "Mysticism." *Wikipedia, The Free Encyclopedia*. Wikipedia, The Free Encyclopedia, 1 Jan. 2017. Web. 5 Jan. 2017. <https://en.wikipedia.org/w/index.php?title=Mysticism&oldid=757775817>

Wikipedia contributors. "Deity." *Wikipedia, The Free Encyclopedia*. Wikipedia, The Free Encyclopedia, 21 Dec. 2016. Web. 5 Jan. 2017. <https://en.wikipedia.org/w/index.php?title=Deity&oldid=756050754>

Wikipedia contributors. "Utopia." *Wikipedia, The Free Encyclopedia*. Wikipedia, The Free Encyclopedia, 10 Dec. 2016. Web. 23 Dec. 2016. <https://en.wikipedia.org/w/index.php?title=Utopia&oldid=754112415>

Wikipedia contributors. "Social issue." *Wikipedia, The Free Encyclopedia*. Wikipedia, The Free Encyclopedia, 16 Dec. 2016. Web. 5 Jan. 2017. <https://en.wikipedia.org/w/index.php?title=Social_issue&oldid=755121187>

Wikipedia contributors. "Standard of living." *Wikipedia, The Free Encyclopedia*. Wikipedia, The Free Encyclopedia, 24 Dec. 2016. Web. 5 Jan. 2017. <https://en.wikipedia.org/w/index.php?title=Standard_of_living&oldid=756483046>

Wikipedia contributors. "Universalism." *Wikipedia, The Free Encyclopedia*. Wikipedia, The Free Encyclopedia, 13 Dec. 2016. Web. 23 Dec. 2016. <https://en.wikipedia.org/w/index.php?title=Universalism&oldid=754528247>

Wikipedia contributors. "Heaven." *Wikipedia, The Free Encyclopedia*. Wikipedia, The Free Encyclopedia, 21 Dec. 2016. Web. 23 Dec. 2016. <https://en.wikipedia.org/w/index.php?title=Heaven&oldid=756027587>

Wikipedia contributors. "Vacuum state." *Wikipedia, The Free Encyclopedia*. Wikipedia, The Free Encyclopedia, 4 Oct. 2016. Web. 11 Jan. 2017. <https://en.wikipedia.org/w/index.php?title=Vacuum_state&oldid=742584453>

Wikipedia contributors. "Fine-tuned Universe." *Wikipedia, The Free Encyclopedia*. Wikipedia, The Free Encyclopedia, 22 Dec. 2016. Web. 27 Dec. 2016. <https://en.wikipedia.org/w/index.php?title=Fine-tuned_Universe&oldid=756128234>

Wikipedia contributors. "Timeline of the formation of the Universe." *Wikipedia, The Free Encyclopedia*. Wikipedia, The Free Encyclopedia, 22 Dec. 2016. Web. 3 Jan. 2017. <https://en.wikipedia.org/w/index.php?title=Timeline_of_the_formation_of_the_Universe&oldid=756152107>

Wikipedia contributors. "Variable (mathematics)." *Wikipedia, The Free Encyclopedia*. Wikipedia, The Free Encyclopedia, 2 Dec. 2016. Web. 6 Jan. 2017. <https://en.wikipedia.org/w/index.php?title=Variable_(mathematics)&oldid=752579469>

Wikipedia contributors. "Equation." *Wikipedia, The Free Encyclopedia*. Wikipedia, The Free Encyclopedia, 5 Jan. 2017. Web. 6 Jan. 2017. <https://en.wikipedia.org/w/index.php?title=Equation&oldid=758448341>

Wikipedia contributors. "Equation solving." *Wikipedia, The Free Encyclopedia*. Wikipedia, The Free Encyclopedia, 29 Dec. 2016. Web. 6 Jan. 2017. <https://en.wikipedia.org/w/index.php?title=Equation_solving&oldid=757179659>

Wikipedia contributors. "Future of Earth." *Wikipedia, The Free Encyclopedia*. Wikipedia, The Free Encyclopedia, 22 Dec. 2016. Web. 23 Dec. 2016. <https://en.wikipedia.org/w/index.php?title=Future_of_Earth&oldid=756144196>

Wikipedia contributors. "Andromeda–Milky Way collision." *Wikipedia, The Free Encyclopedia*. Wikipedia, The Free Encyclopedia, 21 Jan. 2017. Web. 21 Jan. 2017. <https://en.wikipedia.org/w/index.php?title=Andromeda%E2%80%93Milky_Way_collision&oldid=761147409>

Wikipedia contributors. "Earth's location in the Universe." *Wikipedia, The Free Encyclopedia*. Wikipedia, The Free Encyclopedia, 5 Oct. 2016. Web. 7 Jan. 2017. <https://en.wikipedia.org/w/index.php?title=Earth%27s_location_in_the_Universe&oldid=742783075>

Wikipedia contributors. "Prejudice." *Wikipedia, The Free Encyclopedia*. Wikipedia, The Free Encyclopedia, 29 Dec. 2016. Web. 7 Jan. 2017. <https://en.wikipedia.org/w/index.php?title=Prejudice&oldid=757258019>

Wikipedia contributors. "Religious intolerance." *Wikipedia, The Free Encyclopedia*. Wikipedia, The Free Encyclopedia, 13 Oct. 2016. Web. 7 Jan. 2017. <https://en.wikipedia.org/w/index.php?title=Religious_intolerance&oldid=744230160>

Wikipedia contributors. "Cooperation." *Wikipedia, The Free Encyclopedia*. Wikipedia, The Free Encyclopedia, 12 Dec. 2016. Web. 7 Jan. 2017. <https://en.wikipedia.org/w/index.php?title=Cooperation&oldid=754487382>

Wikipedia contributors. "Paramita." *Wikipedia, The Free Encyclopedia*. Wikipedia, The Free Encyclopedia, 3 Dec. 2016. Web. 9 Jan. 2017. <https://en.wikipedia.org/w/index.php?title=P%C4%81ramit%C4%81&oldid=752776631>

Chapter Nine

Wikipedia contributors. "World view." *Wikipedia, The Free Encyclopedia*. Wikipedia, The Free Encyclopedia, 10 Jan. 2017. Web. 13 Jan. 2017. <https://en.wikipedia.org/w/index.php?title=World_view&oldid=759307171>

Wikipedia contributors. "Biomolecule." *Wikipedia, The Free Encyclopedia*. Wikipedia, The Free Encyclopedia, 4 Jan. 2017. Web. 1 Feb. 2017. <https://en.wikipedia.org/w/index.php?title=Biomolecule&oldid=758349503>

Wikipedia contributors. "Rare Earth hypothesis." *Wikipedia, The Free Encyclopedia*. Wikipedia, The Free Encyclopedia, 30 Dec. 2016. Web. 17 Jan. 2017. <https://en.wikipedia.org/w/index.php?title=Rare_Earth_hypothesis&oldid=757456351>

Wikipedia contributors. "Planetary system." *Wikipedia, The Free Encyclopedia*. Wikipedia, The Free Encyclopedia, 26 Feb. 2017. Web. 27 Feb. 2017. <https://en.wikipedia.org/w/index.php?title=Planetary_system&oldid=767572167>

Wikipedia contributors. "Drake equation." *Wikipedia, The Free Encyclopedia*. Wikipedia, The Free Encyclopedia, 4 Jan. 2017. Web. 17 Jan. 2017. <https://en.wikipedia.org/w/index.php?title=Drake_equation&oldid=758257808>

Wikipedia contributors. "Intelligence." *Wikipedia, The Free Encyclopedia*. Wikipedia, The Free Encyclopedia, 4 Jan. 2017. Web. 25 Jan. 2017. <https://en.wikipedia.org/w/index.php?title=Intelligence&oldid=758237957>

Wikipedia contributors. "List of distinct cell types in the adult human body." *Wikipedia, The Free Encyclopedia*. Wikipedia, The Free Encyclopedia, 29 Dec. 2016. Web. 21 Jan. 2017. <https://en.wikipedia.org/w/index.php?title=List_of_distinct_cell_types_in_the_adult_human_body&oldid=757187739>

Wikipedia contributors. "Social Darwinism." *Wikipedia, The Free Encyclopedia*. Wikipedia, The Free Encyclopedia, 15 Feb. 2017. Web. 11 Mar. 2017. <https://en.wikipedia.org/w/index.php?title=Social_Darwinism&oldid=765543334>

Wikipedia contributors. "Socialism." *Wikipedia, The Free Encyclopedia*. Wikipedia, The Free Encyclopedia, 16 Jan. 2017. Web. 17 Jan. 2017. <https://en.wikipedia.org/w/index.php?title=Socialism&oldid=760365283>

Wikipedia contributors. "Psychology of self." *Wikipedia, The Free Encyclopedia*. Wikipedia, The Free Encyclopedia, 15 Jan. 2017. Web. 31 Jan. 2017. <https://en.wikipedia.org/w/index.php?title=Psychology_of_self&oldid=760200313>

Wikipedia contributors. "Gaia hypothesis." *Wikipedia, The Free Encyclopedia*. Wikipedia, The Free Encyclopedia, 27 Jan. 2017. Web. 28 Jan. 2017. <https://en.wikipedia.org/w/index.php?title=Gaia_hypothesis&oldid=762214875>

Wikipedia contributors. "Human impact on the environment " *Wikipedia, The Free Encyclopedia*. Wikipedia, The Free Encyclopedia, 3 Jan. 2017. Web. 18 Jan. 2017. <https://en.wikipedia.org/w/index.php?title=Human_impact_on_the_environment&oldid=758143592>

Wikipedia contributors. "Cancer." *Wikipedia, The Free Encyclopedia*. Wikipedia, The Free Encyclopedia, 23 Jan. 2017. Web. 28 Jan. 2017. <https://en.wikipedia.org/w/index.php?title=Cancer&oldid=761475312>

Wikipedia contributors. "Galaxy cluster." *Wikipedia, The Free Encyclopedia*. Wikipedia, The Free Encyclopedia, 20 Dec. 2016. Web. 18 Jan. 2017. <vhttps://en.wikipedia.org/w/index.php?title=Galaxy_cluster&oldid=755759701>

Wikipedia contributors. "Vitalism." *Wikipedia, The Free Encyclopedia*. Wikipedia, The Free Encyclopedia, 21 Dec. 2016. Web. 28 Jan. 2017. <https://en.wikipedia.org/w/index.php?title=Vitalism&oldid=756029746>

Wikipedia contributors. "Organicism." *Wikipedia, The Free Encyclopedia*. Wikipedia, The Free Encyclopedia, 25 Nov. 2016. Web. 28 Jan. 2017. <https://en.wikipedia.org/w/index.php?title=Organicism&oldid=751413724>

Wikipedia contributors. "Anthropic principle." *Wikipedia, The Free Encyclopedia*. Wikipedia, The Free Encyclopedia, 25 Jan. 2017. Web. 28 Jan. 2017. <https://en.wikipedia.org/w/index.php?title=Anthropic_principle&oldid=761902756>

Wikipedia contributors. "State of matter." *Wikipedia, The Free Encyclopedia*. Wikipedia, The Free Encyclopedia, 27 Dec. 2016. Web. 28 Jan. 2017. <https://en.wikipedia.org/w/index.php?title=State_of_matter&oldid=756880079>

Wikipedia contributors. "Volition (psychology)." *Wikipedia, The Free Encyclopedia*. Wikipedia, The Free Encyclopedia, 18 Dec. 2016. Web. 25 Jan. 2017. <https://en.wikipedia.org/w/index.php?title=Volition_(psychology)&oldid=755577104>

Wikipedia contributors. "Will (philosophy)." *Wikipedia, The Free Encyclopedia*. Wikipedia, The Free Encyclopedia, 5 Nov. 2016. Web. 25 Jan. 2017. <https://en.wikipedia.org/w/index.php?title=Will_(philosophy)&oldid=747938229>

Wikipedia contributors. "Unmoved mover." *Wikipedia, The Free Encyclopedia*. Wikipedia, The Free Encyclopedia, 1 Dec. 2016. Web. 18 Jan. 2017. <https://en.wikipedia.org/w/index.php?title=Unmoved_mover&oldid=752431640>

Wikipedia contributors. "Relationship between religion and science." *Wikipedia, The Free Encyclopedia*. Wikipedia, The Free Encyclopedia, 26 Dec. 2016. Web. 19 Jan. 2017. <https://en.wikipedia.org/w/index.php?title=Relationship_between_religion_and_science&oldid=756679637>

Wikipedia contributors. "Cosmological argument." *Wikipedia, The Free Encyclopedia*. Wikipedia, The Free Encyclopedia, 10 Jan. 2017. Web. 21 Jan. 2017. <https://en.wikipedia.org/w/index.php?title=Cosmological_argument&oldid=759374149>

Wikipedia contributors. "Creationism." *Wikipedia, The Free Encyclopedia*. Wikipedia, The Free Encyclopedia, 17 Jan. 2017. Web. 19 Jan. 2017. <https://en.wikipedia.org/w/index.php?title=Creationism&oldid=760546363>

Wikipedia contributors. "Creation myth." *Wikipedia, The Free Encyclopedia*. Wikipedia, The Free Encyclopedia, 29 Jan. 2017. Web. 31 Jan. 2017. <https://en.wikipedia.org/w/index.php?title=Creation_myth&oldid=762641974>

Wikipedia contributors. "End time." *Wikipedia, The Free Encyclopedia*. Wikipedia, The Free Encyclopedia, 20 Jan. 2017. Web. 31 Jan. 2017. <https://en.wikipedia.org/w/index.php?title=End_time&oldid=760974748>

Wikipedia contributors. "Circle." *Wikipedia, The Free Encyclopedia*. Wikipedia, The Free Encyclopedia, 23 Nov. 2016. Web. 19 Jan. 2017. <https://en.wikipedia.org/w/index.php?title=Circle&oldid=751134758>

Wikipedia contributors. "Book of Genesis." *Wikipedia, The Free Encyclopedia*. Wikipedia, The Free Encyclopedia, 11 Jan. 2017. Web. 19 Jan. 2017. <https://en.wikipedia.org/w/index.php?title=Book_of_Genesis&oldid=759414928>

Wikipedia contributors. "Big Bounce." *Wikipedia, The Free Encyclopedia*. Wikipedia, The Free Encyclopedia, 26 Dec. 2016. Web. 19 Jan. 2017. <https://en.wikipedia.org/w/index.php?title=Big_Bounce&oldid=756676230>

Wikipedia contributors. "Cyclic model." *Wikipedia, The Free Encyclopedia*. Wikipedia, The Free Encyclopedia, 1 Dec. 2016. Web. 14 Feb. 2017. <https://en.wikipedia.org/w/index.php?title=Cyclic_model&oldid=752419491>

Wikipedia contributors. "Absolute time and space." *Wikipedia, The Free Encyclopedia*. Wikipedia, The Free Encyclopedia, 16 Jan. 2017. Web. 21 Jan. 2017. <https://en.wikipedia.org/w/index.php?title=Absolute_time_and_space&oldid=760387442>

Wikipedia contributors. "Point at infinity." *Wikipedia, The Free Encyclopedia*. Wikipedia, The Free Encyclopedia, 28 Dec. 2016. Web. 21 Jan. 2017. <https://en.wikipedia.org/w/index.php?title=Point_at_infinity&oldid=757009421>

Wikipedia contributors. "Object-oriented programming." *Wikipedia, The Free Encyclopedia*. Wikipedia, The Free Encyclopedia, 17 Jan. 2017. Web. 23 Jan. 2017. <https://en.wikipedia.org/w/index.php?title=Object-oriented_programming&oldid=760511418>

Concept Progress

Wikipedia contributors. "Infinite loop." *Wikipedia, The Free Encyclopedia*. Wikipedia, The Free Encyclopedia, 17 Dec. 2016. Web. 19 Jan. 2017. <https://en.wikipedia.org/w/index.php?title=Infinite_loop&oldid=755281914>

Wikipedia contributors. "Chicken or the egg." *Wikipedia, The Free Encyclopedia*. Wikipedia, The Free Encyclopedia, 18 Jan. 2017. Web. 19 Jan. 2017. <https://en.wikipedia.org/w/index.php?title=Chicken_or_the_egg&oldid=760674559>

Wikipedia contributors. "B-theory of time." *Wikipedia, The Free Encyclopedia*. Wikipedia, The Free Encyclopedia, 8 Nov. 2016. Web. 21 Jan. 2017. <https://en.wikipedia.org/w/index.php?title=B-theory_of_time&oldid=748435303>

Wikipedia contributors. "DVD." *Wikipedia, The Free Encyclopedia*. Wikipedia, The Free Encyclopedia, 17 Jan. 2017. Web. 19 Jan. 2017. <https://en.wikipedia.org/w/index.php?title=DVD&oldid=760468506>

Wikipedia contributors. "God and eternity." *Wikipedia, The Free Encyclopedia*. Wikipedia, The Free Encyclopedia, 15 Aug. 2016. Web. 24 Jan. 2017. <https://en.wikipedia.org/w/index.php?title=God_and_eternity&oldid=734644264>

Wikipedia contributors. "Conceptions of God." *Wikipedia, The Free Encyclopedia*. Wikipedia, The Free Encyclopedia, 4 Jan. 2017. Web. 24 Jan. 2017. <https://en.wikipedia.org/w/index.php?title=Conceptions_of_God&oldid=758205635>

Wikipedia contributors. "Human Potential Movement." *Wikipedia, The Free Encyclopedia*. Wikipedia, The Free Encyclopedia, 27 Jan. 2017. Web. 29 Jan. 2017.
<https://en.wikipedia.org/w/index.php?title=Human_Potential_Movement&oldid=762231794>

Wikipedia contributors. "Immanuel Kant." *Wikipedia, The Free Encyclopedia*. Wikipedia, The Free Encyclopedia, 24 Jan. 2017. Web. 28 Jan. 2017. <https://en.wikipedia.org/w/index.php?title=Immanuel_Kant&oldid=761789335>

Wikipedia contributors. "God." *Wikipedia, The Free Encyclopedia*. Wikipedia, The Free Encyclopedia, 19 Jan. 2017. Web. 19 Jan. 2017. <https://en.wikipedia.org/w/index.php?title=God&oldid=760838476>

Wikipedia contributors. "Universal evolution." *Wikipedia, The Free Encyclopedia*. Wikipedia, The Free Encyclopedia, 21 Jul. 2016. Web. 21 Jan. 2017. <https://en.wikipedia.org/w/index.php?title=Universal_evolution&oldid=730926710>

Wikipedia contributors. "Intelligent design." *Wikipedia, The Free Encyclopedia*. Wikipedia, The Free Encyclopedia, 19 Jan. 2017. Web. 19 Jan. 2017. <https://en.wikipedia.org/w/index.php?title=Intelligent_design&oldid=760898544>

Wikipedia contributors. "Creation–evolution controversy." *Wikipedia, The Free Encyclopedia*. Wikipedia, The Free Encyclopedia, 6 Jan. 2017. Web. 24 Jan. 2017.
<https://en.wikipedia.org/w/index.php?title=Creation%E2%80%93evolution_controversy&oldid=758635498>

Wikipedia contributors. "19th century." *Wikipedia, The Free Encyclopedia*. Wikipedia, The Free Encyclopedia, 23 Jan. 2017. Web. 24 Jan. 2017. <https://en.wikipedia.org/w/index.php?title=19th_century&oldid=761521155>

Wikipedia contributors. "Names of God." *Wikipedia, The Free Encyclopedia*. Wikipedia, The Free Encyclopedia, 14 Jan. 2017. Web. 24 Jan. 2017. <https://en.wikipedia.org/w/index.php?title=Names_of_God&oldid=760064840>

Wikipedia contributors. "Abrahamic religions." *Wikipedia, The Free Encyclopedia*. Wikipedia, The Free Encyclopedia, 15 Jan. 2017. Web. 19 Jan. 2017. <https://en.wikipedia.org/w/index.php?title=Abrahamic_religions&oldid=760128564>

Wikipedia contributors. "Richard Dawkins." *Wikipedia, The Free Encyclopedia*. Wikipedia, The Free Encyclopedia, 24 Jan. 2017. Web. 28 Jan. 2017. <https://en.wikipedia.org/w/index.php?title=Richard_Dawkins&oldid=761819100>

Wikipedia contributors. "Physical cosmology." *Wikipedia, The Free Encyclopedia*. Wikipedia, The Free Encyclopedia, 6 Jan. 2017. Web. 30 Jan. 2017. <https://en.wikipedia.org/w/index.php?title=Physical_cosmology&oldid=758579858>

Wikipedia contributors. "Philosophy of religion." *Wikipedia, The Free Encyclopedia*. Wikipedia, The Free Encyclopedia, 10 Jan. 2017. Web. 27 Jan. 2017. <https://en.wikipedia.org/w/index.php?title=Philosophy_of_religion&oldid=759346920>

Wikipedia contributors. "Existence of God." *Wikipedia, The Free Encyclopedia*. Wikipedia, The Free Encyclopedia, 24 Jan. 2017. Web. 24 Jan. 2017. <https://en.wikipedia.org/w/index.php?title=Existence_of_God&oldid=761704154>

Wikipedia contributors. "Image of God." *Wikipedia, The Free Encyclopedia.* Wikipedia, The Free Encyclopedia, 7 Dec. 2016. Web. 19 Jan. 2017. <https://en.wikipedia.org/w/index.php?title=Image_of_God&oldid=753428072>

Wikipedia contributors. "Personal god." *Wikipedia, The Free Encyclopedia.* Wikipedia, The Free Encyclopedia, 27 Dec. 2016. Web. 29 Jan. 2017. <https://en.wikipedia.org/w/index.php?title=Personal_god&oldid=756885739>

Wikipedia contributors. "Love of God." *Wikipedia, The Free Encyclopedia.* Wikipedia, The Free Encyclopedia, 15 Dec. 2016. Web. 29 Jan. 2017. <https://en.wikipedia.org/w/index.php?title=Love_of_God&oldid=754901890>

Wikipedia contributors. "Chosen people." *Wikipedia, The Free Encyclopedia.* Wikipedia, The Free Encyclopedia, 24 Jan. 2017. Web. 29 Jan. 2017. <https://en.wikipedia.org/w/index.php?title=Chosen_people&oldid=761804935>

Wikipedia contributors. "God becomes the Universe." *Wikipedia, The Free Encyclopedia.* Wikipedia, The Free Encyclopedia, 1 Nov. 2016. Web. 21 Jan. 2017. <https://en.wikipedia.org/w/index.php?title=God_becomes_the_Universe&oldid=747295239>

Wikipedia contributors. "Capitalism." *Wikipedia, The Free Encyclopedia.* Wikipedia, The Free Encyclopedia, 12 Jan. 2017. Web. 20 Jan. 2017. <https://en.wikipedia.org/w/index.php?title=Capitalism&oldid=759656393>

Wikipedia contributors. "Communism." *Wikipedia, The Free Encyclopedia.* Wikipedia, The Free Encyclopedia, 18 Jan. 2017. Web. 20 Jan. 2017. <https://en.wikipedia.org/w/index.php?title=Communism&oldid=760708511>

Wikipedia contributors. "Fear of God." *Wikipedia, The Free Encyclopedia.* Wikipedia, The Free Encyclopedia, 29 Jan. 2017. Web. 30 Jan. 2017. <https://en.wikipedia.org/w/index.php?title=Fear_of_God&oldid=762557161>

Wikipedia contributors. "Positivism." *Wikipedia, The Free Encyclopedia.* Wikipedia, The Free Encyclopedia, 18 Jan. 2017. Web. 20 Jan. 2017. <https://en.wikipedia.org/w/index.php?title=Positivism&oldid=760769634>

Wikipedia contributors. "Social order." *Wikipedia, The Free Encyclopedia.* Wikipedia, The Free Encyclopedia, 1 Dec. 2016. Web. 27 Jan. 2017. <https://en.wikipedia.org/w/index.php?title=Social_order&oldid=752472556>

Wikipedia contributors. "History of human rights." *Wikipedia, The Free Encyclopedia.* Wikipedia, The Free Encyclopedia, 26 Nov. 2016. Web. 31 Jan. 2017. <https://en.wikipedia.org/w/index.php?title=History_of_human_rights&oldid=751590574>

Wikipedia contributors. "Socioeconomics." *Wikipedia, The Free Encyclopedia.* Wikipedia, The Free Encyclopedia, 17 Jan. 2017. Web. 27 Jan. 2017. <https://en.wikipedia.org/w/index.php?title=Socioeconomics&oldid=760486028>

Wikipedia contributors. "Bertrand Russell." *Wikipedia, The Free Encyclopedia.* Wikipedia, The Free Encyclopedia, 28 Jan. 2017. Web. 28 Jan. 2017. <https://en.wikipedia.org/w/index.php?title=Bertrand_Russell&oldid=762327766>

Wikipedia contributors. "Dark Ages (historiography)." *Wikipedia, The Free Encyclopedia.* Wikipedia, The Free Encyclopedia, 14 Jan. 2017. Web. 20 Jan. 2017. <https://en.wikipedia.org/w/index.php?title=Dark_Ages_(historiography)&oldid=759959759>

Wikipedia contributors. "Age of Enlightenment." *Wikipedia, The Free Encyclopedia.* Wikipedia, The Free Encyclopedia, 20 Jan. 2017. Web. 20 Jan. 2017. <https://en.wikipedia.org/w/index.php?title=Age_of_Enlightenment&oldid=760978990>

Wikipedia contributors. "Cogito ergo sum." *Wikipedia, The Free Encyclopedia.* Wikipedia, The Free Encyclopedia, 16 Dec. 2016. Web. 20 Jan. 2017. <https://en.wikipedia.org/w/index.php?title=Cogito_ergo_sum&oldid=755063732>

Wikipedia contributors. "Freedom of religion." *Wikipedia, The Free Encyclopedia.* Wikipedia, The Free Encyclopedia, 15 Jan. 2017. Web. 20 Jan. 2017. <https://en.wikipedia.org/w/index.php?title=Freedom_of_religion&oldid=760176822>

Wikipedia contributors. "Natural and legal rights." *Wikipedia, The Free Encyclopedia.* Wikipedia, The Free Encyclopedia, 24 Dec. 2016. Web. 24 Jan. 2017. <https://en.wikipedia.org/w/index.php?title=Natural_and_legal_rights&oldid=756473939>

Wikipedia contributors. "Toleration." *Wikipedia, The Free Encyclopedia.* Wikipedia, The Free Encyclopedia, 7 Jan. 2017. Web. 25 Jan. 2017. <https://en.wikipedia.org/w/index.php?title=Toleration&oldid=758754140>

Concept Progress

Wikipedia contributors. "Atheism." *Wikipedia, The Free Encyclopedia.* Wikipedia, The Free Encyclopedia, 26 Jan. 2017. Web. 30 Jan. 2017. <https://en.wikipedia.org/w/index.php?title=Atheism&oldid=762082455>

Wikipedia contributors. "Intellectual." *Wikipedia, The Free Encyclopedia.* Wikipedia, The Free Encyclopedia, 13 Jan. 2017. Web. 20 Jan. 2017. <https://en.wikipedia.org/w/index.php?title=Intellectual&oldid=759884469>

Wikipedia contributors. "Emotional intelligence." *Wikipedia, The Free Encyclopedia.* Wikipedia, The Free Encyclopedia, 17 Jan. 2017. Web. 20 Jan. 2017. <https://en.wikipedia.org/w/index.php?title=Emotional_intelligence&oldid=760439256>

Wikipedia contributors. "Major religious groups." *Wikipedia, The Free Encyclopedia.* Wikipedia, The Free Encyclopedia, 24 Dec. 2016. Web. 20 Jan. 2017. <https://en.wikipedia.org/w/index.php?title=Major_religious_groups&oldid=756474890>

Wikipedia contributors. "Special relativity." *Wikipedia, The Free Encyclopedia.* Wikipedia, The Free Encyclopedia, 7 Feb. 2017. Web. 16 Feb. 2017. <https://en.wikipedia.org/w/index.php?title=Special_relativity&oldid=764233746>

Wikipedia contributors. "Quantum Darwinism." *Wikipedia, The Free Encyclopedia.* Wikipedia, The Free Encyclopedia, 5 Dec. 2016. Web. 17 Feb. 2017. <https://en.wikipedia.org/w/index.php?title=Quantum_Darwinism&oldid=753113362>

Wikipedia contributors. "Universal Darwinism." *Wikipedia, The Free Encyclopedia.* Wikipedia, The Free Encyclopedia, 7 Nov. 2016. Web. 17 Feb. 2017. <https://en.wikipedia.org/w/index.php?title=Universal_Darwinism&oldid=748257476>

Wikipedia contributors. "Enlightenment (spiritual)." *Wikipedia, The Free Encyclopedia.* Wikipedia, The Free Encyclopedia, 24 Dec. 2016. Web. 1 Feb. 2017. <https://en.wikipedia.org/w/index.php?title=Enlightenment_(spiritual)&oldid=756486362>

Wikipedia contributors. "Buddha-nature." *Wikipedia, The Free Encyclopedia.* Wikipedia, The Free Encyclopedia, 14 Nov. 2016. Web. 20 Jan. 2017. <https://en.wikipedia.org/w/index.php?title=Buddha-nature&oldid=749392152>

Wikipedia contributors. "Prayer." *Wikipedia, The Free Encyclopedia.* Wikipedia, The Free Encyclopedia, 17 Jan. 2017. Web. 20 Jan. 2017. <https://en.wikipedia.org/w/index.php?title=Prayer&oldid=760586015>

Wikipedia contributors. "Search for extraterrestrial intelligence." *Wikipedia, The Free Encyclopedia.* Wikipedia, The Free Encyclopedia, 20 Jan. 2017. Web. 20 Jan. 2017. <https://en.wikipedia.org/w/index.php?title=Search_for_extraterrestrial_intelligence&oldid=761001580>

Wikipedia contributors. "Wave." *Wikipedia, The Free Encyclopedia.* Wikipedia, The Free Encyclopedia, 26 Jan. 2017. Web. 30 Jan. 2017. <https://en.wikipedia.org/w/index.php?title=Wave&oldid=762081028>

Wikipedia contributors. "Antenna (radio)." *Wikipedia, The Free Encyclopedia.* Wikipedia, The Free Encyclopedia, 14 Jan. 2017. Web. 20 Jan. 2017. <https://en.wikipedia.org/w/index.php?title=Antenna_(radio)&oldid=760097146>

Wikipedia contributors. "Grey matter." *Wikipedia, The Free Encyclopedia.* Wikipedia, The Free Encyclopedia, 28 Jan. 2017. Web. 1 Feb. 2017. <https://en.wikipedia.org/w/index.php?title=Grey_matter&oldid=762314795>

Wikipedia contributors. "Superintelligence." *Wikipedia, The Free Encyclopedia.* Wikipedia, The Free Encyclopedia, 29 Nov. 2016. Web. 30 Jan. 2017. <https://en.wikipedia.org/w/index.php?title=Superintelligence&oldid=752158603>

Wikipedia contributors. "Electromagnetic theories of consciousness." *Wikipedia, The Free Encyclopedia.* Wikipedia, The Free Encyclopedia, 22 Dec. 2016. Web. 25 Jan. 2017. <https://en.wikipedia.org/w/index.php?title=Electromagnetic_theories_of_consciousness&oldid=756141164>

Wikipedia contributors. "Space probe." *Wikipedia, The Free Encyclopedia.* Wikipedia, The Free Encyclopedia, 15 Jan. 2017. Web. 25 Jan. 2017. <https://en.wikipedia.org/w/index.php?title=Space_probe&oldid=760183498>

Wikipedia contributors. "Cultural mandate." *Wikipedia, The Free Encyclopedia.* Wikipedia, The Free Encyclopedia, 2 Oct. 2016. Web. 20 Jan. 2017. <https://en.wikipedia.org/w/index.php?title=Cultural_mandate&oldid=742183865>

Wikipedia contributors. "Coincidence." *Wikipedia, The Free Encyclopedia.* Wikipedia, The Free Encyclopedia, 11 Jan. 2017. Web. 29 Jan. 2017. <https://en.wikipedia.org/w/index.php?title=Coincidence&oldid=759555229>

Wikipedia contributors. "Religious and philosophical views of Albert Einstein." *Wikipedia, The Free Encyclopedia.* Wikipedia, The Free Encyclopedia, 20 Jan. 2017. Web. 20 Jan. 2017.
<https://en.wikipedia.org/w/index.php?title=Religious_and_philosophical_views_of_Albert_Einstein&oldid=761008756>

Wikipedia contributors. "Hidden variable theory." *Wikipedia, The Free Encyclopedia.* Wikipedia, The Free Encyclopedia, 23 Jan. 2017. Web. 25 Jan. 2017. <https://en.wikipedia.org/w/index.php?title=Hidden_variable_theory&oldid=761512616>

Wikipedia contributors. "Quantum limit." *Wikipedia, The Free Encyclopedia.* Wikipedia, The Free Encyclopedia, 21 Jan. 2017. Web. 26 Jan. 2017. <https://en.wikipedia.org/w/index.php?title=Quantum_limit&oldid=761220127>

Wikipedia contributors. "Agnosticism." *Wikipedia, The Free Encyclopedia.* Wikipedia, The Free Encyclopedia, 29 Jan. 2017. Web. 30 Jan. 2017. <https://en.wikipedia.org/w/index.php?title=Agnosticism&oldid=762580758>

Wikipedia contributors. "Quantum tunnelling." *Wikipedia, The Free Encyclopedia.* Wikipedia, The Free Encyclopedia, 16 Jan. 2017. Web. 21 Jan. 2017. <https://en.wikipedia.org/w/index.php?title=Quantum_tunnelling&oldid=760389881>

Wikipedia contributors. "Quantum mind." *Wikipedia, The Free Encyclopedia.* Wikipedia, The Free Encyclopedia, 4 Jan. 2017. Web. 25 Jan. 2017. <https://en.wikipedia.org/w/index.php?title=Quantum_mind&oldid=758240785>

Wikipedia contributors. "Curved space." *Wikipedia, The Free Encyclopedia.* Wikipedia, The Free Encyclopedia, 27 May. 2016. Web. 30 Jan. 2017. <https://en.wikipedia.org/w/index.php?title=Curved_space&oldid=722324701>

Wikipedia contributors. "Euclidean space." *Wikipedia, The Free Encyclopedia.* Wikipedia, The Free Encyclopedia, 14 Aug. 2016. Web. 21 Jan. 2017. <https://en.wikipedia.org/w/index.php?title=Euclidean_space&oldid=734465338>

Wikipedia contributors. "Imaginary time." *Wikipedia, The Free Encyclopedia.* Wikipedia, The Free Encyclopedia, 18 Oct. 2016. Web. 13 Feb. 2017. <https://en.wikipedia.org/w/index.php?title=Imaginary_time&oldid=744919334>

Wikipedia contributors. "Progressivism." *Wikipedia, The Free Encyclopedia.* Wikipedia, The Free Encyclopedia, 11 Jan. 2017. Web. 27 Jan. 2017. <https://en.wikipedia.org/w/index.php?title=Progressivism&oldid=759415176>

Chapter Ten

Wikipedia contributors. "World population." *Wikipedia, The Free Encyclopedia.* Wikipedia, The Free Encyclopedia, 10 Jan. 2017. Web. 3 Feb. 2017. <https://en.wikipedia.org/w/index.php?title=World_population&oldid=759341386>

Wikipedia contributors. "Earth Day." *Wikipedia, The Free Encyclopedia.* Wikipedia, The Free Encyclopedia, 7 Feb. 2017. Web. 15 Feb. 2017. <https://en.wikipedia.org/w/index.php?title=Earth_Day&oldid=764141812>

Wikipedia contributors. "Choice." *Wikipedia, The Free Encyclopedia.* Wikipedia, The Free Encyclopedia, 27 Jan. 2017. Web. 3 Feb. 2017. <https://en.wikipedia.org/w/index.php?title=Choice&oldid=762279438>

Wikipedia contributors. "Fight-or-flight response." *Wikipedia, The Free Encyclopedia.* Wikipedia, The Free Encyclopedia, 27 Jan. 2017. Web. 3 Feb. 2017. <https://en.wikipedia.org/w/index.php?title=Fight-or-flight_response&oldid=762150889>

Wikipedia contributors. "Faith and rationality." *Wikipedia, The Free Encyclopedia.* Wikipedia, The Free Encyclopedia, 29 Dec. 2016. Web. 10 Feb. 2017. <https://en.wikipedia.org/w/index.php?title=Faith_and_rationality&oldid=757192212>

Wikipedia contributors. "Axiom." *Wikipedia, The Free Encyclopedia.* Wikipedia, The Free Encyclopedia, 27 Dec. 2016. Web. 17 Feb. 2017. <https://en.wikipedia.org/w/index.php?title=Axiom&oldid=756960637>

Wikipedia contributors. "Yin and yang." *Wikipedia, The Free Encyclopedia.* Wikipedia, The Free Encyclopedia, 1 Feb. 2017. Web. 3 Feb. 2017. <https://en.wikipedia.org/w/index.php?title=Yin_and_yang&oldid=763074592>

Wikipedia contributors. "Id, ego and super-ego." *Wikipedia, The Free Encyclopedia.* Wikipedia, The Free Encyclopedia, 25 Jan. 2017. Web. 3 Feb. 2017. <https://en.wikipedia.org/w/index.php?title=Id,_ego_and_super-ego&oldid=761969595>

Concept Progress

Wikipedia contributors. "Dualism." *Wikipedia, The Free Encyclopedia*. Wikipedia, The Free Encyclopedia, 31 Jan. 2017. Web. 11 Feb. 2017. <https://en.wikipedia.org/w/index.php?title=Dualism&oldid=762863282>

Wikipedia contributors. "Faith." *Wikipedia, The Free Encyclopedia*. Wikipedia, The Free Encyclopedia, 30 Jan. 2017. Web. 3 Feb. 2017. <https://en.wikipedia.org/w/index.php?title=Faith&oldid=762793832>

Wikipedia contributors. "Bad faith (existentialism)." *Wikipedia, The Free Encyclopedia*. Wikipedia, The Free Encyclopedia, 10 Jan. 2017. Web. 24 Feb. 2017. <https://en.wikipedia.org/w/index.php?title=Bad_faith_(existentialism)&oldid=759279312>

Wikipedia contributors. "Trust (emotion)." *Wikipedia, The Free Encyclopedia*. Wikipedia, The Free Encyclopedia, 22 Jan. 2017. Web. 3 Feb. 2017. <https://en.wikipedia.org/w/index.php?title=Trust_(emotion)&oldid=761431732>

Wikipedia contributors. "Risk." *Wikipedia, The Free Encyclopedic*. Wikipedia, The Free Encyclopedia, 31 Jan. 2017. Web. 3 Feb. 2017. <https://en.wikipedia.org/w/index.php?title=Risk&oldid=762848234>

Wikipedia contributors. "Decision-making." *Wikipedia, The Free Encyclopedia*. Wikipedia, The Free Encyclopedia, 5 Feb. 2017. Web. 6 Feb. 2017. <https://en.wikipedia.org/w/index.php?title=Decision-making&oldid=763825194>

Wikipedia contributors. "Investment." *Wikipedia, The Free Encyclopedia*. Wikipedia, The Free Encyclopedia, 1 Feb. 2017. Web. 3 Feb. 2017. <https://en.wikipedia.org/w/index.php?title=Investment&oldid=763173976>

Wikipedia contributors. "Planning." *Wikipedia, The Free Encyclopedia*. Wikipedia, The Free Encyclopedia, 12 Dec. 2016. Web. 3 Feb. 2017. <https://en.wikipedia.org/w/index.php?title=Planning&oldid=754315042>

Wikipedia contributors. "Hedge (finance)." *Wikipedia, The Free Encyclopedia*. Wikipedia, The Free Encyclopedia, 6 Jan. 2017. Web. 3 Feb. 2017. <https://en.wikipedia.org/w/index.php?title=Hedge_(finance)&oldid=758594382>

Wikipedia contributors. "United States one-dollar bill." *Wikipedia, The Free Encyclopedia*. Wikipedia, The Free Encyclopedia, 3 Feb. 2017. Web. 3 Feb. 2017. <https://en.wikipedia.org/w/index.php?title=United_States_one-dollar_bill&oldid=763514056>

Wikipedia contributors. "In God We Trust." *Wikipedia, The Free Encyclopedia*. Wikipedia, The Free Encyclopedia, 29 Jan. 2017. Web. 3 Feb. 2017. <https://en.wikipedia.org/w/index.php?title=In_God_We_Trust&oldid=762634033>

Wikipedia contributors. "Philosophy of happiness." *Wikipedia, The Free Encyclopedia*. Wikipedia, The Free Encyclopedia, 20 Dec. 2016. Web. 8 Feb. 2017. <https://en.wikipedia.org/w/index.php?title=Philosophy_of_happiness&oldid=755849482>

Wikipedia contributors. "Multiple time dimensions." *Wikipedia, The Free Encyclopedia*. Wikipedia, The Free Encyclopedia, 27 Dec. 2016. Web. 9 Feb. 2017. <https://en.wikipedia.org/w/index.php?title=Multiple_time_dimensions&oldid=756881588>

Wikipedia contributors. "Timeline." *Wikipedia, The Free Encyclopedia*. Wikipedia, The Free Encyclopedia, 9 Jan. 2017. Web. 4 Feb. 2017. <https://en.wikipedia.org/w/index.php?title=Timeline&oldid=759102439>

Wikipedia contributors. "Rosa Parks." *Wikipedia, The Free Encyclopedia*. Wikipedia, The Free Encyclopedia, 14 Jan. 2017. Web. 4 Feb. 2017. <https://en.wikipedia.org/w/index.php?title=Rosa_Parks&oldid=759989302>

Wikipedia contributors. "Martin Luther King Jr.." *Wikipedia, The Free Encyclopedia*. Wikipedia, The Free Encyclopedia, 24 Jan. 2017. Web. 4 Feb. 2017. <https://en.wikipedia.org/w/index.php?title=Martin_Luther_King_Jr.&oldid=761641252>

Wikipedia contributors. "Scopes Trial." *Wikipedia, The Free Encyclopedia*. Wikipedia, The Free Encyclopedia, 2 Feb. 2017. Web. 4 Feb. 2017. <https://en.wikipedia.org/w/index.php?title=Scopes_Trial&oldid=763376813>

Wikipedia contributors. "Mary Leakey." *Wikipedia, The Free Encyclopedia*. Wikipedia, The Free Encyclopedia, 19 Jan. 2017. Web. 4 Feb. 2017. <https://en.wikipedia.org/w/index.php?title=Mary_Leakey&oldid=760904243>

Wikipedia contributors. "Evolution as fact and theory." *Wikipedia, The Free Encyclopedia*. Wikipedia, The Free Encyclopedia, 23 Jan. 2017. Web. 4 Feb. 2017. <https://en.wikipedia.org/w/index.php?title=Evolution_as_fact_and_theory&oldid=761496077>

Wikipedia contributors. "Maurice Hilleman." *Wikipedia, The Free Encyclopedia*. Wikipedia, The Free Encyclopedia, 2 Feb. 2017. Web. 4 Feb. 2017. <https://en.wikipedia.org/w/index.php?title=Maurice_Hilleman&oldid=763345149>

Wikipedia contributors. "Irena Sendler." *Wikipedia, The Free Encyclopedia*. Wikipedia, The Free Encyclopedia, 2 Feb. 2017. Web. 4 Feb. 2017. <https://en.wikipedia.org/w/index.php?title=Irena_Sendler&oldid=763244655>

Wikipedia contributors. "Wright brothers." *Wikipedia, The Free Encyclopedia*. Wikipedia, The Free Encyclopedia, 5 Jan. 2017. Web. 4 Feb. 2017. <https://en.wikipedia.org/w/index.php?title=Wright_brothers&oldid=758519622>

Wikipedia contributors. "Yuri Gagarin." *Wikipedia, The Free Encyclopedia*. Wikipedia, The Free Encyclopedia, 3 Feb. 2017. Web. 4 Feb. 2017. <https://en.wikipedia.org/w/index.php?title=Yuri_Gagarin&oldid=763514128>

Wikipedia contributors. "John Lennon." *Wikipedia, The Free Encyclopedia*. Wikipedia, The Free Encyclopedia, 31 Jan. 2017. Web. 4 Feb. 2017. <https://en.wikipedia.org/w/index.php?title=John_Lennon&oldid=763025158>

Wikipedia contributors. "Imagine (John Lennon song)." *Wikipedia, The Free Encyclopedia*. Wikipedia, The Free Encyclopedia, 28 Jan. 2017. Web. 7 Feb. 2017.<https://en.wikipedia.org/w/index.php?title=Imagine_(John_Lennon_song)&oldid=762403843>

Wikipedia contributors. "Bob Marley." *Wikipedia, The Free Encyclopedia*. Wikipedia, The Free Encyclopedia, 30 Jan. 2017. Web. 4 Feb. 2017. <https://en.wikipedia.org/w/index.php?title=Bob_Marley&oldid=762829039>

Wikipedia contributors. "Artistic inspiration." *Wikipedia, The Free Encyclopedia*. Wikipedia, The Free Encyclopedia, 30 Aug. 2015. Web. 11 Feb. 2017. <https://en.wikipedia.org/w/index.php?title=Artistic_inspiration&oldid=678610023>

Wikipedia contributors. "Human evolutionary genetics." *Wikipedia, The Free Encyclopedia*. Wikipedia, The Free Encyclopedia, 5 Feb. 2017. Web. 9 Feb. 2017. <https://en.wikipedia.org/w/index.php?title=Human_evolutionary_genetics&oldid=763811287>

Wikipedia contributors. "List of Nobel laureates." *Wikipedia, The Free Encyclopedia*. Wikipedia, The Free Encyclopedia, 13 Oct. 2016. Web. 11 Feb. 2017. <https://en.wikipedia.org/w/index.php?title=List_of_Nobel_laureates&oldid=744142866>

Wikipedia contributors. "Timestream." *Wikipedia, The Free Encyclopedia*. Wikipedia, The Free Encyclopedia, 30 Jul. 2016. Web. 4 Feb. 2017. <https://en.wikipedia.org/w/index.php?title=Timestream&oldid=732209038>

Wikipedia contributors. "Family tree." *Wikipedia, The Free Encyclopedia*. Wikipedia, The Free Encyclopedia, 14 Jan. 2017. Web. 11 Mar. 2017. <https://en.wikipedia.org/w/index.php?title=Family_tree&oldid=759980744>

Wikipedia contributors. "Four-dimensionalism." *Wikipedia, The Free Encyclopedia*. Wikipedia, The Free Encyclopedia, 10 Dec. 2016. Web. 16 Feb. 2017. <https://en.wikipedia.org/w/index.php?title=Four-dimensionalism&oldid=754006119>

Wikipedia contributors. "Aerobic exercise." *Wikipedia, The Free Encyclopedia*. Wikipedia, The Free Encyclopedia, 4 Feb. 2017. Web. 15 Feb. 2017. <https://en.wikipedia.org/w/index.php?title=Aerobic_exercise&oldid=763625304>

Wikipedia contributors. "Free will." *Wikipedia, The Free Encyclopedia*. Wikipedia, The Free Encyclopedia, 31 Jan. 2017. Web. 4 Feb. 2017. <https://en.wikipedia.org/w/index.php?title=Free_will&oldid=762836518>

Wikipedia contributors. "Pessimism." *Wikipedia, The Free Encyclopedia*. Wikipedia, The Free Encyclopedia, 31 Jan. 2017. Web. 4 Feb. 2017. <https://en.wikipedia.org/w/index.php?title=Pessimism&oldid=762950061>

Wikipedia contributors. "Optimism." *Wikipedia, The Free Encyclopedia*. Wikipedia, The Free Encyclopedia, 31 Jan. 2017. Web. 4 Feb. 2017. <https://en.wikipedia.org/w/index.php?title=Optimism&oldid=762983496>

Wikipedia contributors. "Double-slit experiment." *Wikipedia, The Free Encyclopedia*. Wikipedia, The Free Encyclopedia, 2 Feb. 2017. Web. 4 Feb. 2017. <https://en.wikipedia.org/w/index.php?title=Double-slit_experiment&oldid=763312464>

Wikipedia contributors. "Wave–particle duality." *Wikipedia, The Free Encyclopedia*. Wikipedia, The Free Encyclopedia, 20 Feb. 2017. Web. 24 Feb. 2017.<https://en.wikipedia.org/w/index.php?title=Wave%E2%80%93particle_duality&oldid=766549121>

Concept Progress

Wikipedia contributors. "Observer effect (physics)." *Wikipedia, The Free Encyclopedia*. Wikipedia, The Free Encyclopedia, 8 Feb. 2017. Web. 14 Feb. 2017. <https://en.wikipedia.org/w/index.php?title=Observer_effect_(physics)&oldid=764346502>

Wikipedia contributors. "Wave function." *Wikipedia, The Free Encyclopedia*. Wikipedia, The Free Encyclopedia, 25 Jan. 2017. Web. 4 Feb. 2017. <https://en.wikipedia.org/w/index.php?title=Wave_function&oldid=761884756>

Wikipedia contributors. "Introduction to quantum mechanics." *Wikipedia, The Free Encyclopedia*. Wikipedia, The Free Encyclopedia, 8 Feb. 2017. Web. 16 Feb. 2017. <https://en.wikipedia.org/w/index.php?title=Introduction_to_quantum_mechanics&oldid=764433821>

Wikipedia contributors. "Possible world." *Wikipedia, The Free Encyclopedia*. Wikipedia, The Free Encyclopedia, 23 Jan. 2017. Web. 6 Feb. 2017. <https://en.wikipedia.org/w/index.php?title=Possible_world&oldid=761579428>

Wikipedia contributors. "Many-worlds interpretation." *Wikipedia, The Free Encyclopedia*. Wikipedia, The Free Encyclopedia, 11 Jan. 2017. Web. 6 Feb. 2017. <https://en.wikipedia.org/w/index.php?title=Many-worlds_interpretation&oldid=759532940>

Wikipedia contributors. "Erwin Schrödinger." *Wikipedia, The Free Encyclopedia*. Wikipedia, The Free Encyclopedia, 8 Feb. 2017. Web. 9 Feb. 2017. <https://en.wikipedia.org/w/index.php?title=Erwin_Schr%C3%B6dinger&oldid=764415476>

Wikipedia contributors. "Modal realism." *Wikipedia, The Free Encyclopedia*. Wikipedia, The Free Encyclopedia, 5 Jan. 2017. Web. 7 Feb. 2017. <https://en.wikipedia.org/w/index.php?title=Modal_realism&oldid=758481640>

Wikipedia contributors. "Abolitionism." *Wikipedia, The Free Encyclopedia*. Wikipedia, The Free Encyclopedia, 6 Feb. 2017. Web. 7 Feb. 2017. <https://en.wikipedia.org/w/index.php?title=Abolitionism&oldid=764064742>

Wikipedia contributors. "Gender equality." *Wikipedia, The Free Encyclopedia*. Wikipedia, The Free Encyclopedia, 25 Jan. 2017. Web. 7 Feb. 2017. <https://en.wikipedia.org/w/index.php?title=Gender_equality&oldid=761937094>

Wikipedia contributors. "Imagination." *Wikipedia, The Free Encyclopedia*. Wikipedia, The Free Encyclopedia, 4 Feb. 2017. Web. 14 Feb. 2017. <https://en.wikipedia.org/w/index.php?title=Imagination&oldid=763649243>

Wikipedia contributors. "Chronesthesia." *Wikipedia, The Free Encyclopedia*. Wikipedia, The Free Encyclopedia, 11 Apr. 2017. Web. 14 Apr. 2017. <https://en.wikipedia.org/w/index.php?title=Chronesthesia&oldid=774867087>

Wikipedia contributors. "Alternate history." *Wikipedia, The Free Encyclopedia*. Wikipedia, The Free Encyclopedia, 27 Jan. 2017. Web. 9 Feb. 2017. <https://en.wikipedia.org/w/index.php?title=Alternate_history&oldid=762228657>

Wikipedia contributors. "Simulated reality." *Wikipedia, The Free Encyclopedia*. Wikipedia, The Free Encyclopedia, 12 Feb. 2017. Web. 15 Feb. 2017. <https://en.wikipedia.org/w/index.php?title=Simulated_reality&oldid=765116370>

Wikipedia contributors. "Political sociology." *Wikipedia, The Free Encyclopedia*. Wikipedia, The Free Encyclopedia, 15 Dec. 2016. Web. 7 Feb. 2017. <https://en.wikipedia.org/w/index.php?title=Political_sociology&oldid=755038830>

Wikipedia contributors. "Freedom of choice." *Wikipedia, The Free Encyclopedia*. Wikipedia, The Free Encyclopedia, 24 Oct. 2016. Web. 14 Feb. 2017. <https://en.wikipedia.org/w/index.php?title=Freedom_of_choice&oldid=745926753>

Wikipedia contributors. "Biophysics." *Wikipedia, The Free Encyclopedia*. Wikipedia, The Free Encyclopedia, 16 Jan. 2017. Web. 7 Feb. 2017. <https://en.wikipedia.org/w/index.php?title=Biophysics&oldid=760434342>

Wikipedia contributors. "Is the glass half empty or half full?." *Wikipedia, The Free Encyclopedia*. Wikipedia, The Free Encyclopedia, 17 Jan. 2017. Web. 10 Feb. 2017. <https://en.wikipedia.org/w/index.php?title=Is_the_glass_half_empty_or_half_full%3F&oldid=760517560>

Wikipedia contributors. "Maturity (psychological)." *Wikipedia, The Free Encyclopedia*. Wikipedia, The Free Encyclopedia, 6 Jan. 2017. Web. 7 Feb. 2017. <https://en.wikipedia.org/w/index.php?title=Maturity_(psychological)&oldid=758669287>

Wikipedia contributors. "Reincarnation." *Wikipedia, The Free Encyclopedia*. Wikipedia, The Free Encyclopedia, 4 Feb. 2017. Web. 14 Feb. 2017. <https://en.wikipedia.org/w/index.php?title=Reincarnation&oldid=763718887>

Wikipedia contributors. "Parallel universe (fiction)." *Wikipedia, The Free Encyclopedia*. Wikipedia, The Free Encyclopedia, 9 Feb. 2017. Web. 9 Feb. 2017. <https://en.wikipedia.org/w/index.php?title=Parallel_universe_(fiction)&oldid=764602863>

Wikipedia contributors. "Plane (esotericism)." *Wikipedia, The Free Encyclopedia*. Wikipedia, The Free Encyclopedia, 10 Jan. 2017. Web. 14 Feb. 2017. <https://en.wikipedia.org/w/index.php?title=Plane_(esotericism)&oldid=759336265>

Wikipedia contributors. "Watchmaker analogy." *Wikipedia, The Free Encyclopedia*. Wikipedia, The Free Encyclopedia, 31 Jan. 2017. Web. 10 Feb. 2017. <https://en.wikipedia.org/w/index.php?title=Watchmaker_analogy&oldid=762870936>

Wikipedia contributors. "Detailed logarithmic timeline." *Wikipedia, The Free Encyclopedia*. Wikipedia, The Free Encyclopedia, 24 Jan. 2017. Web. 9 Feb. 2017. <https://en.wikipedia.org/w/index.php?title=Detailed_logarithmic_timeline&oldid=761693296>

Wikipedia contributors. "Thinking outside the box." *Wikipedia, The Free Encyclopedia*. Wikipedia, The Free Encyclopedia, 3 Feb. 2017. Web. 7 Feb. 2017. <https://en.wikipedia.org/w/index.php?title=Thinking_outside_the_box&oldid=763460715>

Wikipedia contributors. "Stellar nucleosynthesis." *Wikipedia, The Free Encyclopedia*. Wikipedia, The Free Encyclopedia, 20 Dec. 2016. Web. 7 Feb. 2017. <https://en.wikipedia.org/w/index.php?title=Stellar_nucleosynthesis&oldid=755920588>

Wikipedia contributors. "Cat's Eye Nebula." *Wikipedia, The Free Encyclopedia*. Wikipedia, The Free Encyclopedia, 2 Dec. 2016. Web. 7 Feb. 2017. <https://en.wikipedia.org/w/index.php?title=Cat%27s_Eye_Nebula&oldid=752712167>

Wikipedia contributors. "Operating system." *Wikipedia, The Free Encyclopedia*. Wikipedia, The Free Encyclopedia, 6 Feb. 2017. Web. 7 Feb. 2017. <https://en.wikipedia.org/w/index.php?title=Operating_system&oldid=763987675>

Wikipedia contributors. "Zen master." *Wikipedia, The Free Encyclopedia*. Wikipedia, The Free Encyclopedia, 5 Feb. 2017. Web. 7 Feb. 2017. <https://en.wikipedia.org/w/index.php?title=Zen_master&oldid=763779431>

Wikipedia contributors. "Koan." *Wikipedia, The Free Encyclopedia*. Wikipedia, The Free Encyclopedia, 30 Jan. 2017. Web. 7 Feb. 2017. <https://en.wikipedia.org/w/index.php?title=K%C5%8Dan&oldid=762797772>

Wikipedia contributors. "Mu (negative)." *Wikipedia, The Free Encyclopedia*. Wikipedia, The Free Encyclopedia, 26 Jan. 2017. Web. 7 Feb. 2017. <https://en.wikipedia.org/w/index.php?title=Mu_(negative)&oldid=761989590>

Wikipedia contributors. "Maimonides." *Wikipedia, The Free Encyclopedia*. Wikipedia, The Free Encyclopedia, 5 Feb. 2017. Web. 7 Feb. 2017. <https://en.wikipedia.org/w/index.php?title=Maimonides&oldid=763758336>

Wikipedia contributors. "Apophatic theology." *Wikipedia, The Free Encyclopedia*. Wikipedia, The Free Encyclopedia, 14 Dec. 2016. Web. 7 Feb. 2017. <https://en.wikipedia.org/w/index.php?title=Apophatic_theology&oldid=754805606>

Wikipedia contributors. "Philosophy of perception." *Wikipedia, The Free Encyclopedia*. Wikipedia, The Free Encyclopedia, 16 Dec. 2016. Web. 15 Feb. 2017. <https://en.wikipedia.org/w/index.php?title=Philosophy_of_perception&oldid=755056128>

Wikipedia contributors. "Pranayama." *Wikipedia, The Free Encyclopedia*. Wikipedia, The Free Encyclopedia, 2 Feb. 2017. Web. 8 Feb. 2017. <https://en.wikipedia.org/w/index.php?title=Pranayama&oldid=763388844>

Wikipedia contributors. "New Year's resolution." *Wikipedia, The Free Encyclopedia*. Wikipedia, The Free Encyclopedia, 3 Feb. 2017. Web. 8 Feb. 2017. <https://en.wikipedia.org/w/index.php?title=New_Year%27s_resolution&oldid=763399297>

Wikipedia contributors. "Destiny." *Wikipedia, The Free Encyclopedia*. Wikipedia, The Free Encyclopedia, 11 Feb. 2017. Web. 16 Feb. 2017. <https://en.wikipedia.org/w/index.php?title=Destiny&oldid=764827025>

Wikipedia contributors. "Rebirth (Buddhism)." *Wikipedia, The Free Encyclopedia*. Wikipedia, The Free Encyclopedia, 7 Dec. 2016. Web. 8 Feb. 2017. <https://en.wikipedia.org/w/index.php?title=Rebirth_(Buddhism)&oldid=753473770>

Wikipedia contributors. "Finance." *Wikipedia, The Free Encyclopedia*. Wikipedia, The Free Encyclopedia, 26 Jan. 2017. Web. 8 Feb. 2017. <https://en.wikipedia.org/w/index.php?title=Finance&oldid=762117775>

Concept Progress

Wikipedia contributors. "Opportunity cost." *Wikipedia, The Free Encyclopedia.* Wikipedia, The Free Encyclopedia, 2 Feb. 2017. Web. 8 Feb. 2017. <https://en.wikipedia.org/w/index.php?title=Opportunity_cost&oldid=763342172>

Wikipedia contributors. "Mount Rushmore." *Wikipedia, The Free Encyclopedia.* Wikipedia, The Free Encyclopedia, 5 Feb. 2017. Web. 8 Feb. 2017. <https://en.wikipedia.org/w/index.php?title=Mount_Rushmore&oldid=763846401>

Wikipedia contributors. "Galápagos Islands." *Wikipedia, The Free Encyclopedia.* Wikipedia, The Free Encyclopedia, 6 Feb. 2017. Web. 8 Feb. 2017. <https://en.wikipedia.org/w/index.php?title=Gal%C3%A1pagos_Islands&oldid=763965471>

Wikipedia contributors. "Rings of Saturn." *Wikipedia, The Free Encyclopedia.* Wikipedia, The Free Encyclopedia, 1 Feb. 2017. Web. 8 Feb. 2017. <https://en.wikipedia.org/w/index.php?title=Rings_of_Saturn&oldid=763089592>

Wikipedia contributors. "Phenomenology (philosophy)." *Wikipedia, The Free Encyclopedia.* Wikipedia, The Free Encyclopedia, 7 Feb. 2017. Web. 16 Feb. 2017. <https://en.wikipedia.org/w/index.php?title=Phenomenology_(philosophy)&oldid=764255305>

Wikipedia contributors. "Life." *Wikipedia, The Free Encyclopedia.* Wikipedia, The Free Encyclopedia, 18 Jan. 2017. Web. 8 Feb. 2017. <https://en.wikipedia.org/w/index.php?title=Life&oldid=760690434>

Wikipedia contributors. "Contemporary history." *Wikipedia, The Free Encyclopedia.* Wikipedia, The Free Encyclopedia, 6 Mar. 2017. Web. 11 Mar. 2017. <https://en.wikipedia.org/w/index.php?title=Contemporary_history&oldid=768867126>

Wikipedia contributors. "Emerging technologies." *Wikipedia, The Free Encyclopedia.* Wikipedia, The Free Encyclopedia, 29 Jan. 2017. Web. 15 Feb. 2017. <https://en.wikipedia.org/w/index.php?title=Emerging_technologies&oldid=762621182>

Wikipedia contributors. "Common descent." *Wikipedia, The Free Encyclopedia.* Wikipedia, The Free Encyclopedia, 20 Dec. 2016. Web. 9 Feb. 2017. <https://en.wikipedia.org/w/index.php?title=Common_descent&oldid=755900855>

Wikipedia contributors. "Darwinism." *Wikipedia, The Free Encyclopedia.* Wikipedia, The Free Encyclopedia, 14 Feb. 2017. Web. 16 Feb. 2017. <https://en.wikipedia.org/w/index.php?title=Darwinism&oldid=765378615>

Wikipedia contributors. "Human genetic variation." *Wikipedia, The Free Encyclopedia.* Wikipedia, The Free Encyclopedia, 4 Feb. 2017. Web. 9 Feb. 2017. <https://en.wikipedia.org/w/index.php?title=Human_genetic_variation&oldid=763642874>

Wikipedia contributors. "Meaning (existential)." *Wikipedia, The Free Encyclopedia.* Wikipedia, The Free Encyclopedia, 12 Jan. 2017. Web. 9 Feb. 2017. <https://en.wikipedia.org/w/index.php?title=Meaning_(existential)&oldid=759686295>

Wikipedia contributors. "Where no man has gone before." *Wikipedia, The Free Encyclopedia.* Wikipedia, The Free Encyclopedia, 18 Dec. 2016. Web. 9 Feb. 2017. <https://en.wikipedia.org/w/index.php?title=Where_no_man_has_gone_before&oldid=755469614>

Wikipedia contributors. "Probability amplitude." *Wikipedia, The Free Encyclopedia.* Wikipedia, The Free Encyclopedia, 27 Nov. 2016. Web. 9 Feb. 2017. <https://en.wikipedia.org/w/index.php?title=Probability_amplitude&oldid=751810347>

Wikipedia contributors. "Greatness." *Wikipedia, The Free Encyclopedia.* Wikipedia, The Free Encyclopedia, 14 Feb. 2017. Web. 15 Feb. 2017. <https://en.wikipedia.org/w/index.php?title=Greatness&oldid=765517369>

Wikipedia contributors. "List of timelines." *Wikipedia, The Free Encyclopedia.* Wikipedia, The Free Encyclopedia, 2 Feb. 2017. Web. 9 Feb. 2017. <https://en.wikipedia.org/w/index.php?title=List_of_timelines&oldid=763341704>

PLEASE VISIT
WWW.CONCEPTPROGRESS.COM
FOR MORE INFORMATION